Claire Rayner was
trained as a nurse at
London; qualified an
when she was awarde
outstanding achievement. She then studied
midwifery at Guy's Hospital and at the Whittington
Hospital where she was Sister in the Paediatric
Department.

She married in 1957 and turned to writing in 1960
when the birth of her first child ended her nursing
career. She now has three children, Amanda, Adam
and Jay.

Claire Rayner is the author of some eighty books
including not only fiction, but also an extremely
broad range of medical subjects, from sex education
for children and adults, to home nursing, family
health, and baby and childcare. Among her fiction is
the twelve-volume novel sequence 'The Performers',
which she completed in 1986 with *Seven Dials*.

Flanders is Volume 2 in the Poppy Chronicles.

Also by Claire Rayner in Sphere Books

REPRISE

MADDIE

JUBILEE: THE POPPY CHRONICLES 1

FLANDERS

THE POPPY CHRONICLES II

CLAIRE RAYNER

SPHERE BOOKS LIMITED

A SPHERE BOOK

First published in Great Britain by
Weidenfeld & Nicolson Limited 1988
Published by Sphere Books Limited 1989

Printed and bound in Great Britain by
Cox & Wyman Ltd, Reading

ISBN 0 7474 0264 7

Sphere Books Ltd
A Division of
Macdonald & Co (Publishers) Ltd
1 New Fetter Lane, London EC4A 1AR
A member of Maxwell Pergamon Publishing Corporation plc

To Tony Field and Ted Algar
with affection

ACKNOWLEDGEMENTS

The author is grateful for the assistance given with research by: the London Library; the London Museum; the Victoria and Albert Museum; the General Post Office Archives; the Public Records Office; the Archivist, British Rail; the Meteorological Records Office; the Archive Department of *The Times*; the Imperial War Museum, London; Marylebone Public Libraries; Lyn MacDonald, war historian, and other sources too numerous to mention.

BOOK TWO

1

At first it had been just little rivulets trickling out of the more remote of the London suburbs, but they had thickened into scurrying, eddying spates, which were further fed as they passed the big railway station and more and more came off the trains to thicken it. A flood of people, most of them women, pushing and chattering, walking as well as riding, on buses and trains, cycles and cabs, all converging on Westminster and Caxton Hall.

It really was, Poppy decided, quite the most absurd congregation she had ever seen. There were smartly dressed matrons of such ultra respectability that their very stays creaked disapproval of their owner's presence in such company, and on such an occasion; pale-faced girls with expressions on their faces of such intensity that they looked as though they were in actual pain; elderly ladies who looked frightened of the crowd and yet determined not to give in to their alarm; skinny spinsters and buxom mothers and obvious shop girls and parlour maids as well as more than a sprinkling of very expensive ornaments of the upper classes. And their voices were even more mixed: she could hear everything from the flattest of Chelsea drawls and the most pinched of precious vowels of the determined-to-be-refined, to the broadest of Cockney twangs and most deafening of County brays. And she wanted to giggle aloud at the sheer excitement of being there and part of it all.

And also at the wickedness of it. If Mama only knew what she was doing this afternoon! Her rage would be monumental, Poppy decided, and then whispered the word almost aloud as she went on pushing her eager way up Whitehall towards Parliament Square. 'Mon-u-ment-al,' and she slid her hand into her pocket yet again, and closed her fingers tightly round the reassuring coldness of the thing she had hidden there so carefully, and tried to hurry her step even more as Big Ben chimed the last quarter before three.

The wind caught its breath and blew even harder so that the rubbish in the gutters blew round her booted ankles and sent dust into her eyes to make them smart; but none of it mattered. She was embarked on a Great Adventure and the devil take Mama and everything else except the Great Cause. And anyway, she reminded herself with a spark of her usual practicality, Miss Sayers would soon sort things out with Mama if she did by any remote chance find out, and there was after all absolutely no reason why she should; Mama who never went out if she could help it, and who never spoke to anyone unless she had to, how was she to know what her rebellious daughter was up to on this blustery March day? Mama, Poppy told herself loftily, was too hopelessly nineteenth century, that was the trouble. How could she possibly comprehend the needs of such a twentieth-century person as Poppy? And from her vantage point of being fully sixteen in bright-as-a-new-penny 1911, Poppy surveyed her world and found it vastly superior to her mother's.

By the time she reached the space in front of Caxton Hall the crowd was almost impassable and she stood still for a moment to peer over the heads around her to work out her strategy for getting in. It wasn't hard to see: her unusual height of five feet nine inches, which was generally such a bore – especially when the pretty little empty-heads at school twitted her about it from the cosy security of their own five feet two inches of normality, on occasions such as this was a decided asset.

Above the nodding feathers and shiny straw of the bonnets that surrounded her, she became aware of the fact that there were a great many more policemen than she had ever seen in one place before and she caught her breath with yet another thrill of excitement. Just seeing them there, stolid and watchful in their dark blue, with the thin March sunlight glinting off their helmets, filled her with a sense of foreboding. This was supposed to be a peaceful meeting – well, she amended inside her head, *reasonably* peaceful, and certainly so until The Plan was put into action – but seeing the policemen there seemed to suggest otherwise. Could they possibly be considering a repeat of that dreadful day last November when, she had been told, women, just like those here today, had been bullied and manhandled like so many common criminals rather than treated as peaceful protesters? And again Poppy felt that shiver of mixed fear and excitement run through her.

But then she dismissed from her mind the cluster of policemen and recollections of Black Friday, as that dreadful day had come to be called, as she saw, just ahead of her and to her right, a little knot of purposeful people making their way through the women who stood about talking at the tops of their voices and filling the busy square with their shrillness. She recognized several of the leading lights of the Women's Social and Political Union, and most especially Ada Flatman and Georgina Brackenbury, both of whom were to speak this afternoon, even though the meeting was not one organized by the WSPU, being just an 'ordinary' political event under the aegis of the Liberal Party, and she took a deep breath and put her head down almost like a battering ram and pushed determinedly through the hubbub towards them. Most of the women gave way good-naturedly enough to the tall sturdy figure with the thick dark pigtail down her back and dressed in the short serge skirts of the schoolgirl, and so she managed to catch up with the little party just as it reached the steps that led into Caxton Hall, and she pulled a little breathlessly at the sleeve of the woman bringing up the rear.

'Miss Porteous – ' she said. 'Here I am – where do I go now?'

The woman glanced back over her shoulder and looked relieved to see her. 'Oh, splendid – splendid – down on the right, my dear,' she said in a rapid undertone. 'You'll see some seats marked "Reserved" – take the one on the end – I want you to be free to get out if we need you quickly – yes – now, not another word – ' And she raised her voice and said pointedly, 'If you reserved a seat, then I'm sure you will find it easily enough – ' and then swept away after her little group who were now well inside the building.

Poppy, more than a little amused by the doughty Miss Porteous's manner, for she had a considerable taste for melodrama and a great propensity for drawing attention to herself by means of trying to be unobtrusive, waited a moment longer and then quietly made her way through the now orderly groups of women pouring into the hall in the direction to which she had been pointed, found her seat with no difficulty and settled into it to wait. The meeting was actually supposed to start at three thirty so she had a half-hour yet to pass, but that didn't worry her. Poppy Amberly was well used to being alone and to filling long empty hours with such excitement and interest as she could conjure inside her own head. And she dug into her other pocket for the peppermints she had brought with her, tucked one into her cheek and looked around with lively interest.

The hall was large and lofty, and she looked up at the balcony above her head, quite empty, unlike the hall below, and then at the door at the side which she knew led up to it, and a small smile curved her mouth. She could have hugged herself with excitement as she thought of what she had to do about that door and again she reached into her pocket for the precious burden she had hidden there. It was safe, though rather warm now from the heat of her body and, satisfied, she withdrew her hand and looked further afield.

The rows were filling up now, and there were a few men, she noticed, and that made her frown for a moment. This surely was no place for men, she told herself with some censoriousness, and then made a face. That was a silly way to think. This meeting was about votes for women, and getting votes for women must surely be something everyone must care about, men as well as women, children as well as grown-ups. Not that she herself was a child, precisely. She felt every inch an adult, but it was often difficult to hold on to that certainty when so many people insisted on treating her so stupidly.

Mama for a start; to listen to Mama you'd think Poppy was still a six-year-old rather than what she was, almost a woman. And the others at home weren't much better. Grandmama actually treated her the way she treated everyone else, as a potential provider of illicit brandy and someone to cry to about the harshness of her lot, but the Uncles – and Poppy's round young face hardened a little as she thought of her Mama's half-brothers, Harold and Samuel. It had been bad enough when they had all been children. Now they were both young men – even Harold, the youngest, had reached his majority now and was swanking about like a man of the town spending his father's legacy as fast as he knew how – they were just as nasty as they had been as inky schoolboys. Worse, in some ways, especially Harold.

And she shivered a little and refused to think of the particular beastliness of Harold. Perhaps one day it would all get easier; one day when she didn't have to live in that hateful mausoleum of a house with all those hateful people – and then she was, as usual, stricken with guilt. It was wicked to think such thoughts; Mama didn't mean to be hateful, Poppy knew that. Mama was just – well, Mama. She did what she did and spoke as she spoke because she had to. Poppy understood that and tried to make allowances, but it was dreadfully difficult. It must be awful to have to live in so miserable a house with just a bad-tempered stepmama like Grandmama Maud for company and a restless daughter who wanted to do all the things Mildred most disapproved of. But all the same – and Poppy sighed gustily and tried to pull her thoughts away from the problems of home and concentrate instead on the glorious excitement of the here and now.

But there was nothing much happening yet. A few people milled about the stage at the far end of the hall, setting chairs and tables with great pernicketiness and pinning up huge rosettes of the WSPU colours (much to the obvious disapproval of the uniformed staff of the hall who it seemed were meant to be in charge of the arrangements) and Poppy admired the swathes of purple and green and white, and tweaked the rosette in the same colours that she had pinned to her own sensible blue lapel, and looked around at the other people again. And then wished she hadn't, because it happened again. It hadn't happened for a long time, and she had been glad of that because it always left her feeling so – well, odd was the word. Not miserable precisely, nor upset. Just odd.

One of the men in the uniform of the Caxton Hall staff was standing sideways on beside the stage, talking to a self-important and very obvious civil servant in a shiny black suit, and just as Poppy looked at him he turned away from the civil servant and she could see him properly. And he had a row of Boer War medals on his chest and one empty sleeve pinned smartly against the bottle-green of his uniform jacket.

And at once there it was, deep inside her: a great pressing need to run as fast as she could and – what? She didn't know. She just felt a hard push of anxiety inside her chest, felt her muscles tense as she almost stood up and then forced herself to sit still again. She could see the same silly scene, too, inside her head, just as she always did when the feeling came.

She was running along Leinster Terrace, and she could tell she was running because the road was sort of bouncing up and down in front of her. She knew if she could only reach the end fast enough, could get there before the Bayswater Road loomed up in front, she would be all right. She would be able to get there, to catch – who? That was the problem. She didn't know what it was or who it was that made her run so urgently, didn't know why she had this deep inside feeling of struggling to get somewhere, feeling like a bird locked inside a glass cage. And then the worst part of it happened, just as it always did: the road stopped bouncing in front of her eyes and swooped and dipped as she was lifted from behind in a great sudden lurch and someone was shrieking in her ears and shaking her and smacking her, and whatever it was that had made her run was gone, and there was nothing she could do about it –

Poppy shook her head at herself and then ducked it down to tuck her chin into her collar, and with a furtive little movement rubbed her

5

upper lip to get rid of the line of sweat drops that had appeared there. It was a horrid feeling and she was glad it had gone; it left her feeling so empty, though, and dreadfully sad and that was the nastiest part of all. And she closed her eyes and sucked hard on her peppermint in an effort to make the unpleasant feeling fade away and leave her in peace to enjoy the excitement of the afternoon.

And, slowly, fade it did, just as it did when it woke her in the middle of the night – for she had had the same experience in her dreams – and she was able to catch her breath and lift her head to look around her again. One day she would find out, perhaps, what it all meant. One day she would tease out the strangeness of it all. Perhaps Mama would explain – but then she smiled, a little wryly. Mama explain anything? Not Mama, who seemed to live all the time in a state of suppressed anger. But never mind now, she told herself as sturdily as she could. It was over, the bad moment, and there were better things to think about.

And indeed there were, for she now saw – and her eyes widened as she looked – two more women arriving and she longed to jump up and applaud them. There was Dame Ethel Smyth, striding down the centre aisle with her head up, and on her arm the thin frail figure of Lady Constance Lytton. Several other people had in fact stood up and were patting her shoulder as she went by and some broke into the tune of the rousing 'March of the Women' Dame Ethel had composed specially for the WSPU and which had just been published. And Poppy sighed as she looked at that splendid figure and wondered for a moment if perhaps, after all, Miss Campion might be a little bit right. Dame Ethel and Miss Campion actually looked a little like each other, she thought, as she watched the newcomers move into the front row to sit with the other members of the WSPU already there. They were both sensible and bright and just, well, *academic*, and she made a face at that. That was what Miss Campion wanted her to be, and what Mama was agreeing to; if they had their way she, Poppy, would do nothing for the next two years but sweat over exams and then go up to Cambridge to sweat over even more study and all for what? To teach other girls to do and think and live when what Poppy wanted most passionately was to do and think and live for herself.

School was all very well, and so were books – and she had to admit she was bright and fast at her schoolwork and getting to Newsham wouldn't be all that difficult – but would it be enough? And she knew in her heart it would not. She had to be where the world was at its busiest, not in classic book-lined studies. Her life had to be an active one, a doing one, not merely a thinking one, she told herself. Like now, and she almost shouted aloud her delight at the thought of what she was doing here this afternoon. Not just sitting being a demure schoolgirl, but actually doing something very exciting. Oh, if only all these people sitting in the rows around knew what she had in her pocket, and what was to happen this afternoon! How excited they would all be and how they would admire her!

Miss Sayers, her form mistress, understood all that, and Poppy thought affectionately for a moment of Miss Sayers and her willingness to help her be what she wanted to be. After Miss Campion had told Miss Sayers that Poppy was to be one of the school's entrants for college, Poppy had begged her to take her side, and Miss Sayers had sat and listened to Poppy explaining with great eloquence just why she didn't want to go to Cambridge, and then had nodded and said she quite understood. And told her that she should be working with the WSPU because there she would find all the excitement she wanted and perhaps, one day, the inspiration she sought.

'You might even end up choosing to go to Cambridge after all,' she had said then, her endearingly ugly face with its lavish dusting of freckles splitting into a wide grin. 'It's more fun than you might believe. But go to a few Votes for Women meetings. Then we'll talk again about Cambridge. And it's all right. I'll make sure your family don't know what you're doing. You won't be the only person I've lied for in the name of the Cause!' And they had laughed together, the pupil and the teacher barely ten years older, and Poppy had gone back to her dreary Leinster Terrace home and felt better.

And now she was here where it was all happening, with a special task all of her own to do, and it was the greatest moment of her life. Or so she told herself as a sort of whispering sound moved across the big, now jam-packed hall – except for the locked gallery, of course, which remained empty – and people turned to crane and stare at the entrance.

And there he was. The Home Secretary, Mr Churchill, a square pugnacious-looking young man and far from as alarming as Poppy would have expected. And she too stared at him with her eyes wide with interest as someone leaned over the back of her seat and hissed at her, 'You have it safe?'

At once, Poppy was all excitement again and her cheeks blazed with colour as she turned to stare up at the newcomer, someone she barely knew from the WSPU committee.

'Yes,' she whispered, and moved her hand as though to slip it into her pocket, but the other woman shook her head peremptorily and said softly, 'No, be still. We'll tell you when to make your move. Obey now – whatever you do, don't be too precipitate – ' And she hurried away to slip into the last empty seat in the front row.

And as Mr Churchill and several other men in high-collared shirts and well-cut dark suits settled themselves on the platform, the great hall sank into a hush and the meeting of 11 March 1911, on the subject of the issue of Votes for Women, started precisely on time.

2

Poppy was disappointed. This was the first public meeting of this sort she had attended; she had been to several of the WSPU's own meetings, of course, but this was one organized by a major political party, and she had therefore expected it to be much more dramatic and interesting and altogether exciting. But it was far from that. Where the WSPU meetings had been filled with fervour, this one was dull. Where the people on the WSPU platform had almost glittered with the passion of their commitment to their cause, these speakers were clearly bored, and doing a run-of-the-mill sort of job in speaking at all. But the audience felt the same; there was enough pent-up tension and excitement among sections of it, especially in the first rows where the leading WSPU members sat, and Poppy could feel it coming from elsewhere too; particularly from a section at the back, where a group of young, rather gaudily dressed girls were sitting.

She had noticed them earlier and had wondered about them, for they looked interesting, and now she turned her head to look at them as yet another dull speaker droned on and on and caught the eye of one sitting just in front of them; a rather plump girl in a neat yellow straw hat which was noticeably smaller than some of the oversized fashionable ones around her, but still trimmed with a profusion of fruit and a pair of birds' wings which made her look impudent and amusing. She raised her eyebrows at Poppy and then cast a droll glance towards the platform and gave a little chuck of her chin as if to say, 'Oh, what a bore!' and Poppy almost laughed aloud and grinned back at her; and felt better. After all, however dull the speakers so far, there was excitement to come, as well she knew. She just had to be patient, and she settled down in her seat, her shoulders hunched in pleasurable anticipation, and her pulse began to thump just a little faster and a little harder as she visualized how it would be.

The dull man sat down, and now an expectant hush fell on the hall.

The shuffling of the feet and coughing and rustling of toffee papers which had been going on throughout the proceedings stopped, and Poppy pulled herself out of her private thoughts and stared at the platform. And then sat up a little straighter, for it was clear that the star speaker of the afternoon was about to rise to his feet. And she lifted her chin and glanced briefly at the empty balcony and then back at the bulky shape now striding to the front of the platform to be greeted by a burst of applause from some parts of the hall, and a faint hissing sound from others, and paid him her undivided attention.

Why Mr Winston Churchill should attract so much feeling seemed at first to be a puzzle. He was a plump young man with a sleek air but he seemed innocuous enough; even his opening words seemed to be of little real importance. But as he found his pace and began to relax, the words came rolling out in his pleasant rather plummy voice with more warmth and then with some fire and Poppy found she was listening without effort, absorbing the mood of the man as much as what he actually said. And his mood was a reasonable one. He was the sensible middle-of-the-road sort of fellow, he seemed to be saying, who wanted women to have the Vote, of course he did, but he could see, from his special vantage point, problems about extension of the franchise which would not be immediately apparent to his audience. If they could be but patient, however, and leave it to the good will of the men of Parliament who were, of course, quite concerned with it, then all would be well. He counselled tolerance and womanly forbearance and –

Someone – Poppy could not see who – called out at that from the back of the hall, and the nervousness in the voice made it sound squeaky and mouselike, but it was audible for all that. 'We've been patient long enough!' it cried. 'How much longer must we wait?'

'We want the Vote now,' someone else chimed in, just as nervous and shaky but very determined and Poppy wanted to jump up and agree with her to encourage her, whoever she might be; but she had no chance for Churchill said smoothly, 'I cannot say how long – but patience has always been a womanly virtue, and much more effective than the unpleasant militancy of some of your misguided sisterhood – ' and Poppy could see Dame Ethel Smyth rising to her feet to argue with him, her arm up and her very hat seeming to bristle with indignation.

At which point several things seemed to happen at once. The gaudily dressed girls at the back of the hall leapt to their feet and began to shout furiously at him and then began to pelt him with fruit, and Poppy ducked her head in amazement as a large green apple whizzed dangerously close to her. She had not been told this was to happen. The only interruption that had been planned, she was sure, was –

And even as she thought it, the plan was put into action. Above her head there was a sound from the balcony and she looked up, together with the rest of the audience, to see a row of women standing there and waving a vast green, purple and white banner. It read 'Votes for Women!' in large letters and the effect of it was marred only by the fact that it had inadvertently been displayed upside-down. But all the same the message was clear, for the women holding it began to shout at the tops of their considerable voices, 'Votes for Women! Down with Churchill! Votes for Women!' and to stamp their booted feet rhythmically. The noise was satisfyingly loud and reverberated through the wooden balcony and downwards to the floor below so that Poppy could feel it through the seat of her chair, and she leapt to her feet and shouted 'Hooray' as loudly as she could. And simult- aneously, another group of people, all women, and this time in costly and fashionable clothes, had jumped up on the far side of the hall and were shrieking down at the gaudy girls who were still throwing fruit; their cry was 'Down with the Pankhursts! Down with the Pank- hursts!' and Poppy almost jumped up and down in fury. It had never occurred to her that any of the women here today could possibly be opposed to the Great Cause, and she stared at them with amazement and then with even more amazement realized that her own mouth was open and she was shouting her disapproval back at them in no uncertain terms, using every bad word she had ever heard – and that amazed her most of all.

But that was not all. It would not have seemed possible for there to be a greater turmoil, for now most of the audience were up and shouting and stamping as the noise from the balcony above went on becoming ever more thunderous. But it *was* possible, for the big double doors at the back crashed open and a great tide of blue came rushing through to add its own din to the all-pervading uproar.

Now people began to push their way out towards the sides as the blue tide in the centre aisle faltered and broke up into individual policemen who were grabbing indiscriminately for anyone within reach, one or two of them actually waving their truncheons about in a menacing manner, but then, as the would-be escapers realized that there were policemen in the side aisles too and tried to turn back, the tangle of bodies became impossible, and for the first time Poppy felt genuinely frightened. She had been full of pleasurable excited fear so far, a feeling born of the sheer exuberance and drama of the moment, but now, as she saw the big helmeted men with their faces set in grim expressions reaching for women with hands that seemed as big as hams and about as sensitive, and felt the sharp pain of an accidental kick on the shins imparted by a fellow member of the terrified audience, real fear trickled, ice cold and sickening, into her limbs from some central reservoir in her belly. She felt she could not move and for a moment stood clinging helplessly to the back of the seat in front of her as the people buffeted her and bounced off her in their struggle to get out of what was fast becoming a maelstrom.

In the hubbub someone did manage to push their way through towards Poppy, for she felt a hand on her shoulder and heard a voice in her ear, as the words were shouted into it.

'New plan; hold on – don't go up to them yet. Hold on to it – not safe to let them out – ' and then the other woman was gone, pushing away behind Poppy towards the exit doors, and after one startled moment, Poppy turned to try to follow her, needing to know what to do, and when to do it. Above her the din seemed to double itself, for now there were policemen battering on the locked doors of the balcony, trying to get to the women still standing at the front of it and crying their message, so Poppy's attempts to attract the attention of the woman now disappearing in front of her were singularly pointless. However loudly she shrieked, the sound was quite lost in the overwhelming noise.

Now there were people pushing her from behind and she felt herself swept inexorably forward as elbows as sharp as knitting needles ground into her back, while her legs began to feel numb from the kicks they were receiving from all around. But at last she was swept out of the hall and into the lobby and on out into the street beyond where at last she could catch her breath and the noise seemed to lessen as the March wind snatched people's voices and hurled them up into the grey-scudding sky.

She managed at last to stand still, bracing her legs apart to hold herself firm and pulled her coat, which had been tugged awry in the hubbub, back into tidiness and then looked about her; and now a new feeling rose in her. A huge sickening rage, twice as powerful as the anger she had felt inside at the women who had shown themselves opposed to the Cause, for all round there were policemen man-handling people and pushing them along to clear a way and they were not wasting any effort on being careful.

And then she saw her; the plump girl in the impudent hat was being harried by a particularly burly policeman. Her hat had been pushed ridiculously to the side of her head and half over one eye, and the policeman had a grip on her hair, which had come loose, and was pulling her head backwards by it as he propelled the girl forwards with one elbow between her shoulder blades. And she was squealing very loudly indeed.

It was more than Poppy could bear, and she hurled herself forwards and kicked the policeman as hard as she could in the back of one leg, and it was his turn to shout with pain. He let go of the plump girl and whirled on Poppy and seized her by one arm and twisted it behind her with so sharp and shrewd a movement that in a fraction of a second it was bent halfway up her back and the pain was so agonizing that to her eternal shame and horror she burst into loud and furious tears. And as if that weren't enough she felt a great thud in the small of her back that made her feel sick for a moment, and she realized that it was a large constabulary knee, and wanted to kick him again, but caught as she was in an unbreakable grip it was impossible.

But now the plump girl had recovered and was in action again, for Poppy saw her through the blur of her tears come charging towards her with a large umbrella held in both hands like a lance, and she aimed it hard over Poppy's shoulder and she heard the grunt as well as felt the impact as the man let go at last and threw both hands up to protect his face from this sudden and unexpected onslaught.

Poppy, rubbing her almost numb shoulder and still with tears falling down her cheeks, felt her other arm seized as the plump girl, without seeming to draw breath, tugged on her and pulled her away from the policeman who was now shouting for a couple of his colleagues, who were moving ponderously towards them from the now rapidly thinning fringes of the crowd, to help against this pair of termagants. But the plump girl wasted no time waiting for them; she turned and immediately pushed Poppy into the thickest part of the crowd back towards the hall, and Poppy willingly went with her.

'Come on!' the plump girl panted. 'We can get out this way round through the crowd and the other side – they'll never catch us – '

'Oh, please, no – I can't go – ' Poppy was beginning to catch her breath again now and she managed to get closer to her rescuer as they pushed on against the tide of people which was still trying to push outwards from the hall. 'I have to stay here – I've got something to do – '

'No one has anything left to do here,' the plump girl said grimly.

13

'Do come *on*, for pity's sake – they can still grab us – '

'I can't,' Poppy cried again. 'I can't – not till they say what to do with the key – '

The other looked at her sharply. 'What key?'

Poppy blinked and then sniffed hard to get rid of the last of her tears of pain and reddened. 'I'm not supposed to – Oh, I can't say – I really mustn't – ' she managed and wiped her face with one hand and tried once more to pull her coat tidy, for she felt like a bag of old rags, she had been so pulled about.

'Don't be so soppy,' the girl said curtly and again pushed into the crowd, aiming sideways so that they could escape, but Poppy was quite herself again now and she shook her head firmly.

'I can't,' she said with great determination. 'I have to go back. Thanks most awfully for your help – goodbye – ' And she pulled away from the other's grip and went plunging back into the hubbub towards the door of the hall.

'Hey!' shouted the other after her and stood for a moment, undecided, and then with a grimace cried, 'Oh, drat you! I suppose I'll have to come too, you idiotish creature – ' and went charging after her.

There was a considerable cordon of police still standing protecting the doorway of the hall, pushing women out of the way as they tried to make their own choice of where they wanted to be in spite of the opposition, and Poppy, still very frightened by the roughness of the policeman who had bent her arm back into that vicious half-nelson, almost lost her courage; but not quite for she lifted her chin pugnaciously and went marching up to the cordon and pushed her way in past it and, just as one of the men reached for her to stop her, someone from behind the line called out, 'Let her by – she's supposed to be here.' And, amazingly, the policeman obeyed.

She stood for a moment in the lobby, blinking, and then saw at last the person she had been looking for. Edith Bowman, the organizer of the protest who had given her her special task in the first place.

'Oh, Miss Bowman!' she cried. 'I didn't know what to do! I got swept out of the hall and someone said there had been a change of plan and then I saw this horrid policeman hurt someone so I kicked him and he – ' and again her treacherous tears threatened to engulf her and she could say no more.

'It's all right, my dear,' Miss Bowman said, and patted her shoulder. 'You couldn't help being pushed out – we almost all were – my dear, do hark at them. Isn't it too deevy!'

And Poppy lifted her head and sniffed and then managed a watery grin. For above them the hubbub went on. There were still the women's voices chanting, 'Votes for Women! Votes for Women!' and still women's feet stamping and Poppy rubbed the back of her hand across her nose with a regrettably childlike gesture and nodded.

'Yes,' she said. 'It's very deevy – they are wonderful – when should I – I mean, I don't know what the new plan is. The person who said it had been changed didn't tell me – '

'That doesn't matter now. You did exactly right,' said Miss Bowman and took Poppy by the shoulders and turned her towards the door to the balcony. 'You've come back just when you should – *now*, my dear.' And she stepped back and moved into the crowd again and Poppy looked apprehensively over her shoulder in time to see her vanish – and to see the plump girl emerge, very tousled, from an argument with a policeman who wanted to keep her out.

'I said you were my young sister,' she gasped as she came up to Poppy, pulling her hat straight again over her very tumbled hair. 'And I managed to convince him you were quite mad and I had to take you home. I might as well be mad myself coming back into this to fetch you, but you were so good to try to help me and – anyway, what *is* going on? Can we go now?'

'Not quite,' said Poppy and grinned at her, grateful to see the now familiar face. 'I say, you are a brick – look, I have an important something to do – ' And she slid her hand into her pocket to make sure her precious burden was still safe. It was. 'You can come if you like. But don't try to get too close or they may think you're in on it too and I don't want you to get into trouble even if I do.'

And purposefully she marched to the door that led to the balcony where the noise went on unabated.

There were three plain-clothes policemen standing there – they were easy to identify, Poppy decided, for their suits of serge were so very heavy and their bowler hats so very round and hard and their boots so very shiny – together with a man in the uniform of the Caxton Hall and several of the men who had been on the platform, though there was no sign of Winston Churchill.

'Trust him to get away when the getting's good,' muttered the plump girl behind Poppy and she flashed a glance back at her, grateful for her company. 'If he hadn't talked to us as though we were half-witted children and told us to be patient and womanly, there wouldn't have been this fuss. What's going on up there now?'

Poppy shook her head at her to enjoin silence and stood undecided for a moment, watching what was going on. The man in uniform had a great bunch of keys in his hand, and with dreadful slowness, using movements as ponderous as that of any elephant, he was fitting them one after the other into the lock of the door while the policemen stood shuffling in their impatience as they peered over his shoulder watching with heavy concentration.

'Don't understand it,' the man grumbled in a monotone as he went on with his efforts. 'Locked up, I did, after I searched this 'ere place last night, locked up and 'ung up the keys all shipshape and Bristol fashion down in my cubby'ole, and now it ain't 'ere. Some bugger's bin at my keys, that's the size of it, and when I gets my 'ands on 'oo it was, I'll give 'em such what for they'll wish their mothers never got 'em born. No error, I'll kill 'em. I reely will, bleedin' women, bin at my keys – '

'We'll have to get gelignite,' one of the policemen said, almost in despair now. 'Blow the thing in, it's the only answer. We've got to get those hellcats out of there. Home Secretary's orders, he wants them out fast – '

'You ain't blowing up none of my doors,' the uniformed man said with great pugnacity. 'Not while I'm 'ere in charge. Not without a proper warrant what's got gelignite permission wrote on it proper. Leave the bitches be. They'll get 'ungry and tired soon enough. Leave 'em be, I say.'

'And the Home Secretary says get them out. Until they are, we can't clear this place properly – listen to 'em.' And he lifted his head and jerked it in the direction of the outer door. And now Poppy could hear it too – a great chorus of 'Votes for Women!' – and she realized that the WSPU members had regrouped, as the plan had originally arranged, and were shouting their support for their colleagues in the locked balcony.

'No gelignite,' said the man in uniform again, mulishly. 'Not if I 'as to lie down in front of this 'ere door to stop yer.' And he turned and stood with his back to it in an absurd posture of bravery and glared at the three policemen.

It was more than Poppy could bear another moment, and she took a deep breath and stepped forwards. 'I say,' she said diffidently. 'I think I might be able to – '

The policemen turned almost as one man and glared at her and she wanted to giggle at the silliness of the way they looked, like a sort of theatre chorus line. One of them, who glared the most, said dismissively, 'Go away. You just buzz off home, little miss,' and the patronizing and insulting tone in his voice was so like the Uncles at home when they were being at their most hateful that her face flamed. 'Little girls like you oughtn't to be at a scene like this anyway. Your mother ought to be ashamed letting you out. Go home at once and we'll say no more. You don't want to be taken to the police station, now do you? Run away, my child.'

'I am not your child,' Poppy said with all the dignity she could muster and held out her closed fist. 'I am here to give to you what it is you want. Here it is.'

And she opened her fingers and showed them the key to the balcony door resting in the palm of her hand.

3

'Tea,' said the plump girl firmly. 'Quantities of tea and furthermore crumpets and a muffin or two. What do you say?'

'Oh, yes,' Poppy said fervently. 'Tea would be sheer bliss.' And indeed it would. She was achingly tired now it was all over, and remarkably hungry. She had been too excited to eat any luncheon before slipping away to the meeting and now she felt quite hollow.

'Splendid,' the plump girl said and tucked one hand into the crook of Poppy's elbow and led her out of the now almost empty and darkening square. They had slipped away unnoticed from the balcony door as the police, in great excitement, unlocked it and went charging in, and then, melting into the remains of the crowd, had watched as the triumphant WSPU members, still chanting their battle cry, were led off to the Black Marias. They had planned to be arrested in order to benefit from the ensuing publicity, Poppy knew, and would be happy at the outcome of the day, but it had depressed her to see them go, all the same, and having her new friend beside her had helped a lot.

'Come on,' the girl said now. 'The ABC in Bridge Street ought to do well enough. They aren't too ridiculously expensive and they have the most divine muffins – '

'Oh,' Poppy said and stopped short. 'I say, I'm awfully sorry but – um – ' She disentangled her arm and stepped back a little, bending her head to smooth her coat down with both hands so that she wouldn't have to look at the other girl. 'Actually, I don't think I'd better after all – I mean, it's getting frightfully late and – '

The plump girl peered at her and first frowned and then laughed. 'I know what it is! You've no blunt! My dear, I'm always like that – except at present, I'm not. I can buy you a cup of tea and muffin, for heaven's sake! If only to thank you for being such a great brick and helping me out – the way you did – '

Poppy shook her head, unable to trust herself to speak. She wanted to go and have tea with this interesting new person so very much. But how could she? She had precisely tuppence in her pocket, which was the fare home on the omnibus, and to spend it on tea would mean a dreadfully long walk back and a dreadfully late arrival which would bring down all Mama's ire; it could not be thought of. Nor could accepting the other's charity be thought of, of course, and she tried to say as much, stammering her embarrassment.

'Oh, such stuff!' said the plump girl cheerfully and again tucked her hand into Poppy's elbow and marched her on their way. 'I simply won't be refused. You'll be doing me a kindness, you foolish thing! Do come along now – I'm famished!' And despite Poppy's determination, somehow she could not refuse her.

And when they were sitting on each side of a marble-topped table in the steamy warm restaurant with the gaslight plopping cheerfully overhead and an all-pervading smell of tea and currant buns and cream cakes enveloping them, and the plump girl had ordered a sizeable tea – and Poppy could not help but be a little amused at the transparency of her greediness – she tried again to explain how embarrassed she was; but her companion would not hear of it.

'My dear girl, do you think I am some sort of millionairess? Indeed I am not – I am a working woman with just my earnings for an income, so I know perfectly well how it is to be a little short of the necessary! I dare say there will come a time when you can return the compliment, so not another word about such boring matters – now do tell me – who are you, and how did you come to be at the meeting and how was it you had that key and – oh, do tell me everything! I am quite fascinated – never saw anything so cool as the way you handed over that key, and their faces! Oh, my dear, it was as good as a show!' And the plump girl laughed heartily and then clapped her hands as the waitress arrived with her laden tray.

'My name is Poppy Amberly,' Poppy said as the girl began to deal with the pouring of tea and the sharing out of muffins and raspberry jam with much clatter and bustle. 'And I am not precisely a member of the WSPU but they chose me to look after the key after they locked Annie Kenny and Grace Rae and the others into the balcony last night and – '

'My dear!' The plump girl stared at her, wide-eyed. 'Do you mean they were there all *night*? How too, too exciting.'

'Wasn't it just.' Poppy said and gurgled with laughter suddenly. 'Oh, it was so clever and yet so simple! You see, what they did was go to a meeting at Caxton Hall last night, all about Bible study, I think it was, and they took rugs and sandwiches and flasks of tea and so forth and sat at the back of the balcony. That was the plan, you understand. And when all the other people left, they hung about to stop behind and then hid down between the seats on the floor. And when the man came to see if the balcony was empty before he locked it – for the organizers of the meeting had ordered the balcony not be used for fear of interrupters and displays – ' And again she gurgled with laughter. 'Why, all they did was roll down from row to row to hide from him as he walked along shining his lantern between the rows and – '

'How do you know that? Were you there?' The other girl had her mouth full of muffin, but excited interest quite outweighed any concern for good manners. 'And if you were, how did you get out with the key?'

Poppy blushed. 'No, I wasn't there.' Although I might just as well have been, she thought, for it is all so clear in my mind I feel I actually saw it. 'It was the plan, do you see, and I was there when they made that, and I understood it all so well, it was as though I *was* there. And since they were all safely locked up and made the demonstration as it was arranged, it must have been so, mustn't it?'

'Indeed it must,' her companion said and grinned widely. 'Oh, you are fun, Miss Amberly, indeed you are! You have such a way of telling a person things it is quite as if one was there oneself! And how did they get the key to give to you?'

'Oh, Miss Porteous did that.' Poppy said, still pink in the cheeks, but now for quite other reasons. It *was* agreeable to be admired by someone she already liked as much as she liked this girl. 'She looks very dull and seems terribly – well, like one of the teachers at school, do you see, but she really is quite a *driving* sort of person. And she went to tell the porter there last night after he had locked up that there was a boy who had been knocked off a bicycle outside and could he help and when he went rushing out, why, she just took the key from his cubbyhole as cool as you please and fetched it to me, this morning. They wanted me to hold it, you see – they said no one would expect a schoolgirl like me to be involved – they would be after the known leaders of the WSPU. So I was quite an important part of it all – ' And she tried not to look pleased with herself, but it was difficult.

'You're still at school?' The other girl had started on her second muffin now. 'I hadn't really thought about it but I dare say you are quite young, after all. Tall, of course, but now I look at you – and your hair still down – how old *are* you?'

'Sixteen,' Poppy said after a moment and was mortified to see the other girl nod a little complacently. 'But I am not at all childish, you know! I may look young but really I am – '

'My dear, I am quite sure you are! Terribly grown up, I mean. I was too, at your age. Now of course it's easier to be taken seriously.'

'Why? How old are you?'

'Eighteen,' the other said with great dignity and then grinned. 'Not so very much older than you, after all. I am sure we shall be great friends in spite of all! Now let's shake hands on that – and my name, by the way, is Bradman. I am Mabel Bradman and I work in a newspaper office, don't you know – '

Poppy was quite overawed as she held out her hand in response. 'How do you do, Miss Bradman,' she said fervently. 'I am *indeed* most gratified to meet you. To work in a newspaper office must be very splendid. Do you write the articles and so forth? Is that why you were at the meeting, to write about it? I say! You won't give my name out, will you? If Mama knew I had been there she'd be so waxy – '

Miss Bradman laughed. 'You need have no fear. I wish I were writing for the paper, but I'm not. I am a typewriter – I type out all the stuff the men write. My brother's mostly.' She tried to be casual. 'He is Bobby Bradman, you know. Perhaps you have heard of him? He is the *Dispatch*'s most valued man.'

'Of course I have,' Poppy said, lying stoutly, for she would not have hurt her new friend's feelings for the world. And she determined immediately to start reading the *Dispatch* regularly in order to get to know this splendid person's brother's work. 'And you are in the same office? How very exciting – a newspaper office!' And she sighed. 'That is the sort of thing I would so much like to do. They want me to go to Cambridge, you know, and to get a good education, but it seems so dreadfully dull to me. I want to do – oh, such exciting things. A newspaper office!' And she sighed again even more deeply at the thought of it all. 'I do envy you, Miss Bradman.'

'You must call me Mabel,' the other said firmly. 'And I shall call you Poppy – what a sweetly pretty name that is! – and you need not envy me for it is not so very exciting after all. I sit there and I type all day and at the end of it I am quite as tired as I ever was at school. More so, sometimes. Except I have my salary, you know, and that comforts me a good deal.' She grinned wickedly. 'I spend it mostly on clothes and Bobby says he is quite shocked, but he is the best of brothers and indulges me all he can. Although of course he has such high expenses, with the house and the baby and all.'

21

'Baby?'

'Chloe. My niece, Chloe. Such a dear little thing, a naughty one, you understand, but terribly sweet. My brother is a widower. Barbara – his wife – she died three years ago when Chloe was born. Such a tragedy. And only a matter of a year or so after that Papa died – my Mama died when I was small – and Papa, dear soul, was dreadfully bad with money. So I had not a farthing of my own and Bobby gave me a home with him, and then arranged my employment when I finished school, and we rub along famously, though I do worry about Bobby. He does work so hard.' It was her turn to sigh then. 'But he says I need not worry for he is strong and as long as I am there to be an aunt to his Chloe and to make the house comfortable he is content enough. And we do have darling old Goosey – she is our housekeeper as well as nurse to Chloe, just as she was to Bobby and me when we were little, for she's been with our family for ever – and she does all the hardest work so I have no cause to complain at all, for all I am mistress of the house. It is not easy to be mistress of a house as well as to have employment in an office when you are eighteen, but there – I manage well enough, Bobby says, and he seems content. Now, tell me all about *your* family. Have you brothers and sisters? And what sort of Mama and Papa have you and – oh, everything. And will you be doing more work for the WSPU and if so what will it be and – ?'

Poppy laughed. 'Only one thing at a time,' she protested.

'Well, family first. Where do you live and who with? And are you a happy person or – ?'

'As to happy – ' Poppy said slowly, 'I don't know. It is not a thing I consider very often. I mean, one doesn't. I'm just – life is just the way it is, isn't it?'

'Well, *how* is it for you? You tell me and then I will tell you if you are happy.' Mabel laughed then. 'I am very good at that. The other girls at the office, when we sit and have lunch, we all talk a great deal about our lives and our feelings and so forth, and they all say I am quite the best at judging matters of feeling. It is a skill of mine.' And she smiled with some complacency and, at last replete, pushed her cup to one side, set her elbows on the table, propped her chin on her hands and fixed Poppy with a steady gaze.

Poppy, a little embarrassed again, stammered slightly at first, but then it got easier, for there was no doubt that Mabel, for all her tendency to be a chatterbox, could listen too, and was genuinely interested in what Poppy had to say. So she said perhaps more than she might have on first acquaintance with any other person.

She told of the quiet life she led with her Mama and Step-grandmama (not wishing to sound disloyal she said nothing of Grandmama Maud's predilection for brandy, but did let out that she was captious and difficult and much given to fits of weeping and complaining) and mentioned her Uncles only in passing, saying she saw little of them, for they led their own lives centred on their clubs and their sport, which was true enough. The other unpleasant things about Harold in particular she would never tell anyone, and certainly not so new and delightful an acquaintance.

But she did tell her of the loneliness of the big house in Leinster Terrace and of the way she daydreamed so much and yearned for a real life, a busy life, an active life, and not one that wound its dreary way between home and school, and how Miss Sayers's help in making contact with the WSPU had been so important to her, and how much she yearned for – oh, she did not know quite what, but something –

And Mabel listened and watched her and absorbed it all and when at last Poppy came to an end said abruptly, 'And what of your Papa?'

'Mm?' Poppy looked startled.

'You have spoken of your Mama and your Mama's relations, but said not a word about your father and his family. Is he dead? And did he have no connections of his own, like your Mama's brothers and so forth?'

Poppy stared at her and tried to collect her thoughts. She never considered the matter, that was it. Long ago, when she had been younger, she had asked questions, could remember doing so. Other girls at school had spoken of their Papas and she had wanted to know about hers and that was why she had asked. And she could still remember the coldness that had descended on Mama when she had spoken so and how her Grandmama had fussed and fidgeted and told her to go away and stop pestering. Poppy had never asked the Uncles of course; even when she had been small she had known they had to be kept as far away as possible and she would never have considered seeking any sort of aid from them on any score. And she hadn't asked the servants either, not even Queenie who had been at Leinster Terrace for ever. She was much too bad-tempered to start with and, anyway, Poppy had realized early that these were questions that were not to be asked.

But that had been long ago, when she had been small, not yet seven years old. It was now many years since she had given the matter a moment's thought, and but for Mabel's direct question would not have done so now. But why not? It was a reasonable question. People had fathers; it was a universal experience. Why should she, Poppy Amberly, be excluded from it? And why, she found herself suddenly remembering, why did I once use a different name from Mama? A long time ago – she had forgotten that till this moment.

Now she lifted her brows at Mabel and said as easily as she could, 'Oh, he is dead.'

'And his relations?'

Poppy shrugged. 'I never knew of any.'

'My dear, how romantic! Is he the black sheep of your family?' Mabel grinned at her so warmly there could be no offence in the world meant or taken. 'I always wanted to meet a black sheep, but we Bradmans are dreadfully respectable and desperately dull. Perhaps your Papa was the younger son of a duke who did something wicked before you were born and his family cut him off altogether? Wouldn't that be divine? If it is so, perhaps you can go and seek out your long-lost relations and make them acknowledge you and then you'd be frightfully rich and wouldn't have to worry at all about the price of tea and crumpets! Do let me help you make your search!'

'Oh, Mabel, you are ridiculous!' Poppy said and laughed and Mabel, full of good humour, laughed too. And they started to speak of the work of the WSPU and said no more about Poppy's family; but the thoughts the conversation had mobilized did not go away.

Later, in the omnibus as it trundled its interminable way to Bayswater through the busy Saturday dusk, past the glittering shop fronts and the strolling crowds intent on an evening's entertainment, she thought again about all they had said. And began to make some tentative plans for the future.

First, she would accept Mabel's invitation to visit her own group of women working for the Vote.

'We're different,' she had explained earnestly. 'We don't entirely agree with Mrs Pankhurst and Miss Christabel Pankhurst. We agree with Miss Sylvia Pankhurst and prefer to be less militant – '

Poppy had nodded eagerly. 'I know about that. I was told by Miss Sayers that the family is not entirely in accord about how the work should be done – '

'Miss Sayers is right, whoever she may be. Well, Miss Sylvia likes to work with people who are less well-off than they should be. She says it is all wrong that only rich women can spare the time to work with the WSPU and that – '

'Oh, that is not fair!' Poppy had objected. 'I am not rich but I am not turned away. I can't join yet properly for I am not old enough, but as soon as I am – '

'Oh, you know what I mean.' Mabel had waved her hand airily. 'I don't mean rich precisely – it's really that it's all one sort of woman who joins the WSPU – Sylvia says that in the East End there are many women who suffer dreadfully for want of some sort of – well, *power* – in their own lives and she says it is necessary to take care of them and to help them understand they should have the Vote so that they can run their own lives *properly*. Do you see what she means? It isn't a matter of being poor precisely so much as a matter of – well having the time and the strength to think about things like voting. Poor women are so busy looking after their children and working in factories they can do nothing else – '

'I see,' Poppy had said. But she hadn't. Not really.

'Anyway the thing is that I like Sylvia better than I like the other WSPU people. I've been to some of their meetings and it's all a bit – ' Mabel had shrugged. 'I can't explain, but it's not as much fun as going to Sylvia's meetings. And the police don't follow her as much as they do the others, and that's one of the things that makes me prefer her.'

She gave a little shiver then. 'When that hateful policemen pulled my hair today I could have died. I felt so – it wasn't only that it hurt, you know. I was just so mortified. I felt like – like a slug or something caught by a hateful gardener.'

That Poppy had understood and had agreed fervently. 'Oh, *yes*! That was the worst part of it, the way the policeman pulled my arm.' And she rubbed her still slightly aching shoulder. 'But why did you come today then? I mean, if you don't work with the WSPU – '

'Oh, that was because of the others! Did you not see those rather jolly girls – the ones in hats and feathers?'

Poppy had grinned. 'I did see some who looked a bit – well – '

'Like cockatoos on a holiday,' Mabel had said cheerfully. 'That's right. Well, they are some of Sylvia's girls. Great fun – very rough and noisy you know, in their speech, but as good as gold, and much more amusing than some of those other WSPU women. Such prunes and prisms, some of them are! So boring – anyway, they heard of this meeting and they wanted to come and throw tomatoes at Winston Churchill, although Sylvia would be very put out if she knew – and I said I'd come with them as it is a Saturday and I have the time to spare. I thought it would be a great lark to see the Home Secretary spattered with tomatoes! But they were all such rotten shots – anyway, I came along and there you were! I had my hair pulled wickedly and you saved me!'

'And you saved me even more,' Poppy had said. 'For the way that man pulled my arm was so wicked, I never want to see a policeman ever again.'

'I doubt you'll get *that* wish,' Mabel had said dryly. 'But you won't see so many at Sylvia's meetings. There's one next Sunday – let me take you – '

And Poppy, flushed with excitement at the very idea, had agreed at once. All she had to do now was make a plan that would enable her to get out of the house without Mama knowing and fussing, and that shouldn't be too difficult. She had become very gifted at that over the past few years; she had had to.

But there was something else she had to do, she told herself now, staring out of the omnibus window as it made its clattering way round Marble Arch to reach the Bayswater Road and home. She had to speak to Mama about her father. It was quite absurd to be sixteen and to know so little of him; he must have existed, after all. And surely, as Mabel had said, he had had relations? To know them must be interesting; it certainly could not be any worse than knowing the relations she already had.

And her heart slid down into her scuffed and dusty boots as the omnibus at last stopped at the end of Leinster Terrace and she had to get out to walk the last hundred yards or so to her house and the inevitable scolding from Mama for being out so late on her own. And she began to marshal her necessary lies to make sure the scolding did not go on too long, and felt dreadful. Because accomplished liar to her mother though she had become, she still hated doing it.

4

Mildred had been sitting in the window of the drawing room for a long time; ever since Queenie had taken the tea tray away, in fact. She had made no attempt to find herself any occupation, as she usually did. Sewing or reading or indeed anything seemed to require too much effort by far and, once she had settled herself there to peer out between the Nottingham lace curtains to the street below, it had seemed so right somehow to just sit, and she had wondered a little dreamily just how many hours of her life she had spent here in this embrasure, wasting her years away in nothingness. And hadn't minded at all that it had been so many.

There had been a time, long ago, when she had been young – and how long ago that was it seemed impossible now to remember – when she had resented being locked away in this house, but not now. Now, she told herself, it was a haven, a place of peace and security that she was fortunate to have, a place where she could care for Poppy and give her the sort of home and background that a respectable young lady ought to have and deserved. Especially Poppy.

Oh, Poppy, she thought. I wish you knew how much I worried about you. I wish you knew how much you mattered to me. But she doesn't know; and she sighed, staring down at the dark street and the pool of light thrown by the gaslight outside on to the grimy paving stones. She looks at me with those wide eyes of hers and I can see her thoughts. She thinks I'm a dreary boring stop in her way; not her support and strength. She thinks I am tedious and uninterested in her wishes, rather than as concerned as I am that she should have always and only the best of everything. But she does not know what is best for her, so she thinks I do not care. And I care so much I – and she almost shook herself in irritation. To think so was maudlin. She had a task to do; to be mother and father, friend and mentor, support and guiding hand to this precious child. She had wrought well so far by means of

27

holding her hand hard to the plough and making a straight furrow, she reminded herself. To deviate from her path just to curry favour with Poppy was not the way to rear her to be the sort of woman her mother ached for her to be. It would be too easy to indulge her, to give in to all her whims, to say, 'Never mind, dearest – if you do not wish to do this or that – to stay at school – to go to college – then you need not do it.' That would not be the loving thing to do, even though it would be the easiest. Indeed, it would be a wrong and damaging thing to do to this unique and special person in her life, and, Mildred told herself firmly, I must never forget that.

It was getting even darker outside, for the pool of lamplight had seemed to brighten and now made threatening shadows and she leaned forward to peer further down the street towards the Bayswater Road. How much longer could she be? And she pulled on the fob watch which was on the bodice of her severe grey merino and looked at the time and frowned again. Almost seven, and the dressing bell due to ring in just fifteen minutes. Had something happened to her? Something dreadful?

And in spite of herself her mind took off, as it so often did, weaving a series of images in front of her eyes that were sickeningly real: Poppy, running heedless of the traffic, running under the wheels of a cab – no, worse, a great dray. Poppy destroyed and bloody as people came rushing to see what had happened, and then Mildred herself following a coffin along the dripping cinder paths of Kensal Green cemetery and Poppy gone for ever and ever – And she shook her head sharply and leaned forwards as she had so often this past hour, watching for the familiar figure along the empty street.

And then at last, there she was, a long shadow pushing into the lamplight, shortening, dwindling and then lengthening again as she walked through it towards the front door and Mildred felt a great rush of relief come lifting in her and took a shaky breath and then tightened her mouth; for it was taking longer for the shadows to thin out again than it had to shorten them. Poppy was dawdling. It was almost seven, she had been out all the afternoon and now she was dawdling; and Mildred got to her feet in one sharp little movement and walked out of the room to stand at the head of the stairs looking down into the hall, waiting for her.

It lay there below her, gleaming with the polish on the heavy mahogany furniture and the glitter of the well-scrubbed black and white tiles of the floor, warm and rich and good to look at, and yet again Mildred asked herself with some irritation why it was Poppy was always so anxious to leave this place of comfort and beauty, and so unwilling to come back to it. There had been a time, of course, when she too had felt trapped here in this very same house, but that had been long ago, when her father was alive, her uncaring, selfish, bullying father. But he was no longer here to hurt anyone. There was just Mildred to run the house and see that all was as it should be, Poppy's own mother, Mildred. How could the child feel about this house now as her mother once had? It seemed impossible to Mildred.

And yet Poppy did, and as Mildred stood there, waiting for the sound of the key in the lock, and hearing the moments tick away on the big clock in the hall beneath her, the pain of that knowledge filled her and made her very teeth ache with it, and she folded her lips even more firmly and waited, determined not to let Poppy see how hurt she was.

She came in at last, dragging her feet on the doormat, and slowly hung up her coat on the stand before smoothing her serge school tunic over her hips with both hands and then making the same movement over her rumpled hair. Mildred felt her chest tighten with love as she looked down on that curly head with its escaping tendrils and its thick untidy plait, and saw the drooping shoulders and the turned-down mouth; oh, Poppy, look happy, my dear one, as you did when you were small. Look happy!

'Poppy!' she said then and her voice came out thin and high, and Mildred knew the effect it would have and hated it; but she could not have helped herself. 'Where have you been?'

Poppy lifted her head and looked up and slowly her hands came down from her head and she let them dangle at her sides as she stood there and there was caution and, Mildred felt, hostility, in every line of her. But her voice when she spoke seemed neutral enough.

'I did tell you, Mama, where I was going. I have been at Miss Sayers's house, reading with her.'

'Until this hour?'

'Is it so late?' Poppy sounded surprised, but Mildred was not deceived. Poppy knew quite well what time it was.

'It is almost seven. Queenie will soon be ringing the dressing bell.'

'Oh, Mama, must we be so formal? Could we not just have our dinner cosily in your sitting room just as we are, instead of fussing over dressing? It is such a dull evening – it would be lovely to sit by the fire there and eat our supper from a tray.' She set her head on one side then added with some care, 'The way we used to do.'

'The way we –?' Mildred began and then stopped. It was so rare for

Poppy ever to say anything of past events. She talked to Mildred, when she talked at all, only of her plans for the future. Or rather her non-plans, reiterating over and over again her unwillingness to go to Cambridge, wanting, she said, to do something different without knowing quite what. Mildred had told herself long ago with great relief that Poppy had forgotten all about the past, that she had no need to worry over any inconvenient recollections. But now this; and she frowned sharply.

'I don't know what you mean. Of course we must dress. Supper on a tray? We have never done such a thing.'

Poppy had come upstairs, climbing steadily, one hand on the banister, never taking her gaze from her mother's face.

'Oh, but we did. Long ago when I was very small, I remember – '
She had reached the landing now and was standing beside her mother, looking at her very directly, and Mildred realized with a little shock that their eyes were no longer on a level. Poppy looked slightly down on her; she had grown taller. And, after a lifetime of being herself the tallest woman she knew, that made Mildred feel very odd.

'I was thinking, as I came home,' Poppy went on, and suddenly put out one hand and set it on her mother's shoulder, confidingly. 'I was thinking of how it used to be. When there were just you and me and we didn't live here with Grandmama and the – when it was just us.'

Mildred's mouth had gone dry suddenly and she turned away sharply, afraid her feelings might show on her face, and walked back to the drawing room.

'I really don't know what you mean' she said. 'You know perfectly well I have always lived in this house and you with me – '

'Oh, not always, Mama.' Poppy had followed her into the drawing room and now was leaning over the back of the high armchair, drawn up to the fire opposite Mildred's, into which she had arranged herself with her usual neatness. 'We lived in a much smaller house, once. I –' She smiled then, her whole face lifting into amused lines. 'Oh, Mama, it was so strange. As I came into Leinster Terrace just now, the cook at number three had come out to talk to Roberts – he's the policeman on duty tonight – and she had left the kitchen door open and, as I walked past their area, the most delicious smells came up – coconut and lemon, and caraway seeds, for she had been baking cakes, and it was like being at the Biograph, you know, the way it made me see how it used to be. It was just like seeing a cinematograph picture. The little kitchen and – everything.'

And she stopped and closed her eyes and saw it again for a moment, just as she had there on the corner of the street after getting off the omnibus; the little room glowed inside her head and she could stare round at it and see every detail: the shiny black range with the flickering coals and the mantelshelf over it with the pink china clock and the matching candlesticks; the pretty purple and blue vases with spills of curly paper which Mama used to carry a flame from the grate to the gaslight over the table; the shelves, one each side of the range, tucked away alongside the chimney breast, where the blue and white dishes were displayed and the cups hung on hooks; the big wooden table in the middle where the cakes stood, too many to count – and beyond in the scullery Mama, apron wrapped, pulling freshly boiled plum puddings out of a great steaming copper, with a huge pair of wooden tongs; Mama with her hair tied back and her face shining and wet from the steam that curled round her like a cloud –

She opened her eyes again and looked at Mama, sitting very upright in her chair beside the fire. Her grey merino with the soft cream collar fitted her well, and above it her hair was perfectly arranged in a neat and fashionable – without being *outré* – style that suited her thin face perfectly. She wore her gold fob watch and a discreet but pleasing gold brooch at the throat of the lace collar, and her hands, white and well-manicured, were folded tidily over each other. To imagine so perfectly turned-out a lady of Leinster Terrace wrapped in an apron making plum puddings and with her face red and damp from steam from a copper was ridiculous. Yet that was what Poppy had remembered as she had walked from the omnibus to her home tonight; and whether it was entirely due to the scent of freshly baked cakes, or her determination to speak to her mother of the past, she did not know. All that she knew was that the memory was there and she trusted it. There had been a time when they had lived in a small house and Mama had worked in a kitchen, amazing though that might seem. And she was determined to speak of it.

'And we used to eat our suppers on trays in front of the fire in that little kitchen,' she said now. 'I remember. So can't we do that again tonight?'

Mildred sat, nonplussed, trying to sort out her thoughts, for her head had whirled at Poppy's extraordinary remarks. Not that there was any sign on the surface of the turmoil within her, for she sat and stared in her usual direct and unsmiling manner at Poppy until she in her turn gave a little sigh and straightened up as the bell rang, muffled, from below.

'Another time, perhaps,' Poppy said dully as she turned towards the door. 'I'd better go and dress.'

'Um – wait – perhaps you are right, Poppy,' Mildred said suddenly and her voice was a little cracked. 'I dare say it will not be a great matter to do as you ask. Just touch the bell, will you?'

Poppy blinked and turned and gazed at Mildred, but she simply sat there and looked back at her, her face expressionless and Poppy, rather pink now, hurried to ring the bell, and they both remained silent as they waited for Queenie.

Who arrived looked disgruntled, which was far from unusual, and startled, which was. The house normally ran as sleekly as quicksilver in a barometer's channels, and nothing ever changed the pattern of its days; for the drawing room bell to be rung after the dressing bell was unheard of, and Queenie's face showed her disapproval of this change of arrangements.

'We shall not use the dining room tonight,' Mildred said. 'Serve our dinner in the morning room, if you please, on the small table. Set it on the hearth. There will be just myself and Miss Poppy. Mrs Amberly will take her dinner in her room as usual, and the gentlemen are out. That will be all, Queenie.' And Queenie opened her mouth to argue and catching Mildred's eye thought better of it and went, while Poppy stood and waited, delighted, till she had gone.

'Oh, Mama, I am so glad!' she burst out. 'It will be so agreeable!' And she ran across the room and hugged Mildred and, after one startled moment, Mildred let her straight shoulders soften and droop, although she made no move to return the hug. But Poppy felt new warmth in her and for just a moment the barrier that had been between them for so long seemed to thin out a little and lose some of its power.

The softening between them lasted all through supper. Mildred said no more about Poppy's late arrival home, and she, though conscience-stricken about telling that lie about being with Miss Sayers (a lie she knew would be supported by Miss Sayers if Mama ever thought to make any checks on it) knew better than to refer to it. The fragile bubble of accord around them was too precious to spoil by any such action.

They ate split-pea soup and steamed sole and collops of mutton while Poppy chattered of inconsequentials, longing to speak of all that had happened this afternoon, and also to start the conversation about her father that she had promised herself. But some native caution told her that the time was not yet ripe. So she talked of news items she had seen in the paper, such as the planned expedition to the South Pole by Amundsen (and she waxed lyrical on that, thinking it quite iniquitous that women could never be such intrepid explorers; now that would be something worth doing!) and of the new opera she had heard about which sounded so charming – *The Jewels of the Madonna*, such a mysterious title, didn't Mama agree? And the film of *Pinocchio* which Miss Sayers had seen and told her all about – and so the hour passed agreeably and Mildred watched her and listened and wished that she had the ability to be as free and comfortable with her child as she longed to be. But perhaps, just perhaps, tonight could be the beginning of a new closeness between them. And as she poured the coffee which a still highly disapproving Queenie brought to them she promised herself that she would try to be less serious, while of course still making sure that Poppy was kept to the most careful of lines, and encouraged to be what she was born to be – the sort of woman that Mildred herself had always yearned to be. Free and independent and strong.

She had relaxed much more than she had realized, for when Poppy said it, Mildred was as shocked as if the child had suddenly jumped up and shouted an obscenity, and she sat and stared at her for a long moment and then very carefully set down her coffee cup.

'What did you say?' she said, almost stupidly.

Poppy was still sitting there holding her own coffee cup between both hands and staring at her over the rim.

'I said, please, Mama, tell me about my father,' Poppy said, and her voice was a little unsteady, however composed she seemed.

'That is a very unexpected question, Poppy,' Mildred said, and folded her hands on the table in front of her. There was a lamp beside her, and the other lights in the room were off, and by dint of leaning back she was able to shade her face from Poppy; but the flicker of the firelight leaping busily from wall to wall and across the low ceiling showed it brightly from time to time, and Poppy could see clearly just how discomfited she was.

'Hardly unreasonable, though, Mama,' Poppy said, emboldened by the effect she had had. Usually Mildred was well able to turn away any subject she did not wish to discuss, but Poppy now had her at a disadvantage and, well realizing that fact, made the best use of it. 'After all, every person in the world has a father. I must have one too. But no one ever tells me anything about him or about his family. It is as though he disappeared from everyone's minds when he died, and surely that should not happen? A person may be dead, but he shouldn't be well – wiped away, the way you wipe chalk from a blackboard. Should he?'

'I – Sometimes that is what happens,' Mildred said.

'Then he *is* dead?' Poppy pounced. 'No one has ever actually said so, but I supposed that was the case. But then I couldn't be sure – *is* he dead?'

'I – what an absurd question, Poppy! He is not here, is he?' Mildred leaned even further back in her chair and turned her head away from the firelight in an attempt to hide her expression even more.

'Oh, Mama, that is no answer!' Poppy said and set down her coffee cup with a little clatter. 'Either he is dead or he isn't. If he is, then say so! It is no shame to die – or is it?'

'No, of course – oh, dear, this is so difficult.' And the sound of Mildred's voice made Poppy jump from her chair to come to her mother and kneel in front of her, reaching for her hands.

'Oh, Mama, I am sure it is – but we cannot be silent on this any longer! I knew when I was small that there were matters not to be spoken of regarding this, so I did not. But I used to think about it so many times! And today – well, I thought some more. I wondered about not only my father but about his relations. I mean, have I no other connections apart from Grandmama and the Uncles? I know there were your other brothers who died in the war in South Africa and I have heard of the various cousins of Grandmama, for she speaks of them often enough, but no one has ever said a word about the other relations. I must have some, mustn't I? Who are they? Where are they? Why are they never spoken of? Were they poor? Or wicked? I must know, Mama, surely!'

'What must you know?' Mildred was beginning to regain some of her confidence now. 'Why is it necessary? For all purposes that matter, there are just you and me. Grandmama is our cross which we must bear and we must do all we can for her, and as for my half-brothers – well, they are as they are – as most men are. They care nothing for us. They use this house, of course, and I am content enough to provide their care, but for any real purpose – there is just we two, Poppy. Can that not be enough for you? Must we spend time dealing with other people who know nothing of us and care less? I do beseech you, my dear, be content! We have this comfortable house and all we can possibly require. Caring for Grandmama is not so onerous, after all, and you have your education to consider, and your future to work for. When you have been to university and – '

'I am not going to college,' Poppy said, dismissing that. 'I am quite determined. And I am equally determined to know the answers to my questions, too. If you cannot tell me, there must be someone who can. Queenie perhaps – she has been in this house for ever, hasn't she? She will know and tell me if I ask – '

'She will not,' Mildred said swiftly. 'Indeed she will not.'

'Then there is a secret to be told!' Poppy again pounced like an eager cat. 'I am right to be so interested! It is not just a matter that he is dead? Are my other relations of such importance that you cannot tell me of them?'

Could Mabel be right? she was thinking, highly excited as she stared at Mildred's drawn face. Could it be possible that my father was indeed the younger son of a duke or some such? Could I be a rich heiress? And then somewere inside herself she laughed and pushed the notion away as absurd. But that there was something to be known was far from absurd and she was quite determined now, having breached Mildred's defences, not to give in.

So now she leaned closer forwards and said with all the guile she could put into her voice. 'Come, Mama, you might as well tell me. I will not let you be until you do, you know. Who was my father? Was he a Mr Harris? For I have remembered, you know, that once you told me that was my name. And then not long after told me I should forget it, for it was not my name after all. But I never shall forget now, Mama. Just as I shall never stop asking you about my father. So you might as well tell me now, might you not?'

5

'Oh, do tell me more!' Mabel said. 'It's too divinely thrilling!'

'You might think so,' Poppy said with some spirit. 'For me it is mortifying.'

Mabel was at once all compunction. 'Oh, my dear Poppy, I am sorry! Of course you are right – I should be ashamed of myself. Indeed, I meant no harm.'

'Oh, I'm sure you did not. And I suppose you're right, really. It *is* rather thrilling, such a mystery, isn't it? I just wish, though, that it weren't. I mean, I wish Mama would have told me all I wished to know instead of leaving me with so many questions. But I suppose I should be grateful for what I have discovered.'

'I cannot help but think that there must be some splendid story there somewhere if she is so secretive. It *is* strange, don't you think?'

'Yes, very strange,' Poppy said and leaned forward to stare out of the window of the omnibus. At first there had not been a great deal to see, for the shops they passed were shuttered and wrapped in Sunday afternoon rectitude, and there was only a small amount of traffic on the streets; but as the omnibus trundled ever farther east the scene outside began to change and Poppy was fascinated by all she saw – and not only by that. There was a curious familiarity about it all, even though she had never to her knowledge travelled this way before.

They were going to one of Miss Syliva Pankhurst's meetings in the East End; the plan which she had made with Mabel had been adhered to but despite the definite changes in the situation at home between Mildred and herself, Poppy had still chosen to be discreet about her interest in the Women's Suffrage movement, and had told her mother merely that she was to meet a new friend who wished to spend the afternoon with her. And Mildred had agreed meekly enough, accepting that Miss Campion and her staff, including Miss Sayers, whom she trusted completely, would not permit her daughter to associate with unsuitable girls. Poppy knew Mildred had assumed she had met her 'new friend' at Miss Sayers's house, and did not disabuse her of that notion. It was easier that way. One day, perhaps, if the ice continued to thaw, she would be free to be quite honest with Mama. That would be a very comfortable thing, and she looked forward to it with pleasure; but it was not yet the right time.

So, she had left the house in her neat brown ribbed wool costume with the black braid trimmings on the skirt and the cream cambric shirt with tucks that she had had made last autumn and which still looked well enough, and would have felt very grown up if only she had been able to put up her hair. But on that she knew Mama would be adamant. No decent girl put her hair up until she was seventeen at least, according to Mama, and perhaps not even then. She must wear her hated pigtail for some time yet, and though she pushed it up and tried to hide it under her hat, a rather dull one, she felt, in matt black straw, it made no difference. She looked dreadfully young and felt dreadfully dowdy when she met Mabel at the omnibus stop.

Mabel was wearing a most elegant costume in a rich purple with a divine hobble skirt, and over it one of the new very large hats that were all the rage. She looked most *soignée*, Poppy told her smilingly, from the tips of her beautiful lilac gloves to the toes of her pointed *glacé* kid boots.

And Mabel had preened a little and then, as they had settled into their seats at the front of the omnibus, had asked her why she looked like a chicken about to burst if she didn't lay an egg; and Poppy, badly needing a confidante, had blurted it all out, and after that the fact that Mabel was dressed killingly in the latest mode while she, Poppy, was still every inch a dowdy schoolgirl, mattered not a whit.

But it had been difficult to explain, because Poppy herself was not sure, as she looked back, precisely what her mother had told her. It had clearly been difficult for her, Poppy had said to Mabel, staring with glazed eyes out of the omnibus window and seeing only Mildred's strained white face in the flickering light of the morning room fire that Saturday evening when she had said – well, *what* had she said? Only that she did not know whether or not Poppy's father was alive or dead.

'I have not seen him for many years, Poppy. We – we could not agree, you understand. We tried, but we could not. He was in the Army during the war – he was at Spion Kop, like your Uncle Basil and – we could not agree.'

And her face had become very hard and closed and she had looked up at the photograph on the mantelshelf, the one of two rather doughy-faced boys in school clothes who were, she knew, her mother's own true brothers, Basil and Claude, both long-since dead.

'Was he killed there too?' Poppy had ventured after a while, and Mildred had after a long moment shaken her head and turned it to look at Poppy again. It was clear then to Poppy how very distressed her mother actually was behind her hard façade and for the first time felt a pang of guilt at having had the temerity to push her so hard. She had been concerned only with her own will, her own curiosity, her own restlessness. She had given no thought to what her mother might be suffering with all this probing into the past and suddenly she had felt quite dreadful, and impulsively leaned forwards, opening her mouth to speak. But Mildred had put up one hand to stop her and said sharply, 'No, he was not killed – I saw him once more, after the war. Just once.'

Poppy had said nothing, just crouching there, sitting on her heels and watching her mother's face, for now she had started it would have been, she felt obscurely, more unkind to stop her than to allow her to go on.

'He came here to see me, and I told him that – we decided then that – well, suffice to say we saw no more of each other after that day. I remained here with you and for a while I tried to arrange matters so that you used your father's name, Harris – but you seemed so unwilling to do so, and kept forgetting it and paid no attention when the teachers at school used it, so – ' Mildred had shrugged slightly. 'It was simpler to send you to a new school and use again just the name to which you were accustomed. Mine – ' And then she had slid into a silence that Poppy at length had to break somehow.

'So he might be alive yet?' she ventured at last.

'It is possible,' Mildred said. 'I suppose it is possible. But I think probably not – he was not a healthy man. He – he lost an arm in the war, you see and – '

'Oh!' Poppy had cried and rocked back on her heels and then had jumped to her feet, to stand and stare down at her mother with one hand set to her mouth.

'What is it? My dear child, whatever is it?' Mildred had cried out in alarm, for Poppy had gone quite white, although she herself was not aware of it. And after a while Poppy had told her, haltingly at first and then with more energy, of her recurring experience during both sleep and waking, and how the sight of a man with an empty sleeve had set it off this very afternoon (and even in her agitation she had managed not

38

to give away to her mother where this had happened). And Mildred had closed her eyes in distress and said heavily, 'I thought you had forgotten.'

'Forgotten what?' Poppy had cried. 'I thought it was just a sort of dream – I wanted to know what it meant, I always did, but I never liked to ask – I thought it was a dream.'

'No.' Mildred had shaken her head. 'It was a memory. The day he came here you – I don't quite know how, but you saw him and got out of the house and ran after him. Why, I shall never understand, for you – you did not know him. Because of his absence at the war you did not know him, yet you had run down the street after him. You were only a baby, Poppy! A little baby of just five years old! You did not know what you were doing! And Queenie, thank God, saw you and ran after you and caught you before you reached the corner, and brought you back – '

Now, sitting in the omnibus with Mabel beside her waiting eagerly to hear every word of what had happened last Saturday, Poppy felt again the sick emptiness that she had known then, listening to her mother's bald account of the source of that horrid running vision she had suffered for so long. It had been bad to have it, but it had been worse, somehow, to lose it. For she had known at once as she had listened to her mother's halting explanation that it would never happen again. Now she had been told what it was, and why it occurred it had vanished into some impenetrable void, and with it some sort of contact that was important to her. It was like waking in the morning after a disturbing dream, and knowing it had been disagreeable and yet wanting very badly to remember it to deal with it. And not being able to.

'So you still do not know about him? About his relations?'

'Mmm?' Poppy said and dragged her eyes from the window of the omnibus to look at her. 'Oh, the relations – I did ask her about them – '

'And what did she say? Oh, do, please tell me! It is like reading the most thrilling of stories to hear this! You must tell me all. What did she say? *Are* they rich and important? Is that why – ?'

Poppy shook her head. 'I tried. I really did, but by this time she was indeed past talking of anything, I believe. It seemed unkind to persist, so I – ' She shrugged. 'I said no more. And ever since – '

'Yes?' Mabel said eagerly. 'Ever since what?'

Poppy's gaze had drifted back to the window. Outside the view was quite different. No longer were the shops shuttered and empty; now they were busy with doors standing invitingly open and many people bustling in and out, and the kerbs were lined with market stalls, doing just as roaring a trade as the shops with eager customers. And such customers! Lively, busy people in cheap but gaudy clothes, for the most part, though some were dressed in the rusty black and tattered boots of the truly poor, and hordes of children as well as adults, and all shouting and talking at the tops of their voices and gesturing busily to add emphasis to their speech; even here inside the omnibus Poppy could hear the hubbub, and she realized that they were not all speaking English. Words she could not understand came to her out of the underlying counterpoint of din, and though she knew they were foreign words, yet still they did not seem unfamiliar. Indeed none of it seemed as unfamiliar as it should; and she stared, fascinated, as again the omnibus gathered speed after depositing passengers at a stop, and moved on its way.

'Poppy!' Mabel said again. 'Ever since *what*?'

'Mm? Oh, yes – well, all this week Mama has been different. I can't say how, but she is.' She shrugged. 'She is not so – well, severe as she was. She is still definite, you understand, on what is proper to be done and how matters should be arranged at home – we live a very ordered life, do you see – but she is not so severe. I see her watching me sometimes and it is so strange – it is as though – ' and she stopped, suddenly feeling disloyal in saying all this to Mabel. She liked her a great deal, but she was after all only the most recent of acquaintances. To pour out all the family history to her like this, on just their second meeting, was really rather disgraceful. And she bit her lip, annoyed with herself.

'I do not wish you to think she is a bad Mama, you know,' she said now a little abruptly. 'She is very definite in her opinions, but I must respect her for that. And she has a great care for me.'

'I'm sure she has,' Mabel said, now embarrassed herself as she felt the discomfort that filled Poppy. 'I mean no criticism in asking you these questions. It is just so – I live so humdrum a life, you understand, that any new information is an adventure to me!'

'Humdrum? You? Working in a newspaper office and being the mistress of your brother's house? That cannot be called humdrum when you are only eighteen!' Poppy said.

'Everything is, I suspect, when it is part of your own life,' Mabel said sapiently. 'What happens to other people always seems so much more exciting. Your life seems more interesting to me and mine to you – but I suppose it's easier in some ways to be me.' And she reached up to tweak her huge hat into position, and to prink a little at her reflection in the omnibus window. 'I must say I should find it very disagreeable to have no money of my own. My salary is a great comfort to me! I would hate to have your problems about money, dear Poppy, indeed I should – '

Poppy went a little pink. 'Actually I have no further ones now,' she said. 'Mama only yesterday – she said that it was time I had a small allowance. She said she understood quite well that I have greater needs than I had and must have some more interests in my life. She said – '

She stopped as she remembered the conversation, over breakfast the day before.

'I know you are not certain about your future, Poppy,' Mildred had begun. 'And I dare say you become very irritated with my insistence that you should complete your education to a high level. I am sure, however, that you will come to see the matter sensibly in due course – No!' she had lifted her hand to stop Poppy's attempts to interrupt her. 'No, let me finish. I have been considering the matter carefully and realize that I had forgotten the wisdom of the old adage. It is indeed the case that all work and no play – anyway, I have thought most carefully of the matter and it is time, I think, that you should have a little more pleasure in your life. I shall speak to your teacher Miss Sayers, who seems to have your welfare at heart and whose company you seem to enjoy so much and suggest to her that she arranges more entertainment for you. You must still attend to your books, of course, and complete your studies, but in between some pastimes are clearly necessary for you. Theatres and concerts and so forth – '

She had waved her hand in an oddly stilted little gesture. 'I am sure you would enjoy that. And perhaps you need some new clothes. You are growing so rapidly that all you have seem to look skimpy. I shall ask Mrs Winkworth to come and discuss some new costumes for you, perhaps next week, in time to make you something new for Easter. And you will need some money in your pocket for such outings, so I propose an allowance of half a sovereign each week. I imagine that will suffice – '

And she had gone to the kitchen to give the day's orders leaving Poppy open-mouthed and elated, and yet somehow anxious. For Mama to have changed so very much, to have thawed quite so suddenly, was alarming indeed; but perhaps, she told herself, she would get used to it? And her natural optimism lifted in her and she almost hugged herself as she thought of the great many things she

41

could do with half a sovereign each week. Knowing about her father and his relations suddenly seemed far less interesting; there were other things to think about after all.

'She has given me an allowance,' she said now to Mabel, who made her mouth into a keyhole of excitement and opened her eyes wide.

'My dear Poppy, how splendid!' Mabel said. 'Is it a good one?'

'It is not for clothes, you understand,' Poppy said. 'Mama will deal with those still. Mrs Winkworth, who does our sewing, is to come next week to see us and I am to have some new ensembles for Easter. So this is just for theatres and so forth – it is half a sovereign. Every week.'

'That's very handsome!' Mabel said after a moment. 'Why, I earn only seventy-five pounds a year in my employment, which gives me a little over a sovereign and a half each week and I have to work from ten until six for that, although my brother has arranged I need not work on Saturdays, which is good of him. So I am greatly in awe of you – to have so much for not working at all must be very agreeable!'

There was a slightly waspish note in Mabel's voice and Poppy said at once, 'Oh, I do agree, I feel quite indulged, indeed I do. And the first thing I shall do with it, after paying for this journey, of course, is to give you tea. Is there a nice ABC tea shop anywhere near where the meeting is to be held this afternoon?'

Mabel laughed at that. 'Oh, no, my dear! There are none of those in these mean streets! This is the slums, you know! No, we shall not take tea in a tea shop here. We shall go instead back to town and find somewhere there, perhaps where there is music. That will be delightful.'

Poppy turned again to the window and looked out. They had reached almost the end of their journey now, for the omnibus was wheeling down the Whitechapel Road and once again Poppy was struck by a powerful sense of familiarity, and an agreeable one at that. The road was wide and lined with some sizeable buildings, but down the side streets it was possible to glimpse a very much more squalid scene, where tiny houses were pressed close together and the pavements were filled with people who seemed much less well dressed than those she had noticed earlier. After the peace and elegance of the Bayswater Road and Leinster Terrace such streets should have filled her with disgust; but they did not. It all seemed to her to be exciting and attractive, even welcoming, and she wrinkled her brow as she stared out.

But then her thoughts drifted away again back to all that she had been telling Mabel. It had indeed been an eventful week in her life, ever since she had first met this delightful new acquaintance. Mabel had, in a sense, brought her good fortune, for now she was to have new clothes and an allowance and that was very splendid indeed. What did it matter that she still did not know all she would have liked to know about her father and his family? Perhaps he was not rich, nor the son of a duke as Mabel had hoped, but he had been a brave soldier and that was a great thing to know.

One day, perhaps, Mama would tell her more, when she felt less agitated but, meanwhile, Poppy was content enough with the way her lines were falling. And she followed Mabel off the omnibus as at last it reached their destination, well satisfied and looking forward with great anticipation to the meeting that was to come, because Mabel had promised her it would be a great deal more fun than the one at Caxton Hall and certainly a good deal less alarming.

6

Mabel had been quite right. This meeting was a lot more fun than Caxton Hall had been. First of all, Poppy had no responsibility for any action, and although her involvement with last Saturday's events had been immensely exciting, it had also been very alarming. To be able to sit at this meeting as just a member of the audience with no need to concern herself with anything else was much nicer, Poppy told herself, as she perched on the edge of a wooden form and stared about her. And in such a place, too!

For it was an open-air meeting. They were in the middle of a green square of rather worn grass and ragged bushes just off the main road where Whitechapel met Mile End. Wooden forms had been dragged out of a nearby school for people to sit on, though many were squatting at the front on spread-out potato sacks near a central rather ramshackle dais, apparently built of tea chests, while a few younger people had scrambled up the stunted trees that grew at the edge of the square to sit on branches and peer down at the crowd below and jeer at them and pelt them with apple cores. But there was no malice anywhere; the crowd was clearly good natured and there was much cheerful badinage among the young people, who were in the majority. There were almost as many men as women, unlike last week's more elegant Westminster meeting, and best and exceedingly colourful clothes were much in evidence.

'It's as good as a party to them,' Mabel remarked, and she pulled her dress aside a little fastidiously as a large young woman in a very vivid acid yellow and emerald green ensemble came and plonked herself down beside her. 'There can't be a great deal for people to do in these parts for entertainment and they're really frightfully poor.'

'They don't look it,' Poppy said, matching her tones to Mabel's low ones. 'Everyone looks well fed enough and the clothes the girls are wearing are very jolly.'

44

'That's as may be,' Mabel said a little loftily. 'They're certainly garish enough, aren't they? And as to well fed, I really can't say I know about that. But this is a famously slummy part of London, you know, so it can't be a very agreeable place to live, can it? And no one would choose to live here unless they were dreadfully poor?'

Prudently Poppy didn't answer, but she disagreed profoundly with her new friend. She and Mabel might live in the so-called respectable part of the town but that did not, she told herself, make it better than this part. Here she felt a great energy wrapping round her and an excitement that would have greatly improved the dreariness of Leinster Terrace. The buildings here might not be very splendid – indeed the houses were, she had to admit, mean and narrow – but that didn't seem to matter. Everyone she saw was relaxed and noisy and seemed quite oblivious of all the things she had been brought up to believe were extremely important. They talked loudly, they looked around them at others and stared shamelessly at what interested them, they laughed easily and, horror of horrors, they ate in public and with great abandon for everywhere she looked there seemed to be rotating jaws and a lively trade was carried on by sellers of pasties and Italian ices and toffee apples and heaven knew what else besides. And she gazed at it all and wished passionately that she was part of it properly, instead of just an onlooker. It would be fun to shout to acquaintances and wave at them and cry out loud greetings and –

'I say,' Mabel said. 'Here she is – look – '

And Poppy looked and saw pushing her way through the crowd towards the dais a short rather dumpy figure in a somewhat old-fashioned and untidy costume of donkey grey, but hatless. Her hair was pinned on top in an unruly bun so that wild tendrils curled everywhere and her face bore an expression of good-humoured anxiety. The people she passed seemed to know her and patted her on the back and called out to her and she bobbed her head and smiled at them in an abstracted fashion as she ploughed her way determinedly on.

'That one?' Poppy asked. 'Is *that* Miss Sylvia Pankhurst?'

'Indeed it is!' Mabel said and began to applaud with her gloved hands as others around her took up the welcome and shouted mightily at the untidy woman now scrambling inelegantly on to the dais.

'Oh!' said Poppy, a little surprised, and more than a little disappointed. Quite what she had expected she did not know. Certainly, she had not thought to see someone quite so unprepossessing. Mrs Pankhurst, the divine Emmeline, and her daughter Christabel were both very handsome women, even beautiful, with sculptured high-cheekboned faces and deep dark eyes that seemed positively to burn as one looked into them. They dressed with great style and were well known for their appreciation of fashion. Many were their followers who copied their appearance as much as they copied their principles, and many were those who came to meetings just to admire those two splendid creatures. But no one would ever come to a meeting to admire Sylvia Pankhurst, Poppy decided. She seemed much too dull.

And, at first, it seemed she was an equally dull speaker. She started hesitantly and used a rather thin little voice that had none of the trained resonance that both Emmeline and Christabel could command. And she hesitated a good deal, again quite unlike her forthright and very eloquent mother and sister.

But after a while that stopped mattering. She was so very agreeable a person and so very sincere, Poppy decided as she listened to her talking; and what she had to say while not particularly inspiring was very important. And moving too –

For she said little about the battle for Votes for Women. She was much more concerned with the problems of poverty. She spoke of hungry children and hard-pressed mothers trying to earn enough in the sweatshops to buy food for them. She spoke of dispirited men struggling to earn a living in the docks, but held down and exploited by a most cruel system of controls over labour. She spoke of the sort of landlords who made fat profits out of buildings which were barely fit for humans to live in and yet into which they packed as many tenants as they could get. She spoke of factory owners who made their workers slave for twelve hours a day for a pittance to make clothes that would sell for large sums in West End shops. She spoke too of loneliness and despair and hunger – and yet everyone cheered her.

Eventually, however, she began to speak of more political matters, and of how the Vote might give women some chance to improve their lot by having an effect on Parliament, and then the meeting really did become amusing. Many of the men started to heckle, still cheerfully and without malice but very noisily, and at first Sylvia Pankhurst struggled to ignore them; but then she gave up and began to reply to their sallies with some spirit. And then some of the girls joined in and soon there was a great deal of laughter as Sylvia neatly capped point after point and some of the crowd started jeering at and teasing each other instead of her.

Yet there was still no unpleasantness. There was none of the tension that had crackled so alarmingly at Caxton Hall and which had seemed to Poppy at the time to be so exciting. She had noticed a brace of policemen at the back of the crowd, but they were not at all threatening. They stood and listened and watched and showed no signs of being as belligerent as their massed colleagues had been in Westminster and no one paid them any attention, and that comforted Poppy greatly. So she relaxed and listened and laughed and even, after a while, joined in the heckling, somewhat to her own surprise, feeling quite unable to prevent herself from crying out, 'Nonsense!' when a man not far from them had shouted out, 'Wimmin wiv eddication is a blot on the landscape. Why don't you put a sock in it, lidy?'

At Poppy's interruption the man turned and stared at her and then bawled out, 'See what I mean, gents? 'Ere we 'as one o' these 'igh-class school madams, an 'ellcat in the makin' and much good it's done 'er! Don't she look a fright?'

'At least I have more sense than to wear as regrettable a hat as yours, sir!' Poppy cried in great indignation. 'But I dare say it is all you *can* wear when you have so little inside the head it covers!' It was so mortifying to look so obviously what she was that her tongue ran away with her and gave her a courage she did not know she had. But her mortification melted away as someone else in the crowd shouted, 'That's it, missie – you tell 'im wot an ugly moosh e's got! Send '*im* to school for the next forty years and 'e'd still be ugly and stoopid!'

And everyone cheered and Poppy blushed as Mabel nudged her, half-shocked by her temerity and half-applauding, as someone on the far side joined in. 'I'd a sooner look like an 'igh-school miss than like Tosher Evans, an' no error. You show 'im 'ow to be a gent, miss – go on, you show 'im!'

Poppy sank back on her seat, quite speechless now, and Mabel beside her giggled and said in her ear. 'Oh, my dear, that was delicious! You've only taken on a man they all hate. Last time I came to a meeting here they almost carried him off in a barrel, they were so incensed by him!'

'Why do they dislike him so?' Poppy asked, still blushing as the crowd exhorted her to respond to Evans, who was now shouting very loudly indeed on his own account. 'I agree he's very rude, but then so is everyone else!' For now the insults were flying thick and fast amid a great deal of laughter. 'He seems no worse than they are!'

'Oh, but he is! You see there was a burglary at Miss Sylvia's

Settlement house and it is generally thought around here that the man Evans was behind it, and she is very well liked indeed – so – '

She was interrupted by even more noise and they turned to see Evans being carried shoulder-high from the square and out to the edge of the crowd, where he was unceremoniously dumped by the three large men who bore him there, after which he swore loudly and went off to much ribald laughter and applause. And the crowd then returned its attention to Sylvia Pankhurst, who had been quite inaudible for some time.

But now she was ready for them and after a little more talk of the importance of improving the lot of the women and children of the East End, she announced that the hat was coming round, and an ironic cheer went up.

But many of the people there contributed willingly enough, and Poppy dug into her own pocket and brought out one of her precious shillings – a good sum when most people were dropping ha'pennies into the hat – and felt it was well worth the expenditure. Mabel had been right. Miss Sylvia Pankhurst's meetings were far more to her taste than the more political ones she had hitherto experienced. And she promised herself that she would come back again to the East End whenever she could and help her. There were quite enough well-off people working in town for Votes for Women; here it seemed the only people willing to help the poor to obtain anything, including the Vote, were the poor themselves, and she looked round at the crowd, now beginning to wander off to pubs and cafés and yet more of the itinerant food sellers, and thought how interesting they all looked, and how much she would enjoy being one of them.

'I am glad I don't live here myself,' Mabel said, uncannily echoing her thoughts. 'But I must say the people here are much more fun than they are in Holland Park. There everyone is so precise and proper that it is very boring. Shall you come here again, Poppy?'

'Oh, yes!' Poppy said fervently. 'I should like to very much. There must be a lot of work to be done for those women and children Miss Sylvia spoke about. It is dreadful to think of children being hungry –' and her eyes glistened a little as she went on, 'Imagine what it must feel like to be truly empty.'

'It feels very nasty indeed,' a voice said behind them and they both turned to stare. A pale thin girl in a long black duster coat that underlined her pallor and with her brown frizzy hair loose and flowing over her shoulders was standing gazing at them.

'Oh,' Poppy said, nonplussed. 'I – I'm sure it does.'

'Why, hello, Flora!' Mabel said with a rather strained *bonhomie*. 'I wondered if we should see you here today. Poppy, this is Miss Gordon. She works a great deal with Miss Pankhurst, for she is a pupil of hers. Flora, this is Miss Amberly. She held the key for them at that meeting last week – you know, at Caxton Hall – did you hear about it? It was a great drama, indeed. And then she saved me from a hateful policeman – '

'Oh, I did little enough,' Poppy said, abashed. 'And then you helped me – how do you do, Miss Gordon?'

'How d'you do,' the pale girl said abruptly. 'Miss Sylvia sent me. You are to come to tea.'

'Oh!' Mabel said and grinned widely, her round face glistening a little with pleasure. 'I say, how jolly! Did she like Poppy joining in that way?'

'Yes,' the pale girl said shortly and turned to lead the way out. 'We are to meet her there.'

'Where?' Poppy said, obediently falling into step beside her. She was not sure she wanted to go somewhere unknown to tea; it seemed so very sudden an invitation that she wanted time to think about it, but she had been given none. Mabel had gone to the girl's other side with alacrity and was stepping out with her as cheerfully as her hobble skirt permitted. 'I mean, I much appreciate the invitation, but I must not be away too long. I told Mama I would be home again by seven, you see, and – '

'Oh, it is barely four now,' Mabel said airily. 'And we should have had tea in town somewhere, anyway. We shall have to do that another time – you owe me that, Poppy! But you will enjoy tea here. I have been before, and it is all very delicious. Is Mrs Braham still – ?'

'Oh, of course,' Flora said contemptuously, still striding ahead and looking neither to right nor left. They had left the square now, and had reached the Mile End Road which was heavy with traffic, in spite of it being Sunday afternoon, and with its pavements thronged with strollers. 'You know how she is always around! And there is nothing she likes better than to feed everyone – it is quite disgusting, indeed it is!'

'Oh, Flora, we cannot all be as high minded as you!' Mabel said, a little spitefully. 'You may be far above such commonplace things as food and drink but, for my part, they make life very agreeable. And I remember the perfectly delectable cakes we had last time I was asked to tea at the settlement house, and Mrs Braham had made them.' She peered round in front of Flora to Poppy, who was almost running to keep up with the pale girl's stride. 'She is an American, you know, Poppy, and owns a food shop near here, and whenever there is a special meeting she arranges to look after everyone afterwards. She says that it's her contribution – but I believe she is generous with money as well. She is quite rich, I understand.'

'Many Americans are, I am told,' Poppy said and looked back at Mabel, and almost laughed aloud for she looked so very absurd. Her hobble skirt was of course quite impossible to hurry in; it hardly permitted a walk, let alone an almost-run like that demanded by Flora, so she had hauled it half way up her calves so that her little *glacé* boots quite twinkled with the speed they were making. Her hat had slipped slightly – not surprising, since it was so very large – and her face was damp with her efforts. But she seemed to be enjoying herself greatly and Poppy relaxed. She could still reach home in time, and it would be fun to meet Miss Sylvia after all.

'She is not precisely American,' Flora said unexpectedly. 'She was born here, and lived here in these parts all her life until she married and went to America. Now she has returned as a widow with a very strange manner of speaking, but a good heart. I am afraid, however, that she does encourage greed among some people.' And she looked sideways at Mabel, who seemed oblivious of her disapproval, and then hurried them both on their way, across the crowded road ahead before plunging into the side street on the far side.

And Poppy hurried along beside her, looking round with lively interest, as Mabel chattered on on Flora's other side.

'You must ask Flora to show you her sketches, Poppy, for she is a very gifted artist.' Mabel sounded a little condescending now. 'Aren't you, Flora? She is destined to be a great success, I am quite sure. Miss Sylvia thinks highly of her work, and she should know after all, since she teaches her. Isn't that so, Flora?'

'Yes,' Flora said with great scorn and still stared directly ahead of her as she strode on her way, and Poppy had to giggle. She was so very intense a girl and so determined not to show any of the responses that were expected of her that she was quite funny. Poppy had never met anyone quite like her, and certainly no one who looked so determinedly artistic in clothes and style, but at the same time she felt she understood her well enough. She was a person who needed to make herself important, and had chosen this way to do it. It would be interesting to see her work and to discover whether or not she was a real artist; but it would not surprise Poppy to find that she was merely competent.

She turned her attention away from Mabel's chatter and Flora's contemptuous silence and stared about her again, and then, oddly, felt the same way she had done earlier in the omnibus. These narrow streets were foreign to her, so very unlike the wide pavements of home and the tall cream stucco of the house she lived in, and yet they were not foreign at all. Everything seemed pleasantly familiar and she frowned a little, trying to work out why that should be. And then, as Flora speeded up even more and she had to take a deeper breath to fuel her own efforts to keep up, Poppy realized what it was that made her feel so comfortable. It was the smell. It was that which was so reassuring and she lifted her chin and drew in a long breath through her nose, trying to analyse what she smelled.

Ordinary street smells of course – soot and horses and some petrol fumes from the occasional rattling van and dust and people – but there was more than that. There was a great collection of food smells, of frying fish and sour vinegary pickles and cooked onions and spices and baking yeasty bread and she half-closed her eyes and let the amalgam of odours fill her and felt a deep sense that seemed compounded of both comfortable security and an enjoyable anticipation. It was known to her, and it presaged good things, and she found herself smiling as at last Flora Gordon slowed her headlong stride as they reached a tall narrow building on a corner.

'Here we are,' Mabel panted, with considerable relief in her voice. 'I am sure we have returned before Miss Sylvia, you have made us go so fast.'

'Possibly,' Flora said curtly. 'You are to wait in the back room,' she said, 'the others will be here directly.' And she marched into the house, pushing open the door with a sharp little movement, and disappeared into the darkness, and they heard her footsteps go pounding upwards as she left them behind.

'Oh, thank heavens she has gone!' Mabel said, with heartfelt relief. 'She is so very wearing a person! Now we can be comfortable.' And she led the way down the narrow hallway towards a door at the back.

'Is she always quite so curt?' Poppy asked as she followed her.

'Oh, yes – such a poseur! She thinks that because she is an artist she is so far above everyone else that even talking to humble mortals like us is an insult to her! But she works hard for Miss Sylvia and loves her very dearly, so we all put up with her. Now do come in. This is where we are to wait. It is good of Miss Sylvia to invite us, isn't it? Do you like this room? It looks very interesting, doesn't it?'

They were in a small space, which seemed full of paper, for on every table and on most of the chairs there were piles of papers and books, and on every inch of wall there were posters and drawings – some of which Poppy thought looked very good indeed and she wondered fleetingly if they were the work of the odd Miss Gordon – which seemed to make the place feel as though it were much smaller than it actually was.

And then it shrank even more, for behind them the door opened and when Poppy turned to look there in the doorway stood quite the largest and reddest woman she had ever seen.

7

'So how come you got back so soon? Ain't the others with you?' the large woman said and Mabel jumped to her feet – for she had cleared a chair to sit on by means of the simple expedient of putting its contents on the floor – and hurried across the room with one hand outstretched.

'Hello, Mrs Braham. How good to see you again! Yes, we are the first. Flora brought us, you know, and said Miss Sylvia and the others would be here directly. She said we were to have tea –'

'So what else should you have?' the big woman said and looked over Mabel's shoulder at Poppy. 'Why else have I been spending the whole afternoon slicin' and spreadin' an' bakin' and fixin', that you shouldn't have a bite to eat when you got back from your cockamamie meetin'? So you're hungry, hey? Good – good. You'll come and eat –' And she stepped back to indicate they were to follow her from the room.

She had a strange voice, Poppy thought, warm and deep and yet with a faintly nasal twang to it, and her accent was quite the most peculiar she had ever heard. A Cockney accent was not unfamiliar to her, for she had spent enough time with her mother's servants, heaven knew, but this was not just Cockney. There was an overlay of something more that she had to assume was American. But she couldn't be sure, for she had never before met an American and certainly never spoken to one.

'Shouldn't we wait for the others?' Mabel said with dubiety in her voice, but frank greed on her face. 'I mean, it would be more polite –'

'Polite, polite, who cares polite?' the big woman said, and moving with a swiftness and grace a little startling in one so very bulky, she turned with a swish of her red velvet skirts and a creaking of her even redder satin bodice and led them out of the room towards the front of the house and the staircase.

53

Poppy followed, and as they went up the stairs a great waft of the smell came back to her; food again, as delectable as before, but also an almost overwhelming wash of attar of roses and she took a deep breath, enjoying it, for it was the most delightful scent she could imagine and a little bubble of happiness seemed to form deep in her belly and begin to grow, slowly but very steadily.

The big woman was still talking as she led the way up the stairs. 'You wait till they all come in and what we got? We got a rumble, that's what, we got people all over the place all fighting to get food at the same time. An' that ain't no good for no one. Better already you should eat first. You're here first, you eat first, okay? Then you make space for the others, right? Right. Now, you settle in, and me, I go and fetch the tea. Easier up here for so many of you – but me, I got to shlap up and down the stairs, up and down, to keep the kettle goin' and fill the urn. I tell you, who'd be a woman, hey?' And she pushed them both through the door that led to the room at the front of the house on the first floor.

Inside the smell of food was quite overpowering and not surprisingly so, for there amid a clutter of sofas and chairs was a long table that spread the length of the whole room. And it was a big room for it ran from the front to the back of the house, with a pair of doors between the front and back segment, now pushed back against the walls. And the table was laden with more eatables than Poppy could ever remember seeing. There were plate after plate of slices of bread and rolls on which were spread all manner of things that looked strange and yet – perhaps not so strange. Pieces of silvery fish which she knew without being told were raw pickled herrings, set in rings of pale onion, and cheeses ranging from the pure white of cream to the gently golden, and the rich crimson gleam of sliced tomatoes against the equally beautiful clear green of sliced cucumbers. There were cakes galore, and scones and jams and biscuits and fruit of all kinds, and Poppy stared at it all and then at Mabel and then at the woman at the door, who was now standing with her arms folded as she watched them looking at her efforts, her round face creased widely with pleasure as she caught Poppy's eye.

Poppy could see her more clearly now, for this room was brightly lit, with the gaslight plopping cheerfully overhead to lift the greyness of the now dwindling afternoon that pressed against the net-curtained windows. She was a handsome woman, for all her size, round-faced and very smooth- and rosy-cheeked and with bright glinting eyes that seemed to laugh as she looked at Poppy. Her hair was dark and lustrous and piled high on her head in ringlets and waves and curls of quite terrifying complexity. It must take hours, Poppy thought, trying not to stare too obviously, hours and hours and hours to arrange it in the morning, for it looks too perfect to be true. And then she saw among the curls and waves little pins bearing artificial butterflies which were artfully concealed so that it looked as though the little creatures had just hovered there for a moment and then decided to stay. They seemed almost alive for the wings quivered with every breath the large woman took, and she laughed as she saw Poppy's glance steal towards them again.

'You like them?' she said complacently, reaching up to touch one of them with a large and very well-manicured finger. 'I bought 'em at a little shop on Sixth Avenue in New York, I can't tell you what a treasure house, to die for! I got a feather boa there, too, a real dilly – some day, maybe, I'll show you. So eat, dollies – the rest'll be here, there won't be none left, you see if there will, so eat while you got the choice!'

And she beamed on them happily and turned to go, and her great red velvet skirt surged and swished, sending another wave of attar of roses over Poppy as she disappeared.

'I say, Mrs Braham,' Mabel called. 'This is Poppy Amberly and –' But it was too late for they could hear the footsteps clumping down the stairs and Mabel shrugged and unpinned her great hat and set it neatly on the windowsill.

'Well!' she said. 'I suppose we had better do as we are told! And I must say I'm uncommonly hungry. An afternoon in the cold March air does sharpen one's appetite. And didn't I tell you that there'd be a great spread here?'

'Indeed you did,' Poppy said and watched as Mabel seized a plate and began to load it with some of the open sandwiches. 'But perhaps we ought to wait after all –'

'Not at all,' Mabel said in a rather muffled voice, for she had already sunk her teeth into one of the slices, and was chewing ecstatically. 'She said to start, so why not? My dear do have one of these! It is quite, quite delicious. I thought it was sardines the first time I had it, though rather more delicate in flavour, but Mrs Braham tells me it is a concoction she makes herself, from finely chopped pickled herrings and apples and so forth. Quite delectable!'

And Poppy, who although she was a little embarrassed by Mabel's eagerness, had to admit that she too was more than ready for something to eat, unpinned her own hat and let her pigtail fall comfortably down her shoulder, for it had been feeling uncommonly heavy piled on top of her head under the unyielding black straw for so long, and joined her friend at the table.

They were both perched side by side on the windowsill, their mouths full, when they heard the sound of new arrivals from below followed shortly after by the clatter of Mrs Braham's heels on the stairs, and they sat and watched as several women came chattering into the room, unpinning their own bonnets and hats as they came, and Mrs Braham came swinging in behind them, bearing a large tea urn in her capable hands.

'So move already!' she was shouting loudly as she pushed through the chattering women. 'You want you should get scalded tochusses? Believe me, this pot is hot, hot, hot! Make way, and come and eat –'

At once it was all hubbub again as people rushed to help her settle her urn in place and cups began to clatter as she started to pour tea and voices rose as the women – about a dozen of them – fell on the table as though they had not eaten for weeks, without for one moment stopping their eager talk. And Poppy, a little dazed by it all, watched and listened and went on eating her own delicious herring sandwich as she listened. Were all the women in the East End as noisy as this? she wondered. Did everything they did have to be accompanied by eating and drinking? Certainly all her experience this afternoon seemed to point that way, and she swallowed the last of her sandwich and rubbed the crumbs from her mouth and smiled at Mabel, still busily chewing beside her.

'Now, my dear, it was you, I think, who spoke up so bravely against that unpleasant Evans man!' Poppy looked up to find Miss Sylvia Pankhurst standing in front of her, and she jumped to her feet at once, and felt the familiar sense of embarrassment that came as Miss Sylvia had to tilt her chin to look up at her, for she was, Poppy realized, at least four inches shorter than Poppy herself.

'Yes, Miss Pankhurst,' she managed. 'I did not realize, of course, that he was a man who made others so – so alarmed. Perhaps if I had I wouldn't have been so outspoken, so I am not so very brave after all –'

'Of course you are!' Sylvia said warmly and smiled at her, and at once her rather dull face seemed to be lit from within, for her eyes glowed and her mouth curved very prettily. 'Now, Mabel, you must introduce us properly! I hope we are to see your young friend here on other occasions, but first I long to hear all about her and how she comes to be here with you – and –'

Mabel too was on her feet now. 'Oh, yes, Miss Sylvia! She is really a delightful girl and I know we shall all be great friends here. We met at the meeting at Caxton Hall last week, don't you know, and – oh, it was all terribly thrilling.' And Mabel launched herself into a highly coloured account of Poppy's doings with keys and policemen at last Saturday's meeting, which Poppy herself could do nothing to halt – although she tried, pulling rather ineffectually at her friend's sleeve – her eyes glowing with excitement and reflected glory as the rest of the women in the room slowly stopped their own chatter and came to listen, sipping their tea and watching Poppy over the rims of their cups so directly that she felt her cheeks turn the colour of her name and wanted very much indeed to be anywhere in the world except where she was.

'So there you are, Miss Sylvia!' Mabel finished triumphantly. 'She is very young, of course, but she is a very sensible person, is she not? And has already shown herself to be of great value – I do hope you will be able to make use of her in the work we do, for she has already told me she wishes to do more for us!' And she beamed at Poppy much as a proud mother beams at her toddler when he has managed to take an unsteady step without adult aid.

'I am sure I shall be able to make excellent use of so resourceful a person!' Sylvia said and pushed her hair back out of her eyes with what was clearly a familiar gesture. 'And – oh, thank you, Mrs Braham! I am indeed ready for a cup –' For the big woman in red had pushed her way determinedly to Sylvia's side and was thrusting a cup of tea towards her. 'And I am delighted you are interested in our work, Miss –' And she stopped, her head tilted in query.

'Oh, if that isn't me all over!' Mabel said and laughed heartily. 'I've told you all about her and not yet introduced her. This is Poppy, Miss Sylvia, Miss Poppy Amberly and my very good friend –'

And they all turned and stared for there was a sudden crash of china and they saw Mrs Braham standing with her head up and her eyes wide and very dark in a face which had gone a quite sickening white above the crimson of her clothes. Sylvia's cup and saucer lay smashed at her feet, but she stood quite heedless of the splash on her skirt as she stared at Poppy, who, alarmed at the intensity of that gaze, looked back and then embarrassed, looked away.

'My dear Mrs Braham!' Sylvia was all concern. 'My dear, are you all right? Are you ill? Come and sit down at once! You look quite dreadfully unwell – do you feel faint? Make way, my dear – just pull that chair forward, will you? And fetch me some cool water and help me undo these stays –'

But Mrs Braham waved away her attentions and refused to move, still standing staring at Poppy with her eyes so wide and dark that they seemed as though they were about to leap out of her white cheeks.

'What did you say your name was?' she said after a moment and her voice was quite husky. 'Listen, tell me I didn't imagine. Tell me I ain't hearin' things on account I want to hear 'em. What's your name, boobalah?'

She was still staring at Poppy, who again looked away, unable to meet the intensity of that glare.

'This is my friend Poppy Amberly,' Mabel said, staring equally intensely at Mrs Braham, but with naked curiosity in her expression rather than the shock that was so clearly part of Mrs Braham's. 'Why? You seem very –'

'Oh!' Mrs Braham said and threw up both her hands to clutch at her cheeks and now Poppy had to look at her, for there was something very commanding about the emotion that this woman was clearly experiencing. 'Oy, oy, oy! God is good, believe me, God is good! I've prayed, I've hoped, but God is good and listens! Poppy, my boobalah – Poppy!'

And to Poppy's combined horror and amazement she hurled herself at her bodily and enfolded her in an embrace so engulfing and so crushing that she could hardly breathe and began to thrash about to escape.

She felt rather than saw Sylvia jump forwards and with help from the agog other women pull Mrs Braham away and stood gasping a little and setting herself straight as they led the big women gently but very firmly to a chair. Mrs Braham was now weeping copiously, with tears running down her cheeks and streaking her powder and rouge cruelly, and Poppy could see that she was not quite as smooth and young as she had at first assumed, but was nearer fifty years of age than forty. And a women gripped by feelings so intense that she could not give them speech. Poppy stood hovering by the windows, deeply mystified, and not knowing what to do as the other women soothed and fussed over Mrs Braham.

She wanted suddenly very much indeed to go home to the peace and stillness of Leinster Terrace. Mama might be a severe person, even cold and rather harsh, but at least she did not expose a person to this sort of experience, Poppy found herself thinking, as anxiety lifted in her. To have to watch a grown person – and one of quite such generous proportions – swept by a storm of powerful emotion was a rather alarming experience. And she stole a sideways glance at Mabel to see what she thought, but Mabel was just standing and staring at Mrs Braham with amazement on her face.

At last, the loud sobs began to ease, and Mrs Braham pushed her attendants aside and paddled in the bosom of her gown to find a handkerchief. She rubbed her cheeks and eyes furiously to the further detriment of her complexion and then took a deep breath.

'Listen, everybody. I'm sorry,' she said huskily. 'I tell you, it's just that I've had a shock.'

'What sort of a shock?' Sylvia asked and crouched in front of Mrs Braham to look up into her face, and took her by the hand. 'Come, you must explain.'

'I don't think – listen, it's kinda private, this. You know what I mean?' And she looked over Sylvia's shoulder at Poppy. 'I don't want I should cause no one no embarrassment. It's just that – listen, Sylvia, be a friend already. Ask this young – ask her to come downstairs –' And she jerked her head towards Poppy. 'Ask her to come downstairs and we'll sit in your room and talk, eh? I can explain then. But everyone wants their tea – I made a nice tea for you all, it's wicked to let it go waste. Eat already – the urn's full. Help yourselves, please. I'll be back later – believe me. I'm fine. I'll be back –'

And she pulled herself to her feet and now moving a little heavily, went to the door. 'You'll come and talk, boobalah?' she said then, turning her head to look once more at Poppy. 'There's something I got to explain –'

And after a moment Poppy nodded. She had no idea what all the fuss was about, and was deeply alarmed, wanting more and more to go home to her mother, but clearly this was a matter of some importance to this very odd and somewhat overwhelming person, and she would have to agree. And she reached for her hat from the windowsill and made a small *moue* at Mabel and then turned to follow Mrs Braham from the room.

'I'll wait for you, Poppy,' Mabel hissed eagerly, her eyes wide and her very nose glistening with excitement. 'If you aren't out of that room in the next fifteen minutes, why, I promise I shall come and fetch you – shall I?'

'Oh, yes *please*,' Poppy whispered back gratefully and turned to go, but her legs felt a little shaky as she walked and she had an odd sensation as though she were not actually there, but was watching all that was going on from somewhere outside. It was almost as though she were perched high on a shelf in a corner of this odd room watching all that was happening but not being really part of it, and she thought absurdly of how she had once asked Mama to explain what had happened to Alice in *Through the Looking-Glass* when she had felt so strange, and how Mama had said she couldn't explain, but perhaps one day Poppy would understand. And now she did –

The small cluttered room at the back downstairs seemed smaller and more cluttered than ever, somehow, as the big woman, now moving with some slowness as though she were exhausted by her feelings, settled herself in a chair beside one of the desks and Miss Sylvia, who it seemed had appointed herself as some sort of supervisor of the proceedings, sat on another. And Poppy stood in the middle of the room and looked from one to another and didn't know what to say.

There was a short silence as Mrs Braham, breathing rather heavily, sat and gazed at Poppy, looking at her with a sort of hunger that made Poppy feel even more uncomfortable. It was as though she were taking stock of every inch of her, Poppy thought with some indignation, and she lifted her chin and tossed her head so that her pigtail, which had been hanging over her shoulder in front, was flipped over to lie down her back. And Mrs Braham's face crumpled as she did it and for one dreadful moment she seemed to be about to burst into noisy tears again.

But she did not. Instead, she sniffed lusciously and said with the same husky note in her voice, 'You know something? When you was little more'n a scrap of a baby you used to do that. You'd toss your head to get your curls out of your eyes, you little dolly. Oh, my Poppy! All grown up and so beautiful. And I've found you!'

And Poppy felt her eyes widen until she thought they would never stop and heard her own voice, strangled and amazed, saying stupidly, 'What?'

And Mrs Braham beamed and held out her great arms and said simply, 'Boobalah, I'm your Auntie Jessie. Don't tell me you've forgotten me altogether? I'm Auntie Jessie – and I've found you again and I've never been so happy in all my life.'

8

The most difficult thing that Poppy had to cope with was not so much the information she was given by Jessie Braham as the determination that was fixed in her not to speak to anyone else about it.

Miss Sylvia Pankhurst had promised her she would say nothing, and indeed made sure she could not for once she had realized that Jessie Braham was about to speak of purely personal matters, she had tactfully left the two of them alone, and gone away, quietly closing the door behind her. And anyway Poppy felt she could trust her. But there was no one else in whom she could confide at all and that made her feel quite dreadful, for she had a burning need to share the burden of this amazing piece of information about herself. Yet how could she share it? She had to pretend both that there was none, and that anyway it did not matter.

The difficulties started on the omnibus going home through the dark of the early evening with Mabel by her side. She, of course, had been avid for news of what had transpired in the small back room downstairs, and had shown strong signs of becoming decidedly huffy when at first Poppy had declined to speak of it, and so Poppy had felt herself forced to tell lies, which she did not enjoy. Not because of any powerful notions of the wrongness of lying – she could not pretend to such high-mindedness, being a most practical person – but because she was rather bad at it. She lacked the natural deviousness that made lying easy for some people, and which protected them from lapses of memory of the sort which Poppy knew would soon reveal her as mendacious. But with Mabel prodding at her for information what else could she do but lie?

'It was all rather absurd,' she said as lightly as she could. 'Though I found it dreadfully embarrassing. It seems Mrs Braham had a – a niece once, a child with whom she lost contact when she was very small. The niece was small, I mean. I gather Mrs Braham and the

61

child's mother had some sort of disagreement.' So far so true, Poppy thought. I'm being honest up to a point, after all. 'And she thought I – it was that I looked like the child, you see, and had a similar sounding name.'

'Oh!' Mabel said, a little nonplussed. 'What was the niece's name, then?'

Poppy had not expected that and she floundered for a moment, grateful for the dim lighting in the omnibus which hid her face from easy view. 'Mmm? Oh, I didn't ask her that – it didn't seem important. Anyway, once we had talked, Mrs Braham decided it was not as she thought after all and apologized for the disturbance she had made and went home.'

'Well!' Mabel said, clearly dissatisfied and more than a little disappointed. 'I had thought it all something much more interesting, she made such a scene upstairs! But there, I suppose it was not likely – I mean, that you should be a relation of hers.' She laughed merrily then. 'You could hardly have such a one as a connection, could you? Imagine what your Mama would say at such a claim!'

'Oh, it would not necessarily be so strange!' Poppy said, suddenly nettled. 'After all, we are not so very special, Mama and I. And I doubt there are many people in the world who can claim they are connected only to the rich and fashionable – such as that duke you spoke of!'

'Well, I know that, of course!' Mabel said and laughed again. 'But my dear, that woman! So noisy and so Jewish! It really is an absurd notion, isn't it?'

'I suppose so,' Poppy had said, not knowing what else to say, and then had lapsed into silence as Mabel had gone on to talk of other things, especially the clothes the women at the tea party had been wearing, grateful for the opportunity to gather her thoughts about her.

For she needed to clear her head and to decide what to do about Mama, for what Mrs Braham had told her – and she supposed from now on she would have to think of her as Aunt Jessie, which was very difficult at present – had been so very startling. And yet – and yet, perhaps not. Now so many things seemed to click into place that she knew without doubt what the large red woman had told her was true, incredible though it all sounded. She knew now why these mean streets seemed to her eyes so friendly and welcoming. For had she not spent her earliest days here? She knew why the smells and the tastes of the exotic food, so unlike the fare at home at Leinster Terrace, made her feel so comfortable and so eager, although she was not usually a greedy person; it was because these were the scents and tastes of her infancy. And she knew too why she saw so vividly in her mind's eye that small glowing kitchen. It was not what she had thought, mainly a creation of her own overactive imagination, but a true and honest memory. And she stared out at the reflection in the dark omnibus window of her own face and Mabel's chattering image, shadowy against the passing street lights outside, and marvelled. Mama, her stiff and proper Mama, to have worked as a cook, to have lived in a small almost slum house, alone except for herself as a baby? It seemed unimaginable thinking of the cool, neat and self-contained Mama who now spent so much time sitting and sewing while servants waited on her and cleaned and cared for her large and comfortable home. Clearly, there was still much more to be explained and understood.

Not that Mrs Braham had been mean in her explanations; far from it. Facts and names and news had poured from her in a small flood. She herself, she told Poppy, had gone away just after the war in South Africa had ended to marry and live in America. 'In Baltimore, with Nate Braham, as good a man as drew breath, believe you me, for all he was a bit of a dull fella. But you can't have it all and he was good to me, and took care of me, and gave me my Bernie, such a boy, my Bernie – your cousin, yet! You'll meet him, you'll love him, believe me, he's a real lobbus and with so much cheyn –' And Poppy hadn't liked to ask her to explain what she meant for she did not fully understand the words she used, though she had the impression that Bernie was energetic and charming in his mother's estimation.

'And then Nate died, God rest his sweet soul,' Mrs Braham had gone on. 'And left me well provided for and I thought, why should I stay here with a bunch of in-laws as don't care a busted dime for me? I'll go home, take my Bernie home to London, open a business, maybe, find the family again –' And she had stopped then and sniffed lusciously and said with her eyes glinting with unshed tears, 'And I won't hide from you, boobalah, I thought – maybe I'll see *you* again My Bernie is my life, you understand this, my life, but you, you were the first baby I loved. And did I love you! But your Momma, Millie, she didn't want to know me after she went back to her own family. I can understand up to a point, but only up to a point – whatever had happened to her, why make me suffer? Why make you suffer? You loved me as much as I loved you, believe me you did – you remember?'

And Poppy had looked at her and tried so hard to remember and to tell this large, eager and almost overwhelming woman what she wanted to hear, for the appeal in her voice and in the tight expression on her round face was very poignant. But she knew her own expression remained merely polite, for Mrs Braham had sighed gustily and smiled – a brave little smile that had made Poppy want to cry, suddenly – and had said as cheerfully as she could, 'Well, you was just a baby! How can I expect you should remember? It's ridiculous, a real idiot, I am – anyway I came back and here I am, got a nice little place over on Cable Street, building a big clientele – the best bagels and pickled herring anywhere in London, believe you me –and you should just try the cheesecake. They come all the way from Golders Green to buy my cheesecake, you know that? And there's my sister Rae's kids – also your cousins, you should meet them one day – they're doing very nicely now, got houses over in Stoke Newington and Stamford Hill, though Rae, God rest her soul, died three years back, and I always thought, maybe one day I'll see my Poppy again – and now I have –' And she had stopped as much for want of breath as anything else and beamed at Poppy, who tried to smile back but knew that she made only a poor stab at it.

'I – it all seems so strange to me,' she ventured at last. 'I remember some things about the past, of course – but not a lot. It all seems –' She shrugged a little. 'I have asked Mama about my father, but she does not say much – though I know his name was Harris –' And she stopped expectantly and looked at Jessie Braham, wanting to know what she could tell her, but suddenly shy about asking outright.

For the first time the big woman was silent, leaning back in her chair in such a way that her face was in more shadow so that Poppy could not easily see her expression.

'So listen,' she said after a long pause. 'When she's ready she'll tell you. It's not for me to interfere. It's caused me enough trouble in the past, interfering. It's why she wouldn't let me come to see you when I come back to London again. I tried, you know that? Sure I tried! I wrote her a nice letter, I said as how here I was, in a nice way of business, plenty of capital because my Nate left me well provided for. He was a good man for the insurance polices, you know what I mean? And the business in Baltimore had been good and I got a good price for it, so I said to Millie in my letter, I'm back, we should be friends again and she wrote back –' She had stopped then and after a moment gone on a little flatly. 'Anyway she wrote back, you was well, you was happy, I was to leave you alone, don't interfere. She wanted only a quiet life, I should keep away. What could I do? I can't force a woman to make friendly, can I? I got no rights. What am I? I got no rights – I ain't her family –'

'But you're my aunt,' Poppy said after a moment. 'Isn't that family?'

Again that strained little silence and then Jessie Braham had said, 'As to that, it's up to Millie. She don't want no connection and I got no way I can force her. But now I found you, Poppy – or really, you found me – listen dolly, you won't make strange, will you, like your Momma? It's beshert – you know what I mean? Meant, that's what it is, it's meant. If the good God hadn't wanted us to meet again, believe me, he wouldn't have sent you here this afternoon, of that I am as certain as I sit here and breathe. It's beshert – so keep in touch with me, hmm? And, er –' She had shifted a touch awkwardly in her chair so that it had creaked a little and leaned forwards so that once more Poppy could see her face, warm and damp with earnest sweat in the overheated little room with its plopping and hissing gaslight and glowing fire. 'Listen Poppy, I don't want you should do nothing that don't feel right, you understand me. But I want so much you should keep in touch – but don't tell your Momma. It's not I want you should lie, you understand. It's just – what the eye don't see, the heart don't grieve over, ain't that what they say? It won't hurt Millie if you and me see each other now and again, hmm? And it might hurt her if she – oh, you know how it is, Poppy, you must do. She's a strong-minded person, your Momma. I got a lot of respect for her. But sometimes, she's stubborn. And I know what I say because we were close, she and I, very close.'

She stopped then and bent her head to look down at her hands clasped on her lap before continuing with an obvious effort. 'I miss her too, you know. I was never that close to my sister Rae, and as for the rest of my family – believe me, far and wide they are. But Millie – I cared for her. We shared a lot back when you was born – It was me that gave you your name, for pity's sake! You was so rosy, you looked so round and red. I gave you your name – but – ' She lifted her head then and managed a grin. 'But that was a long time ago, and things change, hmm? So don't tell your mother – '

And Poppy had known she wouldn't. She had already decided that, without being asked. She could not imagine speaking to Mama of the day's events, would not know where to begin. It wasn't being deceitful to keep this quiet. It wasn't wicked, she told herself with some passion, sitting on the omnibus as at last it left the East End behind and brought her to the more familiar wider streets of home. It's just the way it has to be. One day perhaps she would be able to find out more about her own past and fit it into what she knew of her mother. One day she would unravel it all and be able to understand. That would be soon enough to talk to Mama. In the meantime, she would keep her own counsel.

And that embargo on talk she extended to Mabel. She was a delightful new friend and Poppy was deeply glad to have found her. They shared much in the way of interest, not just Votes for Women, for Mabel talked cheerfully of music and books and plays of the moment and was also deliciously frivolous on matters to do with clothes, which Poppy could not deny amused her a good deal. She felt the need for a real friend, someone as unlike as possible the insipid people of her own age with whom she went to school. They were very dull, and she could hardly make a close friend of Miss Sayers, even though she was not that much older than Poppy herself, for after all she was a teacher, and Poppy her pupil. Mabel, with her almost three years of seniority and rather exciting job and interesting home situation was exactly the friend Poppy felt she needed, and she would not jeopardize their new intimacy with talk of these new relations she had discovered she had. At least, not yet. Perhaps one day it would be possible – except that – and she had dragged her thoughts away from Mabel's somewhat scathing comments about Jessie Braham, and also from her own eventful afternoon, as at last the omnibus drew nearer to the stop by Lancaster Gate, where she would have to leave it.

'Mabel, thank you so much for taking me this afternoon,' she said. 'It was really awfully interesting and I think it would be very good to return at some time. I said I would like to help Miss Sylvia and I really would. It was sort of fun last week at the Caxton Hall meeting but somehow – '

'I know,' Mabel said cheerfully. 'A bit too serious. And those policemen – ' She shuddered prettily. 'I wouldn't have been there myself if the girls from the Settlement hadn't wanted me to go with them. Anyway, it is settled. I shall let you know when the next meeting is and perhaps you can come to one of the planning afternoons that are held in advance. And there are always things to do in the office there, you know. Miss Sylvia sends out a lot of letters and pamphlets and she needs help with that. Can you use a typewriting machine?'

'Heavens no!' Poppy was on her feet now as the omnibus swayed towards the stop. 'It sounds very complicated to me.'

'Well, of course it is,' Mabel said. 'I took ages to learn – but I dare say I can teach you and then you can help us with that sort of work. Goodbye, dear Poppy. I am glad that there was nothing to worry about with Mrs Braham – it was all so dramatic, wasn't it? It seems that dramatic things tend to happen when you are about! Now, take care – and I shall send a note soon to let you know of the next meeting! Goodbye – '

And she waved Poppy on her way, and then waved again as Poppy stood on the pavement under the snapping dark branches of the trees in Hyde Park which were swaying over her head in the sharp evening breeze. And Poppy waved back, and then turned to walk home to her mother and supper, painfully aware of how carefully she would have to watch her tongue if she was to avoid any sort of clash with her over her new-found aunt. And not enjoying the prospect.

But in the event it was not as difficult as she had feared. Mildred's new attitude to her seemed to last; Poppy felt that she was no longer being treated as a child, but as an almost-equal adult, and although she felt no closer to her mother in any real sense, she welcomed her new status and was grateful for it. And since Mildred said nothing about how Poppy had spent her afternoon, and showed no interest in anything other than purely domestic details, there was no need to tell active lies, which comforted Poppy greatly. She had only to avoid speaking on a certain subject, and that was easy enough after a lifetime of private thoughts.

And in the ensuing weeks there was also the fun of new clothes to occupy her mind. True to her promise, Mildred had arranged for the dressmaker to come to visit, and long and very agreeable hours were spent over discussion of a new summer wardrobe for Miss Poppy, with Poppy pushing hopefully for hobble skirts (which her Mama forbade, but did agree at least to a much narrower hemline than she had hitherto worn) and even for the new harem skirt with its trouser effect, even though she knew she had no hope at all of having such a thing. But though fashion was forbidden there were the fabrics to enjoy. Figured silk and braided jersey, soft chiffons and delicate lawns were all discussed and long deliberations were entered into on the matter of colour. Everyone was wearing, Mrs Winkworth decreed, the new *Schéhérazade* colours this spring. No more the pale pinks and swooning mauves of 1909 and 1910, but golds and emeralds, crimsons and rich blues were the only possible hues for this year. And the shapes, too, were different; no more tightly laced waists and rigid bodices, but softness and drapery and a sense of mystery; and Poppy revelled in it all and learned how to pin up her thick curls behind a forehead fillet, hoping that one day she might be invited to the sort of evening party where such a mode would be permissible, and generally dreamed all the things other girls of sixteen dreamed about.

And what with that, and the pressure of the work she still had to do at school for Miss Campion, she had little time for any other activity until Mabel wrote her a gushing little note three weeks after the East End meeting to tell her there would be no further meetings at the Settlement for some weeks because Miss Sylvia was going to Florence on a drawing holiday with some of her pupils and would be away some weeks.

'She's taken, of course, Miss Gordon,' Mabel had written, her already untidy handwriting becoming even more excitably looped and exuberant as she dealt with the irritating Flora. 'Really, I sometimes wonder how Miss Sylvia tolerates her, however excellent she may be at her drawing board – such a tiresome person. Perhaps we may meet and go out for that tea you suggested one Saturday afternoon soon?' she went on. 'I should enjoy that, and I would like to see the exhibition at the Grafton Gallery and I am sure you would enjoy it greatly, too. And perhaps we could even get a couple of seats at the Palace Theatre to see Pavlova dance her "Dying Swan" – I hear she is all the rage and quite entrancing. My brother Bobby says if we wish to go he will try to obtain Press tickets for us – so it will not make too much of a hole in your weekly half-sovereign!'

And Poppy had agreed with great excitement and asked Mama if she might go on these expeditions and been told, with Mama's strange new willingness, that indeed she might and furthermore could wear her new ensembles when she did. So plans were made for three separate entertainments. One to the Zoo, for a stroll among the animals, followed by tea at the Langham Hotel. ('Dreadfully expensive, I know,' Mabel had said gaily. 'But so fashionable and you see such divine people!') Another to the Grafton Gallery after lunch one Saturday, to push their way among the very smart crowd to see what they could of the pictures, which wasn't much and, finally, the special event for which Poppy chose to wear her very best and most delightful new clothes, which made her look, she was convinced, quite twenty: a visit to the Palace Theatre with Mabel and her brother Bobby followed by supper at their house in Holland Park.

It was a great deal to look forward to and, as the trees in Hyde Park blushed ever greener with the coming of spring and talk of the Coronation filled the air with crackle and excitement, Poppy revelled in it all, so much so that it was not difficult for her to push to the back of her mind her meeting with her new-found East End connections. There was plenty of time to think about that, Poppy told herself, and resolutely refused to consider it now. Now there were dresses and outings and the ballet to think of. What more could any girl possibly want?

9

It was clear to Poppy right from the start of it that the evening was going to be magical. First of all, Miss Sayers had a severe migraine headache, so her English class were sent home from school early, and that meant that Poppy had had the entire afternoon in which to take a leisurely bath and pin up her hair (about which Mama had relented, for she was now permitted to put it up for special occasions) and get dressed. Her hair had gone up easily and prettily, instead of demanding the arm-aching hour of struggle it so often took to get it to look just the way she liked it, and her dress when she put it on appeared even to her critical eyes quite perfect. It was a narrow-skirted swathe of deep kingfisher blue silk, caught high under the bust with the prettiest matching silk braid across the yoke and short sleeves and she knew it made her look wonderfully grown-up. No one could possibly think her just sixteen, and for almost the first time in her life Poppy began to be actually glad she was so tall. All the irritating years of teasing and remarks about her loftiness that had so plagued her seemed to melt away as she admired herself in her cheval glass. She looked wonderfully willowy, she decided, in spite of the fact that she knew she was really quite sturdily built, and immensely sophisticated.

And things got better still. When she had put over her dress the cream brocade evening coat with the silk fringes and pulled on her long buttoned gloves, also in cream, and had gone downstairs to the drawing room to show herself to Mama, she had looked up at her over her thin-rimmed spectacles and had actually smiled.

'You look very well, Poppy. I am sure your friends will be most impressed,' she said and then took off her spectacles and pulled her reticule from her waistband. 'You certainly cannot travel on the omnibus in such splendour! Tell Queenie to fetch you a cab from the Bayswater Road. This will be enough to pay for it, and to bring you home from your friends' house. Holland Park, I think you said?'

'Yes, Mama,' Poppy said, gratefully taking the half-sovereign. 'Norland Square. It is quite near the main Holland Park Road, Mabel says, and not too far from here.'

'Well, enjoy yourself, and remember to be suitably polite about your entertainment. And you must make an arrangement soon to invite your friends to tea here. It would be agreeable to meet them.'

'Yes, Mama,' Poppy said, as some of the glitter slid out of her. To invite Mabel here? To have her listen to Mama being severe? That could spoil everything; and then she felt compunction, for hadn't Mama been immensely kind and generous tonight? And she hurried across to her and leaned over and kissed her cheek – a rare salutation these days – and said impulsively, 'Oh, Mama, yes I will! She's a dear girl and I know you will like her! Thank you so much –'

'There, there, no need to fuss,' Mildred said and moved her head back a little to escape the embrace, though Poppy could see she was not displeased by it. 'And really you do not need quite so much eau-de-Cologne, you know. I hope most of it will have worn off by the time you arrive, for indeed you are quite overwhelmed with it.'

'Yes, Mama,' Poppy said again, and turned and went, not a bit put out by the criticism. That was just Mama needing to be Mama. She smelled delicious and she knew it. And she waited in the hall as patiently as she could while Queenie, muttering a little under her breath, went to the corner to hail a cab and almost hugged herself with excitement as she stood in the patch of evening sunshine which spilled on the black and white tiles of the hall floor. It was all going to be wonderful, quite, quite wonderful!

And so it was. The cab clattered through Bayswater Road and then past Marble Arch and along Oxford Street, past all the fashionable shops so that she could stare at their elegant windows, on its way to Cambridge Circus and the glories of the great and wonderful Pavlova. And she sat there deeply aware of her own perfect appearance, of the silk of her gown whispering so sweetly against her stockinged legs, of the sweet scent of the cologne in her nostrils, and of something more; of her own youth and hopefulness and vigour and excitement. As she sat there, one hand elegantly raised to hold the dusty leather strap to keep her steady, staring out at the passing scenery with as languidly fashionable an air as she could muster, she knew that to be Poppy Amberly on this April evening in 1911 was quite the best and most exciting thing in the whole world that she could possibly be. She gently pitied all the people she passed who were not Poppy Amberly, going to the theatre with her friend and her interesting brother. She was sad for everyone in the world who could not be inside her skin and know the joy of it.

And at the theatre, as she stepped out of the cab, it all got better and better. The pavement outside was milling with people, mostly as carefully dressed as she was herself, but there were enough of the poorest sort in dull shabby clothes to make her feel even more aware of her own splendour and good fortune, and she drew her cream coat closer to her bosom in one gloved hand and stepped across the pavement with her head up and her toes turned out in the approved manner, thus using all the style she could muster, to walk under the great glass canopy and into the interior of the theatre.

She was never to forget the way that moment felt. She had been to theatres before, of course, but never had it been like this. A wash of warm air greeted her and filled her nostrils with a heady mixture of scents: cigar smoke and costly brandy and hot perfumed bodies and dust and – faintly – disinfectant and ancient unwashed curtains and carpets in need of beating. And there were even more people inside, all talking in polite accents and with great mannerliness but at the tops of their voices so that it sounded like the most vulgar of brawls. There were trills of artful feminine laughter and male guffaws and little screams of excitement and greeting and she stood for a moment, quite bewildered by it all; and then heard a shriek that managed to lift itself above the general hubbub.

'Poppy! Poppy – over here, my dear – over here – Poppeee!'

She blinked and turned her head to look and then at last saw her amid the mêlée; Mabel, one arm stretched high in the air above her and her head bobbing absurdly as she jumped up and down to make sure she could be seen above the heads of the people hemming her in. It was indeed, Poppy thought briefly, useful to be tall. And she began to make her way towards the upstretched arm as politely as she could, but without much success, for most people quite ignored her murmurs of, 'Excuse me!' as they stood and brayed cheerfully at each other.

'Let me –' someone said in her ear, and she tried to turn and look, but could not manage to do so for the crowd was really quite thick here, and then she felt her elbow taken firmly but far from roughly and was propelled swiftly forwards as behind her the voice said loudly – and with great determination, '*If* you please – kindly make way – thank you *so* much – if you would *just* let us through – *too* kind!' until in a very short time indeed she was standing beside Mabel who threw her arms about her as eagerly as though they had not seen each other for months, even though they had actually spent last Saturday together at the Grafton Gallery, giggling like babies, and greeted her with a smacking kiss.

'Oh well done, Bobby!' she cried. 'Didn't you manage that beautifully! Poppy my dear, this is my good old bro, Bobby. I know you two are going to be the greatest friends, just as you and I are!'

At last Poppy was able to turn her head to see her companion. What a most agreeable looking person, was her first thought. A rather square face – much the same shape as Mabel's, but firmer than hers of course – with a hardness about the cheeks that made her think of the nicest kind of sculpture. Rather dusty looking hair, rough and clearly unruly for there lay across his forehead one long and rather lank lock and she had a sudden urge to put out her hand and push it out of his eyes, and almost as though he knew what she was thinking he tossed his head in what was clearly a well-schooled trick and the hair lifted and flopped back into position on his head. And he smiled, a very nice smile, Poppy decided, which made his eyes almost disappear, for they became mere slits, but still managed to be expressive, radiating cheerfulness and calm good humour of a most engaging kind.

'How do you do,' she said. 'It was most clever of you to get me through so quickly. How did you know I was the right person? Why, I could have been anyone, perhaps wanting to go in the opposite direction!'

'Oh, that was easy,' he said and now she could see his eyes, although he was still smiling, if not so widely now. They were hazel coloured, a warm, rich browny green and she liked the look of him even more as she saw the way the light seemed to twinkle in their depths. 'There was my asinine young sister leaping up and down like a jack-in-the-box and shrieking, "Poppy!" at the top of her not inconsiderable voice, and there you were looking positively dismayed by the sort of exhibition she was making of herself – it had to be you. So, I decided to cut short dear May's performance by getting the two of you together as soon as I could. How do you do, Miss Amberly. I have heard much about you, and it is indeed a pleasure to meet you at last!' And he held out one hand and she gave him hers and they shook solemnly. His hand was warm and hard and even through her glove she felt the strength of it and shivered a little inside. What a very nice person indeed he was! And to her own surprise she felt her face redden into a blush.

'Oh, pooh!' Mabel said and leaned across Poppy and gave him a sisterly tap on the cheek. 'I was not at all making myself an exhibition. Merely making sure we found our dear Poppy. My dear, I *adore* that ensemble. You look quite divine! Doesn't she, Bobby?'

'Totally divine,' Bobby said promptly and lifted his hand towards a programme seller on the far side of them. 'And I vote we get ourselves to our stalls and settle in so that we can admire each other to even greater advantage. Now come along, you two!' And again he turned and began to push towards the entry to the stalls, once again calling out his authoritative 'If you pleases' and 'Kindly make ways' which people obeyed just as they had before, paying no obvious attention and not losing one syllable of their conversation, yet moving enough to make a pathway all the same.

They settled themselves at last, Mabel chattering non-stop as they did so, unwrapping themselves from their coats, finding their precise seats and sitting down, one on each side of Bobby. 'I shall have to arrange you so, I imagine,' he said cheerfully, 'or I shall be plagued by the uproar of your chatter all through the performance, no doubt!' And he winked at Poppy as he held her seat down for her to slip into it.

And her spirits for the first time that evening took a little dip. She didn't want this splendid person to wink at her and make jokes about her chattering to his sister. That made it all too commonplace, somehow. She wanted him to look at her with some awe in his eyes, to treat her as though she were made of spun glass, to regard her as she had herself on the way here – as the most exciting thing in the whole world that any person could be.

But the thought went away in a little burst of laughter as he leaned towards her and murmured, 'Say a little prayer, my dear Miss Amberly! See the lady in the hat as broad as Table Mountain? Pray she sits elsewhere, for if she comes to be in front of us that will be the end of our entertainment, I fear!' And she turned her head and had to giggle, for the hat in question was indeed monumentally large, and was causing much confusion among the clutter of people now making their way down the aisles towards their own places, for it was so much wider that its wearer's shoulders that passers-by kept knocking it awry, much to the lady's irritation. And then that laughter increased as the woman and her hat sat down three or four rows ahead of them and at once the man in the seat behind her leaned forwards and tapped her on the shoulder, and an obviously lively discussion ensued, and Bobby leant towards Poppy and began to speak in a low voice, giving a rapid account of all that was happening, although they could not in fact hear a word of the actual discussion.

'Aha! Our Hero is remonstrating with Table Mountain! The Mountain objects and is very ferocious – but what is this? Reinforcements, by Jove! Observe the chap on Our Hero's right joining in. His view of the proceedings is *also* jeopardized by the Great God of Fashion! Table Mountain tires, persists – ah, capitulates! Off comes the hat – Our Hero and his Reinforcements retire satisfied. Table Mountain's evening quite ruined now she is little more than a pimple on the landscape! A Tragedy in Three Acts, no less. What an evening we shall have if this is but the start of it!'

'Bobby, you are in one of your wicked moods this evening! Heaven help us all! Beware, now, Poppy – when he is like this he is capable of all sorts of villainy. Last time we came out he tied together the sleeves of the silk chiffon coat the lady in front of us was wearing and which she hung over the back of her seat – she was so waxy when she discovered it!'

'I had every right.' Bobby said with great dignity. 'The sleeves were excessively long and were tickling my knees quite shamelessly, even through my serge trousers! Now, let us see what we have in store – there, such a photograph, isn't it, Miss Amberly? Isn't she quite the loveliest creature?'

'Indeed she is,' Poppy said, looking at the picture of Pavlova in her most celebrated role that dominated the centre pages of the special souvenir programme. 'And I wish you would call me Poppy. It is so dispiriting to be Miss anything – '

'Aha! An egalitarian like myself, perhaps? A lady after my own heart, if so. If I had my way, Poppy, there would be no such things as Mr or Mrs or titles or even surnames. We would all be ourselves, just our given names. None of this nonsense of what sort of family you had, and using your father as a yardstick for your abilities! No titles, no labels of any kind – ' And he turned his head and smiled at her and Poppy thought suddenly – he's testing me – this isn't just a joke. He's testing me –

'I need time to consider that idea,' she said after a moment. 'On the surface it sounds an excellent one in many ways. I think it quite absurd how much people fuss about such things sometimes.' And she thought confusedly of Mama and her new-found Aunt Jessie and the contrast between them and the way she had once had a different surname and it all melded together in her head and she went on suddenly, 'No, I do not need to consider it! I feel you are right! Perfectly right. It would indeed be wonderful if we were all new from the moment we were born and no one judged us at all on anything but what we are.'

'And how should we manage to sort ourselves out when we needed to?' Mabel said, looking up from the programme she had been reading carefully. 'Bobby has said this before to me, and I have told him it will not work. Why, there are four girls named Mabel at our office alone! It is tiresome enough to have so popular and fashionable a name, but imagine how much more difficult it would be if we had no surnames with which to identify ourselves!'

'And, anyway, you would miss being able to be Miss Bradman and so showing off to the others that you are my little sister!' Bobby said and laughed again as Mabel reddened a little.

'Well, why shouldn't I?' she said spiritedly. 'If doing so is of use to me! There are enough times when being your sister brings considerable opprobrium down on my head, when you are being particularly waspish as only you can be when you choose.'

'I am sometimes justifiably irritated, Poppy,' Bobby said and again grinned at her. 'I am sure you would be, too, in my shoes. Why, these girls sit there at their typewriters and chatter away like so many demented hens and are then aggrieved when I point out I am waiting for my copy and they must make some shift to do some work – you see how difficult it is for me to be Mr Bradman when my sister is one of such a crew?' And he turned to Mabel and patted her hand in a friendly fashion. 'Never mind, May, dear. When I am king, we shall do away with all surnames and all will be peace and joy for you, and we will still know who you are!'

'But I thought you were doing away with titles,' Poppy murmured. 'How can you be king in a land where there are no lords and such?'

Bobby twisted his head and looked at her sharply and then lifted his chin and laughed with great pleasure. 'Oh, *touché*,' he said. 'It is clear that Mabel has chosen a splendid friend in you! Now, hush – here is the overture – '

And indeed the lights in the house had faded, and the curtain, that great wall of red velvet so near to them – for they were in excellent seats – had lifted into a vibrant life of its own as the music began.

The music was not particularly well played for even at the Palace Theatre the musicians who made up the pit orchestra were not of the standard of true orchestral players, but it captivated Poppy. She heard far too little music, in her estimation. Occasionally Mama played the piano, but it was rare enough. And when she did it was melancholy stuff she usually chose, and there was no gramophone in the drawing room at home. Her Uncles had their own, Poppy suspected, and probably jolly records to go with it, but she rarely saw them and hardly ever heard them for they lived their private lives outside their home, using it entirely as an hotel. So, most of the music she heard was at school, where it tended to be sepulchral and religious, or in the park in the summer when the military bands came, and then it was delightful, sprightly and jolly and full of drama. She enjoyed that hugely.

But not as much as she enjoyed tonight's music. The orchestra carried itself away on a great soupy wave of luscious strings, using the music of Saint-Saëns as though it were a vast feather bed in which they could wallow. The sounds lifted and swelled, swooped and rose again, and inside herself Poppy moved with it, though she sat very straight and with her head up and her eyes fixed on the curved swathes of the velvet curtain. She no longer saw or had any awareness of the other people around her. There was herself and the music and that was enough.

And then with a great swishing sound the curtain shivered, heaved and rose and there was the stage – vast, shadowy, tree bedecked and enchanting in its artificiality. Poppy sat entranced as the *corps de ballet* trembled on from the wings, arriving in great bursts of tulle and twinkling ankles, and she caught her breath as they began to weave their patterns of movement in the shape of the music; here and there, round and round, up and down, and still she sat with her back as straight as a ramrod and her eyes fixed almost unblinkingly on the stage for fear of missing a single movement, a solitary note.

It went on and on: the music; the male dancers, handsome and virile in their tights and loose open shirts, swaggering about the stage like so many clockwork toys, and then the various other principals in the ballet. Poppy knew little of the story or what was happening and was only aware from her perusal of the programme that this was just a *divertissement*, but it didn't matter. She wasn't interested in stories tonight. It was movement and colour, sound and mood that had clasped her tightly and would not let her go, and she was almost transfixed with the pleasure she was experiencing.

And then there was Pavlova herself. Pavlova as slight and fragile as Poppy was tall and sturdy. Pavlova with her pale long face and those strong dark brows and that anguished look, and as Poppy watched her she stopped being herself and moved into that incredible body up there on the stage. When Pavlova used her outstretched limbs and pleading face to show her yearning for her love, it was Poppy's heart that was breaking. When Pavlova's long hands and incredible arms began to move into the death throes of the sad swan, it was Poppy who felt herself in feathers, unable to speak, mute and suffering. When Pavlova's legs slid and crumpled beneath her as she subsided into her last moments, it was Poppy who felt herself shrink and die by inches.

And then it was over and vast waves of thunderous sound broke over Poppy's head and she blinked a little, dazed and dazzled, and turned her head and saw Bobby looking at her a little quizzically.

'I think, you know, that you enjoyed that. I do not think I shall bother to enquire further about your opinions or reactions,' he said and began to clap, and then after a moment leaned forwards and picked up Poppy's hands in both of his and set them together and she realized with a start that she had been quite unmoving, and began to applaud as violently as she could, banging her hands together in an ecstasy of appreciation until her shoulders ached and her hands burned with the impact even inside their gloves.

'There my dear – how was that? I shall have to enquire after all. It really is a delight to see someone so entranced. You are a most satisfactory guest in every way.' And there was some laughter in his voice, but it was kind, and not in the least mocking as she had for a brief moment feared.

He was standing up now and holding out a hand to her, encouraging her to join him, as Mabel impatiently egged him on from the other side.

'Do come on, Poppy!' she cried. 'I'm dying for an ice – and we have just time to get one – come along now, do.'

Obediently Poppy let Bobby hand her out of her seat and into the shuffling crowd in the aisle. She was still dazzled by all she had seen, and could still feel the movement of that heartbreaking dying swan inside her and she took a deep and rather tremulous breath as Bobby leaned over her shoulder – for he had insisted that she lead the way out – and murmured, 'I wish I had been able to take you to see Karsavina in *Le Spectre de la Rose*. And Nijinsky – I think you would have enjoyed them too – '

'As much as this? I can't imagine – where? When?'

He smiled and again urged her forwards. 'In Paris. Two years ago. Diaghilev was there and such a *succès d'estime* that the paper chose to send me to see what all the fuss was about. They expected me to be a little sharp, I think, with all that French decadence mixed with Russian barbarism, but I was quite bewitched. I had never before been at all interested in ballet, but that quite cured me of any lack of taste I suffered. As soon as I am able to get tickets, then we shall go to see *Schéhérazade* – Diaghilev has brought his company here, for the Coronation season, you see, and we are all agreed, those of us who are balletomanes, that it will be the greatest ever – I am very eager to see it – '

'*Schéhérazade*,' Poppy murmured and ran her hand across the bodice of her gown. 'Mrs Winkworth, my dressmaker, said that was why these colours are all the rage this season.'

He blinked at her and then as they reached the lobby at the back and Mabel at last could have her ice, some of the life seemed to leave him. 'Mrs Winkworth,' he said in a rather flat voice.

She could have bitten her tongue off with mortification. To have spoken so was childish, a silly missish sort of comment. He would think her a stupid empty-headed creature with nothing in her head beyond fashion. She had not meant to diminish the importance of what he was saying with so banal a comment – yet she had, and there was no way she could recall the comment, hate it though she did.

'It is difficult for me always to know what is happening in the theatre and –' she began, wanting to excuse her own idiocy and not knowing how to, but he smiled at her, a little vaguely this time, and with none of the warm amusement he had shown hitherto, and shook his head.

'Why should you, after all?' he said lightly. 'I understand from Mabel you have your schoolwork to fill your time – it must be difficult for you to do all you would like to do apart from that.'

She had been a woman for a little while, a grown woman responding to the music and the dance as only a woman could. And now she was a child again, a schoolgirl interested only in schoolwork and fashion, and eager for an ice – for he had purchased two of them and set one in her hand as well as his sister's – or so he made her feel. And she stood there with her ice in her hand, feeling the chill coming through her glove from the little glass dish and for the first time on this wonderful evening lost her sense of the magic of it. It had all been so very special and she had liked him so much and now he had made her feel like a child again, all because of one unguarded stupid remark. She could have wept with fury at herself, but she did not. Instead she took her little spoon and mechanically began to eat her ice. There seemed little else she could do.

10

But the magic came back, or at least some of it did. The second half of
the programme was a series of *divertissements* which, although they
lacked the emotional power of Pavlova's Swan, still proved delightful.
The music was sprightly and the dancing amusing, and they laughed
a good deal and applauded just as happily at the end of it, though
Poppy missed that moment of closeness to Bobby she had felt when
she had been so very moved by Pavlova. But, she told herself, when it
was all over and they at last got unwillingly to their feet and began to
put on their wraps again, she had probably imagined it anyway. She
had allowed herself to be carried away by the music and the
movement and had wanted to feel someone else shared her emotion,
and had cast Bobby in that role. Which was silly really; and mentally
she shrugged her shoulders and tried not to think about it any more.

But it wasn't easy, for he proved himself an ever more diverting
conversationalist and excellent company and made her laugh so much
that it was difficult not to want to be closer to him. Quite what it was
that made her laugh she could not say; his jokes were not that
brilliant, nor his sallies that remarkable, and yet, he had so droll an air
about him that laughter was inevitable; and what was more he drew
from both Mabel and herself a matching swiftness of repartee that
made him laugh a good deal. So it was a happy trio that emerged from
the taxi cab that Bobby had managed to get outside the theatre –
'positively stealing it from under the nose of the most frightful old
General, as cool as you please!' as Mabel had said admiringly – at the
Bradman house in Norland Square where they were to eat supper.

Number twenty-two was, Poppy decided, the most delightful
house she could imagine. Much smaller than her own rather
forbidding home in Leinster Terrace, it was stuccoed in cream and set
neatly behind a set of spiked railings which were pierced in the centre
by the five carefully whitened steps that led up to the front door.

There was a pretty balcony in front of the first-floor drawing room windows, and below the railings it was possible to see into the area and the cosiest of basement kitchens, lit by a glowing fire in a shining blackleaded range in front of which a vast brindled cat lay curled up in a positively storybook pose. The house was exactly like its neighbours and was, Poppy decided, precisely the sort of jolly place she would most like to live in.

Inside was just as charming. No wide hallway paved with handsome black and white tiles here, nor heavy mahogany furniture and a green baize door that led towards the servants' quarters, but a narrow passage, cheerfully papered in a bright rose-strewn design, and floored with an even more cheerful dark red carpet strip set on polished wood. Over the door that led to the dining room on the left, a matching dark red velvet curtain was suspended from large brass rings, and looped back to show the room within, where a cheerful fire showed a table set with good linen and tolerable silver and glass, and a wide sideboard on which some delicious looking food was waiting: a couple of large pies and a bowl of chicken salad and a well-boiled ham on a wide platter. But first they trooped upstairs to the drawing room to enjoy, as Bobby put it 'a little preprandial refreshment', and here Poppy's enchantment was complete.

The room was a large one, considering the size of the house, running from back to front in the usual manner, but was so cleverly decorated that it seemed even larger. She stood in the door and stared, as both Bobby and Mabel watched her, with amusement on his face, and positively smug pride on hers.

There were fabric hangings in rich deep colours completely covering the walls in heavy golds and sultry blues and sumptuous greens and crimsons and the floor was strewn with cushions which glowed in the same jewel colours against most richly patterned Persian carpets. There was remarkably little furniture in the sense that Poppy understood the word – a few low tables and leather-covered stools and just one vast sofa upholstered in purple that dominated the space before the fireplace. The lighting was, she thought, strange and exotic in the extreme, coming as it did from pierced and twisted brass containers within which lamps glowed very prettily. Each light was rather dim but there were so many of them dotted about the room as well as hanging from the ceiling that there was no lack of illumination; everything seemed to gleam richly in the soft ambience, leaving only the most delightfully tantalizing of shadows in the corners. There was a fire burning in this room too for all it was an April evening, for it was cool out of doors, and the overall effect was quite breathtaking. And when she did draw breath, it was to take in scented air, a faintly spicy yet delicately flowery redolence that seemed to linger on the nose and tongue and to fill her head, and she realized incense pastilles were being burned.

'Oh, my!' Poppy said and that was all, and Mabel laughed delightedly.

'Isn't this ridiculous?' she crowed. 'When Bobby first did it I told him he was quite mad, but you know, I have come to like it immensely, and so have our friends. Goosey thinks it dreadful of course – heathen wickedness she says. But then, if she had her way, we'd still be living in the most stuffy of styles, positively mid-Victorian!'

'Why?' Poppy said, not stopping to think. 'I mean – I do think it looks wonderful, but why do it? Where did you get the ideas?' She looked at Bobby a little timidly. 'Am I being stupid to ask that? Did you just decide to do it, out of your own head?'

He smiled at that. 'No, of course you aren't being stupid! It is a reasonable question. I wish I had such a head that I could invent such things out of it. No, this is the result of seeing Diaghilev's company in Paris, as I told you I had. They have a designer, Leon Bakst, and it is his work that I so admire and in my own small way tried to reflect. Now, what will you drink? A little sherry perhaps? Or –'

'Oh, Bobby, let's be wicked and have some champagne! It is the first time Poppy has been here to our house, and that is a good enough reason for extravagance. I shall see if there is still some in the cellar and, if so, I am sure it will be quite cold enough – I shan't be long –' And Mabel went hurrying out of the room, in the little rushing run that was all she could manage in her most elegantly hobbled skirt – and tonight she looked delightful in buttercup yellow, Poppy thought – and left them there. And at once Poppy felt totally tongue-tied, and was furious with herself for being so childish yet again.

But Bobby seemed not to notice and indicated the way to the sofa, and she crossed the room and sank into it a little gingerly, for it was very low, while he threw himself lazily on to the heap of cushions beside the fire.

She looked at him covertly and decided that delightful person though he was to talk to, he wasn't precisely good-looking; it was easier to see him here on his own than it had been in the crowded Palace Theatre, and now she could take proper stock of him. The round face was somewhat lined, she now realized. They weren't the

lines of age, for he was, she knew about thirty and therefore they must
be lines of sadness. That puzzled her a little for so far all he had been
was jolly and chattering, but now as he sat staring at the fire the
laughter seemed to have gone, and she wondered why. It could not be
the fact that he was a widower, could it? she asked herself. After all,
that had happened three years ago, Mabel had told her. An eternity of
time, it seemed to Poppy from the vantage point of her sixteen years.
He must surely be quite cured of any grief in his bereavement by now.
There had to be, she was sure, another reason and came to the painful
conclusion that the trouble was that he was bored with her company.
After all, she was just a silly girl, interested more in fashion than
anything else; he was entitled to think that after her foolishness this
evening and she took a little breath and began to try to set matters
right.

'Please, tell me more about – what was his name? Leon Bakst? The
man from whom you got the ideas for the lovely room. Is he a friend of
yours?'

At once he was all attention, almost visibly pulling himself out of
the little reverie into which he had sunk. 'Mmm? Oh, dear me no! I
wish he were! I am sure he must be a splendid chap to know but I'm
not so fortunate. No, I first saw his work, as I said, when I saw
Schéhérazade and it quite bowled me over. I remember that when the
curtain rose that night I was quite literally breathless. I sat there and
stared and did not believe what I saw. After all the things one usually
sees on stages – you know, all that plush and velvet and so forth, and
such heavy colours – to see all this newness was – well, I cannot tell
you. It was like being dropped into the middle of a rainbow and the
more one splashed about to keep one's balance, the more colours
appeared and made one feel drunk and generally – well, it was a
positively physical experience –' He stopped then and looked at her
and then away and she thought, startled, he's embarrassed – and
could not imagine why. But he collected himself soon enough and
went on, 'So after that, I saw as much of his work as I could, both on
stage and in print. There were exhibitions, you know, in Paris, once
the ballet was launched, and the town went wild for them, and I did
too. I went to them over and over again. You do not find it – vulgar, all
this?'

'Vulgar?' She stared at him. 'How could I? It's beautiful. It's, it's so
– *alive*,' and he clapped his hands softly and said, 'Well done!' as
Mabel arrived at the door, followed by a large woman in a grey gown
and with a ferociously white apron pinned over it. She was bearing a

tray with champagne and glasses on it and a face with a very disapproving expression.

'Here we are then – our little celebration!' Mabel cried gaily. 'Goosey says we are wicked to be drinking such stuff at eleven o'clock at night but I told her it will do us no harm at all –'

'You'd be better off eatin' your vittles and gettin' to your beds,' the old woman grunted and shot a black look at Poppy who reddened. 'But if you make up your minds to behave silly, who am I to put you right? Only the one as had the rearing of you, but that don't mean I got no sense, of course. I'm just a nuisance, old Goosey what doesn't know what's what, that's who I am –'

'Yes, Goosey darling,' Bobby said easily and got to his feet. 'This is Miss Amberly, Goosey, who likes to be called Poppy, and I am sure you will want to welcome her here for her first visit, just as we do. We shall pour the wine here, but take it downstairs with us, Goosey, and then honour will be satisfied.'

'Pleased to meet you miss, I'm sure,' Goosey grunted and then glowered at Bobby. 'And don't you think your sweet talkin'll make no never mind, neither! I still think it's wrong to be drinking like this at this hour of the night – nasty gassy stuff too – Miss Mabel ought to be in her bed and –'

'You see, Poppy? She thinks I'm still her baby! Never mind, Goosey.' Mabel seized the glass Bobby gave her after opening the bottle with a practised twist of his fingers. 'I'll be in bed soon enough and it will be Sunday soon and I can so easily catch up on my sleep then –'

'And more shame to you, miss!' Goosey said tartly. 'Ought to go to early church, you ought. Do you more good. Goodnight to you. I'm away to my bed. You've got all your supper there ready and I'll clear in the morning. Be sure to lock up, Master Bobby. We don't want no tramps walking in to kill us all.' And she went stumping out of the room, her back eloquent of disapproval, to a chorus of goodnights from Bobby and Mabel and a belated one from Poppy.

'She's not so bad really,' Mabel said and slid her hand into Poppy's elbow to lead her downstairs. 'It's just that she likes us to remember that she has looked after us all our lives and especially shows off when we have strangers here. She'll get used to you and then you'll find she's delightful. She isn't really cross at all – just swanking a bit.'

'Miss Mabel!' Goosey reappeared at the door. 'I never said – there's a tureen of my good barley soup on the kitchen range waiting to come up. Do you want me to fetch it or –'

'No, it's all right, Goosey. I'll bring it up. You go to bed, you old darling.' And Mabel let go of Poppy's arm and went to the door to kiss the papery dewlaps of the old woman who snorted and sniffed and then went off up the stairs, as Mabel hurried down to see to the soup.

'I'll just bank up the fire,' Bobby said. 'Do go down, Poppy, and then we shall take some food. You must be very hungry –' and after a moment Poppy turned to follow Mabel downstairs. But she had barely reached the first tread when she heard a sound behind her and turned to look.

At first she could see nothing in the dimness of the landing and then, as she blinked, a little white blur appeared and she saw standing on the lowest step a small figure in a nightgown. She was clutching a small blanket to her cheek with one hand, and holding on to the banisters with the other.

'Oh!' Poppy said and smiled. The child stared at her with large round eyes, and then pushed out her lower lip and blew upwards so that the curly hair on her forehead lifted and settled out of her eyes and suddenly Poppy remembered Bobby's head lifting gesture to clear his own eyes of errant locks and smiled even more widely at the resemblance she could now see to him in this small face.

'You must be Chloe. Hello. I'm Poppy,' she said.

The child said nothing, staring at her with her lower lip still stuck out in a way that now made her look sulky and Poppy, unused to the ways of children, paused nonplussed, not sure what to say next.

'Er – how do you do,' she managed at last and then, annoyed with herself for being so banal, went over to the child and crouched in front of her. 'What's the matter, dear? Can't you sleep?'

'Go away,' the child said distinctly. 'Hate you. Go away.'

Poppy blinked but she didn't move.

'Hate you,' the child said again. 'Want my Daddy. Daddy! Daddy!' She said it louder in a little wail and Poppy heard a little clatter of fire irons in the drawing room and then he was there beside her, looking down at the child who at once put up her arms to him.

'Oh, Chloe, you naughty little wretch,' he said softly. 'You should be in bed fast asleep,' and he scooped her up and held her close and Poppy got to her feet, her face blazing with the embarrassment that had filled her. There had been so much love and pleasure in his voice when he had spoken, so much eagerness in the way he had picked Chloe up, that she felt herself to be an intolerable intruder who had come between two very private people. She had no right to be here and she stepped back into the dimness, wanting very much to escape downstairs as fast as she could.

He was holding the small body close, his head down and crooning into her neck as he rocked her and the child stared at Poppy over his shoulder and suddenly spoke very distinctly.

'Poppy,' she said. 'Soppy Poppy. Soppy Poppy –'

'Chloe!' He lifted his head and looked into the child's face and then over his shoulder at Poppy. 'Oh, Poppy my dear, I do apologize! Chloe, that is very naughty! Where do you get such a word from? Miss Amberly is our guest and you must be polite –'

'Soppy –' the child began again and now he was clearly fussed and almost shook her and at once the child burst into noisy tears and began to kick her feet against his chest, and Poppy put out one hand, wanting to help and not knowing how to.

'Go 'way,' Chloe shrieked. 'Hate you – Go 'way – Daddy – Daddy.' And again she bawled loudly but Poppy could not help but notice that there were no tears to be seen. The little girl was still watching her with those wide alert eyes and Poppy lifted her chin and said softly, 'I shan't go away. Not till I want to.'

Amazingly, Chloe stopped her bawling and stared at Poppy again and said once more, 'Soppy Poppy –' but she sounded a little doubtful now, and Bobby shook his head at her and began to climb the stairs to the upper floor. But Poppy put out her hand and held him back for a moment.

'Say it again, Chloe,' she commanded in a clear firm voice. 'Say Soppy Poppy, Loppy Poppy, Boppy Poppy – say it, Chloe –' And the child stared again and then laughed, and Bobby looked over his shoulder once more at Poppy and smiled in gratitude as above them the stairs creaked and the large shadowy shape of Goosey appeared. She was wrapped in a dressing gown of grey as her day gown had been and had her hair confined in an old-fashioned nightcap.

'You little limb!' She was panting a little at the exertion she was making as she came down the stairs and took the child from Bobby's arms. 'Sneakin' out of your bed that way when Goosey's back is turned! You come away now to bed and back to sleep. Little girls oughtn't to be running about at this time of night this way –'

'Daddy, Daddy, Daddy!' shrieked Chloe, clinging to her father with great ferocity. 'Hate Goosey, hate Goosey, hate Goosey –'

'No doubt you do, madam mischief!' Goosey said loudly. 'But you'll love me again in the morning when it's breakfast time and I say you can have some jam with your bread and milk – yes, I thought that would get you! Let her go now, Master Bobby. She's a little monkey twisting you round her little finger, as I've told you till I'm breathless, and it isn't right! Let her go now –'

Unwillingly, Bobby did and with masterful movements Goosey tucked the small girl on her shoulder and held her there with one large hand and turned to climb the stairs as the child kicked and bawled lustily. But Goosey was clearly not at all put out and at last the sound of Chloe's protests were muffled as a door above them opened and then closed.

Bobby stood there staring upwards for a little while and then the sound of weeping stopped, and there was a little burst of shrill laughter and Poppy said softly, 'There! She's all right, then!'

'Yes –' Bobby sounded abstracted. 'I suppose so. But it makes me feel so –' He stopped and took a deep breath and then turned and smiled at her, all politeness once more. 'But we really must let you have some supper. Come along, Poppy! I'm sorry my naughty baby was so rude to you but –'

'Oh, pooh!' Poppy said. 'You can't call it rudeness in a child. How old is she? Three? Very young! I dare say she woke and was frightened and that made her scratchy.'

'Oh, she does this most nights when I come home,' Bobby said a little wearily. 'Whatever time it is. It's as though she hears me come in, and yet we are not so very noisy after all, and her nursery is well tucked away. She has no mother, you see, and I am sure that is what causes the problem. Goosey says I spoil her, but she is so very sweet a child and how can I not when I must be both mother and father to her?'

'But she has her aunt,' Poppy ventured, remembering the wide-eyed and almost calculating stare the child had given her as she produced her tearless bawling. 'And she seems very well looked after by Goosey. I am sure you worry needlessly.' And suddenly she wanted to tell him that she too had had only one parent, but had not misbehaved quite so outrageously even when she was very small. And then told herself wryly that Mama was hardly the person to permit it, and decided to say nothing. After all, what help would it be?

'Yes, she has her aunt,' Bobby said. 'But that is not quite the same, is it, as a mother? A child needs her mother so badly – but enough of such domestic matters! I insist – supper. You have your champagne? Excellent –' for Poppy was still clutching her glass in one hand. 'I shall fetch mine and supper shall be attacked. I hope one of those pies down there is Goosey's special veal and ham. I can do a good deal of damage to one of those! Come along, Miss Poppy! Your supper awaits!'

And he led her downstairs to the dining room with never a backwards look to the nursery floor. But for the rest of the evening there was no doubt in Poppy's mind that the absent child was the person who was receiving most of her host's attention. And deep inside herself that made her more than a little irritable. Because she liked this man very much indeed.

11

I should not have done it, Mildred thought, as she watched Poppy pinning the trimmings to her new hat. I should have stood firm and made her do as I bade her, I have given her too much leeway, given her money in her pocket and too much time to go about with her own friends. I should not have done it –

But even as she thought it she knew she was wrong. For she could not have helped what had happened. That had become ever more clear to her as she had watched her beloved child grow her way through this hot summer. Last winter, she had been still very much a schoolgirl, rounded of cheek and leggy and coltish, but now as June had arrived she already looked more adult, with her cheeks thinning down to show interesting planes and her movements becoming more elegant than awkward.

Some of the transformation Mildred had recognized might be due to the fact that she had worn down her mother's objections and now had her hair pinned up all the time. It sat on her crown in rich dark waves, revealing a long and well-shaped neck, and its heaviness made her hold her head well up so that she walked with more grace than she had been used to do; but that was not all. There was a new thoughtfulness about her now, and she had stopped being quite so watchful, and for that Mildred was grateful. It said to her that her daughter was less fearful of her and that was important. It had hurt her badly to discover, as she had that evening when Poppy had told her of how much of her childhood she actually remembered, how secretive the child had become. To see her now, in her more relaxed open mood, was much more agreeable. So perhaps, she thought again, perhaps it was all just as well. Oh, if only I could persuade her to go to college!

But on that score Poppy had become ever more adamant. Even this afternoon, when she had come to tell her mother – not ask her, but tell her – that her friend Miss Bradman and her brother together with some others she knew from school were to go to watch the Coronation procession from Whitehall, she had referred to the subject, even while she had been searching through her work basket for some sort of nonsense with which to 'wake up' as she put it, her white straw for the Great Day.

'Mama,' she had said, her head down over the feathers and artificial fruit she had managed to unearth. 'I have been talking to Miss Sayers about the sort of work I should like to do when I leave school next summer.'

'But you are not leaving school.' Mildred had tried to sound as hard and determined as she could, but Poppy had just lifted her head and looked at her and said quietly, 'But I am, Mama. I am quite certain of it. Even if I have to behave quite badly towards you, I should have to, for I am quite certain I am right in this matter. I should not be happy in Cambridge.'

'Why not? How can you be so sure?' Mildred was beginning to sound flustered and she knew it. 'At least try!'

Poppy had sighed and set down her needle to sit and stare directly at her mother. 'Because I have no use for the academic frame of mind, Mama. I see no sense in searching for dead facts in dead books. I am concerned with now and here and –'

She had stopped then and considered and then gone on with a little rush, 'Actually, Mama, I should like to work in a newspaper office.'

Mildred, looking now at Poppy's bent head, felt again the little shock of amazement that had filled her.

'A – what? What sort of office?'

'A newspaper,' Poppy had said firmly and now there was a little spot of colour in each round cheek. 'I – my friend, Miss Bradman, you know, she works in one. She is a delightful girl – you said so yourself when she came to visit and every time she comes again you say she is a good person to be my friend and –'

'Indeed, I do agree. She is a most charming girl, of excellent manners and – but she says herself that she is not so clever as you are, Poppy! Perhaps she chose to work in that office because she could not succeed at her books –'

'Not at all,' Poppy had said, almost curtly. 'It is the case that she prefers to work in the busy world, just as I should like to do. Not to be locked away in dull colleges. I am learning to use a typewriter, you know, Mama! Mabel is teaching me on her very own machine at her house. Her brother had bought it for her –' She had become very pink then and gone on quickly, 'And he works on the same newspaper, so you can see it is all quite safe and proper. He chaperones her, and would do the same for me if I were there. They have said, Mr Bradman and his sister, that they will help me obtain employment there and I am quite determined, Mama!' She had stopped then. 'Even if I had to live alone in just a rented room to do it, Mama, I must tell you my mind is made up.'

And it had been that which had finally defeated Mildred. Her own girlhood situation had been so different, of course it had. She had been the butt of a cruel and uncaring father and under the care of a weak and useless stepmother. She had had every cause to choose to leave her family home and seek her own way outside. And she had done it. The fact that her own dear child had no such compulsion, was not being ill-treated as she herself had been, made no difference. Mildred recognized in her what had been there in herself, once. The courage and the determination and the ability to do as she chose with her life, even if it meant leaving home with just a few clothes in a bag –

And Mildred sat there in her rich Leinster Terrace drawing room as the hot June sunlight outside fried the trees to a dull lassitude and left the pavement almost too hot to walk upon and remembered so vividly her own cold winters after she had done precisely what Poppy now threatened to do that she had shivered.

'I see,' she had said abruptly then, and got to her feet. 'If that is your determination then there is nothing more to be said. I trust you will at least wait until you are seventeen, Poppy, before taking this employment. I would like to see you complete your courses and sit your examinations even if you do not at once avail yourself of the opportunities they offer. You may one day change your mind and choose to go to Newnham after all –'

And Poppy had flamed into excitement and jumped up and hugged her mother warmly – which helped Mildred's pain a good deal – and thanked her and then returned to her hat, humming softly beneath her breath 'The Pipes of Pan' from the show she had seen last night at the Shaftesbury Theatre and which, she had told Mildred eagerly, 'was quite the most delightful spectacle which you should go and see, for I'm sure you would enjoy it immensely.' And Mildred, who had once loved the theatre but who had not attended one for many years now had actually thought, just for a moment, of agreeing to buy tickets for *The Arcadians* and then had pulled herself back from such nonsense to sit and watch Poppy finish her hat. And still thinking, I should not have done it, I should have stopped her, even though she knew perfectly well that she had not had that sort of power over her daughter. Poppy had taken her life into her own hands, and Mildred could do nothing about it.

Poppy herself was not nearly so aware of her new status. In the weeks since she had first met her Aunt Jessie and then Mabel's brother Bobby, strange things had happened to her. She found herself spending far more time in speculative daydreaming than she had ever been used to do and was actually reprimanded in class sometimes for her inattention, something which had never happened before. But she had not minded at all, even when it was her dear Miss Sayers who showed irritation with her, for thinking as she did about these two new people was so enthralling that criticism of any outside kind did not matter at all.

Aunt Jessie first. Poppy had considered going back to the East End to visit her very soon after that first meeting, not so much to see the lady herself – she had to admit that she found her a little over-whelming and was wary of getting too close to her too soon – but to get more information from her about her other relations. Notably her father. But she had not done so.

First of all, she had thought that her interest in this shadowy person would wane once she knew some more about him. He had been a brave soldier – she knew that much. He had also been a rather exotic person, a Jew – such a strange thought, that! – no doubt with all Jessie Braham's colourful style and attack. But it seemed it was no longer a case of had been; he actually *was*. From surprising hints that Jessie had offered it appeared he was still alive somewhere. And that meant, Poppy had thought uncomfortably, he could be an embarrassing person to know.

She could not hide from herself the fact that she felt some dismay about Jessie Braham's connection to her. It wasn't just Mabel's casual dismissal of her as an absurd sort of relative for such a person as Poppy to have; there was inside herself a deep shrinking from Jessie's size and noisiness and general manner, and she was ashamed of that. It could not be right to feel so alarmed simply because a person was different in style from the usual run of people she met. And yet, that was how she felt; so there were clearly things she had to sort out in her head about her feelings regarding her Aunt Jessie, she decided.

And while she tried to do that, she kept her distance, refusing with various excuses Mabel's invitiations to meetings at Sylvia Pankhurst's Settlement and contenting herself with sending occasional polite letters to her aunt at her shop in Cable Street, not wishing her feelings to be hurt because of her failure to return. Poppy realized perfectly well just how confused and foolish her behaviour was about her new-found aunt but could do little about correcting it. It would be, she told herself with some shrewdness, sorted out in time. She just had to get used to the idea of her, that was all.

But it was different when she thought about Bobby Bradman. There was no confusion about her feelings there. Had she been able to have her own way, she would have seen him at any time and on every possible occasion, for she could not hide from herself what had happened. She had become quite absurdly obsessed with him; she who had laughed at and scorned the girls at school who sighed and shivered over the boys they met at each other's parties and to whom they were introduced by husband-hunting mamas at tennis parties and *thé dansants*; she who had always thought such things ridiculous and not at all worth wasting any time over; she it was who now ached to be asked to a tennis party where Bobby Bradmam might be playing or to a *thé dansant* where she could be taken in his arms to dance a waltz – and she would shiver with excitement at the very idea and her eyes would fill with tears as she realized how absurd such yearnings were.

For Bobby Bradman was totally unaware of her in the way she wanted him to be. Oh, he was friendly when they met, which was fairly often, for she and Mabel had become almost inseparable, and always greeted her with all the *bonhomie* anyone could possibly expect. If, that is, they were content to be regarded as a kid sister's best friend, a silly schoolgirl.

Because, of course, that was all she was in his eyes. Mabel's dear chum, someone to be included in family outings for Mabel's sake, who clearly enjoyed having her friend's company; someone to laugh with and make jokes with, but certainly not someone to yearn over as Poppy yearned over him.

The year moved on through the hot months of Coronation excitement and she went with Bobby and Mabel and also with Goosey and baby Chloe to watch the procession. The afternoon was much marred by Chloe's usual ill behaviour, for she clung to her father quite ferociously and refused to do anything anyone else said, not even Goosey who had the most ability to control her, and cried a great deal. That wouldn't have mattered too much to Poppy who quite liked the child, despite her behaviour, had not Bobby showed in every way in his dealings with her on that afternoon, and on every other that followed, that he was the root of the child's difficulties.

Clearly he felt so sorry for her in her motherless state that he indulged her shamefully and actually created in her the uncertainty that made her so fractious, and it was a matter of some amazement to Poppy that even though she saw all this, and felt quite angry with Bobby for being so silly in his handling of his small daughter, her adoration of him never wavered.

Life would be so much easier, she would tell herself in the long hot nights when sleep eluded her, if she could get so annoyed with him that she ceased to feel such attraction to him. But that she knew was a forlorn hope; if she adored him even when he was being silly with Chloe, it was clear to her that she would adore him for ever. And that for the usually equable Poppy was a dreadful prospect, for it was quite obvious to her that Bobby would never ever adore her in return. How could he when he so cheerfully failed to see her now as the woman she was? He would always see her as a silly schoolgirl even if they both lived to be ninety, she would tell herself furiously, and then would weep helplessly into her pillow until sleep at last took pity on her.

In September she managed to find the courage to go again to a Sylvia Pankhurst meeting and was greatly comforted to find that Aunt Jessie was after all far less fearsome than she had remembered. She was delighted to see Poppy again when the meeting was over and everyone had adjourned as usual for tea, but made no public mention of the connection between them and did nothing to cause Poppy a moment's discomfort or to single her out for particular attention, and that made Poppy warm to her greatly.

She sat and sipped her tea and ate the cake she had been given – a particularly delicious sponge which Jessie told her was called plaver – and wondered if perhaps she had been unnecessarily unfair. It would not hurt to visit her more often, after all, now it was so clear that the big woman, dressed today in an even more vivid red gown than she had worn the first time they had met, would do nothing to cause her any distress.

So, after the party had drawn at last to a close and people were bidding Miss Sylvia goodbye at the door, Poppy hung back a little to speak to Jessie. She was cleaning the long tables and piling the plates of food high, clucking as she worked.

'Will you look at this? They eat like birds, these women, like birds! How do they expect they can do a decent job on an empty stomach? It's food makes you work hard, makes you lively, makes you *do*, ain't that true? And look at how much I got left here! Oh, well, the kids down at the Brady Street club'll be glad enough to get it, I dare say.'

She looked briefly over her shoulder at the now virtually empty room and went on in a low voice, 'So how you been, Poppy? Busy at your schoolwork, hmm? You was always a clever girl, you know –' And she looked sharply over her shoulder yet again to make sure no one was within earshot. 'I don't want to upset no one letting on as we're related, you know? It wouldn't do, would it?'

Poppy reddened as the big woman so clearly reflected her own thinking and said quickly, 'Oh, I don't suppose it matters –' but Jessie Braham grinned at that, a little wryly.

'Well, one day I hope it won't, I truly do, dolly. But right now you're too young to deal with the sort of fuss people'd make if it got out you and me was aunt and niece. A Jewish balabuster like me and a smart West End lady like you? I should cocoa! It never worked for your Ma and your Pa so it won't work for us. We got to be more sensible –'

Poppy drew a sharp little breath. 'That was something I wanted to talk to you about, Mrs – er – Aunt Jessie,' she said softly as she saw Mabel reappear at the door, clearly looking for her. 'I – there are things I'd like to know. I'm entitled to know, too, aren't I? So can I come and see you – in your own home, you know, or the shop or somewhere where we can talk? Not here –'

Jessie's face split into a vast grin and Poppy stepped back a little hastily as she showed every sign of surging forwards to engulf Poppy in a hug, but fortunately she was still holding the dishes of food and that hampered her; and anyway she remembered her promised discretion just as Mabel came determinedly towards them from the door.

'Sure you can come and see me. You know the address? Nineteen Cable Street – you can't miss it – best lookin' shop in the whole street – Braham's, it's got written up outside. Come soon – whenever you like. I'll be there. You can phone me!' She sounded proud suddenly at having so elegant a piece of modernity in her home. 'Here, I'll write down the number. Wait here –' And she went hurrying away as Mabel tugged on Poppy's arm to tell her it was time to go home.

So it was that Poppy, late one afternoon in October when the leaves on the trees in Hyde Park were curling into the rich glory of their approaching death, set out carefully dressed in one of her more classic tailored suits in a golden brown as rich as any of the leaves over her head, to visit her aunt's shop in Cable Street, determined that now she would force the issue. It was high time she met her father. The evasions had gone on long enough. Especially her own.

12

But it took a little while to get to the point of her visit. Jessie welcomed Poppy warmly when she arrived in Cable Street that afternoon, but she talked so much Poppy hardly had a chance to say anything, and indeed at first there was so much to look at and so many new pieces of information to absorb that she chould not have framed her own questions anyway.

The shop on the outside gave the impression of being a cave that was bursting out of the brick of the buildings in which it was set. The entrance door was small, and flanked on one side by a window, but it was impossible to see inside through it, for it was covered in white painted messages in large letters which shrieked invitations which were more like summonses to the passing customers. 'Best Schmalz herring, only a penny each!'; 'Salt beef, home cooked, only threepence a portion!'; 'Jessie's famous cheesecake, you can't get better, come in and try!' jostled with lively crude drawings of herrings and cakes and sides of beef, while outside on the pavement there were boxes and trays and arrangements of food piled so high that it seemed impossible to Poppy that all of it could ever be sold. Great barrels reeking of garlic and brine and apparently filled with pickled cucumbers sat beside salt-encrusted tubs that reeked of ancient fish while boxes of sweet biscuits sat in serried rows, their glass lids showing all too invitingly their rich contents.

And when she had taken a deep breath of this harmony of scents and found the courage to step inside the dark little doorway, with the noisy bell on a spring that bounced, jangling, above her head, there was even more to see: salamis and sausages of all kinds hung from a bar that was set over the long counter that ran all the way down the right-hand side of the shop, and the counter itself was heaped with a vast array of cheeses and dishes full of appetizing mixtures of salads and vegetables and fruits of all kinds. The shelves on all sides were groaning with cans and packages, and on every remaining area of wall space there were lively posters advertising all kinds of foods from instant soups to canned beans. And Poppy blinked and looked around and felt as though she had just got up from the table after eating a vast meal, even though she had in fact lunched very lightly this afternoon, for the smells of it all were so powerful they seemed positively edible.

'Poppy!' The voice came in a shriek of delight from the back of the shop and suddenly there was Jessie, emerging from the gloom like a vast glowing sunrise with arms outstretched, and involuntarily Poppy stepped back. All the caution and self-effacement Jessie had shown when they had last met at Sylvia Pankhurst's Settlement had totally vanished and been replaced with all the exuberance that Jessie could display, and that was a formidable amount. Poppy found herself swept into a bear hug that left her breathless, which sent her hat to the back of her head, and from which she emerged crimson-faced and confused.

'I did promise I'd come,' she murmured, setting herself to rights. 'I hope I haven't chosen a bad time –'

'No time is a bad time to see you, dolly!' Jessie cried and then lifted her head and shrieked, 'Bernie! Bernie, where are you, already? Come here and meet someone very important.'

'You should be so lucky he'll come runnin'!' a voice said and Poppy turned her head and saw standing behind the counter a very diminutive figure and at first she thought it was that of a child, until she looked closer and saw a woman of some fifty years, with a pointed sharp little face and a mop of frizzy hair carefully arranged on top of her head with girlish lavishness. Her eyes were as bright as a bird's and just as shiny and black, and looked startlingly wrong under the ferocious carroty redness of the hair and Poppy stared at the odd little thing, with her bony cheeks and her scrawny little neck, and she wondered in a confused sort of way why there were so many strange people to see in the East End. All the people she saw in her own part of London looked so dull and ordinary; here everyone seemed to be like a character out of her childhood's story books. This one was positively witchlike.

'I beg your pardon?' she managed and Jessie laughed and said comfortably, 'Oh, take no notice o' Lily! This is Lily, worked for me ever since I got home from Baltimore. Never stops complainin', eh Lil? Bernie!' and again she lifted her head and shrieked.

'She'll never learn, that one,' Lily said in a conversational sort of tone, and her voice was ridiculously deep for so small a woman. 'That kid of hers runs her ragged, treats her like she was a toe-rag and still she thinks he's the best –'

'And what you wouldn't give to have such a boychick,' Jessie said, but her tone was amiable. Clearly this was a conversation the two women had had many times. 'Listen, so weigh out the new sack o' sugar, and call me if you get busy. I'm goin' in back and I want to stay as long as I can to visit with my –' and she looked sideways at Poppy and grinned at her. 'With my young friend here, all right?' And she guided Poppy towards the back of the shop leading the way through the piles of boxes and sacks full of lentils and beans and split peas that cluttered the available space and made it almost impassable, just as the shop door again pinged itself open and a little flurry of women came in, all talking at the tops of their voices.

'What can I say? You're the guv'nor,' the little woman said and turned to the arriving customers. 'So shut up already! What are you? A lot o' demented fowls? Give me a bit o' peace, do me a favour! So, Mrs Arbeiter, the usual two ounces o' cream cheese and weigh the paper first, God forbid you should pay for the weight of a bissel paper, hey?'

Jessie laughed fatly as at last she and Poppy reached the back of the shop and she lifted a red curtain that shrouded the door there. 'Listen to her! Insults my customers like there was no tomorrow, and you know something? They love it! I taught her that trick. They got a lot o' sense about these things in America, and they taught me that. Be rude to the customers, it makes 'em feel like family and they buy more – come in, now, come along and be comfortable –'

Poppy halted in the doorway and stared round at the room with much the same sense of shock she had felt when Bobby and Mabel had shown her their drawing room in Norland Square, for the contrast between the shop they had just left and the room she now saw in front of her was very startling.

It was, of course, mainly red. Poppy had realized this much about her aunt; her passion for this hot colour in all its shades was clearly something that was deeply entrenched in her. The curtains that were looped back on each side of the broad window at the back of the room were deep crimson brocade and the lace curtains that hung over the panes between them were a soft shell pink. The carpet was equally crimson, and thick underfoot, and the cloth on the central table was made of the same heavy velvet as the window drapes. But the furniture was splendid. A deep mahogany sideboard made in the most modern of designs, rich with sinuous curves and carved lilies, sat against the wall and on it was arranged more gleaming silver than Poppy had ever seen outside a jeweller's shop window. A tea tray with an engraved teapot and coffee pot and vast matching creamers and sugar bowls sat proudly between a pair of exceedingly elaborate candlesticks and behind that equipage stood yet another candlestick, this one with nine branches, four on each side and one standing forward in the centre. There were flat dishes with chased edges and little pots and pictures in engraved silver frames and a canteen of cutlery with its lid up to display proudly the rows of heavy knives and forks and spoons inside. But that was not all; there was a wide fireplace with the most modern of pink tiles and more polished mahogany, and above it an overmantel on which even more silver was spread, this time in the form of vases filled with elaborate paper flowers – red ones of course – and little mirrors with silver frames.

On each side of the fireplace stood a large deep armchair, upholstered in crimson velour, and sitting in one of them with his legs hooked over one arm and his back carefully arranged against the other was a small boy, his head bent over a comic paper.

'Bernie, why didn't you come when I called ? Didn't you hear me?' Jessie cried and she urged Poppy forwards into the sumptuous interior. 'I want you should meet someone!'

'I heard you,' the child said, never taking his eyes from his comic paper.

'So, why didn't you come?' Jessie cried, a note of raillery in her voice now.

'Busy,' the boy said and turned a page and Poppy felt Aunt Jessie beside her stiffen a little and felt her own face flame to match the curtains of this ridiculously expensive looking room.

'Good afternoon,' she said clearly, and she knew her voice sounded loud and even a little arrogant in this place where an accent like hers was one that was not normally heard. And she went on, making her syllables as drawling as she could, and clipping her consonants with all the elegance she could muster. 'How very pleasant to make your acquaintance.'

The boy looked up and stared at her and then after a moment swung his legs over the arm of the chair to sit with his elbows on his knees as he fixed her with a very direct stare.

He was, Poppy decided, quite the most extraordinarily beautiful child she had ever seen. His hair was richly glossy, thick and curly, and drooped in pretty locks over a wide creamy forehead. His brows were straight and silky, like black parentheses against his fair skin, and his eyes were amazing: large, darkly lustrous and fringed with lashes so thick and curled that any woman anywhere would have killed to have them for herself. His cheeks were lightly tinted with the softest rose, and his mouth was a vision of tremulous vulnerability above a round little chin that bore a charming dimple. And then he spoke.

'And 'oo the hell are you, then?' he said, and his voice had a thin whining quality about it that grated against her ears. To hear it coming from that exquisite mouth, which was now seen to display the most even and white of teeth, seemed an affront barely to be borne.

'Now, Bernie,' Jessie said and Poppy could hear the unease in her tones. 'Be nice, already! Say hello to your cousin! A long-lost cousin, would you believe! This is Poppy –'

'So?' the vision of childish beauty said and turned to swing his legs back over the arm of the chair and settled again into his comic. 'Big deal –'

'Sure it's a big deal!' Jessie said and went surging over to the armchair to bend and pick up the child bodily and plump herself down with him in her lap. 'How many relations you got, for pity's sake, what you can talk to as nice as Poppy'll talk to you? You don't like seein' the Rose cousins and you say you hate the Sayleses –'

'That load o' garbage!' the boy said scathingly and pulled away pettishly from Jessie's grip to stand with legs akimbo and his hands thrust deep into his trouser pockets on the hearthrug. In this posture he was still beautiful, with straight legs beneath his shorts and well-shaped knees and a compact body which had grace as well as strength in it, and even though he was now scowling at his mother, his face remained as beguilingly beautiful as ever. 'Listen, are you goin' to sit there and drive me meshuggah with talk? I got better things to listen to than a lot o' wimmin' yatterin' –' And again his voice had that thin whining quality which made Poppy want to grit her teeth.

'Sure we're goin' to talk!' Jessie said. 'This is my little Poppy I used to look after when she was a baby – she was my baby before you was, you know that, Bernie? Not mine, you understand, but I used to look after her a lot – oh, did I look after her!' And she looked fondly at Poppy. 'So she's come to visit with us! Sit down and talk and be nice, Bernie –'

'Ah, I'm goin' out –' the boy said disgustedly and made for the door, and Poppy stepped aside to let him pass. 'It's wimmin what sits and talks – me, I got other things to do –'

'Bernie, where're you goin'?' Jessie called after him, but the boy just pulled on the door and said briefly, 'Out,' and disappeared and Jessie sat and stared blankly after him as he slammed it behind him and called, 'Take care – keep out of the road – don't get hurt –' to its blank panels.

There was a short silence and then Jessie said a little awkwardly, 'It's because he's a boy, you know? A boy needs a man to deal with him, show him how to be a *good* boy. There's me and there's Lily, but that's all – he needs a man. And me, I don't meet the sort of men that Bernie takes to. I don't know how it is. I bring 'em home – not all the time, you understand, but I meet a nice man at a friend's place, invite him here to a little family dinner, so Bernie can meet him and there it is – it never seems to work out – but he needs a man –'

Her voice trailed away and then she looked up at Poppy and her face had an expression of appeal on it. 'But he's a beautiful boy, my Bernie, a good beautiful boy, believe me. No mother could want more. He's lovely, eh?'

'Oh, yes,' Poppy said fervently, grateful to be able to speak no more than the simple truth. 'He is quite the most beautiful child I've ever seen.' And the most hateful, she thought privately as Jessie went a little pink and almost bridled and then got to her feet to go across to the far side of the room and a door that led into what was clearly a small kitchen. Why is it that so many apparently nice people have such dreadful children? 'I'm sure I envy his eyelashes – the most lovely lashes ever!' she added, wanting to comfort this big woman who was now clattering round in the kitchen with cups and saucers. 'His father – your husband – must have been very handsome!'

Jessie gave a great shout of laughter and reappeared at the kitchen door to stare out at her. 'Hey, there's a backhander, then!' she cried, but there was no rancour in her voice at all. 'I can tell you my Nate was a good man, a caring man, a great provider, but handsome? That he never was. My Bernie, he's the image o' what I was when I was a little girl, the image! My sister Rae's grandchildren, they've got the same look – you had a lot of it yourself, of course, when you was little – my family was always the best lookin' in the neighbourhood. Now, of course –' And she pulled her gown down over her billowing hips and gave a gusty sigh. 'Now of course, you'd never know. Run to seed an' no mistake, I have. But so what? Looks don't matter so much as makin' a decent livin', take it from me. You'll take a bissel sponge cake with your tea, boobalah? Or would you rather honey cake? I got the best honey cake you ever tasted – here, try both –'

And she went back to the kitchen to re-emerge with a great tray in her hands, as Poppy did her best to recover from the deep embarrassment she felt at her unwitting insult. And then, as she sat down and steeled herself for the assault of food that she knew was now to be thrust upon her, she seized on one of the things that Jessie had said.

'You say you think I looked like your son when I was a child?' she ventured as Jessie began to pour tea into the big flowered cups. 'In what way?'

'Oh, the curly hair, the cheyn –'

'The what?'

Jessie laughed. 'The cheyn! The charm, the cuteness, the look in your eye when you want to get your own way – it's all cheyn! I know my Bernie's a lobbus – a naughty little boy, you understand. A lobbus is a naughty person who's – well, lovable. I'll have to teach you some Yiddish, hmm? It's a rich language, believe me –'

'Then it's as I thought – you're my – my father and you – brother and sister?'

There was a little silence and then Jessie sat down heavily and pulled her own cup and saucer in front of her and began to sip, carefully avoiding Poppy's eyes. 'Well, as to that –'

'Oh, please!' Poppy said, sharply, nettled now. 'I'm not a baby, you know! I am quite sensible and do understand matters once they are explained. I just want to be sure, that's all. I want to know about my father. I have a right, surely? And if you are as I understand it his sister, then you can give me the answers I want.'

'It's not me as you should be asking,' Jessie mumbled. 'It's Mildred's affair, not mine. It's up to her. She said in her letter to me I wasn't to interfere –'

'So, do you always do what other people tell you?' Poppy said and there was a scathing note in her voice now. 'I am sure I don't, and I am not yet seventeen! Mama is always telling me what I should do and what I should not, but I do not always agree with her so I say, "No, Mama," and there is an end of it. Do you agree with Mama that I should be kept in ignorance of all matters that concern my own history? If you do, then of course that is up to you. I cannot imagine it is so dreadful that I cannot be told, but there it is. If it is your own decision not to speak, then I must accept it. But from all you say it is not so. You are doing as you do simply because of my Mama. Why are you so frightened of her? She is severe, I know, but not so very alarming.'

Jessie had set her cup down and was staring at her, her eyes wide and now she began to smile, very slowly, until her whole face was split by a great beam of delight.

'Oh, I always knew as you were a special one!' she crowed. 'You got a way with words, you have, that I always knew you'd have. Even when you was just a baby you tried to use the longest words ever – I can't tell you! And reading those books of yours before you even started at school! Oh, you was clever and you still are! Such a way with words –'

'That's no answer,' Poppy said firmly and leaned forwards and after a moment reached out one hand and set it on one of Jessie's which was resting on the table. The fingers felt a little rough and dry, but they were warm and radiated a sort of friendliness and Poppy tightened her grip and leaned even further forwards to stare directly into Jessie's eyes.

'Please tell me,' she said coaxingly. 'If it's only Mama's opinion that holds you back – well, I long ago learned that it is often wisest to take my time before telling Mama of some matters. I am not lying to her, you understand – just making sure the time is right. Tell me now what I need to know, and I promise I will not say a word to Mama until we both agree it is right to do so. Will you agree?'

Again there was a silence and then Jessie nodded. She was no longer smiling now, but all the same her face was filled with a warm friendliness that Poppy felt envelop her just as the warmth of a coal fire did when she sat before it on a cold night. And she in her turn smiled and said softly, 'Now, tell me from the start, Aunt Jessie. How did they meet? And when did they marry? And why did they –'

She stopped suddenly, for all the warmth seemed to have drained from Jessie's face. 'What is it?' she cried. 'Why do you look at me like that?'

'Oh, boobalah, I am sorry. I thought you knew –' Jessie said and Poppy frowned and shook her head.

'Knew what?'

'Well, you see, the thing of it is – well, they never did marry, you see. I'm sorry, boobalah, but there it is. They never got married at all. So you're a little mumsah.'

13

'A what?' Poppy said, and stared at her blankly, but she knew what the answer was. However it was expressed, in either English or Yiddish, she knew the meaning of what she had been told. She was a bastard. Illegitimate – and she let the word trundle round and round her mind and tried to take in the real meaning of it. Illegitimate – Il-legit-im-ate –

But it made no sense. She could not look at the mental image of her mother, her upright and oh-so-strict Mama in her neat gowns with the pleated fronts and the harsh tightness of her back as she sat there in her upright chair, and see her as any sort of fallen woman. Mama, a wicked slut who ran about with strange men and – ? And she closed her eyes and tried to impose some sort of sense on what whirled there.

The things she had heard the servants say about other women who had 'got into trouble' and how they were usually servants like themselves, and how they would hush each other and look sideways at her and send her away so that they could talk more comfortably in her absence all came back to her as she sat there in Jessie's glowing little room behind her shop and tried to understand. For once Jessie did not talk, but sat and watched her and let her take her time about speaking, and Poppy sat very still and set her mind to collecting herself into a quiet coherent person, the person she wanted to be seen to be. She was Poppy Amberly – and now the fuss about her surname all made sense as well, at last – and she was a well-brought-up young lady who could go to Cambridge to study if she chose, but who was going to work in a newspaper office with her friend (and what would Mabel say to news such as this? The thought of telling her was impossible) and who lived a quiet decent sort of life. She was not a bastard, the unwanted result of a slut getting herself into trouble with a heedless man. She was not, she was *not*, she could not be –

And then she felt Jessie's arms around her shoulders and realized

she was crying, that tears were running helplessly down her cheeks
and she had not been aware of them. But now, as Jessie crouched
beside her with that great beefy arm holding her firmly, she felt the
misery inside her rise to meet the tide of tears and it all came out in
great sobs; and she turned her head and buried her face in Jessie's
large and comforting bosom and let the distress take its own route.

She stopped at last, as suddenly as she had started, but remained
there held in Jessie's warm clasp. The room was quiet, and all she
could hear was the soft wheeze of Jessie's breathing and the muffled
sounds of voices coming from the shop beyond the curtained door.
There were the deep tones of Lily's odd voice and the yatter of the
customers, and the occasional ping of the door bell, and still Poppy
stayed there, letting it all wash over her together with the mixture of
smells which enveloped her: Jessie, mostly, a not disagreeable meld
of warm body and attar of roses perfume and cooking odours; and
beyond that the smell of the shop, the pickles, and cakes, the cheeses
and cooked meats; and underlying all that the smell of the beeswax
polish that had been used on the mahogany furniture. And after a
while she took a deep and rather shaky breath of it all and sat up. And
Jessie after trying for one brief moment to hold on to her let her go.

'Well,' Poppy said after a while and her voice was husky in her own
ears, and she coughed. 'Well, I am sorry. I do not usually behave so
stupidly.'

'You don't usually get such news as that, either,' Jessie said dryly
and got to her feet heavily, and her corsets creaked a little as she
moved. 'I'm sorry, dolly, I should ha' torn my tongue out before I
said such a thing to upset you. I didn't think – I thought you really
knew, I suppose, and I was so surprised you didn't, that it just sort of
popped out. I'm sorry, dolly –'

'No need to apologize,' Poppy said. She felt very weary now and
wanted only to crawl off on her own somewhere to sleep. Nothing
seemed at all important any more, only the need to sleep. And she
almost yawned. 'No need –'

'Well, maybe you're right at that,' Jessie said, a little surprisingly.
'The sooner you get things like this all in the open the better. I can see
that now. Millie was wrong to keep all these secrets so long. You was
right tellin' me not to be afraid of her. It's been stupid, eh, to carry on
that way? That's what upset you. The secrets, more'n what the secrets
was about.'

Poppy stared at her, the tide of weariness falling back a little,
'What?'

Jessie nodded sagely. 'Believe me, doll, what's upset you most isn't not knowing what your Ma and Pa got up to – and why shouldn't they, bein' normal healthy people after all? – No, it's not that. It's that no one never told you. I was as bad as they was, and seein' you so upset proves it to me. Never again, dolly. You want to know anything, ask your Auntie Jessie. All these secrets – they don't do no one any good at all. They make people go rotten inside, all eaten up.'

And suddenly Poppy felt better. Could Jessie be right? Was it just the sense of having been shut out of her own life history that had hurt her so much and pushed her into that shameful flood of tears? Perhaps it didn't matter all that much after all that she was illegitimate – and she made herself think the word without flinching – for after all what had that to do with her? She was not a person who had chosen to be born in such a manner. *She* had not been a fallen woman. It was no fault in her if her mother had – but again her imagination baulked at the vision of her mother as a heedless slut and she almost laughed aloud at the confusion of it all.

'That's better,' Jessie said approvingly. 'You've got your colour back now. You looked peaky there, really peaky, for a while and it didn't suit you one bit. Listen, dolly, have some more tea, you'll feel better – a little cake –'

Now Poppy did laugh. 'You'd cure everything with food, wouldn't you?' she said and took her handkerchief from her pocket and blew her nose firmly. 'No more to eat or drink, please. I need to go home and – and think a little. But first –' And then she stopped. Hadn't she heard enough for one day? Did she really want to ask more questions, even those which had risen to the forefront of her mind?

And as though she had read that mind, Jessie said, 'He's alive and he's well. This much is easy to tell you. He's here in London – where else should he be, after all? – And he's running a pub over at the Isle of Dogs. Not a very nice place, to tell you the truth, but he seems happy enough there. And who am I to tell a fella how to run his life? Lizah was always one to go his own way –'

'Lizah –' Poppy said and wanted to giggle.

Jessie sighed. 'I know, I know. It made your mother laugh too, as I recall. It ain't so funny. His name was Lazarus when he was born, and o' course everyone shortened it, and when you say Lazar London style, it comes out Lizah. In America, fellas called Lazar is Lazar, but not here. Here it sounds like a girl's name – but believe me, he ain't no cissy. Fought at Spion Kop he did, in South Africa, lost an arm there saving an officer's life –'

Here she lifted her chin then with an odd little spurt of pride. 'Not bad, eh, to be a hero? But it didn't do him no good, o' course. He was a boxer, you see. A really good boxer. Could ha' been a real topliner, but there it is – you don't win no prize fights with only one arm. So after the war –'

'A prize fighter,' Poppy said, feeling dazed again. Was there no end to the surprises this afternoon was to give her?

'It's a respectable livin',' Jessie said firmly. 'And if you're one of the lucky ones, you can be rich and famous and get out in good time to keep your wits about you. One good thing about the war hero thing, though – it made Lizah get out before his brains got mushed to puddin'. But he had to make a livin' and he chose the pubs. I can't say I like it, but he does. An' there he is, down in Limehouse, with a nice little gaff. Some of the people there are a bit more'n I'd like to meet on a dark night, mind you, even me, but being I'm Lizah's sister they treat me well enough when I go down that way. Which isn't often –'

'Take me there,' Poppy said. 'I think – it's time I met him, isn't it.'

'Take you there?' Jessie was horrified. 'Are you out of your mind? A girl like you in a place like that? Not this side o' the end o' the world, dolly, as I live and breathe! Meet him, of course. I'll arrange it, a pleasure for all of us that'd be. A nice little supper here, he'll come, you'll come, you'll talk decent and easy like a man and his daughter should –' And she beamed at her. 'Oh, Poppy, I know you was upset, but I tell you this could turn out to be the best thing that ever happened. You'll see! It'll all turn out fine – I give you my word –'

It was another six weeks before Poppy was able to wear down her aunt's resistance. Just as Jessie was determined that Poppy should never go anywhere as disreputable as Limehouse and the Isle of Dogs, right out on the eastern rim of the city, so was Poppy herself determined that she would. She refused adamantly to co-operate with the many elaborate plans that Jessie made for her to meet her father under Jessie's roof, and went on doggedly asking for the address of her father's public house so that she could make direct contact there. And Jessie went on refusing, making it very clear that this was nothing to do with any anxiety about how Mildred might feel if she did so. It was entirely her own decision, she told Poppy firmly, that it just wasn't suitable for her to visit there.

All through those weeks Poppy kept her distance from Mabel and Bobby. She ached to talk to Mabel, her dearest and closest friend, about all that had happened and wanted badly to share her fears and her feelings with her, but she could not. She remembered all too vividly Mabel's first reaction to the suggestion that the exuberant Jessie Braham might be a relation of hers. How would she react to the news that her dear friend had a father who was a one-armed boxer who kept a disreputable pub in Limehouse? The very name of the place sounded mysterious and wicked – didn't Edgar Wallace say so over and over again in his exciting stories? – so how could Poppy speak to Mabel about him? So, hurt though it did to refuse her invitations on the grounds that she had extra schoolwork to do, or that her mother was demanding her company at home, that is what Poppy did. And if it hurt her more to miss seeing Bobby than to miss seeing his sister, she did her best not to admit that fact to herself.

It was only when Poppy at last told Jessie that unless she was given the chance to visit her father in his own home rather than in his sister's she would stop visiting that Jessie caved in. She was voluble with her complaints, told Poppy over and over again how wrong she was, and how stubborn, but she agreed. And Poppy suspected she was actually secretly pleased that her beloved niece showed so much determination. There was something about Jessie that was still very young and very responsive; she almost seemed to be playing at being a grown-up sensible person sometimes, it seemed to Poppy and she set out on their visit to Limehouse with a sense of adventure that filled Poppy with a matching excitement.

And that was just as well, for now she had won her battle to do what she wanted, she was rapidly losing her determination. Would he turn out to be a person she could like? It was fine with Jessie now – and she no longer attempted to call her by anything but her first name, dropping the label 'aunt' by tacit agreement – because she liked her a great deal. Jessie was funny and warm and in her own way a very shrewd person. Talking to her, which was something Poppy did more and more as the frequency of her visits to Cable Street increased, was a rewarding experience. Would it be as comfortable to be with her father? She couldn't know, and as she and Jessie made their way out of the shop one dark Saturday evening in late November, she almost turned to her and told her that, after all, she had changed her mind, she didn't want to see her father at all.

But she had to. She knew that until they had actually met, until she had seen him in his own world as the person he was, she could not get on with her own life as she wanted to. Her plans to leave school next year were now firm, and she was determined to join Mabel in the

Dispatch office if she could; and, if she could not, would find a similar occupation elsewhere. But thinking about her father and her past had seemed to get in the way so much, cluttering up her mind with silly imaginings. She had to know the real facts before she could set them on one side as unimportant –

So, she and Jessie walked to the end of Cable Street and out into Cannon Street Road to turn sharply left and make their way up to Commercial Road and the omnibus stop that would start them on their journey east. It was a raw evening, cold and biting, with an acrid fog lowering just overhead and threatening to come down and fill their lungs with even more of its choking miasma, but at present it was still possible to see the end of the street, and as they hurried past the brightly lit shops and pushed past the crowds set on spending their week's money in them as fast as possible, Poppy felt a little lift of exhilaration. It was an exciting experience she was having, after all; none of the girls she went to school with ever came to streets as raw and dramatic as these. None of them ever saw the oily slicks lit to rainbows in the gutters by the naphtha flares over the stalls where fruit and vegetables were being sold so noisily to passing housewives. None of them had anything in their lives as interesting as a one-armed boxer in a Limehouse pub to call Father. And as their boots clattered along the greasy pavements she hugged the thought to herself that it was all *right*; whatever happened, it was all living and that to be here, breathing this heavy air and feeling its acid in her throat, was what life was about. It was better than sitting demure and bored in a West End drawing room, that was certain.

The omnibus journey was long and bumpy as the vehicle ground its slow way in a series of jerks from stop to stop along Commercial Road, and then down the West India Dock Road to the Isle of Dogs, and on along West Ferry Road towards the tip of the island. It was quite dark now and outside the brightly lit interior of the bus the docks loomed black and menacing on their left, and the river heaved, oily and reeking of refuse and dead cats, on their right. She couldn't actually see the river from here but she felt its presence, both watchful and menacing, and shivered a little inside her thick winter coat and settled more deeply into her seat, as Jessie went on chattering, as she had all the way from Commercial Road, and demanding no answer.

But now as the omnibus reached the end of Manchester Road Jessie fell silent and sat peering out into the road beyond the window, looking for the landmarks that would tell her when to leave the omnibus and at last she said in a rather flat voice, 'We're here,' and got to her feet.

The conductor who had been leaning dreamily against the pole that guarded the exit from the vehicle straightened up and peered at the two women as they signalled they wanted to get down. The omnibus was almost empty of people; there was no one here on the lower deck apart from themselves, though they could hear laughter and shouts coming from outside, up the little staircase, where several men were sitting smoking their journey away.

"Ere, you goin' to be all right 'ere, lady? Not a very nice part o' the world for the likes of you, is it?' And it was Poppy he was looking at when he said it.

The omnibus drew up with a rattle of its wheels and Jessie surged forwards. 'My niece is safe enough with me,' she said a little grandly, but there was none of the usual gusto she displayed in her voice and Poppy thought – she's more nervous about this meeting than I am. The discovery gave her extra strength and she stepped down into the gutter beside Jessie and slid one hand into the crook of her elbow.

'It's all right, Jessie,' she said. 'We'll be fine! Please don't worry. I shan't cry or anything, I promise.'

'Hmmph,' Jessie said in a muffled voice. 'I wish I could say the same. Come on – we're nearly there – Ferry Street and then Barque Street and the next'll be Schooner Street – there it is –'

'All those ship names!' Poppy said and gave a breathy little giggle.

'They're all like that round here,' Jessie said. 'The next one's called Brig Street. Well, there it is.' She had stopped on the corner of the street and was staring down it, towards the river. At the far end they could just see the tops of the masts in the rigging of ships tied up in Greenwich Reach and Poppy took in a deep breath and tasted the smell of the river, dank and heavy and even more threatening than it had been before, and stepped a little closer to Jessie.

About halfway down the street on the right-hand side they could see lights coming from an unshaded window, and Jessie began to walk towards it. Just as they reached it a door burst open and a cluster of people came hurtling out, shouting and swearing as they went. Jessie pulled hard on Poppy's arm so that she was safely tucked against the wall with Jessie's bulk to guard her and she had to peer over her shoulder to see what was happening.

There were two women and four men who were wearing what seemed to be the uniforms of sailors, though the women were dressed in tight brightly coloured clothes that even in this fitful light looked cheap and rather dirty. Poppy could see the face of one of the women clearly and it made her want to pull even further back into the wall, for it was a tired and old face, but painted so heavily that it looked clownlike, and her teeth were little more than blackened stumps. They were easy to see, for she had her mouth open as she shrieked obscenities at the man who was clearly throwing them out, but Poppy was too fascinated by the woman to pay him any attention at first. The other woman had joined in the screaming now, and the two of them seemed to be about to throw themselves bodily at their ejector, but one of the sailors pulled them away and after a little more shouting the six of them went reeling away down the street, leaving a rich effluvium of beer and tobacco and sheer dirt behind them.

And the man who had thrown them out put up one hand to push his hair away from his eyes, and to tug his tie straight, and now Poppy did look at him and thought – this is him. It's my father. For his other sleeve was pinned neatly against his chest and was clearly empty, and his face was a lined and heavier version of the face she knew so well as Jessie's.

'Hello, Lizah,' Jessie said heavily beside her. 'I'd ha' thought you'd try to keep the place decent tonight, seeing I told you I was coming down. I told you I didn't want no trouble when I came tonight, I told you that particular.'

'So, what can I do, Jessie? These lousy koorevers, they come round here – what am I supposed to do? Smile at 'em and say, so it's all right, you can use my place tonight, no problem, my sister says she wants no fuss made?'

'It wouldn't have hurt,' Jessie said. 'And don't use language like that in front of ladies. Koorevers – you should be ashamed. Listen, Lizah – I brought someone with me.'

'What?' He had turned to return to the pub, and was standing now right in the light and Poppy could see him clearly. He had a square stocky figure, and a wide heavy face that looked as though it had been cut out of very old wood it was so deeply lined, especially across the forehead where the lines ran in parallel tracks that made her think absurdly of Paddington Station. His hair was thick and curly and tinged at the tips with grey and his eyes seemed to be dark and were certainly watchful. He looked a little tired and she thought tentatively – poor man. He's tired. And felt nothing at all.

That this was her father was undoubted. She knew it as certainly as she knew she could taste the river on her lips and could feel the fog thick in her throat and hear the distant wailing of the foghorns downriver, yet there was no emotional response in her at all, no sense of gladness or of sadness. Just nothing. And she stepped forward composedly from behind Jessie's shadow and said politely and with no difficulty at all, 'Good evening. I am, I think, your daughter. I'm Poppy Amberly,' and held out her hand to be shaken.

14

That foggy Saturday night in the Isle of Dogs was the night that Poppy discovered she had power. All her life hitherto, it seemed to her, she had been a subservient person; she had obeyed her mother and accepted her control of her, only circumventing it by telling untruths and being devious. She had bowed her head beneath the yoke of the servants' demands while learning how to dodge them and use her wits to get her own way in spite of them. She had accepted unquestioningly the domination of her schoolteachers and had never doubted she had to do as they told her. But now, for the first time, she found herself to be a person others deferred to, others needed, others begged for favours and permissions. And it was a heady feeling.

Her father's reaction on being introduced to her had been the first intimation. He had stood and stared at her, with his eyes huge and dark beneath his heavy brows, looking totally amazed and then had flushed a brick-red and had almost leapt forward to seize her hand in his and shake it up and down as vigorously as though it had been a recalcitrant pump handle.

'Oh, my word,' he said. 'Oh, my word – my word, I really can't – my word!'

'Ain't she something?' Jessie said complacently from behind Poppy.

'Oh, my word,' said Lizah, and then shook his head as though to clear it. 'Oh, my –'

'Let's come in, Lizah, for Gawd's sake!' Jessie said. 'It's getting so cold out here I could stick to the pavement. You can't stand out here gibbering all night –' And at once he let go of Poppy's hand, much to her relief, and turned and led the way into the crowded saloon bar of his pub. The small room was jammed with people and the air was blue with tobacco smoke, and Poppy ducked her head as she followed his square back through the hubbub, blushing a little as she felt curious

113

eyes on her from all sides. The smell was so thick it was almost palpable, with the reek of beer and hot fried sausages fighting a queasy battle with unwashed bodies and oily clothes. There was an undertow of river in it too, and she was glad when Lizah reached the bar and made his way behind it to a small glassed door and led them through.

They found themselves in a small, very warm, room, where a huge fire was built up in the grate and roaring up the chimney, and where the furniture was so massive and in such a quantity that there was hardly room to move between the pieces.

'Come in, come in – I'll send for some champagne, we'll really celebrate – this is such a – oh, my word, what a turn-up for the book! You've knocked me right off my twig and no mistake,' he said and bustled away to the fireplace to lead Poppy to a comfortable chair. But there was already someone there, a girl in what looked to Poppy to be a particularly thin wrapper of shiny blue artificial silk with rather grimy lace frills. She stared up at them insolently, particularly at Poppy, raking her with a gaze that went from head to foot and back again, and which carried a very obvious sneer.

'Out, you –' he said curtly.

The girl looked at him, her chin up, and said coolly, 'Why?'

'Because I blo – Because I said so. Out. And don't come back till I say.' His voice was a deep one, and had a rich note to it that Poppy rather liked, and she thought – it's easier to listen to the sound of him than to what he actually says, and realized that she was suddenly embarrassed. This girl, who had bright red hair, even brighter than Lily's in Jessie's shop, and who was displaying more of her body than Poppy had ever seen any woman show in public, was clearly the sort of person one pictured when one heard the word slut. Or illegitimate – and that was something she did not want to think about.

'Maybe I won't come back if I go.' The girl's voice was thin and reedy and had a spiteful note to it.

'Suits me,' Lizah said shortly. 'Make sure you don't leave nothing behind if you do.'

''Ere, Lizah –' The girl was on her feet now, pulling her wrapper around her and staring at Lizah with a slightly doggy expression in her eyes. ''Ang about! I never meant no –'

'Out, I said,' Lizah shouted, and now Poppy could see he really was angry and tried to step back, so that she was out of earshot, but that was impossible, and Lizah, clearly seeing her discomfiture, suddenly took the girl by the elbow and propelled her with considerable vigour towards the door.

'I told you and I meant it!' he said wrathfully. 'I got family business here. Out of the way, now –' And he slammed the door behind her and then stood with his back to Poppy and Jessie while he composed himself.

'I told you before, these people ain't no good to you,' Jessie said in a conversational tone and he turned round and threw a furious look at her. 'Well, didn't I? You want to get a proper arrangement made. Settle down –' And she threw a sideways look at Poppy who pretended she hadn't seen.

It was so odd that an adult person should be so embarrassed, even ashamed, in this way in front of her. To have matters hidden from her was not unusual, but it was normally only ever done by people trying to dismiss her in order to leave themselves free to do as they chose; never before to her knowledge had people wanted to hide matters from her eyes in order to protect their own sense of worth. And she moved to the armchair the girl had vacated and sat down, trying to fit this new awareness of her own importance into her scheme of things.

'So, you're Poppy,' he said and sat down opposite her. 'You're Poppy.'

'Yes,' Poppy said. 'I – do you remember me?'

He stared at her with almost catlike intensity. 'I remember about you, of course I do. But I never *knew* you. I wasn't allowed –'

A little silence hung between them and then she said carefully, 'I think I remember you.'

'How can you? If I was never allowed, nor was you, was you?' And he grinned suddenly and she thought, almost in surprise, he's fun. And he's not as old as I thought, either.

'It was one day at our house. You came to us, I think –' she said and she told him about what had happened, about the memory she had not realized until recently was a memory but had thought was just a bad dream. And he stared at her unblinkingly all the time she talked and then nodded heavily.

'Yes,' he said. 'I remember that day.' He was silent for a long moment and then burst out. 'She sent me away. You know that? She wouldn't let me try to – she sent me away. I had it all worked out. We could have been really happy, her and me. I wanted to make it all right, that was the thing of it, wanted to set things as they should be. You could ha' had brothers and sisters of your own –' And he looked over his shoulder then at Jessie and managed a thin grin. 'Sisters is all right, you know. Ta, Jess. It was good of you to arrange this. After all this time, to see my own little girl –' And he turned back to Poppy and

115

she saw the glitter in his eyes and wanted to look away, embarrassed again. And felt her power over him growing. How important she was! How much she meant to this man! It was an extraordinary notion and she smoothed her gloves on her knee with careful fingers and tried not to feel both exhilarated and frightened of the way he needed her so much.

'Not so very little,' she said lightly. 'I'm quite tall and very strong you know! And I shall be leaving school next summer and starting a job.'

He frowned then. 'Starting a job? A lady like you? What's Millie thinking of? You shouldn't have to do that! You should stay at home and go to parties and balls and –'

Now she did look at him. 'Nonsense,' she said crisply. 'That is a very old-fashioned idea. I am a modern woman, and I will do as I think best for myself. Which is not to go to college but to take an interesting job. I shall be working on the *Dispatch*. A newspaper office you know.' And she looked at him challengingly and went on, 'I am not one of those old-fashioned females who just sit about being decorative. I can take care of myself and I shall.'

'You talk just like Millie used to,' he said almost gloomily. 'She was that blo – that independent you couldn't get near her. That was why –' And he stopped.

'Why what?' Poppy said and lifted her eyes to stare at him and he looked away, reddening a little.

'Why I wasn't there,' he mumbled after a moment. 'Why we never lived together as we should and –'

'Why you never married, you mean,' Poppy said clearly.

'Jessie! You never told her that?' Lizah whirled and stared at Jessie, who was sitting beside the centre table fanning herself gently with her hat. 'Or was it your Ma that told you?' He whirled back to Poppy. 'No, it couldn't ha' been. She played all her cards much too close to her chest, that one, and was too bleedin' respectable to breathe. She'd never have said to you anything so –'

'She got it out of me, but I'm not sorry,' Jessie said equably. 'She's a bright one, this girl o' yours, you know. There isn't much misses her sharp eyes and never you think it. But it's all right, ain't it, boobalah? You don't blame no one for it –'

'It's not really anything to do with me,' Poppy said as coolly as she could. 'What happened all those years ago – why should it be my affair?'

He stared at her and then laughed, and again she felt the little shock

116

of pleasure that came from seeing him happy, even for a moment.

'You're a cool one, an' no error,' he said admiringly. 'There's more of me in you than you know, and so I tell you! You'd have made a great boxer, with that sort of way of thinking. Dead cool –'

'A boxer? Well, if there were lady boxers, it might be fun, at that,' she said judiciously and now Jessie laughed too and she joined in herself and a little bubble of accord hung there around them, enclosing them in its warmth, and she felt a sudden surge of deep happiness. She belonged with these people; however different she might seem on the surface, with her ladylike clothes and her West End voice, she was one with them. There were no rules here about how one should behave or how one should speak; she could say whatever she liked with them and they'd treat her remarks as real ones, not as silliness, the way Mama so often did when she said such things –

But she didn't want to think of her Mama, not now. It seemed wrong somehow to let her intrude and she said instead, 'Are you well – er – Lizah?'

He went on staring at her, as though unable to take his eyes away. 'Well? Well enough, for a bloke that used to be the most fighting fit there was but never gets no chance to turn out any more. Hey, listen, you aren't going to call me that, not really –'

She looked at him very levelly. 'Why not? It is your name, isn't it?'

He looked uncertain. 'Well, yes, but you know that – I mean, the thing of it is – I'm your father, you said, and –'

'People get used to calling their fathers Father when they are small. It is impossible to learn when you are a grown-up,' Poppy said and looked at him very directly. She had actually thought a good deal about this matter, and had come to the conclusion long before getting here tonight that she could never learn to say Papa and any other form of address would be equally uncomfortable, if not impossible. So, she had decided quite definitely that she would address him by his first name; it seemed the easiest way.

'Oh,' he said and then stopped, clearly nonplussed.

'So, listen, Poppy, you've got your own way, all right?' Jessie cut in. 'I wanted her to meet you at my place, Lizah. It seemed to me better than coming here, to this sort of gaff and meeting Gawd knows who, which let me remind you, she did. But she's stubborn, like her mother – anyway, Poppy, now what? You've met him and you know a bit more about how things was when you was born. Will you go on seeing him, then? Not here – you grant me, not here. It's such a shlap

117

apart from anything else. Took an hour or more to get over here, and it'll be as long goin' back. You get tired out bumping around in those ferstinkeneh buses. So, next time, it's supper at my house, hmm? What do you say?'

Poppy looked round the cluttered little room and thought about the people she had to pass as she came into it, through the pub, and thought, too, about the girl in the wrapper. Jessie had been right, of course. It was a horrid place and she didn't want to come here again. On the other hand, she did want to see Lizah again.

Her first impulse had been simple curiosity. She had wanted just to look at him, to see whether there were any likenesses between herself and him (and despite all Jessie had said on the subject, she could not pretend she saw any at all, even though her own hair was as thick and curly as his, and her face as round) and had not thought beyond this first meeting. But now she knew she would be interested in meeting him again. There was something very vivid about this man, something of strength there. In spite of the empty sleeve and the body that had clearly thickened with a layer of fat over the basic muscularity, he was like a tightly coiled spring, bursting with an energy she liked, and found familiar. And then she thought – we are alike, then, after all. I feel like that sometimes, bursting to go and live more and do more and be more – and he's the same. And she looked at him and saw the appeal in his eyes and thought – he wants to see me again, of course. But it's up to me whether I want to or not. I'm in charge here. And the feeling of power swelled a little and lifted inside her.

'I don't know,' she said judiciously. 'Perhaps we shouldn't meet again after all. I only wanted to say hello, you see, and –'

The expression on his face was almost ludicrous in its intensity, as misery fought with disappointment and for one wicked moment she played with the idea of getting to her feet and walking calmly out of here and never looking back and never speaking to him again. Why not, after all? Hadn't he abandoned her mother, got her into trouble and –?

But she thought then of Mildred and her unyielding back and her tightly closed face and knew that wasn't just. No one could ever have treated her formidable mother so. If anyone had been ill-used, she told herself with some shrewdness, it was this eager restless man sitting here so appealingly in front of her, almost begging her to exercise her power over him with benevolence, almost pleading with her to make him happy by conferring on him the benison of her approval. It was a heady situation to be in, the most exciting she had known in all her almost seventeen years. And suddenly a vivid image of Bobby Bradman slid into her mind and she saw herself looking at him just as this man Lizah, her father, was now looking at her, and knew what it was to be in Lizah's skin, and to be yearning so dreadfully –

'But then again, perhaps, sometimes, at Jessie's house –' And she remained with her head bent, not wanting to see the naked gratitude that she knew had leapt into his eyes, ashamed of herself for even considering being so unkind. There was no need to treat him so, even though she now knew she could do anything she liked to this man. He was a nice man, one she could like and enjoy being with. Treat him well. Don't do to him what some people have done to you –

'Oh, Poppy,' he said now. 'Oh, Poppy!' And then he looked over his shoulder at Jessie and said huskily, 'I don't know what to say, Jess, that's the thing of it. I just don't know what to say.'

'Then don't say nothing,' Jessie said practically and hauled herself to her feet. 'Listen, I got to get out of here. It's as hot as Hades, and I ain't got the build for it, and that's a fact. Come on, Poppy. Listen, you ever eaten Chinese food?'

Poppy stared at her, amazed. 'Chinese?'

'That's right. This is Limehouse, you know. Well, it is up the road. And it's where the Chinkies live. There's places there you can get all sorts of strange nosh, but it's good! The sailors, you see, they go there when they're in port and the Chinese what live round these parts like to make an honest bob or two – don't we all? – and one of the fellas I used to know, he took me once. It was interesting. Maybe we can get Lizah to take us now – what do you say, Lizah?'

At once he was all eagerness. 'You're asking me about Chinese food? Believe me, there's nothing you want to know about it I can't tell you! I got some of the biggest spielers there is come in here – and they spiel big, you've no idea – these Chinese they spiel very big – and they've shown me –'

'Spielers,' Poppy said, still dazed.

He laughed. 'Gamblers, Poppy. That's the big thing in these parts. And one or two others you should never know about. But there are good places you can go where'll you'll come to no harm and it'll be an education for you. Better'n any education you'll get in that Leinster Terrace of yours.' He had pulled on a coat, shrugging it over his empty sleeve with an experienced jerk of his shoulders and was now standing with his hand on the glass door, waiting to lead them out. 'Is

it still as miserable there as it was, Poppy? Those brothers of Millie's –
are they still there?'

She reddened then. 'Yes,' she said shortly. 'They're still there.'

'Never could be doing with any of them,' Lizah said, apparently
reflectively but watching her with eyes which were very bright. 'It was
the older ones I knew, o' course. Dead now. Basil and me –' He
seemed to be about to say something more and then stopped. 'Well,
never mind that now.' And he touched his empty sleeve with his other
hand. 'And I heard as Claude had died too?'

'There are Harold and Samuel now,' she said a little woodenly.
'There was Wilfred but he went to live in Australia, so it's just
those –' And her voice drifted away as she tried not to think of Harold
and Samuel.

'Well, if they ever give you any trouble just let me know,' he said,
still watching her with those sharp eyes as though somehow he knew
what it was about the Uncles that she so hated. 'I'm here. You can
always let me know –'

'I hardly ever see them,' she said. 'Fortunately. They're usually at
their offices or at their clubs. We see them occasionally on the stairs –'

'Lizah, can't we talk and eat at the same time, already?' Jessie
sounded plaintive. 'It's gone seven and to tell you the truth, my
stomach thinks my throat's been cut. Take me to these Chinese pals of
yours and we can talk there, yes, Poppy?'

'Yes,' Poppy said fervently and at last Lizah opened the door, held
it wide for Poppy to lead them out of the pub, and they both fell in step
behind her. And now she knew just how important she was to both of
them; the leader, the one in charge, and suddenly it didn't feel quite
so comfortable any more.

15

She returned home that night in a state of great confusion, trying to tidy in her mind all the new experiences she had been through. And, absurdly, all she could think about as she slipped silently into the house and crept past her mother's room to her own was the supper they had eaten: the strangeness of the vegetables and noodles, and the oddness of the exotic flavours in the fish and chicken she had been given. She remembered Lizah's laughter as he tried to show her how to eat her food with just two sticks held in one hand, instead of a knife and fork, and how Jessie had laughed too and refused even to try, until one of the smallest and oldest of the Chinese men had come and stood on tiptoes behind her, and almost forced her to use them, reaching round her great bulk with his sinewy little arms in such a comical fashion that all of them had laughed till they had wept. Oh, it had been such a funny evening, so amusing, so comfortable, so very grown up! How could she think of anything else but that?

And she had fallen asleep, managing not to think of all that had happened, but had woken in the dark well before six, a sudden awakening that was so thorough she knew she would not sleep any more. So, she lay on her back with her hands hooked behind her head, listening to the distant sound of the servants starting their day, the clink of copper jugs and basins as they brought up the Uncles' hot shaving water, and the rattle of brooms and dustpans outside her door. The housemaid came in to light her fire and at once she closed her eyes, pretending to sleep as the sticks caught with a cheerful crackle and the room filled with the warm scent of a new day, and then she was alone and free to think. And could no longer evade the question that she knew she had been dodging ever since she had first set eyes on Lizah last night, even before he had asked her directly to consider it.

Was she to tell her Mama? Was she to go to her and say calmly,

'Mama, I have met my father. I know that you and he were never married, and really I am not too concerned about that.' (And that, she told herself passionately, would be a lie. You do care, really, you know you do –) 'And I have a message for you from him. He told me last night –'

But how could she convey to her mother not only the fact that she had this knowledge but what it was that Lizah had said to her? How was she to find the words to tell Mama how it had been last night?

After they had eaten their way through the bewildering range of odd little dishes, and she had with some anxiety gingerly eaten strange pale fruits that tasted like the smoothest of scented slipper satin, they had sat on for half an hour, nursing tiny cups of pale milkless tea, which she had rather liked, sipping it endlessly as the little old Chinese padded round and round the table, constantly replenishing them. And Lizah had leaned forward and spoken to her in a confidential sort of way that made her even more aware of how important she had become to him in the few short hours since they had met.

Jessie had been sitting leaning back in her chair, drowsing a little, for she had eaten well and the room was warm, and Lizah had fixed her with those lustrous dark eyes that she already found so compelling and said softly, 'Ah, Poppy – tell me more about your Ma. Does she – umm – I mean, what sort of life does she have now? Does she go out and about a good deal, hmm? See her friends and so forth?'

'Mama?' she had said and ducked her head to peer in the depths of her little cup and watch the big shreds of tea leaves floating lazily in it. 'Oh, she is a very quiet person, you know. She – she visits some of our neighbours very occasionally, and goes to church of course –'

He had lifted his brows at that. 'Goes to church, does she? She never used to have much use for that sort of – well, well. So she ain't having a lot of fun, then? No gadding about?'

Poppy had laughed. 'Mama is not the sort to gad. I doubt she ever was –'

His lips had curved reminiscently then. 'Oh, you'd be surprised, Poppy, the things she and me used to do. The places we went and all. The boxing and the theatre – loved a bit of music hall, Millie did –'

'Mama? Loved *music* hall?' Again Poppy laughed. 'She would never go to anything so vulgar! I wish she would and take me, for I'd dearly love to see some of the great stars – George Robey, you know and –'

'And so you shall, my duck, so you shall! Leave it to old Lizah – I'll take you down the Holborn Empire and to the old Met in Edgware Road any time you fancy. I got mates there, I have, get the best seats in the house, late doors, o' course, just for the asking! Go you shall – but like I say, your Ma used to love that. And *you* say she don't go any more?'

'She goes nowhere, really,' Poppy said flatly. 'It is so – oh, Lizah, it is so dull at home! Nothing ever happens, you see, nothing is ever – Mama sits and sews, you know, and sits with Grandmama and reads, and well, mostly she just sits. She seems content enough, but for me, it is quite dreadful! I could not bear to be so!'

He had nodded slowly, seeming pleased. 'So, she has no special friend, no man who –?'

And then he had stopped, and Poppy had stared at him with her brows a little creased and said, 'Do you mean has Mama admirers?' And then she had not been able to help it. She had put her head back and laughed, a sudden trill of mirth that even in her ears seemed to echo round the little restaurant and bounce off the tables and the low-hung lanterns, and a few of the other diners turned and looked with blank stares and then returned to their incomprehensible jabber, for Lizah and Jessie and Poppy were the only people there who were not Chinese.

'It ain't so funny!' Lizah said, suddenly wrathful. 'Your Ma is a very – is a remarkable woman. It ain't so strange to think she might have a gentleman friend! Lots of women in her situation – people think she's a widder, I dare say, and why shouldn't a respectable widder be courted? Don't tell me no one ever has, and her settled so comfortable and all! There'd be some as'd be after her house and her money, even if she wasn't so well set up a woman!'

Poppy had stopped laughing then and had looked at him wonderingly. 'Did you love my mother then?' she asked suddenly and wanted to kick herself for sounding as silly and sentimental as the stupid girls at school who talked of nothing but love all the time.

But clearly he did not think the question silly or sentimental, for he said simply, ''Course I did! Why else are you and me sitting here this way? You wouldn't be there if I hadn't, that's for damn sure – sorry, I mean, that's certain.' For Jessie had stirred and opened one eye and looked at him sharply. 'Ought to watch my tongue better –' he mumbled.

But Poppy was not concerned with his mild swearing. She sat there and felt a warm glow begin deep in her belly and stretch itself outwards and upwards till all of her was filled with it. Even after Jessie had told her of her status as an illegitimate child she had not really thought about what that had meant in terms of the relationship between her parents, only about how she felt herself. But now the words had come into mind and hung there, glowing as warmly as the feelings inside her. Love child. She was a love child. No matter how cold and remote her mother might seem now, once she had loved this man so much that together they had – But her thoughts baulked at going any further and she only smiled at Lizah, and said softly, 'I'm glad.'

There had been a little silence between them and they had both sat staring into their tea, and now Jessie seemed to have really gone to sleep, for the sound of her breathing had deepened and become more steady and her head had lolled forwards. And then Lizah had repeated abruptly, ' 'Course I loved her! And the thing of it is, I still do. The stupid woman! Do you think a day's gone by this past ten years and more that I haven't thought of her? I came to see her that time, when you was – how old? Four? Five? Something like that – and I begged her to try again, to get married. We'd have had such a good life, her and me, I told her, a lot of laughs, a few more like you – it could have been so good. But she wouldn't and I done nothing but think about that ever since. I won't pretend I've been a monk, you understand. A fella needs a bit o' feminine company – but believe me, not a day gone by but I haven't – ain't that a laugh, hey? Me, Lizah Harris, getting the hump over some stuck-up bitch that – oh, I didn't mean that. But you know what I mean –'

Poppy had said nothing, just sitting and looking at him and then he had burst out, 'So there it is, Poppy. Will you have a word with her? Tell her we've met, like, and tell her you'd like us to be a family? If you really do want that, o' course. I'll give up the pub, find another way to make a livin' – a nice little restaurant, maybe, up West, something with a bit o' real class, hey? And then we can try again. It's not too late, dammit! I mean, we ain't that old, her an' me, I'm just comin' up to forty-two and your Ma's – what? Forty-five or so? I've known women as have had kids then – it ain't impossible! And I got all the time in the world yet, we both have. Tell her for me, Poppy, will you? Ask her to see me, try again –'

Poppy had sat there, almost stunned with amazement. To imagine anyone thinking of her Mama in this way, to imagine her Mama having more children; but that had been an impossible mental feat and she had continued to stare at him and then had shaken her head and he had said flatly, 'Oh. You don't want me then –'

At once she had been overcome by compunction. 'Oh, no! I didn't mean that! I just – it's only that – I mean, Mama! I can't – It's just not –' And she had subsided into silence, ashamed of her inarticulate confusion, and he had managed a grin and said with a brave attempt at lightness, 'Well, never mind, then! It was just a thought. Listen, I got to get you two back, eh? It's getting on, you know. I'll fix a cab, okay? Jessie, hey Jessie, you lazy lump! Wake up already!' And he had leaned over his sister and shaken her plump shoulder and she had opened her eyes and said drowsily, 'I wasn't asleep. Heard every word –' and yawned hugely.

'Sure you did,' Lizah said and laughed at her, a cheerful laugh, but behind it Poppy could hear the remnants of his pain and hated herself for inflicting it. 'Like the cat never drank the cream no matter what everyone could see was hanging on its whiskers! Hey, Lee Ho! 'Ow much do you want, then? Take what you need outa this –' And he had taken a crisply crackling white five-pound note from his pocket and thrown it on the table with a fine air of insouciance and again Poppy thought – he's trying to show me he doesn't care at all, but he does really. He cares dreadfully. Oh, dear, what do I do? What *do* I do?

And now this morning, lying in bed in Leinster Terrace and watching the light creep into the dark November morning through her open-curtained window, she still didn't know what the answer was. Could she do it? Could she march into her mother's room and say casually, 'Mama, I met my father last night and he says –'

And suddenly she rolled over in bed and buried her face in her pillow and shouted her fury at herself into it. To be so stupid and vacillating! It was absurd in someone who prided herself on being so independent and grown up. She who did what she wanted when she wanted, who went to Suffragette meetings and to theatres and concerts, who had made such practical plans to leave school and start at a worthwhile job in a newspaper office and made her mother accept them, to be so childishly unable to make up her mind and to act on it? It was absurd –

The housemaid came back then with her morning tea and she sat up in bed, her arms round her knees and her cup held between both hands as she hunched herself over its steam and sipped it slowly, and went on thinking. But this time she was less confused. The flames from her fire leapt and danced on the ceiling and the light crept higher and higher outside; now she could hear the traffic making its morning din from the Bayswater Road and could almost feel the city stretching out beyond this room. There was the Park spreading away south and west, and beyond the far end of the Bayswater Road to the east there was Marble Arch and Oxford Street and after that the fringes of Covent Garden as the roads went on ever eastwards towards the City. She saw in her mind's eye the streets becoming narrower and busier, and the river looping its way towards the docks and that odd little pub in Schooner Street, and suddenly, without even realizing she had moved, she had set her cup down on her tray with a little clatter and was out of bed and in her wrapper, and pushing her feet into her slippers. It was quite absurd to be so silly, quite absurd –

And she walked out of her room and went padding silently along the thickly carpeted corridor past the heavy oil paintings and the little tables with their ornaments, repeating the words inside her head as she went. It was quite, quite absurd – quite, quite, quite absurd –

Mildred had slept badly, again. It had been, she told herself as she tossed and turned through the night, Maud's fault. Somehow she had managed to get her hands on some brandy – and Mildred strongly suspected that Harold and Samuel were responsible for that, for they seemed to take a delight in making life as difficult as possible for her – and that had meant an evening running up and down to her stepmama's room to lift her back into bed when she fell out and, worse still, to deal with the wet beds that always resulted when she obtained alcohol. By the time Maud had slid into a drunken sleep at last and Mildred had been free to go to bed, she had been so tense with anger, so taut with frustration that sleep had been an impossibility. And now she sat up in bed, her tea tray on her knees, and felt her eyes hot and sandy behind weary lids, and wondered bleakly why she bothered to wake up at all.

When her door opened she thought at first it was Queenie, come to report some new nuisance about Maud and sat up even more straight and glared at the door, ready to tell Queenie that she must manage the old lady as best she could; that she, Mildred, had no intention of going anywhere near her until she was decently bathed and dressed. But it was Poppy who stood there, and Mildred stared at her almost blankly. The child never came to her room; was she ill? And a sudden lift of anxiety sharpened her voice more than she had intended.

'What is it?' she snapped. 'Are you ill? And why are you not dressed? To walk about the house in such a state! What are you thinking?' And somewhere at the back of her mind she thought – why do I do it? Why do I speak to her so? Why can't I just open my arms and say – come and be hugged? But that would not make this beloved child the strong independent woman she wanted her to be; that would make her as useless as all the other women in the world. And again Mildred lifted her brows and said sharply, 'What is it?'

'I have something to tell you, Mama,' Poppy said, standing at the door, her hand still on the knob. 'I – this seemed a convenient moment, before you are busy about the day. But, if it is not, I will go away.'

Mildred stared at her, at the white wrapper, pulled tightly around the strong shapely body and the round face with the rumpled curly hair framing it and the thick plait over her shoulder and thought – Oh, you are so lovely! Oh, Poppy, I do love you so! And tried consciously to soften her voice.

'You had better come in and sit down and tell me whatever it is,' she said and hoped she sounded welcoming. But all Poppy heard was her mother's usual dry tones and she closed the door behind her softly, thinking – I wish I hadn't. Why did I let him beguile me so? And a vision of his face slid into her mind, that heavy face with its carved contours and its friendly lines and above all its rich dark eyes, and her resolve seemed less tenuous and she took a deep breath and walked composedly across the room to sit in the chair in front of the window from which she could see her mother's face clearly while her own remained in shadow.

'Mama,' she said and her voice sounded thick in her own ears, and she could hear her pulse beating thickly, too. But she went on as firmly as she could, using every fibre of strength she had to control her voice and to show no anxiety. And somehow succeeded. 'Mama, I have asked you often about my father, and you have always avoided telling me. I ask you again. Will you tell me now about him?'

Mildred frowned and peered at her in the thin morning light, but it was not possible to see any expression in that shadowed face and she thought – shall I? Tell her, all she wants to know? How can I? How can I possibly explain –?

'This is ridiculous.' she said harshly. 'It is barely seven in the morning and you come asking me this now? It is of no significance – of course I will not discuss it now.'

'I had hoped you would,' Poppy said, and now her voice did shake a little, for inside she felt very young, for all the show of courage and grown-up status she was putting on. 'But there is no need after all. I have discovered for myself.'

There was a silence so solid that it seemed to shout in her ears and then Mildred said carefully, 'What did you say?'

'I have attended some Suffragette meetings with my friend Mabel,' Poppy said baldly, and she swept up the last crumbs of bravery she had and poured them carefully into her voice, holding her shoulders firm by means of clasping her hands tightly in her lap. 'These meetings are held by Miss Sylvia Pankhurst in the East End, and there by chance I met Mrs Braham. She is my aunt, she says. I see no reason to disbelieve her. She took me to meet my father Lizah Harris. And he asks me to ask you to meet him again and to – to – he wishes to see you,' she ended lamely and now at last her courage ran out and she let her head drop forwards, and felt the sweat that had broken out all over her begin to trickle down her body between her breasts and across her back; and had never felt so dreadful in all her life.

And still the silence continued and the two of them sat there as outside in the street the sound of the milkman rattling his churns and shouting down the areas to the cooks and housemaids below the houses while his horse stamped and blew noisily into its bag of oats came up to them, muffled and yet cheerful. In the house itself there were more noises; the thump of feet as the Uncles went downstairs to the breakfast room and the loudness of Harold's voice as he bawled at Queenie to bring him his coffee at once, and the thin wail of Maud's voice as she, now awake, called for Queenie too. And all Mildred could do was sit and stare at Poppy, her face as stiff as a board, and say nothing.

At length Poppy lifted her chin and spoke. Her voice was a little hoarse now and she looked at Mildred wearily and said, 'Will you meet him?'

There was another silence and then at last Mildred said, 'No,' and her voice sounded exactly as it always did, calm, expressionless and cold.

Poppy managed to stand up, and she smoothed her wrapper over her hips and nodded, and went to the door.

'Well,' she said flatly. 'I tried. I was asked to try and I did. I shall continue to see them, you understand, Mama. I must.'

Mildred stared back at her, her hands still clasped on her tea tray, for she had not moved since Poppy had started speaking. Oh, Poppy, she was thinking. Oh, Poppy, please don't look at me like that! Oh, Poppy, please don't see them – they are not your people any more –I took you away from all that, I made a better life for you. I gave you all this, I made you a lady. Poppy, please don't –

But all she said was, 'Very well. If that is what you wish, then you must do it. Please close the door quietly when you leave.'

And Poppy left and Mildred sat there and let the tears slide down her face, unchecked, at last. There was nothing else she could do.

16

And that was the start of Poppy's triple life – or was it, she would sometimes wonder, a quadruple one? – for she still had her inner secret life, her dreams and hopes for her exciting future, in which she would achieve so much. But, be that as it may, there were certainly at least three quite different strands to her existence, which she managed, over the next three years or so, to keep safely separate, only allowing them to run parallel with each other when she felt able totally to control the outcome.

First of all there was the Leinster Terrace Poppy. She was much as the child Poppy had been, biddable, polite, demure even, but very watchful. She spent time with her Mama, sewing and reading, rarely speaking more than the politest 'Yes' or 'No', to which Mildred responded in the same cool detached way she always had, as though there had never been that early morning discussion between them. And Poppy paid lip service to the same pretence, always willing to bear her mother company and always deferring to her, no matter what she said. She was also kind to her increasingly querulous step-grandmama, and would sit with her patiently and talk to her gently even when the old lady wandered in her speech and babbled nonsense and begged for brandy and wept when she didn't get it. She was polite to the servants and unobtrusive as far as her Uncles were concerned, managing to keep well out of their sight at all times, and generally moved around her own home like a wraith, an almost non-existent person.

But outside Leinster Terrace lived the other Poppies, and one of them was the Norland Square Poppy. She was a very different person; merry and quick and with a gift for rapid repartee that made her friend Mabel love her more – though it sometimes moved her to behave in a rather competitive manner; the occasional barbed word from Mabel's lips was something Poppy had to learn to endure – and which even made Bobby Bradman pay her attention occasionally. Not the sort of attention Poppy most craved, of course, but attention none the less, so that the Poppy who visited Norland Square most weeks became almost part of the family.

She could wander into Goosey's kitchen to be greeted with the same sort of affectionate scolding that Mabel received, could visit the tiresome Chloe in her nursery and deal calmly with her frequent tantrums, and sit with Bobby and listen to his gramophone playing his favourite Russian ballet music as though she were as much his sister as Mabel was.

And when she started work at the *Dispatch* office in December of 1912, just before her eighteenth birthday, she became even more part of their life, often sharing poached egg lunches with them in Fleet Street ABC tea shops and wandering around the stores with Mabel while she agonized for hours over which ribbons to buy to trim her new hats, and generally being one of the Bradman clique, as much a part of their lives as their furniture.

The work she did at the *Dispatch* was not as interesting as she had hoped it would be, consisting as it did almost entirely of the typing and retyping of the most tedious of the City pages, in which were listed news of gilt-edged securities, Stock Market activities and banking affairs of the sort that made her yawn with jaw-cracking boredom; but never mind. The job gave her an illusion of independence even though she still had to live with Mama at Leinster Terrace and there was always the comfort of the sixty guineas a year she now earned for herself, no longer needing Mama's allowance. It had given her pride and pleasure to refuse that, and she had glowed for weeks over it, never imagining that Mildred was hurt by the refusal. But she had her own money now, and that felt good. And in the evenings there were theatres to which she and Mabel and sometimes Bobby went, and in the summer months the croquet parties that Mabel got up in their minuscule back garden, and boat trips down the river and music in the park when the Guards band came out to entertain, and then supper parties in the Norland Square dining room. Life was very agreeable for the Norland Square Poppy.

And not only at Norland Square itself; she met other people through Mabel, and continued to go to meetings at Miss Pankhurst's Settlement house and typed some of the material for her leaflets as part of the continuing 'Votes for Women' battle and made several other friends, though none as close as the Bradmans, of course. Life seemed very pleasant as the months pleated into each other and winter fun took the place of languorous summer activities and Poppy went on growing up and changing.

But it was the third Poppy, the Cable Street Poppy, who changed and grew most of all. This strand of her existence was undoubtedly the most exotic, for when she took an omnibus from the West End to travel eastwards it was as though she bought a ticket not just to another part of London but to a totally different world. It was a world where people not only looked different but also sounded different and smelled different. If Fleet Street and the office, Norland Square and the houses of the Bradmans' friends provided three or four times more excitement and noise and jollity than Leinster Terrace, then the East End and Jessie's Cable Street shop provided ten times more than Norland Square. Here everyone seemed to live at a pitch that was so high and intense that Poppy sometimes marvelled that they did not blow their own heads off, much as an engine blows off its safety valve when too big a head of steam builds up. Where the people she lived and worked with murmured or spoke, Jessie and Lizah, Lily and Bernie shrieked and harangued. Where Bobby Bradman explained and described, Lizah delivered great flowery lectures full of imagery. Where Mama lifted a brow and looked disapproving, Jessie wrung her hands and wept. It was all rather amusing, occasionally irritating and always exhausting.

But she would not have given up her East End connections for all the exhaustion in the world. In some ways it became almost like a drug to her. When she did not visit her aunt or see her father for several weeks, as could often happen when other demands were made by the lives of the other Poppies, she became edgy and restless, and could only be soothed by once again taking that eastward-bound omnibus and filling her nostrils with the smells of those narrow streets. That heady combination of fish and cakes, meats and pickles, horses and engines and over it all the reek of the factory where Allen and Hanbury's made their cough pastilles, and the brewery where the heavy yeasty beer was made and from which vast drays trundled out pulled by massive hairy-heeled shire horses which added their own familiar ingredient to the mixture, all gave her comfort.

She never lost her sense of power as far as Lizah was concerned and that too might, she thought, trying to be honest with herself, have been one more element that drew her East so strongly. That he needed to see her was undoubted. If she announced by means of a postcard to Jessie that she was to visit, then she could be sure that Lizah would be there in the silver and mahogany littered sitting room behind the shop, waiting for her. If she arrived unexpectedly, knowing when Jessie could be relied on to be there, then somehow the information would get to him and, within an hour or so, there he would be, greeting her with his wide-mouthed grin and his forehead creased up into its railway lines pattern.

He continued, even though she had told him sharply that her Mama was not at all willing to agree, to ask her, indeed to beg her, to intercede with Mildred on his behalf. This persistence of his was the only flaw she found in being the East End Poppy, and sometimes she would get angry with him; but more often she managed to respond with laughter.

'What's so ridiculous?' he demanded with some truculence, sitting very straight so that the pin that held his sleeve in place on his chest glittered in the lamplight. 'You of all people should know it's the right thing to do! We're a Mama and Papa, we are, Millie and me! It's wrong we ain't married!'

She managed to continue keeping a straight face as she shook her head. 'Mama has changed, Lizah,' she said then as gently as she could. 'She has become – well – I have to say it – she is so very hard now. I cannot know how she was when you first knew each other, but now, there is no – there is nothing you or I could say to her on such an issue that she would ever listen to. Mama is so very – well *proper*, you see. Everything must be just so, and – it really is out of the question –'

But however often she told him so – and he returned to the subject over and over again – still she could not convince him. He threatened to write directly with his proposal to Mildred, to tell her that Poppy was visiting him regularly and that they should marry for their daughter's sake, and Poppy was only able to prevent him from doing so by telling him flatly that if he did she would never ever see him again. That one confrontation she had had with her mother had been quite enough; she never wanted the matter raised again at Leinster Terrace. And she told him that, and made it clear she meant it, fixing him with a glittering gaze until he dropped his own and muttered miserably that all right, he wouldn't. Not yet –

Even Jessie had difficulty in making him see how unapproachable Mildred now was, and could only deflect his determined attacks on Poppy by demanding outings for them all; and always he would agree and off they would go, Lizah and Jessie and often Bernie too – who continued as disagreeable and evil-mannered as ever – to theatres and circuses, dog race meetings and boxing matches and most particularly the music halls, all of which Poppy found entrancing, as much for the audiences as for the shows themselves. She would spend most of her time at the entertainment sneaking glances at all the other people around them and revelling in their exotic looks and behaviour. Here there were real people, she decided, here was excitement and fun and living –

She became so enraptured by all of it that at length she tried to twist this strand of her life into the Norland Square one. She enjoyed the music hall shows and the boxing matches and dog races so much she was sure that Mabel and Bobby would too, and decided to confide in Mabel. Once she knew about her friend's interesting parentage, wouldn't she be entranced too, and come and join them in their outings? But it wasn't as easy as she had hoped it would be.

It was on a warm September Saturday afternoon in 1913 that she made her first attempts to join these two parts of her life together. She could never speak to anyone at Leinster Terrace about the people of Cable Street, of course, but surely she could take her confidences to Norland Square? So she thought about what to say as she and Mabel sat in the garden fanning themselves gently against the heat – for it had been the warmest of summers again – almost exhausted by an hilarious hour of trying to teach themselves the newest dance craze of the foxtrot. Mabel had managed it well enough once or twice and so had Poppy, but never at the same time and the resulting tangle of feet had sent them to the floor over and over again in peals of laughter.But now they sat peacefully over the tea which a grumbling Goosey had brought out to them while Chloe, in a good humour for once and happy enough to play quietly at the end of the garden, surrounded herself by her dolls and organized an elaborate tea party for them.

Looking down the garden at the froth of white frills in which the child was dressed and the pretty way she sat with her curly head bent over her favourite wax doll, Poppy sighed a little. If only she was really as angelically good as she looked at this moment! She was all sweetness and innocence now but no one knew better than Poppy how rapidly that delicious little five-year-old could become a spitting shrieking termagant who was not above biting whichever portion of another person's anatomy happened to be convenient to her sharp little teeth. Poppy had at least two scars on her fingers to show for her attempts to entertain small Chloe, but she had not told Bobby of them, nor made any complaint. If that was the price she had to pay for being part of this charmed household, so be it.

'Mabel,' she said now, still looking at Chloe. 'Can you remember being five years old?'

'Mm?' Mabel squinted down the garden at her small niece. 'Chloe's age? Let me see now – a little I suppose. I had a Mama and a Papa then of course –' She closed her eyes comfortably and leaned back even more lazily in her basket chair. 'But I became a total orphan when I was still quite young. She is only half a one, of course, so she is better off than I was.'

'But you came to no harm being orphaned, did you? You had Bobby –'

'Oh, yes,' Mabel said cheerfully. 'I had Bobby. And Chloe has both of us, so that is all right. Why do you ask?'

'I was just thinking –' Poppy was picking her words carefully. 'I never knew my Papa when I was small, of course –'

'No, you just had a Mama, didn't you? Has she told you anything yet about him?' Mabel opened one eye and peered at her and then closed it again against the sunlight. 'I still think perhaps he is a duke's son or something really romantic. You are so – *different* a person, after all, than the run of the people we know, aren't you? So tall and imposing.' She giggled. 'Except when you try to dance the foxtrot.'

'With you, you clumsy wretch,' Poppy retorted. 'I should have been perfectly upright on my own.'

'Not much use for a partner dance though,' Mabel said.

'No,' Poppy said and stopped to think a little while. 'I don't suppose he was a duke's son, you know,' she said at length.

'Mmm?'

'My Papa,' Poppy said. 'Why, he might have been anyone. A sailor perhaps, or a soldier. Or a sportsman – a boxer perhaps –'

Mabel giggled. 'Oh, Poppy, you are ridiculous! Just look at your Mama! Would *she* marry a boxer?'

'Perhaps she did not marry at all,' Poppy said daringly. 'Perhaps she just – well – *had* me –'

Now Mabel did open her eyes and looked disapprovingly at Poppy. 'My dear, I know you like to be outrageous in the things you say, but that is to go too far! That is servants' talk, very silly and not very nice. Never let Goosey hear you speak so or she'll forbid the house.' But she wasn't entirely joking, clearly, and Poppy subsided.

'Well, I dare say that it was wrong to say that – but suppose she made a *mésalliance*? Someone totally wrong – you know, a –'

Mabel crowed. 'We're back to the duke's son! That would be a dreadful *mésalliance* indeed, I suppose, if you were the duke!'

Poppy made a face. 'Oh, no! I meant a much more romantic thing than that. A gypsy –' and she slid a sideways look at her friend who was now sitting up and staring at her consideringly.

'I suppose he could have been a gypsy – but I don't think so. It sounds romantic, doesn't it? But after all in real life it would not be so. They are quite impossible – I have seen them in their camps, you know when we have been to the country for the holidays on Goosey's brother's farm in Shropshire. They are a dirty lot for all their handsome dark eyes, and they do dreadful things like stealing children – and it is not surprising after all, for they are quite irreligious. They never go to church.'

'Is that so important? I did not think you were so concerned about church. After all, Goosey always has to nag you.'

'Of course! It is what Goosey is for, nagging! But I would go even if she didn't, if not so often. Anyway, it's not a matter of going to church, really. It's a matter of – well, just *belonging* and having the right ideas. Why you might as well talk of your Mama marrying a Moor or Jew as talk of her marrying a gypsy – I know you like to make fun of things, Poppy, but really I do think sometimes you go too far.'

'Do I, Mabel? Well, perhaps you're right,' Poppy said. And did not attempt again to speak to her of her father and his family. There was clearly no possible way in which she could bring the strands of her life together as she would have wished and so she went on as she had begun, keeping the reins of the three horses, which was the way she saw the three separate Poppies which made her, as untangled as they could be. No one must know of what happened in the secret parts of her life. That was the way it had to be, and so it was.

And so perhaps it might have gone on, had it not been for the Archduke Ferdinand in Sarajevo. Or so Poppy would tell herself in later years, even though she knew perfectly well that the Archduke and his assassination was not really so important. The world had been building up to its paroxysm of killing and misery long before the Archduke went visiting and had himself shot for his pains. All through the long contented months that followed her nineteenth birthday, she read the *Dispatch* in her usual casual way, and listened to Bobby talking ominously of trouble in Europe and never gave a thought to the possibility that anything could ever change. Nothing ever did change, after all. In spite of the strangeness of her life and the extreme contrasts that she lived between her three strands, she knew that the structure that underpinned it all was safe and solid. It always had been, so why should it ever change?

But, on a hot afternoon in August 1914, it did change.

17

'I can't imagine war,' Mabel said and sat disconsolately fanning herself, for the afternoon was oppressively hot without a breath of air even out of doors in the little garden under the shade of the laburnum tree which hung over the wall from the house next door. 'I keep thinking of knights in armour and so forth, but that is ridiculous.'

'Very ridiculous,' Bobby said shortly. 'This is a modern war, very violent and very efficient. The machines they now use are quite horrendous, and the guns –' He shook his head. 'People here are underestimating the Germans, and saying such stupid things about the Uhlans. But they are great soldiers and should not be dismissed so easily. Huns they may be, but they're damned efficient Huns.' And it said a lot for the strength of his feelings that he should have sworn so in front of his sister and her friend, and not realized it.

'Then you do not believe it will all be over by Christmas?' Poppy ventured. 'Sammy at the office is mortified, for everyone says it will be, and he is so afraid it will be all over before he gets his chance to go to the Front and deal with them instead of being just our office boy who is dealt with by everyone else! He is just sixteen, you know, and very bloodthirsty.'

'He might well get the chance to drink his fill yet,' Bobby said and reached for another piece of cake. The wreck of their afternoon tea sat on the little table between them, but he was still eating happily enough, and that comforted Poppy. However gloomy his words were, at least he still behaved in his usual way.

'Oh, Bobby, you're just being gloomy!' Mabel said with some vigour. 'You always see the worst of everything. I cannot see it will last all that long, especially as you say we have these efficient guns. How can we go on fighting a long time when we kill so many of these wretched Uhlans you admire so much?'

'I don't admire them,' Bobby said. 'I just do not underestimate them. Our soldiers have already been pushed back from Mons and look how well the Germans did at Lille and Tannenburg!'

'But our men won on the Marne,' Poppy murmured and he threw a sharp look at her.

'Thank heavens that you at least seem to read your papers properly! Yes, there was the Marne, but never forget that long retreat from Mons. And now the Germans are fighting hard on the Aisne and doing well. I tell you, it won't be as easy as the armchair warriors at the office say it will –'

He stopped then and set down his empty cup. 'I think I had better warn you, Mabel, that there may be some problems for us soon.'

Mabel looked up. She had started feeding Chloe, who was becoming extra irritable in the hot afternoon, with morsels of seed cake to keep her quiet, and looked irritable herself. 'Oh, now what, Bobby? Haven't I enough to be concerned about? Here's Goosey complaining most bitterly because the grocer is being quite absurd over what he will and will not sell her, claiming it is his war duty to make sure there is no hoarding – as if she would – and being complaining all morning about his impudence, and Chloe here being quite – well, what is it now? You had better put me out of my misery!'

'I might have to go away,' Bobby said and sat quietly waiting for her reaction and Poppy looked at him, at the way his dust-coloured hair flopped over his forehead and at the rather tight anxious expression on his square face, and felt her chest tighten with that painful and yet so wonderful feeling of need she still had when she was with him. After all this time, surely she should have outgrown her schoolgirl passion? She was, after all, no longer a schoolgirl, and it was high time she learned to see him as he really was: a dear close friend, that was all. And it was clear he thought of her so, for he treated her with the easy camaraderie he used with his sister, laughing and teasing and being very comfortable with her. But she knew that however much she harangued herself on the issue, nothing had changed from the first time she had met him. If anything, her feelings had grown and deepened. She now wanted so much more from him and suddenly her fingers almost ached with the desire to stretch out and push the lock of hair that was across his forehead back out of his eyes. Those eyes, which became slits of laughter when he smiled, but which now were wide and watchful and not at all amused.

'What did you say?' Mabel said and put down the plate of cake, leaving Chloe to reach for it in a most unmannerly fashion and stuff her mouth with cake. 'Bobby? You are not being ridiculous and joining up, are you? It would be so –'

'No,' he said quietly. 'I am not joining up. But I have told old Palfreyman that I am available to take on Jerry's job.'

There was a long silence and then Poppy said carefully, 'Jerry Heath?'

'Yes,' Bobby said. 'Someone has to.'

'It doesn't have to be you,' Mabel cried passionately. 'It is quite absurd that you, with a child to care for and me, and – you can tell Palfreyman you can't, surely! Let it be Meredith or Thomas or –'

'Mabel,' Bobby said gently. 'I have already told Palfreyman I am available. He did not ask me, you must understand. I told *him*.'

Mabel's face crumpled, and she stared at him as two large tears formed in the corners of her eyes and hung there, helplessly, and at once Bobby got to his feet and came to crouch down beside her on the parched grass, holding her close so that he crushed the muslin of her frock. But she just sat there and let the tears roll down her face unchecked.

'I ought to be proud,' she managed to gulp at length. 'I know I did, but – if only Jerry hadn't been – I mean –'

'My dear, he was a foolish man, you know that! I bow to none in my respect for him and he sent back some excellent stuff, but he had no need to go to that section of the Front! He should not have done so, and we all know that. He was being foolhardy, wanted a great scoop and Mons was no place to show off. Jerry was always a dreadful show-off and you know that perfectly well.'

'I know!' Mabel wailed. 'I loathed him for it and that made it all that much worse when they said he'd – when it happened. Oh, Bobby, why must you go? You don't have to, surely – not with Chloe and me to take care of –'

'You are a grown lady now, my dear,' Bobby said, still quietly. 'And sooner or later you must take care of yourself, especially in these hard times –'

'You don't need to go –' Mabel began passionately but he shook her gently and said, 'Yes, I must.'

'Why? It is not as though you are a soldier, or have any wish to be one –'

'I am a journalist and I am one because it is vital people have knowledge. It is especially vital that they know what is happening there. Of course I have no wish to be a soldier, but neither have I any wish to see these Germans take over the whole of the world, as indeed they will if they are not stopped. It is essential that the *Dispatch* have a man at the Front, and I am the best for the job. I am not being vainglorious saying that, you must know that. I just know –'

Mabel pushed that aside and then rubbed her face with one hand, angry now. 'Oh, I know that! We all know you are by far the best man the *Dispatch* has! But to send you to such dreadful danger! How can they do it, and you a father of a motherless child and – and –'

'Do you have to rub that in? Don't you think I've thought about it, agonized over it, in fact? But you have our dear friend Poppy here to take extra care with you, and there is of course Goosey. It is really she who takes care of all of us, as well you know. I shall miss you all dreadfully, you know –' And he looked over her shoulder at his heedless small daughter, still pushing cake into her mouth with great abandon, and Poppy saw the sharp spasm of pain that crossed his face and wanted to cry too. And tried to think of how best to deal with what she had to say herself; and took a deep breath as at last Bobby came back to his own chair and Mabel sat up and set her now rumpled hair straight while sniffing a little.

'I shall probably miss all of you far more than you'll miss me. You'll be busy and happy at the office. And,' Bobby gave a sudden wicked little grin. 'And there is always Georgie, of course –'

Mabel went scarlet and Poppy smiled in sympathy. George Pringle's attentions to Mabel had been very marked for the last six months. He had arrived as a new member of their tennis club that met at the courts in Hyde Park, near Kensington Gardens, and almost from the first day had fixed his somewhat myopic gaze on Mabel and not removed it. At first Mabel had pooh-poohed him and treated him with a marked disdain, but in the past few weeks his attentions seemed to have made some inroads, for they often sat together, he with his eyes glinting behind their thick lensed spectacles, as he stroked with his little finger his neat moustache, and she chattering gaily at him. Poppy had been a little irritated at first, and then resentful – for inevitably the new liaison meant that Mabel had less time to spend with her in the dear old way that had been so much fun – but now, she was glad of George Pringle, and his eternal boring talk of his law practice. If Mabel liked him and enjoyed his company that meant that she, like Bobby, need not feel too concerned about what she was about to do.

'Ah – this may not seem the right time and yet –' she began but Bobby interrupted her, apparently not aware she was about to say something.

'Poppy, my dear, do you think I am a dreadful man to go off to be the *Dispatch*'s correspondent at the Front? Be honest now. I'd value your opinion. I don't think it will do any harm to Chloe or to Mabel – as I say, life will go on much the same for everyone here. It is at the Front that we will be living in mud and misery, after all. It is right I should go, isn't it?'

She caught her breath and tried to think clearly. Of course she didn't want him to go. The casualty lists that had been published after Mons had sobered everyone. The general enthusiasm which had greeted the outbreak of the war had melted away in the face of those interminable lists and the eruption on London's streets of women wearing deep mourning. Everyone knew now, as the Indian summer burned its way through October, that this was a real war, a painful war, and one that meant loss. And she adored this man, even though he didn't know it. For over three years she had dreamed about him, made him the centre of all her most torrid imaginings and now here he was, telling her he was going to the Front where so many other people had been killed – including his predecessor on the *Dispatch* – and asking her approval. How could she give it?

But then she thought of the men she had seen in the streets, men in khaki and in the drab blue of naval uniforms and of the way people lifted their chins in pride as they looked at them. She thought of what had happened in Belgium and of the appalling tales she had heard of what the Germans had done there, though some of them she found almost unbelievably wicked, finding it impossible to think that even the most implacable warmakers could behave so; to spit babies on bayonets? How could it possibly be? Well, people said it was, and everyone agreed that the Germans must be stopped. And it was indeed necessary that people should know the facts of what was going on in Flanders. She might be only a junior typewriter at the office, but she had in her two years there absorbed a good deal of the ethos of a newspaper. It was essential of course that a man from the *Dispatch* be there to give the right sort of reports, honest and true ones. Dispassionate ones, she thought then, absurdly, and almost laughed aloud at her own pun. Dispassionate reports from the *Dispatch* man. She must stop being so silly and answer his question –

'Of course it is right,' she said at length and managed a slightly shaky smile. 'It has to be, doesn't it?'

He looked at her with so much gratitude in his face and with so wide a smile that she almost had to sit on her hand to prevent herself reaching out to him; and then he leaned over and hugged her and kissed her on both cheeks in the approved brotherly fashion and turned back to Mabel.

'You see, my dear? Poppy understands! Take a leaf from her book, kid sister, and learn to be brave and sensible. It has to be. You'll take care of her while I'm gone, won't you, Poppy? And there'll be my leaves at home, of course. I'll get back whenever I can –'

'I –' Poppy swallowed. 'I am not sure I can take care of her, Bobby. I'm sorry, Mabel, but you see –' Again she swallowed as both of them turned and stared at her in surprise. 'The thing of it is, you see, I'm going to be a FANY.'

'A – you're going to be a *what*?' Mabel said, almost stupefied.

'I've signed on with the First Aid Nursing Yeomanry,' Poppy said and bent her head to look down at her fingers entwined in her lap. 'I – I wondered about discussing it with you first, Mabel, but – well, it seemed unfair to burden you with my anxieties, so I just – well, I just did it. It seemed to me that I must do something. After Mons you see, the casualty lists –'

'My dear girl!' Bobby said and leaned forwards and took both her hands in his. 'My dear, I do admire you! But how on earth – surely you are too young?'

'I told them I was twenty-one and they believed me,' Poppy said. 'And if you dare ever to tell anyone otherwise – and anyway I shall be twenty soon, shan't I? So I will only be a year under age and that doesn't signify –'

'But your Mama – how did she –?' Mabel said, staring at her friend, her face creased with amazement. 'Surely she forbade you?'

'No doubt she would have tried had I told her,' Poppy said calmly. 'But I have not.'

'My dear Poppy,' Bobby said dryly, 'there are some things that cannot be hidden. The uniform of a FANY is one of them, I would have thought, as is a prolonged absence in Flanders during a war. I suspect she might get an inkling, you know, whether you tell her or not.'

Poppy laughed a little shakily. 'Ass! I know that! I just prefer to choose my own time, that is all. You know how my Mama is. Rather severe and – well, anyway, she is sensible as well. If she is faced with a fact she cannot alter, then she accepts it. She always has. It is – it is quite an admirable quality in her –'

There was comfort to be found in speaking well of her mother. She had been feeling more and more anxious about the way she was deceiving her. Of course, once it was all a *fait accompli*, she would be able to go; Mildred would do nothing to stop her. Severe as she was, it was not in her nature to deal in confrontations. Poppy could perhaps tell her now and still do as she wished; hadn't she won over the matter of not going to university and getting a job at the *Dispatch* instead? But still she hadn't told her of this new plan, and speaking well of her now to her friends made Poppy feel a little better about her own deceit.

'So there it is,' she went on after a moment. 'I am waiting now to hear when I am to report for training. And once I have, then I will be off to Flanders to drive an ambulance –'

'But you can't drive!' Mabel cried almost contemptuously. 'You know you cannot – this is all a hum!'

'That is why I am to be trained, Mabel,' Poppy said gently. 'I shall learn to drive an ambulance, and also how to look after its engine and put it right if it goes wrong, and I shall learn how to put on bandages and tourniquets and so forth and various other matters. I thought – I want to be useful, you see –'

'And you think I am stupid and useless, both of you, because I am doing nothing.' Mabel flared and jumped to her feet, as Chloe burst into tears at the suddenness of her aunt's cry and added to the noise. And Mabel looked down at her and then shook her head furiously and turned and ran blindly into the house, weeping bitterly as she went, and after a moment Bobby made a little grimace and went after her.

And Poppy sat in the hot garden and waited for someone to return, feeling wretched. The last thing she had wanted to do was distress her friend, and now she had. Perhaps it had been wrong to tell her of her plans now, so soon after Bobby had broken his own news, but she had acted on impulse; she had just thought it had seemed so natural a point at which to do it. And, anyway, a secret little voice whispered deep inside her, you wanted to impress Bobby. You know you did. You weren't at all worried about Mabel and how she might feel. You just wanted to show off to Bobby. You're no better than the man who got himself killed because he showed off. You're just a selfish beast.

And tears began to prick her own eyes as suddenly she remembered what had happened when she had told Lizah and Jessie only three days ago of what she was to do. That they would have to be told was obvious, and she had decided to tell them now rather than later, needing to space the family confrontations as widely as possible. To face what she expected would come from Mama, a cold anger, at the same time as dealing with the inevitable emotional outburst that would come from Jessie and Lizah had seemed to her a dreadful prospect. So she had told them last Saturday when she had gone to the

East End for afternoon tea and unleashed precisely the emotional tidal wave she had expected.

Except that it had been worse in reality than even the most pessimistic of her imaginings had warned her it might be. Jessie had first refused to believe her, and then had wept and then had harangued her. And as if that hadn't been bad enough, then she had been immensely and visibly brave, biting back her tears as she told Poppy how wonderful and good she was and how courageous and how proud of her they would all be. And that had been the worst part of all.

Except for Lizah who had looked at her with his face whitening under the remains of a summer tan, collected in a two-week holiday in Southend, and with an expression in his eyes that had made her feel as though someone had taken her belly in hard fingers and squeezed it tight.

'Oh, you little fool,' he had whispered. 'You crazy fool of a girl! Call them, tell them you're under age, get a doctor to say you're too ill – you mustn't do it! I've been there and I know. You mustn't do it –' And he had touched his empty sleeve with one square finger and stared at her with eyes which looked huge in his white face and she had not been able to look at him.

'I will go,' she had said in as firm a voice as she could. 'It's my war, this one. I'm young and I have no ties to stop me, no responsibilities. It is right that I should do what I can. The men of my age are going, so why shouldn't I? I have been running to meetings which demand votes for women as for men. Well, if I want the privileges of men I must share their work, mustn't I? And anyway, I shan't actually be fighting – only taking care of the sick and the wounded. You can't object to that. I shall be behind the lines most of the time.'

'Most of the time!' Jessie had wailed and wept again. 'Only most of the time! Why not all the time, already?'

But Lizah had looked at her and said in a thin voice quite unlike his usual warm one. 'No ties? No responsibilities? Then indeed you must go –' And had got to his feet and taken his alpaca jacket from the back of his chair and gone, walking quietly out of the shop. And Jessie had pulled her back when she had started to go after him and said softly, 'It's all right. He'll get over it. We'll talk to him again soon – before you go. Oy, before you go!' And again she had begun to weep.

Indeed, the only comfort that awful afternoon had been, amazingly, Bernie, who had launched himself with all the vividness of which his eleven-year-old mind was capable – which was considerable

– into an account of the sort of bloody and ugly wounds his cousin would have to see and deal with, and how – and here he had been very graphic indeed – the men she had to look after would be sick and would lose control of their bowels and be altogether disgusting; until his mother, unable to stand any more had actually been driven to cuff him soundly, something she did all too rarely in Poppy's estimation, and he had burst into floods of noisy tears, much as Chloe was weeping now.

Oh, this hateful war! Poppy thought as she bent to pick up the shrieking child to try and soothe her while they waited for her aunt and her father to come back to the garden. It's only been a couple of months and already it's making us all so dreadfully unhappy. I don't see how it can get much worse.

18

My dear Mabel,

I am so sorry not to have written to you sooner, but truly, my dear, it has been an impossible task. I cannot tell you how hard I have been working, from the very earliest moment in the morning until so late at night that to be honest I can barely fall into bed, and have no energy to write so much as a postcard. But today is a red letter day – I have a half-day holiday all to myself! I am sitting here on my camp bed – which is not quite so uncomfortable as it looks, or is it that I am so weary that even a bed as unyielding as concrete now seems welcoming? It is very possible! Anyway, here I sit, with my poor feet up and my writing case on my knees, and full of so much to tell you that I hardly know where to begin.

Perhaps I should tell you first how I arrived here at Pirbright to be met by a most charming but quite terrifying personage who announced herself as our Commandant and welcomed us. There are seventeen of us, raw new recruits, all laden with luggage about which Mrs Baker – said Commandant – was *most* scathing. We should not need a fraction of it, she told us, and must learn to travel light, and she made many people send their extra bags back on the next train! I had happily brought very little and was permitted to keep it. Anyway there we were and were taken to this camp, which I must tell you is far from comfortable.

In the summer they are all under canvas – poor creatures – very small tents, one of the others who was there in the summer told me, and most damp and horridly full of all sorts of creatures that have a great affection for female stockings – very nasty! But we are more

147

fortunate and are accommodated in huts since it is winter, ten of us to each one, in which we have the aforesaid camp bed apiece, and a small locker arrangement for all our possessions. There is also a small stove for which we are constantly begging coal from the men in the adjoining camp, and where we roast potatoes as well as our toes when we have the opportunity.

Then we were issued with our uniforms. Very fetching! I have a scarlet tunic with a painfully high collar and white braid facings – which get dreadfully grubby while we do our training, of which more anon – and a navy skirt, bell-shaped and not at all fashionable but rather pretty none the less with three rows of braid at the bottom, and the most delicious cap. It is as flat as those the page boys in hotels wear but larger of course, and it has a shiny black peak, which looks divine since the cap is scarlet. Then we have black patent leather riding boots which we wear over thick black stockings that rub most cruelly when our feet are wet – which is often in these muddy fields where we train – and white gloves which I am forever washing, a riding crop – I cannot think why! – and a first-aid kit in a haversack with a water bottle which we wear at our belts at the back. I positively rattle as I walk! They say the uniform will be less cumbersome soon for they are to be redesigned, but then such things are always being gossiped about. And it does not help that all our orders come from France as must the new uniforms. As I told you, our own Government will not permit FANYs to go to France, so we must be under the orders of the French Government, which is really nothing strange, but everyone, including Mrs Baker who should know says we will grind down our Government in time and then we will be British personnel! But meanwhile, I am a French *poilu*! It is all very absurd.

Now to the training – oh, Mabel, I have *never* worked so hard! We are on the wards of the local hospital for set hours of the day learning basic nursing, and I run about with bowls and bandages, pans and pots of all kinds – I will not enter into details here! – and generally am dreadfully bullied by the real nurses who quite despise us, though not as much as they despise the VADs who are always being sneered at.

Then we have classes in ambulance driving and in engine maintenance – do you know about carburettors? I now know more than I ever would have thought possible, and also about such matters as gaskets and cylinders – all very technical. Then we have long sessions on map reading, which is a good deal more difficult than I had imagined it would be. Clearly, to use a map of Belgium and France when you do not speak the language and are unaccustomed to their systems entails considerable effort.

Then we have lectures on so many things – on first aid of course and dealing with shock and so forth and also on how to deal with men who become too familiar. Mrs Baker is a stickler for what she calls the proprieties and seems more concerned that we should always remain as ladylike as possible than that we should be successful at the work. So we try to do both, we are all so eager.

For the rest, we sit and nurse our tired feet – it is amazing how wearing it is to run up and down those long hospital wards – or practise our bandaging, which is very tedious and a great deal less easy than I had imagined, and do the packing of our first-aid kits and read again and again about how to staunch bleeding and so forth and so on. At meals – which are rather dull and stodgy so that I yearn for a delicious poached egg on toast and a cup of tea at our dear old ABC with you beside me to gossip to – we almost fall asleep over our plates, we are so weary!

Enough about me – I shall tell you more in my next letter for I really must write to some other people now and unless I get on with it my half-day will be gone for this week and I will have no chance to do all I mean to. Is your George well? Has he proposed yet? I am sure he will; I never saw a man so taken as he was with you when last I saw you together. And I do hope Chloe is well and that Goosey is not having too much trouble with her bunions in this bitter winter weather. Write soon, dear Mabel, I do so miss our little prosey gossips!

Your affectionate friend
Poppy

Pirbright Camp
Surrey
17th December 1914

Dear Mama,

Thank you for your last note and for the £10. I am sure you meant kindly but I really must return it. We have little opportunity to spend money here, and my allowances are quite sufficient for my needs. To have such a sum by me is an embarrassment, I am afraid, so it will be safer in your keeping.

The work I am doing is arduous but not impossible, and we are told that we shall shortly be sent off to Flanders to put all we have learned into practice. I am looking forward to that, of course; I joined in order to be useful, and it is galling to have to wait so long to be sent where I can be so.

I hope the gift of the money means that you are less angry than you were with me for doing as I did, but I am sure that one day you will understand that I could not have done otherwise. As I did try to explain to you, I do feel that all young people must make an effort in this war or there will be no world in the future for us all.

I trust Grandmama remains tolerably well, and that the Uncles are also well.

Your respectful daughter
Poppy

Pirbright Camp
Surrey
29th January 1915

Dear Bobby,

It was grand to read your accounts in the *Dispatch* this week of what life is like for our Tommies in the Basée Canal and Soissons areas. It was most vivid and human; I almost felt the chill of the mud about my feet, although I cannot lie to you – there is enough chilly mud here to have that effect on its own.

I am enjoying my training in a sort of way. I cannot pretend it is easy but however weary I get I have the comfort of thinking –well, today I have learned something new and soon I will be able to use it. I will not bore you with the details now. Perhaps one day you will choose to return to England for a while and will write an account of life for FANY recruits in the Surrey area.

It was good of you to be so concerned about the risk of bombing here, but I do not think we need concern ourselves. That cowardly attack on the East Anglian ports was a long way away, and I cannot imagine the German airships would come so far inland as we are here, or to London.

I am hoping to have a weekend's leave soon, and I shall of course visit Norland Square then and make sure that all is well with Mabel and Chloe, although I have no fears for them. I receive regular letters from dear Mabel and she seems content enough, with

George much in evidence in all she writes! So she is safely cared for, as is dear little Chloe.

If you can spare the time from preparing your material for the paper, please send me a few lines, I would so much like to hear from you.

Your friend
Poppy

Pirbright Camp
Surrey
11th February 1915

My dear Jessie and Lizah,

It was most good of you to send that magnificent parcel. The other girls here were just as delighted as I was, though some of them were a little startled by the contents. It is not often that a Scottish girl, for example, is offered an East End bagel! The cakes were particularly delicious.

Please do not worry yourself so much over my health. I am indeed working hard and the conditions here are cold and not very comfortable, but I have been perfectly fit since the last cold which I do agree was a horrid one. But clearly I am becoming hardened to the elements and no longer catch cold at all.

There is no need, Lizah, I do assure you, for you to be so alarmed about my officers. Mrs Baker, our Commandant, is a most caring person. She is strict, of course, as is necessary, but she is very fair. We are fortunate in this troop, perhaps, since we are all educated women and as such our officers feel comfortable with us. So you need not think that the sort of unpleasant experiences you describe at officers' hands in the Boer War will be my lot. This is a very different sort of war, after all.

Please give my warmest wishes to Lily and the shop customers and tell her I look forward with pleasure to the gloves when she has knitted them. But please do assure her that there is no need to make more. The scarf she sent last month was most welcome, but I already had the one she had sent me earlier, you'll recall. If you can persuade her and her friends to make comforts for the Tommies instead of me, I am sure they will be very welcome. The weather in Flanders and in France is quite dreadful, I believe, and there is great need there for warm clothing.

I look forward to your next letter most eagerly, but do not feel it necessary to send a food parcel every time you write. I am still dealing with all the good things you sent last time and, even with the help of many good friends here, it is difficult to do justice to your generosity.

Yours affectionately
Poppy

Pirbright Camp
Surrey
16th February 1915

My dearest Bobby,

I know I am mad to write this letter, but I feel I need to. Mad because I shall never post it – but simply saying it all as though you would one day read it will make me feel better.

Dear Bobby, I do miss you so. I know I ought to be missing Mama, but I am not. It is sad to feel so happy to be away from her and from that house in Leinster Terrace. Here I sleep on a hard camp bed, which is covered with the flattest of biscuit mattresses and with a blanket so thin as to make it necessary for me to put my greatcoat on top of it, but I still would rather be here than there in that comfortable prison of a house. There, I've said it! Do you think me wicked?

Dear, dear, dear Bobby, I wish you missed me as much as I miss you. I used to sit there at my desk at the dear old *Dispatch* office and watch for you to come in, and when I saw you walking across the floor between the desks with that odd loping walk of yours and your lovely square shoulders, it was as though the day had at last started. Until then the sky had been dull and my middle quite empty, but once you were there, all tousled and busy at your own desk, all seemed brighter and I felt whole again. It is so unfair that I need you so and you don't even know that I care at all –

Dear, dear, dear, *dearest* Bobby, if only we could go away together somewhere, just you and I. If only you knew how much I love you and how sweet you are in my eyes. If only, if only –

If only I had the courage to post this letter! But of course I shan't. And I feel such a fool writing it –

Pirbright Camp
Surrey
21st March 1915

My dear Mabel,

Such larks! You will never guess who has arrived here as the rawest of new recruits. Only the egregious Miss Flora Gordon! You do remember her, I am sure – Miss Sylvia Pankhurst's protégée and pupil who was so very overbearing to us that first time we went together to a meeting and returned afterwards to tea at the Settlement house. I am now quite a senior personage in this place and have the task of supervising some of the efforts of the newer arrivals and there I was in the ward, dealing with a recalcitrant patient who had taken exception to having his bed made, and was sent a new bug to help me – and there she was! She is not quite so overbearing now, I can assure you, and is turning out to be rather good fun, in fact. She is indeed very shy and I think that is why she was so disagreeable, or seemed so, when we last met.

She tells me that Miss Sylvia, and indeed her mother and her sister Christabel too, as well as the membership of WSPU, have agreed to devote all their energies to war work. They will return to the issue of Votes for Women when we have destroyed the Hun. I do agree they are right, don't you? How long ago it all seems, and how very unimportant! I worried so much about it all once, and now I only worry whether there will be any tea left when I get to my billet!

Flora Gordon agrees with me that it seems unimportant. All that happened before the war feels so, she says. But she is still drawing, all the same, and does such witty sketches of us all. I am sending you this one she did of me, polishing my boots. I do look bedraggled, don't I? You will notice how difficult I find it to keep my hair in order – but it was ever thus!

We are getting new uniforms next week specially adapted for active service, they say. So of course the entire camp is alive with rumours about when we leave. I shall let you know as soon as I do!

As ever
Your friend Poppy

Base Camp Hospital
Calais
2nd April 1915

My dear Bobby,

A most hasty line which I hope will reach you. I understand from people here that most of the journalists are up at Neuve-Châpelle where another major push is expected, so I shall send this letter there and hope for the best.

As you see, I have arrived. The crossing was frightful – we were all so sick and there was so little space on our ship that there was no chance to get any air at all, unless you were unlucky enough to be on deck in which case you froze. But we are surviving and our ambulances have been unloaded. Mine has been called *Queen of Flanders* and I was put in charge of her because of being called Poppy – very embarrassing but madly exciting to have my own vehicle at last – and we're off tomorrow. I've no idea where we're going, but there are people who think it might be Ypres again. They say a new push will come there. If you manage to catch up with me, it would be so very nice to see you.

Yours in haste
Poppy

Somewhere in Flanders
27th April 1915

Dearest Jessie,

You really must stop worrying so! There is no need for I am fine, I really am. I am better fed in fact than I was at Pirbright, for here much effort is made to look after us. There are not many women about and apart from a few VADs and Sisters, who are on the hospital trains, the men don't see many of us, so they take excellent care of us. So please, dear Jessie, don't trouble yourself with parcels – not until I find myself somewhere where I can be sure to stay for a while. Then I will send you the address and we shall see what is possible, if you are determined. Otherwise, the parcels just chase me about and by the time they arrive, frankly, the contents are in no condition to be eaten!

Yes, I have lost some weight since you ask so determinedly but it does me no harm. I now find it easier to slide in and out of tight spaces, which is a real asset in these conditions.

The weather at last is improving. I can't imagine how it is at home, and keep remembering a poem I learned at school for ever ago, 'Oh, to be in England Now that April's there' – but actually I would rather be here than not be here, if you understand me. I know I am useful at last, although driving very injured men is so distressing. One does all one can to avoid potholes but some are inevitable and as one bangs over them the men in the back cry out most piteously and beg me to take care. It is so hard to bear but I must just go on and cannot stop to soothe them for that might make the pain worse. So as I say I am glad to be here for at least I am doing something which I hope is useful, just getting the men out.

I will write again as soon as I can, and please, dearest Jessie, no more parcels yet awhile?

Yours with love
Poppy

Somewhere in Flanders
3rd June 1915

Dear Mama,

I am sorry you have not received letters from me. I have written them and I can only assume that the difficulties with the Army's postal arrangements are to blame. I shall write again as soon as I may – this is just to reassure you that I am alive and well. But I am somewhat fatigued. This is a very hard war we are fighting –

Base Camp Hospital
Calais
20th June 1915

Dearest Mabel,

I cannot believe it! Leave! I am to spend the next two weeks here at base setting up ready for the new intake – I have been promoted you see, and am now in charge of a small group of three vehicles, and the six girls who take care of them and run them – but after that I shall be home for two whole weeks! I cannot tell you how I long to see you. And how I long for such things as hot baths and the chance to wear a gown again, just for a little while. Don't try to meet me at the station, dear, for I am told it is always very crowded there with people anxious about wounded relatives, and I shall be working on the hospital ship and on the train. It is necessary as part of getting my leave, so I do not mind at all that I must work my way home. So I will see you as soon as I may when I get back. I am counting the days, I do assure you.

My love to Goosey and to Chloe.

Yours in great excitement
Poppy

PS I did hope to see Bobby at some time, but we have never managed to be in the same place at the same time –

19

It was not until the train was at last rattling on the last few miles of the suburban route into London that she really believed she was home. Outside in the dusty July sunshine the railway lines gleamed their way between the buildings on each side and the advertisement hoardings shouted their brazen messages at her, and warmed her heart with their familiarity. 'Mazawattee, what a tea!' and 'Stephenson's Inks', with a great blue-black splash of a blot against the white enamelled surface and 'They come as a boon and a blessing to men, the Pickwick, the Owl, and the Waverley Pen –', and suddenly hot tears stung her eyelids and she had to close them hard to avoid making an exhibition of herself.

Home! And she tried then to see what she really meant by home and closed her eyes to visualize it. Her bedroom in Leinster Terrace? She imagined herself in that cream and white room soaking in the big japanned bath before the fire that Queenie had to fill from great copper jugs – for Mama did not approve of changing the old house to put in new-fangled bathrooms – and then stretching out on the softness of her bed. It was an agreeable vision and yet –

And then she saw herself in Jessie's cluttered glittering little sitting room behind her shop, buried in one of her great armchairs with her feet up warming to the glow of the fire and a tray, inevitably, laden with food and drink beside her and thought that though that was pleasant it did not give her the same *frisson* the advertisements had.

And then, without even trying to imagine it, there she was curled up on the multicoloured cushions in the Norland Square drawing room with Bobby lying stretched out on the great sofa with the music of *Schéhérazade* coming in great sensuous waves from the big horn of his gramophone. And then it happened; the hot shiver of excitement and happiness that made her catch her breath and feel so good and which she knew she should be filled with now she was here, so close to

Victoria Station. But it was because of Bobby she had felt it, not just because of home; and he was still somewhere in France.

She opened her eyes to stare out again at the passing warehouses and coalyards as behind her someone called fretfully, 'Nurse!' and she was dragged out of her reveries at once.

'Yes?' she murmured as she stood beside the shelf on which he lay, with a man stowed above him and another beneath him, one of the hundreds the long train held, all of them stretcher cases. 'Has your dressing slipped again? Here, let me just – that's it – ease that leg forward a little, if you can – oh, well done! Not much longer now, old chap. We should be there in about ten minutes, I'd say. And then you'll be popped in an ambulance and away to a really comfortable hospital – it'll be fine now –'

'I know it will,' the man said drowsily and closed his eyes, grateful to be comfortable again. 'Got a blighty one 'ere, I 'ave. I'll never go back to that 'ell'ole again, that's for bleedin' sure –' and then he was asleep and Poppy stood and looked down on the grey tired face and thought – I wonder if he knows he's going to lose that leg? And is it really better to face life as a cripple rather than to go back? And knew the answer.

Because it had indeed been a hellhole. She had never been as close to it as some of these men had – never been inside the trenches, but she had seen enough of those soldiers who had been dragged out of them and packed into her *Queen of Flanders* ambulance to know that all that anyone said about the horrors there was true, and probably understated. She had seen men with sodden uniforms reeking of sour mud and ripped to tatters, with their flesh beneath as torn as the fabric, men with faces drawn and almost green with agony as they tried to breathe after attacks with mustard or phosgene gas had caught them lying low in their dugouts, men with bones so shattered that the pallid jagged ends stuck out through their filthy puttees. She had cradled heads in her arms, knowing the men could not hear the words she crooned into their ears, but needing to try to comfort them all the same until they died, which for many of them took dreadfully long, and had dealt with the cheeky impertinences of jolly Tommies cock-a-hoop because they had an injury severe enough to take them out of the active line and off to a safe hospital, but not so severe as to threaten life. They had been almost the hardest to bear with their flirtatiousness and their transparent gratitude for the most minor of things she did for them. She had wanted to shout at them sometimes, to tell them not to be so mindlessly cheerful about it all. They should protest at the wickedness of what was going on here and refuse to tolerate it another moment –

But then she would smile at them and push that stupid notion aside, for it was obvious that the war had to be fought and had to be won, somehow. The Germans were evil creatures who had to be stopped – and she had managed to hold on to that conviction until the day when a breakthrough in the line at Hooge, not far from Hill 60, had brought injured German prisoners to her ambulance to be shipped back to a dressing station, patched up and then sent to prisoner-of-war camps. They had been men too, and just boys as well, just like the Tommies. They too had cried and been grateful and had died too, and she had been confused and miserable for a long time after that. For if both sides were really the same, as it appeared to her now, why were they fighting at all?

But there had been no time to continue to think such foolish thoughts, for she and her small fleet of three ambulances had been sent south to the Messines ridge and there the shelling had been so fierce that for three days and nights she had been able to think of nothing but driving or filling her ambulance and then taking it back to the dressing station before setting out on another run, over and over again, until sheer exhaustion drove all thoughts from her, let alone doubts of the value of the War.

But now as she stood swaying in a hospital train, thick with the smell of exhausted sick men and carbolic and dirt and ether, holding on to the window strap as she peered out at the curving lines taking her into the city of her birth, there was time to think, and the words came into her mind again   Why? What is this stupid war *for?* And shook with the effort of not crying because she knew there was no answer.

The next hour or two as she helped unload the men and hand them over to the crisply clean waiting nurses, who looked at her with awe in their eyes and bobbed their heads but did not speak, were at least busy. That gave her no time to think, which was good, and then at last she was free and could go about her own affairs. And she picked up her small kit bag, and tugged her soft forage cap over her eyes, and began to walk down the platform towards the main concourse. A taxi, that was the answer; she had plenty of money for such a thing, that was one comfort, for she had been paid at Calais when she had picked up her leave warrant and her travel permit. And she came out into the glow of the summer afternoon at the front of Victoria Station and stood blinking as she looked around.

It was incredible. There were buses and newspaper sellers and flower women and people with children and shopping baskets and hurrying heedless crowds and she couldn't believe it. She had left behind her, just a few miles away across the strip of the Channel, such squalor and pain and misery, and here there were people buying flowers and scolding children who dragged their feet, and cooing over pet dogs. And she shook her head a little as a cabbie leaned out of his window and called, 'Where to, missie? You look as you be in need of a ride.'

'Hmm?' she said and then nodded. 'Yes – yes, of course.' And she opened the door and threw in her kit bag and followed it in and the man said again, 'Where to, miss?'

'Cable Street,' she said. 'In the East End. I'll show you the place when we get there –' And she leaned back in the cab and closed her eyes against the brightness of the sun which seemed such an affront to her memories of the past three months.

'Just shows yer.' The driver had pushed back his connecting window and was leaning back a little so that he could chat affably to her. 'It's amazin' how wrong you can be, even after all my years in the trade. Even with the uniform on an' all I took you for a real West Ender. And you talk right too, but there it is! You can get it all wrong, can't yer? Ambulance driver, eh?'

'Yes,' Poppy said. 'Ambulance driver.'

'See what I mean? I'd ha' thought you was a real lady, like most drivers are, and not one of us at all. Our girls are working 'ard, all right – my two daughters is at Woolwich makin' guns an' bullets. But there can't be many from our end o' the town as are ambulance drivers.'

'I'm afraid you've got it wrong,' Poppy said, ashamed to have to say it. 'Actually I'm just visiting Cable Street. My home's in Leinster Terrace in Bayswater.'

'There!' the cabbie said in high good humour. 'Didn't I know it? Not often wrong I ain't, sorting out the wheat from the chaff. Took you for what you was, didn't I? A lady. Knew you couldn't be no East Ender.'

'I am in a sense,' Poppy said, nettled. 'I am to visit my aunt there. It is her shop we are going to.' And put that in your nasty old pipe and smoke it, she thought viciously as the man cocked a sharp glance at her and then pulled his window to and left her in peace. What difference does it make where people come from, East or West? And she thought of the men she had been caring for and how little it mattered what a man's class was when he was bleeding to death, and felt sick. Clearly, it was high time she came home for a rest –

And then she sat more upright and stared out of the cab window. Home. She was supposed to be going home. She had sent Mama a letter saying she was to come on leave today and she would be expecting her. Yet here she was going to Cable Street! And she bit her lip as the cab went careering on up High Holborn towards the City, amazed at her own foolishness. But she did not instruct the cabbie to turn around, for all that.

Mildred had been sitting in the drawing room window ever since lunch. She had been told, when she checked with Victoria Station, that the trains came in steadily all through the day, and that they could not possibly tell her when her daughter's might arrive, but, the man said sympathetically, 'I can tell you that most of the heaviest train loads come in the afternoon. And they're the ones they send the leave nurses and drivers on, so they can look after the men on the way. I wouldn't start worrying yet, Madam. Just be patient –'

And patient Mildred had been, for now it was almost seven o'clock and the afternoon had dwindled to a soft blue evening and Queenie was moving about the house restlessly, clearly thinking about organizing dinner, and not knowing when to start for fear of having it all ready for the returning heroine too soon.

They were all desperately excited below stairs, Mildred knew; no one had said as much to her, but she was not a fool and she had for a moment actually thought of speaking to Queenie about her own excitement; but had stopped herself. It never did to become too friendly with servants. They took liberties if you let your guard down for a moment and with only three of them there now, for the rest had gone rushing off to join up or to make munitions and a great deal of money, it was imperative she kept a firm control on her household.

So she sat wordlessly waiting, staring down into the street as she had on so many evenings and for so many different reasons. But tonight's was a good reason, and she twisted her hands in her lap, trying to imagine how it would be. And how this time she would indeed put her arms around her daughter and hold her close and tell her it didn't matter what she did, Mildred loved her and was proud of her, headstrong though she was –

When she did arrive Mildred wasn't ready. Indeed, she did not realize at first it was Poppy, for the cab pulled up outside and the door swung open and a large figure got out into the dusky evening light. And that could not possibly be Poppy.

But then the large figure leaned back into the cab and after a moment emerged again, this time with someone on her arm and Mildred stood up sharply and let go of the curtain, and then after one frozen moment turned slowly and made her way to the head of the stairs to wait.

Queenie was at the door to answer it even before the echo of the pealing bell had died away, standing back with her face wreathed in the most unusual grin as the other two servants peered out of the baize door that led to the kitchen and stared and whispered to each other. But Mildred said nothing, keeping her eyes fixed only on the scene in the hall below.

The dying sun poured in through the stained glass of the front door and reflected in the hall with its tiles and darkly polished furniture and gleaming brass and for a moment Mildred saw it as an outsider might and filled with pride. It was a good house, a rich house; it was one any sensible person must admire. She down there must admire it too –

But she down there did nothing of the sort. She stood in the hallway, peeling off her kid gloves and looking directly upwards as though she had known at once that Mildred was up there watching her and she saw her in the shadows and called genially, 'So, there you are, Millie! It's good to meet on happy occasions, eh? After all these years – I brought her home to you, Millie. And ain't she wonderful, hey? Ain't she a boobalah and a half?'

Behind her Poppy was standing, her soft forage hat held in one hand and her head drooping a little as she stared round at the hall in precisely the way that Mildred had wanted Jessie to do; it was as though she had never seen it before, for there was a faint look of puzzlement on her face.

'Well, Jessie,' Mildred said after a moment and then came down the stairs, setting each foot carefully on each tread, needing to control herself, to control her hurt and her anger. 'So Poppy came to you first? Poppy dear, it is good to see you. Come upstairs and rest yourself. You look tired.'

'No, she didn't come to me first,' Jessie said smoothly. Too smoothly? wondered Mildred, her senses sharpened by her pain. 'I did what she said I shouldn't. I went to Victoria to meet her. Yes, I know, she said no one was to go. But you know me, eh, Millie? It may be over fifteen years since we talked, but I don't change at all. Just get bigger – ' And she laughed and smoothed her heavy mulberry coloured coat over her billowing form.

'So, Poppy? You were met? You should have let me come. I accepted your refusal when you wrote – how are you, my dear?' and she leaned forward to kiss her daughter's cheek, longing to hold her close but totally unable to do so with Jessie standing there.

'I – I'm well, Mama. A little tired. Mama I – ' And she looked over Mildred's shoulder at Jessie who cut in swiftly.

'It's enough chatter already! Let the child sit down, eh Millie? Well, well, nothing looks to have changed, hey? You still look well, Mildred. It's good to see you after so long.'

'That will be all, thank you Queenie,' Mildred said and turned to lead the way to the stairs as the agog Queenie, her face ludicrous with disappointment, closed the front door and went laggardly across the hall towards the green baize door. 'You may start dinner now. Poppy dear, would you like something now, some tea perhaps or – '

'I've had some,' Poppy said and again Jessie jumped in.

'At the station, Millie, at Victoria, in the buffet. Crowded it was, but she's had a nice cup o' tea – '

'Well, thank you for bringing her, Jessie.' Mildred looked over her shoulder again, but Queenie and the other servants had disappeared at last and now she looked directly at Jessie. 'I don't think we need detain you.'

'I ain't going that easy, Millie, doll.' Jessie said. 'Not now I'm here. Come on then. Where are we to sit down in this great house? Such a palace as it is – so many rooms – it's a pleasure to see. But it must take a deal of looking after   '

Poppy had started to make her way upstairs and without hindrance from Mildred, Jessie followed her and after a moment Mildred herself brought up the rear. Her face showed no sign of her anger; to have her meeting with her daughter after so very long marred like this – but there was nothing she could do, clearly, to alter the situation at the moment, so she would not try. That was not her way.

By the time she reached the drawing room Poppy had unbuttoned her tunic and was stretched out in one of the high-backed armchairs, her booted legs outstretched. Mildred could see she was at the end of her tether; her face was tight and closed and her eyes had a hot glitter to them that she had only ever seen before when Poppy had been ill.

And suddenly memory assailed her: Poppy, small and hot and flushed, propped up on pillows, her breathing thick and noisy and her eyes half-closed in her fever, and she and Jessie on each side of her, taking care of her, watching over her; and she lifted her chin and looked across the room now to where Jessie sat in one of the smaller chairs, overflowing it a little and looking at Poppy with an expression as concerned and watchful as it could possibly be. And Mildred felt the anger inside her ease and soften and the pain loosened and began to drain away. She cared for Poppy so much, always had. Why be so angry because she had been the one who had met her at Victoria? Mildred herself could have done so had she not been so punctilious about doing as Poppy had asked her. Just like Jessie not to care, to do what she wanted to do and to benefit from it –

'Well, Jessie,' she said and the big woman looked at her sharply and then relaxed and grinned.

'That's better, Millie! Oh, it's good to see you! I've always wanted to see you that much these past years, you'll never know. We was that close, wasn't we? And here's me with a boychick of my own now, and you never met him – a real little villain he is, a proper lobbus – '

'I'm sure he's charming,' Mildred said.

'Oy, such a word for my wicked little Bernie, eh Poppy?' And Poppy lifted her head and smiled a little wanly at her.

'He is a bit of a handful, Jessie,' she said and then looked at her mother.

'Mama, I hope you didn't mind Jessie bringing me home. I must tell you it wasn't my idea. I meant to come in a cab on my own, indeed I did, but she – ' and she looked across the room at her aunt and then her smile widened. 'I dare say you know how hard it is to control her.'

'I know,' Mildred said and a little of her anger came back. There was a bond between these two that had no right to be there; it ought to be between Mildred and Poppy not Jessie and Poppy –

'I know,' she said again. 'She has always been a forceful person.'

'Hmph.' Jessie made a contemptuous little sound in her throat. 'I should cocoa! Look who's talkin'! I never knew no one like your Ma, Poppy, for bein' stubborn! That's why I'm here. I know you never wanted me to, but these are bad times. Anything could happen, God forbid, to any of us. We could be killed in an air raid, God knows what. That's why I come, Mildred. I looked at this boobalah here and I thought – this is crazy. She has to shlap to and fro, to and fro, to see her own people. It ain't right, and I said to myself, soon's I saw her this afternoon, I said to myself – no, Jessie. Enough is enough. I'm going to tell Mildred, whether she likes it or not. I'm going to tell her. You hear me out is all I ask, okay? And then I'll go away. But I hope you'll hear me out and you'll agree and then we can be a bit like we used to be in the old days. Good friends, eh, Millie? Wasn't I there when you gave this baby here her first breath? Didn't I look after the two of you all those years ago? Ain't we *family*, for God's sake?'

'What is it you are going to tell me, Jessie?' Mildred was still standing by the door, her hands folded in her usual fashion in front of her, and her face was as still and contained as ever it was.

'Why, ain't it obvious?' Jessie cried and flicked a look at Poppy and then at Mildred. 'It don't take no massive brain to work it out, and you was always clever. It's time already, Millie, that's what I want to tell you. Time to forget old scores and to start again. Here's Lizah breakin' his heart to see you again and here's you all on your own, and here's our boobalah who needs a family as tight together as it can be. She *deserves* it. What do you say, Millie, eh? Let Lizah come and see you again, be friends again at least! What do you say?'

20

She leaned on the rail of the ship and watched as the men cast off, and listened to the shouted instructions that echoed all over the dock, concentrating on what they were doing as though it were a matter of great importance that she should do so, almost as though her supervision was necessary for the success of the operation. And then, as the first few inches of space appeared between the ship's side and then widened and stretched as the shore began to diminish, so at last did her own tension begin to loosen. And she pulled back her shoulders and lifted her chin to take a deep breath of the warm evening air.

All around her there were other people staring back at the shore too, leaning on their kit bags with their hats pushed to the backs of their heads, many with cigarettes dangling from the corners of their mouths, as they watched Dover vanish. But they all looked bleak and bereft, and she felt yet another stab of guilt. Oh, it was dreadful to be actually glad to be going back to the horrors of France, glad to be leaving home behind; but she could not help feeling so. And it was not, after all, entirely her own fault. They had behaved so stupidly, all of them, and she almost stamped her foot in rage as she remembered.

At first she had felt dreadful about her mother. To have gone directly to Cable Street from Victoria to see Jessie instead of home to Mama had been a wicked thing to do. Yes, she had been tired, and not thought clearly, yes it was something that just had happened, but once she realized what she had done, she ought not to have compounded it by letting Jessie behave as she had.

Not that it was always possible to control Jessie, she thought now, staring with glazed eyes at the blue water of the Channel creaming away from the sides of the ship below her. She had taken one look at Poppy's face when she had climbed out of the cab, and rushed her into the shop, past the cries of delight and excitement from the customers and from Lily, and virtually pushed her into her usual armchair. She had fussed over her, fed her tea and sandwiches, chattered at her, soothed her, and then, when she had fallen abruptly asleep – for she had indeed been exhausted – had let her sleep as long as she wanted to. And when she had woken suddenly at almost seven o'clock to find the sun lengthening the shadows outside and had been so filled with compunction that she had wept, Jessie had again soothed her and told her firmly she was taking her home –

Oh, it had been dreadful. She could still see Mama's face as she stood there at the head of the stairs looking down at her, still see the anger in it. It had made her feel so alarmed, had actually speeded her heartbeat, that face, and she remembered now the matching anger that had been kindled in her by the whole silly situation. After all, what had been so dreadful about what Jessie had tried to do? To heal breaches, to bring people together – could that be so bad a thing?

Mama thinks so, she told herself miserably then. Mama will not budge from her determination. No matter what Jessie had said, she had sat there implacable and silent. She would not meet Lizah, thank you very much, and did not particularly wish to see Jessie again either. She had almost said as much though thanking her again for bringing her daughter home – and oh, thought her daughter, why did I let Jessie lie like that and say she had met me at Victoria? Why didn't I stand up and say what I felt? That I too was painfully aware of the rifts in my life and would like Mama and Lizah to be friends again, and to let Jessie be part of our lives so that I could stop being a person torn into three separate pieces – why didn't I?

But she hadn't and there was an end of it. But the beginning of her leave had clearly destroyed the rest of it. Mama had tried hard; Poppy had known that, had almost felt the effort she was making, but it had been too late. There lay between the two of them a barrier so wide and so deep that it was impossible. And Jessie, in all her clumsy good-heartedness, had been the one who had made it so much worse than it need have been. And Poppy closed her eyes against the brightness of the glittering sea and tried to think of other things about her leave, other things that might make her feel sad to be going back, like everyone else on this shipload of returning soldiers and nurses and ambulance drivers and airmen. To feel one with them would be comforting; to be as yearning to stay at home as they were would make her feel less strange, a normal person. A *sensible* person.

So she began instead to think about Mabel and her times with her, but that didn't help. Oh, Mabel had been glad enough to see her, had positively whooped with delight when she had found her waiting in the drawing room on her return from the office on Poppy's first full day in London, and had hugged her so warmly and eagerly that for the first time since leaving France Poppy had felt really good. And the evening that followed had been agreeable too – at first. Goosey had been plainly delighted to see her and had cooked a special supper for them all, making Poppy's favourite boiled salmon patties and raiding her precious hoard for the ingredients for a burnt cream pudding, and even Chloe had hugged her and been affectionate for a little while.

But then the evening had drifted away into loneliness, for after supper George Pringle had arrived to take Mabel out, and though she had insisted they remain at home to keep company with her heroic friend, newly returned from Flanders, the fun and closeness were gone. Mabel had eyes and words only for the tiresome George (and the more Poppy saw of him the more jaw-crackingly dull she thought him) and Chloe became very fractious and had to be sent to bed early in disgrace, from which she shrieked at full blast for the remainder of the evening, much to Goosey's fury. It had actually been a relief to slip away and go home to the chill unfriendliness of Leinster Terrace, leaving George and Mabel sitting canoodling foolishly in the drawing room at Norland Square, guiltily glad to be rid of her.

And then there had been the Uncles – and now her face reddened suddenly and she could not stop herself from thinking of what had happened there. At first she had been a little flattered – if uneasy – when Mama had told her that as she was on leave they had made a point of saying they would dine at home one night, a rare thing for them, and Queenie had worked hard to make a special occasion of it for them, producing a beef pie and a piece of crimped cod. But the beef had been tough and gamey and the cod tasteless and that seemed to have made Harold more than usually irritable; for he had started to tease her in the same old hateful way, while staring at her with those sharp knowing eyes of his, with that horrid expression in them that she had learned to fear long ago when she had been just a child.

She had managed not to rise to his taunts and teases, as he made silly jokes about the uselessness of women in general when it came to internal combustion engines, implying that with ambulance drivers drawn from the ranks of women, it was no wonder the death toll in Flanders was so high. She had bitten her tongue when he had made Samuel guffaw as he painted a verbal picture of a troop of women drivers with laden ambulances being defeated by an urgent desire to drive to Paris to see the gowns in the shop windows of the Rue de la

Paix. But when he had said carelessly that, 'Not that the average Tommy would expect any better treatment anyway –' she finally lost her temper.

'What do you know about the average British Tommy?' she had blazed. 'You, sitting here, cosily safe and pretending to be engaged on essential work at your damned bank, while other better men than you are killed to keep you safe, what do you know?'

'Poppy!' Mama had actually gone white at her choice of language, and Samual had guffawed again, but Harold had sat still and silent and stared at her with an ugly look on his face; and then had said with as scathing a sneer in his voice as he could manage, 'My dear girl – don't you think we all know how it is you know so much about Tommies and their likes and dislikes? Clearly you find yourself in your element, mixing with the riff-raff of the world! You see, Mildred? In spite of your efforts, you have reared a hoyden with a tongue like a guttersnipe. You will excuse me. I find the atmosphere less than agreeable –'

And he had pushed back his chair and gone out of the dining room, leaving Samuel looking uneasy and Mildred stricken, and after another long moment Poppy had got to her feet, almost unable to walk with the shakiness in her legs – for she had been swept by such anger at his words that she had been unable to speak – and gone to look for him, to demand that he apologize not just to her but to her mother; and he had been standing in the hall outside, waiting for her, and grinning that hateful grin to which she was so accustomed and which she had learned so long ago to fear.

And at the sight of him her legs had felt even less able to support her, and she had held on to the banisters staring at him, and he had grinned again and said softly, 'You want me to apologize, don't you? I insulted you, didn't I? But there, I dare say you'll be used to it by now, so let me insult you again –'

And he had moved so fast she had been unable to stop him and he had put arms like iron hoops about her and kissed her mouth so suddenly and so roughly she had frozen into immobility. She could still feel the sense of sickness that had risen in her, could still feel the rage that had almost paralysed her, but it wasn't as bad now, for she could also remember what she had done. How when he had let her go she had found her muscles again and swept back her arm and hit him so hard that his eyes had actually watered, and then had hit him again before he could move away.

'If you ever come near me again, I shall tell everyone what you tried to do to me when I was a child,' she had blazed as loudly as she could, wanting people to hear, hoping they would. 'You're a sick, slimy excuse for a man fit only to pester small girls with your lewd attentions, picking on those smaller and weaker than you are. You're not fit to soil your lips with talk of the men I have known in Flanders and been privileged to care for. The lowest Tommy from the dirtiest gutter in the worst of the slums is a better man that you can ever hope to be. Stay in your bank and keep away from the dangers and chances of war. We don't need your sort – it would be better to let the Hun win than to have something as evil as you amongst us!'

And she had managed to make her way back to the dining room and sit down again opposite her mother, who sat in frozen silence, staring down at her plate. Had she heard what she had said to him? Poppy hadn't cared then, and didn't really care now. She had not set eyes on Harold for the rest of her leave, for he had gone to stay at his club, taking Samuel with him, and her mother had given no sign of any awareness that there was anything amiss between her half-brother and her daughter other than that short exchange of words they had had over the dining table.

But it's odd, Poppy thought now, as the gulls wheeled and shrieked overhead and the ship rocked a little more heavily as it met the mid-Channel swell, it's really odd that I feel as I do now. All those years when I was so afraid of him, when I hid away from them both as much as I could, all those years of being miserable about him; none of it mattered any more. He had been horrible, indeed, when she had been about eleven and he had been eighteen or so; he had hidden around corners and jumped out at her, and pretended to be a bear and wrestle her, seeming to play childish games for his little niece's amusement, but all the time being hateful, kissing her with great wet sloppy kisses on her mouth and rubbing himself against her, and trying to reach beneath her skirts. She had hated him and all he was doing and had learned to kick and scratch and bite back in silence for fear of alerting the servants or her mother and being blamed for what was happening, so he had never been more than a nuisance to her; but she had never told anyone and had always felt so bad about it, so sure was she that it was her fault that he had behaved to her so dreadfully.

But now she didn't feel like that. What had happened that night at dinner had somehow put an end to all the bad feelings. She had told him, she had given him some of what he had given her, and she felt cleansed and easy inside herself in a way that was deeply comforting. It was the only good thing she could remember about her leave.

Apart, perhaps, from the afternoons she had spent sitting with Grandmama, listening to her murmur and chatter her usual disconnected nonsense. Poor old Grandmama seemed quite unaware of anything outside her own bedroom, indeed her own bed. She knew nothing of any war, and talked at Poppy only about the balls and parties she had gone to as a young girl back in the seventies; and Poppy had found that soothing.

For the rest of her leave she had spent some time with Mabel, choosing to meet her for lunches mostly, and going to Norland Square only once or twice again to play gooseberry while George Pringle fussed over her friend, and going to the theatre in the evenings, content to be alone and enjoying what she saw. She would pretend sometimes that Bobby was with her, but that was too depressing, so instead she spent her mornings writing long accounts of all that she saw and all that was happening in London, prattling of *The Bing Boys* and George Robey, of *A Little Bit of Fluff* at the Criterion and Alice Delysia in *Odds and Ends* at the Ambassadors, and, in more serious vein, of Mrs Patrick Campbell in Shaw's new shocker, *Pygmalion*, filling page after page of her notepaper with her big scrawl, and sending the resulting packages off to the *Dispatch* who forwarded all his mail, hoping he would receive them but knowing there was every chance he wouldn't. All she knew about Bobby was that he was behind the lines somewhere. The war correspondents were supposed to be bear-led always by someone from Staff and to be told where to go, but she knew from his dispatches to the paper, which she read avidly, that he was far too independent a man to tolerate that. He was everywhere, she found, sometimes at an airfield and reporting what was happening with the dog fights the pilots involved themselves in when they went up ostensibly to reconnoitre and take photographs over the enemy's lines; sometimes well up to the Front where the shelling was thickest; occasionally behind the lines at Headquarters, pestering senior officers for opinions, news and comments. A good journalist, she thought with a glow, when she put the paper down. He's a *good* journalist. And I wish he wasn't. I wish he was here at home, with me. I wish, I wish –

But now her leave was over and she turned her head to squint over her shoulder against the orange glow of the setting sun at the approaching docks of Calais. She was back and London and all the people there were so far away; just a few miles in reality, but an eternity away in her thoughts. And she felt good about where she was. It may be a hellish stupid war where decent men were senselessly destroyed and she might have deep doubts about what the war was for and whether it was justified, but that didn't matter at the moment. She was here where she was needed and where she had an important job to do, and she pulled her war-worn tunic more snugly about her hips, and tugged her forage cap more neatly over her curly hair, and picking up her kit bag moved into the crowd of people now slowly making their way forward to the gangplank. There was some joking going on around her now; it was as though the men, now that Dover and home were far behind them, had found once more their resilience and were expressing it in laughter, and she was jostled by a cheerful squad of corporals who once they realized what they had done, made way for her with great care and insisted on carrying her kit. And she thought only briefly of Harold's sneers at these young underfed and unhealthy-looking Tommies, who treated her as though she were a duchess, and smiled warmly at them. Yes, it was good to be back with all these marvellous men. They were hers, people she cared about and cared for, and they made her life worthwhile in a way it had never been before. And she actually linked arms with one of the corporals – an unheard-of gesture by a lady ambulance driver – and walked steadily down the gangplank and back into hell.

21

Within two days she felt she had never been on leave; within a week it was as though England didn't even exist. There was only the here and the now, and the stench of illness and purulent wounds, ether and carbolic, the taste of rough hospital food and the ache in her back and legs and feet.

She had returned to find that the Commandant, a distracted lady who had been an acceptable committee worker in her home village, but who in France was sorely out of her depth, and who had to struggle to maintain full control of her troop of twelve ambulances and their personnel, and who generally failed to create anything more than a muddle, had promoted her.

'I do so wish Mrs Baker had been able to come out here to take command. I was so much happier there at Pirbright dealing with the Commissariat – but there it is. She is needed there to continue the training, so I must manage as best I can,' Miss Jessamy said, and pushed her hair back under her cap with a vague gesture, and not for the first time Poppy ached to pin her senior's hair up properly for her, so that she could spend less time fiddling with it and more on sorting herself out. 'So, I shall take you from the active driving roster, my dear, and bring you in here to assist me. I cannot deal with the muddle at all without help. And I believe you speak tolerable French?'

'I learned at school,' Poppy said guardedly, not at all liking the way this conversation was going. 'But I am by no means fluent –'

'That's no matter,' Miss Jessamey said and waved her hand vaguely. 'You can read these wretched orders they send us and deal with the requisitions and so forth and then –'

'But please, Ma'am, I joined to be a driver,' Poppy ventured to argue, knowing that Miss Jessamy was weak as well as disorganized and would be hard put to it to withstand any resistance. 'I would be most unhappy to –'

'Oh, please, Miss Amberly, you must understand – I am not taking you from driving for always! It is just that at present it is more vital we sort out the confusion here and get ourselves running smoothly. And then I promise you, you shall drive again. I know how much you would hate to be tied to a desk – I do so loathe it myself –' And she peered at Poppy with anxious myopic eyes and Poppy capitulated. It was indeed high time the place was better organized, and she looked around the office, set up in a roughly converted hut in the grounds of the school which had been taken over to act as base hospital, and saw the heaps of papers on chairs and on the floor, the out-of-date notices on the board, and sighed.

'Well, if you are sure, Ma'am,' she said and Miss Jessamy beamed at her.

'Oh, indeed I am. You will drive again as soon as may be. But first let us see what we can do to reorganize ourselves –'

So the work had begun. She came on duty at six in the morning, an hour and a half before the rest of the day staff while the night nurses bustled about the wards and dealt with such of the morning cleaning that could be done, and set to work tidying the dreadful tangle of orders, counter orders, requisitions and dispatches that had built up into a great drift of paper on Miss Jessamy's desk. Then she handed over to Miss Jessamy who came yawning into the office at nine, with strict instructions about what she might and might not touch (and to Poppy's relief she did as she was told) and went on duty in the wards.

It had almost been arranged by the French authorities that the British FANYs would at last be handed over to the British Staff to add to their forces, since the Government had finally agreed to send women to the war, but while the last details of the transfer were being dealt with, work went on as it had under the French, and that meant that the lady drivers, in addition to their responsibility for and work with their vehicles, would work shifts on the wards at the Calais base hospital. While half of the troop, some twenty girls allowing for sickness and Blighty leave, shared the labour of driving the twelve ambulances with occasional help from semi-trained orderlies when there weren't enough FANYs to permit two to each vehicle which was the rule, the remainder worked alongside the Army nurses in the hospital wards. At first there had been some snobbery on the part of the fully-trained British Sisters about these first-aiders, as they tended to call the FANYs, but that had been in the early days. Now, almost two years into the war – could it really be so long? – they accepted all the help they could get, gladly and eagerly, and treated people only on the quality of what they did. And Poppy was well liked by the Sisters, for she was quick and resourceful and seemed to have an unending store of energy. When frailer, more delicate, girls began to wilt and burst into tears of fatigue after an eight-hour shift, Poppy, sturdy and determined, seemed able to go on without too much trouble, and was usually willing to do so; and that being so, she was put upon a good deal. She knew she was, but it didn't matter; she enjoyed working with the men, enjoyed taking care of their needs whatever they were, and even began to think seriously of taking her nursing training when the war was over – would it ever be over? – and she would be seeking a new life.

But meanwhile she worked hard, usually until well after six in the evening. And then, after a quick meal snatched in the canteen – and by the time she got there it was usually only left-overs she was offered – she went back to Miss Jessamy to sort out whatever tangles she had made that day, and to set all right that she could for the next morning. It was exhausting, it was draining, and it left no room for any thoughts other than work. But that was one of its major virtues. While she laboured so hard, there was no opportunity to think of the way things were at home, and slowly the problems of her mother and Jessie and Lizah slid away into the deepest background of her mind. And she liked it that way.

The summer slid away into a rich autumn and the food improved a little; butter and meat began to come up to the base hospital from Norman and Breton farms away to the west, and then fruit began to arrive and sometimes wine and Calvados, and everyone began to cheer up. The war seemed to have moved away a little; now people talked of Gallipoli and Salonika rather than of Flanders and France, though there was the battle of Loos, which the British seemed to have won and which lifted the soldiers' hearts considerably. But then news came of a nurse being executed as a spy in Brussels and that threw the whole hospital into angry despair. One of the Sisters had been a friend of Miss Edith Cavell when they had worked together at the Archway Hospital in Highgate, and she took the news hard, and could no longer work for a while. And as a result, for one alarming week, Poppy was left in charge of a ward because of the lack of someone more senior to take over. She dealt with dressing suppurating wounds, with applying hot packs and poultices to men with swollen legs and feet, gave out the necessary medicines and saw that all her patients were fed and kept clean and warm, with the help of just one wiry little orderly and those of the patients who were fit to help. It was an horrendous week, and yet deep down she enjoyed it. The responsibility suited her, and the effort she put in seemed so worthwhile that she didn't mind the way her whole body shrieked its weariness at her.

In December, there were great upheavals everywhere: Joffre became French Commander-in-Chief and Sir Douglas Haig came out to take over from Sir John French as British Chief-of-Staff and this led to all sorts of ripples at the hospital. Several of the senior Sisters were transferred to other hospitals up the line and all the French personnel left to be replaced with raw new people from England though, for administrative reasons, the FANYs continued to be attached to the French Army. And, once again, Poppy found herself working flat out, for she was now one of the most senior people there, for all her lowly status as just a FANY. The new Commandant was fortunately a more efficient woman, however, so at least Poppy was relieved of the need for office work, and for that she was grateful. But she was pressed into service as an extra pair of hands in the operating theatres, where they were extra busy as they often were as winter weather brought in more and more sick men from the trenches, suffering as much from the effects of exposure as from war wounds. And she learned a lot, and she grew up even more in those long hard weeks of working long hard hours day after day. Sometimes she felt so old it was as though she had never been young –

She was offered leave, in a rather half-hearted fashion, in January but refused, much to the Commandant's obvious relief, for there were rumours of a big push coming somewhere to the south-east, and she needed all the staff she could get.

But when she realized that it was Poppy's birthday and actually her twenty-first, in the last week of the month, the Commandant managed to find time to make a party for her. The wiry little orderly scrounged several bottles of Calvados as well as some *vin du pays*, the kitchen managed to obtain, no questions asked, a couple of scrawny chickens and a piece of fat bacon and made a good enough *choucroute* from them and the only easily available food, cabbage, and everyone who could be spared from the wards came to the main mess hut to help celebrate Poppy's coming of age, amused because clearly she had joined up under age. And she looked at them all holding their glasses up to her and wept, much to her own fury and to everyone else's amusement, for she was very touched by the affection and support of all these strangers who were now so close to her, and so important a part of her life.

She was given many presents, too; some of the Tommies in the wards heard of the party and offered her precious cigarettes and soap and bars of chocolate, and one gave her the much prized Uhlan helmet he had salvaged from a battle last year. It wasn't easy to find a way to insist he kept it, but she managed by asking him to take it back to blighty when he went next week – he had lost a leg – and promising that one day she would come to see him in Middlesbrough and collect it.

And then there were the presents from home; the inevitable food parcel from Jessie, groaning with goodies of all kinds, enough to feed half the nurses in the hospital, and a small gold wristlet watch from Lizah, which made her eyes prickle with tears. Mabel sent her an absurd spangled scarf in pink silk chiffon which made her laugh aloud with pleasure at the sheer irrelevance of it, and Chloe sent a hand-painted picture of herself sadly blotted, but almost recognizable. Goosey sent her warm hand-knitted gloves which were very welcome, and her mother – Mama sent a letter saying she could not think what would be the most suitable gift for her twenty-first birthday, so she had deposited fifty pounds in her name in the bank to spend later as she chose. A munificent gift indeed; but Poppy ran the silk-spangled scarf through her fingers and put her gold watch around her wrist and tried on her gloves, and didn't think about the money at all.

After that, settling down to the slog of routine work seemed more difficult, until, almost as though the fates in the form of Sir Douglas Haig had known how she was feeling, orders came in February that the whole FANY troop was to move on.

'We're going to Revigny,' the Commandant said crisply at a specially called meeting of all those who were available. 'There is an Urgent Cases hospital being set up there, and we are to service it as ambulance drivers and as first-aiders when necessary in the wards. You are to load each ambulance with as many stores as you can get in, and set out in a convoy. You'll be accompanied by an Army unit, who will give you any necessary cover. You have just four hours to be ready to go. Miss Amberly!' And she looked round to find Poppy. 'You are senior in command. I cannot follow until the new Commandant arrives here to take over. So, here are your orders and the necessary maps. However, the Army Major giving you cover will deal with the route planning so it shouldn't be too difficult – as fast as you all can now, move!'

And move they did. Poppy supervised the loading of all the ambulances with bedding and dressings, drugs and medicines and some clothing, for the men who were brought in from major battles often had their clothing virtually blown away, together with the FANYs' own kit and some essential food supplies, in case it was not possible to victual on the road. And at dawn on 20 February they were ready to set off.

Poppy was driving the *Queen of Flanders* for the first leg. The old vehicle was showing signs of wear now; the canvas cover was frayed and shabby and the bodywork was pitted and chipped from shrapnel and some bullet holes. But the engine was running sweetly, thanks to the careful overhaul Poppy had managed to give it in the last hours before the convoy left, and driving was easy. She stretched a little, luxuriating in driving again; she had not realized how much she had missed it. They were to liaise with their Army column at Amiens, and there was a long drive ahead through the wrecked roads over which the armies had fought and refought every yard; but today she did not see the stunted dead trees or the ruined houses. These were things she was so used to they made no real impact any more. All she thought of now was the job she had to do.

Her companion for this journey was the taciturn Flora Gordon and for that she was grateful. Flora had proved herself to be a much more agreeable person than their first meeting, all that time ago in the East End of London, would have suggested. She was energetic and quick to learn, and Poppy was glad to have her support. But she was also glad that she felt no need to chatter, and sat there beside her wrapped in her greatcoat and with half-fingered mittens on her hands as she clutched a pencil and a drawing block. She always had one in her pocket, and Poppy had long ago decided to close her eyes to the rules that forbade such activity when the ambulances were on the move. She knew that Flora could be relied upon to know when to stow away her drawing and to concentrate on the work they were there to do, and in the meantime produced excellent sketches of much that they passed. Right now, Poppy saw, as she stole a sideways glance, she was drawing the rear of the ambulance in front, in which one rather anxious looking and very new FANY fresh out from England was perched uneasily on a pile of folded blankets, clutching her kit in her arms and with her feet set awkwardly on the spare drums of petrol every ambulance carried. It was a good drawing, witty, in spite of its bleakness, and caught exactly the ambience of their journey: the rutty pit-holed road, the grey wet fields streaming past them and their own breath hanging in white clouds before their faces. Let Flora draw, thought Poppy; it kept her happy and there was all too little happiness here in France now.

At Amiens they picked up their convoy, a British Division fighting with the French Army for this sector of the Front, and it proved to be of seventeen lorries all loaded to their axles with ammunition. Poppy looked wryly at the Major who was leading it and said, 'They could have chosen a safer escort for us!'

He grinned. 'I wouldn't have minded a safer load myself! Still never mind, Sister. If we get a direct hit we all blow together. There'll be no trouble – we'll just meet on the other side of the pearly gates. Now, I'll lead, you sandwich your girls in one and one, a lorry on each side of 'em, and there'll be four right behind you to bring up the rear. You'll be safe enough – '

'I have no doubt of it, Major,' Poppy said. 'And – er – when we bivouac – I've got some Calvados here we didn't like to leave behind at Calais. You might like a little of it?'

'We have an appointment, Sister,' the Major said and grinned widely and Poppy grinned back. He looked little older than she was herself, she thought, though with his rank he had to be at least twenty-five or so; though it was hard to say these days. So many officers had been killed at Ypres and Loos and on the Marne that many men who were much too young to be more than the merest lieutenants found themselves sporting crowns on their sleeves.

The journey seemed interminable. They reached Laon on the first night and bivouacked there, boiling tea over oil stoves in the back of their ambulances, well away from the vulnerable ammunition convoy, and settling for the usual bully beef and rough bread as their main meal. But the Major remembered the Calvados and came and shared it with them, bringing some of his men with him (as Poppy said dryly, 'It's as well it was more than just a single bottle, wasn't it?') and afterwards they sat huddled in their heavy coats, their hats pulled down over their ears, and sang softly all the popular songs they could think of. When the Major led them into 'If You Were The Only Girl In The World' Poppy felt her eyes sting suddenly. It had been such a long time ago that she had sat in a London theatre and watched *The Bing Boys* and heard that song; such a long time since she had written that long letter to Bobby telling him all about it. And where was he now? She still hadn't heard from him, still didn't know where she could reach him. That he was all right was clear – copies of the *Dispatch* only three or four days' old at Calais had borne his articles, and that had comforted her. But listening on a bitter February night to the banal words – 'There would be such wonderful things to do, I would say such wonderful things to you' she felt alone and miserable as though nothing would ever be right and happy ever again.

But then she slept, albeit uneasily, in her sleeping bag in the back of the *Queen of Flanders* and next morning they had to set off again, on their way to Reims and then to Châlons-sur-Marne, trundling their noisy grinding way through the muddy snow and the frozen fields left ruined by the war.

They reached the railway line at Vitry-le-François at midnight on 21 February and as they pulled off the road into a muddy field where they were to spend the night before pushing on in the morning towards Revigny, and switched off their engines and climbed down stiffly from their driving seats, Poppy lifted her head and listened. There was a sound of shunting from the railway, and the shouts of people working on the lines, and a certain amount of traffic on the road, but beyond that she could hear a soft distant rumbling and she thought with a sudden lift of fear – guns. They're shelling somewhere; but then the rumbling seemed to stop and she thought – I imagined it.

But when she woke next morning after another uneasy and hungry night, she heard it again and once more tried to tell herself she had imagined it, but when she came stomping back to her ambulance from the hastily organized latrines at the far end of their field she found the Major standing, legs akimbo and head up, listening at the side of his lorry.

'It's started,' he said shortly. 'They told us it was on the way. Oh, God, this one will be hell.'

'What is it?' She was alert, feeling his fear crawling into her belly.

'Verdun is my guess. It was what they were expecting anyway. Listen to it – It's like a giant carpet being beaten – thud, thud – '

They set out in sharp order, not stopping to make hot tea but settling for cold milk begged by Flora from a nearby farm, and Poppy, who was driving again now, settled grimly to the remains of the journey. They were snaking along a long road that ran beside the railway line, and which, the map told them, would bring them to the outskirts of Revigny-sur-Ornain, where the Urgent Cases hospital was, and all the way the noise of the shelling got louder and louder. Clearly, they were driving into the bombardment, wherever it was, and looking at the maps, Verdun seemed a likely place. The ambulance shuddered and jumped as the combination of potholes in the road, slippery frozen mud and the reverberations of the guns attacked it, and she hung on to the steering wheel grimly, as though her hands were glued to it.

And then they met the refugees. At first it was just a trickle of people pushing carts, with here and there a few horses to help them, but then the trickle thickened to a steady stream as people with bundles on their backs and babies' perambulators full of household goods came trudging towards them. Poppy saw one man who had clearly brought the whole contents of his shop in his child's perambulator, for his wife stumbled alongside with a large and clearly heavy baby in her arms, while he, tight-mouthed, pushed his ribbons and laces and bolts of silk and cambric away from the noise of the guns and the threat of the Germans. There were old women with birds in cages and children with struggling pet dogs, and crying women and angry shouting men. And none of them paid the convoy any attention, only pulling to the side of the road and walking steadily on as they passed.

Soon the convoy caught up with marching troops, and though Poppy in the *Queen of Flanders* was set well to the back of the procession she could see, when the road curved, what was happening ahead, and there they were, French colonial troops, pushing their way through the dreary morning towards the even heavier noise of bombardment.

A runner came back up the convoy to carry information from the Major to the ambulance drivers and Poppy leaned out precariously and shouted, 'What's happening?' and the man, breathless with his efforts shouted, 'German attack – definitely Verdun, the Major says – you're to spread out in case one of us gets hit. Not far now – ' And he was off again, loping down the line of slowly moving lorries and ambulances, disappearing into the line of refugees who pressed them on both sides.

Soon, Poppy thought, soon; another couple of hours and we should be there. And please, let there be time for a hot meal and maybe a bath and a little rest before we go to work. I'm getting tired – very tired – and she blinked her hot red eyes to try to clear her vision, and still all she could see was that stream of sullen refugees and the next lorry, now fifty yards in front at a safer distance.

'It's another seventeen kilometres,' Flora said, lifting her head from her map. 'Not long now. We'll get some coffee if we're lucky once we're there. Shall I take over?'

'No,' Poppy said and managed a sideways grin. 'I can do it. Just keep reminding me about the coffee, that's all. With that in sight I can manage anything.'

And by five in the afternoon she had managed it. The line of ambulances hooted a melancholy goodbye to the ammunition convoy which went on towards Verdun, and turned into the grounds of the small château that was the hospital. And thirty-seven exhausted, grimy FANYs tumbled out of their ambulances and stretched and grinned at each other and shouted congratulations at their safe arrival over the din of the guns, which still pounded in their ears like an eternity of mad drumming. But never mind, Poppy thought, suddenly elated. We're here. A little rest is all we need and then we can get to work.

22

But there was to be very little rest before a great deal of work. Poppy led the way into the hospital, her troop of weary FANYs following at her heels, and stopped aghast at what she saw. Clearly, the place had been caught in a flood of casualties, for there was uproar everywhere. The main hall of the once stately château was now a litter of stretchers, set side by side on the ground for the most part though some were put up on makeshift beds, and it was clear to Poppy at first glance that most of these men were severely injured. There were few of the minor wounds that were swift and easy to deal with. Each and every one of these men would need prolonged treatment if they were to survive; and many would not. The whole place seemed to reverberate with the tension of that awareness of death, and the stench of blood and cordite and sweat and oil was thick in her nostrils and the sound of crying and groaning was so loud and pitiful it made her feel a sensation in her belly that was more like anger than anything else. There were nurses rushing about everywhere and doctors working doggedly over stretchers and one man in the uniform of a French medical officer bounced up and down in the middle of it all, shrieking and waving his arms around a good deal as he tried to organize operations in some sort of logical fashion. Poppy stared at him and then at the scene around her and said curtly to Flora, 'Take the girls back outside for a moment. I'll see what is happening here –' and went plunging in through the hubbub towards him

He was a short fat man with pince-nez incongruously perched on his nose and his face was gleaming with sweat as he stood there in the middle of the vast room shouting at the top of his voice; not that it made much difference for there was so much noise anyway that however loudly he shouted few people could hear him.

'Sir,' Poppy shouted at him, knowing she had to try to top his shrill tones. 'Sir, I've brought the twelve ambulances from Calais –'

He ignored her, berating a passing doctor who paid him no attention at all, and Poppy reached out and tugged on his sleeve.

'Sir,' she bawled. 'I've brought the ambulance troop – but they're very tired and need rest. If you'll note we've arrived, I'll –'

'*Que'est-ce que vous dit?* the man roared at her and then went on in French so rapid and so disjointed that Poppy could hardly comprehend a word of it and she shook her head and roared back at him, 'English ambulances, sir – just arrived from Calais – twelve of them –'

'Ambulances?' The little man blinked and then peered more closely at her. '*Grâce au ciel! Combien? Douze? Bon – allez! Immédiate-ment – tout de suite, à –*'

'No!' Poppy shouted back. 'We're not going anywhere yet. My girls need some rest and some food or they'll be unfit for anything at all. I'm just reporting on duty – but I have to take them to be fed and rested before we do another thing. And the ambulances need petrol and a clean-up. Then we'll be ready for whatever you want –'

Again the little man shouted at her in his incomprehensible French and she stood there shaking her head stubbornly as he ranted on, suddenly very aware of her own fatigue and needing badly to get away from this dreadful place to curl up somewhere and sleep. And she was about to turn away and ignore this stupid man the way everyone else seemed to do when someone stopped beside her and said in a low voice that somehow made itself heard in spite of the din, 'May I be of help?'

Poppy turned gratefully to the sound of that quiet English voice and said, 'Oh please! I'm trying to report to him – I gather he's the Commandant, the way he's bawling at everyone – but I can't send my girls out again immediately, which he seems to want. They've just driven all the way from Calais with the barest minimum of rest on the way and they're at their ropes' ends, truly they are. Can't they be sent to rest just for a few hours? That's all I want but he just doesn't seem to understand –'

'Poor chap hasn't had much rest himself this past thirty-six hours,' the other said and grinned at her. He was a young, fresh-faced man in the uniform of a British medical officer, as far as she could see under the rubber apron he had tied round his middle, and he winked at her and then turned to the little man, who was still standing jabbering between them, and spoke to him in a low voice in French as rapid and apparently perfect as the little man's own. And at last he listened and then after a moment nodded and turned away after one last look of cold dislike at Poppy. He threw some curt instructions back over his shoulder and then went hurrying away into the mêlée in hot pursuit of a nurse who had caught his attention and who was clearly doing something of which he disapproved.

'You'll have to be patient with people here,' her rescuer said. 'The French are taking a terrible pasting at Verdun, and there are very few of our chaps here to help. They weren't ready for this bombardment and they didn't expect anything like this volume of wounded. But we'll manage, somehow – look, there are rest quarters of a sort at the back of the château. They're the old stables, actually. Follow the building round to the right and you'll find 'em. There's a tanker of petrol round there too, so you can top up your ambulances, and there should be Army cooks around about who'll give you something to eat. Come back when you feel you can, hmm? We're going to need you soon. Some of these chaps can be taken out down to the railhead to be trained back to Calais, and then I dare say they'll need you further up the line towards the Front to bring out the men being injured up here. If it goes on the way it started, then we're going to need every spare space we can get here –'

'Thanks,' Poppy said. 'We'll get going as soon as my girls are fit. I'm Poppy Amberly, by the way –'

'Joe Pomfret,' the other said. 'Off you go then – lucky girl. I could do with some rest too –' And then he was gone, hurrying through the serried rows of stretchers towards a room at the far side, which Poppy suspected was some sort of operating theatre, going by the traffic of stretchers in and out of it.

She felt considerable guilt as she made her way back to the outside. To have insisted so firmly on rest for her girls when everyone else here was clearly at the edge of exhaustion was a little selfish, perhaps – but then she saw them standing huddled there in the fitful light of a few burning torches in the courtyard and the sickly gleam of the occasional Very lights overhead, and knew she had been right. To let these girls out on the roads again would be sheer murder. They were in no fit state to drive and would not be till they had food and sleep.

They managed to find a comparatively dry corner of the stables and a pile of straw palliasses and, to everyone's intense joy, a small primus stove on which water could be heated for washing as well as for tea, and for the next hour there was a quiet bustle as they washed in a rather sketchy fashion, but at least got some of their grime off, and drank with thirsty gratitude hot stewed tea well-laced with thickly sweet condensed milk. One of the Army cooks spotted them, and arrived with piles of bread and plum-and-apple jam, which they ate greedily, they were so hungry, and then they slept, curled up against each other on the straw, as Poppy lay beside them and thought sleepily – I've got to get proper quarters for them somehow. This is dreadful – they can't cope like this – and then fell asleep herself with the suddenness of an exhausted baby.

And when they woke to the bitterness of a February dawn that was spangled with frost and thick with mist she was still fretting over her responsibility to the girls of whom she had been given charge. There were the wounded too, to think about, of course; soon they would be filling their ambulances and ferrying those groaning bleeding wrecks away towards the railhead and also back from the Front, but right now all that seemed to matter to her were these white-faced girls drooping so wearily around her as one after the other they struggled awake; and she was short-tongued with them as she urged them to dress and make tea, needing to hide her concern under a brusque exterior.

And that seemed to help, for her sharp words needled them and gradually they lost their droopiness and began to be a little more alert, even perky, and at just after seven they came out of their stables to the even more bitter cold of the yard to check their vehicles and top up the petrol tanks, ready at last, in Poppy's anxious estimate, to do the work they had come to do.

There was no sign of the excitable little Commandant when she reported back into the hospital, nor of her new friend Joe Pomfret, and she was obscurely glad of that, feeling ashamed of her helplessness the night before. The place was as busy as ever, though, with even more stretchers now lying there, impossible though it had seemed last night to get in any more, and she lifted her head and listened again to the din of the guns which had started once more to pound the air; the very walls seemed to shake and those men who had been dozing stirred uneasily on their stretchers and some of them began to cry out with their pain again.

One of the senior nurses spotted her and beckoned her over with relief.

'Ambulances?' she said. 'Glory be! Listen, can you clear that far room there? There's a train leaving Revigny at ten to take them north – and then there are three of the forward dressing stations which can't cope because they're choked with stretchers. You'll need to get their men down here as fast as you can. It's about ten miles to Le Petit Monthairon, which is the clearing station, so it shouldn't be too bad a journey though they tell me the roads are bad – anyway, see what you can do, please –' And she turned back to the dressings she was doing on a leg so mangled that Poppy couldn't bear to look at the mess of muscle and bone splinters that lay there.

'I'll split the troop,' she said, thinking fast. 'Each ambulance can take six stretchers – we've got equipment to layer them – and even a couple of walking wounded – how many to go to Revigny railhead?'

'About sixty,' Sister said, not lifting her eyes from her work.

'And I've got about three hours to do it in. Right – six ambulances for Le Petit Monthairon, and six for the railway run. Where's the paperwork?'

'Sister in charge in there – Mary McLeod – she'll accompany them together with a couple of sisters already there at the station – all right, old chap – almost there now,' as the man beneath her hands groaned and tried to push her away. 'Almost there –'

The next few hours were a wilderness of busyness for Poppy; making sure that all the men she loaded on to the first six ambulances were properly documented for their return to Calais and then to French hospitals in Normandy and Brittany; checking that adequate supplies of dressings were packed for each man, and that accommodation for the accompanying Sisters was found in each ambulance, took great concentration, and the task wasn't helped by a sudden new influx of wounded brought by stretcher bearers directly from the road. A low-flying German plane had shot up a section of the main artery to Verdun and had done so with no discrimination at all. Soldiers were mixed up with refugees, including women and children and even some Germans who had been taken prisoner and were being shifted down the lines towards the camps in the rear. Poppy managed to get her contingent of men out of the big second room being used as a ward just in time to allow this new wave of wounded to be brought in, and she hurried past the screaming figures on the stretchers, trying not to show how the sight and above all the smell of them affected her; for their anguish was indeed sickening.

But once the first six ambulances were away, with clear instructions to come back to shift the next batch of patients to the railhead in good time, she was free to lead the remaining six on the road north to Verdun, and she pulled out into the main road from the château with a load of extra dressings to supply the forward stations and stretchers ready to bring back as many wounded as she could possibly carry; and her heart sank as she saw what lay ahead.

The road was filled with traffic; a slow-moving stream of lorries, armoured vehicles and supply wagons oozed along the cracked surface as columns of marching infantry eddied and swirled round them, travelling in all directions. There was even a trickle still of refugees, though how there could be any civilians left in the war after so many long hours of appalling shelling Poppy could not imagine. There was only one thing for it, she decided, and she did it; she pulled the *Queen of Flanders* out on to the left-hand side of the road and with her klaxon blaring as constantly as she could make it do so, she pushed her way through the oncoming people, forcing them to the muddy frozen fields at the side of the road.

Some of the drivers of the lorries they were passing leaned out of the cabs and cursed her, but others grinned and waved her on, once they saw the red crosses that proclaimed their task on the sides of the vehicles, and somehow, by dint of the maddest driving ever, she managed to push her little troop the ten miles up the road to Verdun in just two and a half hours – an effort which, she was to discover later, was regarded by everyone who had been on the road as little short of superhuman.

Getting back wasn't quite so bad. They had plenty of willing hands to help load the ambulances with the wounded at Le Petit Monthairon; outside the canvas lean-tos that made up the forward station there were stretchers bearing men waiting to get into the clearing station to be dealt with and until those who had already been patched up ready for the journey to the Urgent Cases hospital were sent on their way, there was nothing that could be done for them. So everyone who was able to help was only too eager to set to. And she was ready to take to the road back to Revigny again within an hour.

And again, with klaxon blaring and Flora beside her leaning out to look ahead and to make sure the way was clear, she pushed her way through the hubbub towards Revigny and delivered her wounded at around four in the afternoon. Neither she nor any of her girls had stopped for food, but while the Sisters supervised the stretcher bearers carrying the men into the hospital they snatched hot tea and bully beef sandwiches and then set out again; if they could get in one more run between now and midnight, they might be able to fit in yet another before stopping for the night for, as Poppy told Flora hopefully, there was surely a let up in the pressure of the traffic on the road once it was dark?

But there wasn't, and it was almost one in the morning before she once more jumped out of her cab, stiff and awkward and with every muscle in her shoulders and back aching from her battle with the steering wheel over the potholed roads, to see her wounded into the hospital.

The little French Commandant had reappeared now and was out in the yard of the château still shouting as hysterically as ever, but now he seemed to be having more effect. People were obeying his screamed orders, and Poppy looked at him with withering contempt before turning away to call the stretcher bearers to start pulling her men out of the ambulances. She was tired, but all the same it ought to be possible to go back just once more; the road was indeed easing up now, and she might manage another run before four in the morning? Then they'd give up in order to get some sleep while the other girls, with the six ambulances which had had the easier railhead run, took over the collection of troops from Verdun and Le Petit Monthairon.

But, suddenly, the little fat man was behind her once again screaming as usual and she shook her head at him, trying to make him see she did not understand, as the stretcher bearers who had come when she had waved at them hesitated and stopped work.

'C'est impossible.' the little man cried. 'Impossible! Il n'y a pas de lits, ici – prenez ces blesses autre part – il n'y a pas de lits, ici – c'est impossible –'

'Somewhere else?' Poppy stared at him blankly. 'Take them somewhere else? Where, you silly little man? Where am I supposed to take them?' The strain of the day, and indeed of all the long days that had led up to it ever since she had come to France, seemed to come to a great final tension and she actually knew it as a physical thing. Her belly felt tight as a drum and her head seemed about to burst with fury. 'You tell me to take them elsewhere? Are you out of your mind? I've just brought them down from the line – there's nowhere else to take them! This is the only place – so I'm unloading them and then I'm going back for more – and more, do you hear me? There are hundreds of them up there – hundreds and hundreds, and you're going to have to take them here, every last damned one of them, so stop your stupid shrieking and get out of my way!' And she actually set both hands in front of him on his chest and pushed him hard and called back over her shoulder at the stretcher bearers, 'Get them out – get these men out and inside! At once, you hear me? At once!'

The stretcher bearers, who were also French, began to shout back at her, and at the Commandant who also started his shouting once more and the din was excruciating, almost drowning out the ever-present pounding of the big guns up the line, and Poppy's head seemed to swell even more with the tension of it all. And then, as she turned to push her way back to the ambulance and to start unloading the wounded herself, if need be, she saw a man come darting out of the crowd of stretcher bearers, one hand held high with a sort of T bar held in it and the other close to his face and for a moment she couldn't understand what was happening. And then there was a great flash of blinding white light and she knew and turned and shouted at the man at the top of her lungs.

'Come and help, you blithering idiot. Don't stand there taking damn fool photographs! Come and help!'

And after one startled moment the man did just that, stowing his camera and his flash stick into the knapsack that hung from one shoulder and then coming with a will to help her pull the first stretcher out of the interior of the ambulance.

It was an action that seemed to operate like a log pulled out of a jam. After one brief moment the stretcher bearers surged towards the ambulance too and in a matter of moments, every ambulance was being unloaded as the little man almost jumped up and down in his fury, his face growing redder and redder as he screamed at them to stop. But now no one took any notice at all.

It wasn't until the ambulances were at last emptied and she had found an English-speaking Sister to hand the paperwork to and was ready to take the ambulances back to the Front again that Poppy suddenly realized what had happened. Someone had helped her – but not just someone; it was someone she badly needed to talk to; and she went running out of the château to find the man with the camera.

Outside in the yard there was the usual din, with only the flash of lights in the sky from the bombardment to show what was going on and she stood there uncertainly for a moment, staring round eagerly and then feeling sick with disappointment. He was nowhere to be seen, and suddenly it was the most important thing in the world that she should find him again, and she almost wept with the fear that she wouldn't.

And then it happened again; that great blinding flash of light as a magnesium flare went up and she turned and ran headlong towards it. Where magnesium burned there would be her photographer.

And she found him, almost knocking him over as she ran into him and he held out one hand warningly, guarding his camera with the other and protested, 'Hey, take it easy, young lady! You tryin' to kill me, for God's sake? And me a non-combatant too!'

'You're an American –' she said and the wave of bitter disappointment that rose in her was like a wash of cold water, and she bit her lip and turned away. 'I'm sorry.'

'Sorry you battered me, or sorry I'm an American?' His voice was friendly and cheerful and she shook her head at him in exasperation. He had no right to be so cheerful when she was so disappointed.

'Sorry you're an American,' she snapped. 'I'd hoped you were with the British Press corps –'

'But I am,' he said and grinned at her in the darkness so that his teeth glinted a little. 'David Deveen, at your service, Ma'am, working for the *New York Trib* but what the hell – we're all in this together! I'm bivouacked with the whole damn British Press corps, and with the French, and I wouldn't be one bit surprised we had a few Canucks and Aussies too in amongst us. Very democratic, we warriors of the word and picture are –'

She caught her breath with a surge of hope as physical as the disappointment had been, and reached out and grabbed at his sleeve. 'Oh, that's wonderful – wonderful! Are – is there anyone there from the *Dispatch* in London?'

'The *Dispatch*?' He frowned. 'Now let me see. *The Times* we have – and a more boring fella – well, never mind. And the *Daily Herald* – he's a great guy – and the *Morning Post* and – oh, sure we have! That is, if the guy I'm thinking of is the *Dispatch* man. Bobby Bradman – d'you know the name?'

23

She was never to feel a greater fool in all her life, or so she was convinced at the time. She stood there in the dirty churned-up mud of the château yard at Revigny Urgent Cases hospital, cold and tired in the darkness as guns pounded madly at her ears, and wept with joy, holding on to a total stranger's arm with both hands as tears coursed down her cheeks in a stream, and while she laughed at the same time. And he stood there peering at her in what seemed a friendly sort of way, making no objection to her clutches and saying nothing at all.

Which helped her regain her equilibrium and after a while she managed to sniff mightily and catch her breath and let go of his sleeve to go digging in her uniform pocket for a handkerchief. And rubbed her face and eyes dry and blew her nose and then looked at him and said huskily, 'I'm sorry! It was just that I'm so happy –'

'You could have fooled me, honey,' he said and now his American drawl was very pronounced. 'All that weepin' and wailin', and you were happy? Well, well! You English sure are remarkable people.' He patted his knapsack in which his precious camera was tucked. 'That's why I wanted a picture of you – there you were, a right little spitfire, giving that screwy little French Major what was coming to him, and getting away with it – A great picture, I reckoned – I got masses of Our Brave Boys and Their Ambulance Units so I wanted something different. Have you met our lads from the American Field Service Ambulance Section yet? They've been working out here a good while now – good guys, all of 'em –'

She shook her head and managed a shaky smile. 'I've only just got here. I had no idea – is he all right – Bobby, I mean? Is he all right?'

'He was just fine last time I saw him,' David Deveen said. 'Which was – well, let me see – what day is this? Wednesday, I reckon – yeah, Wednesday, February the twenty-third – and I saw Bobby last Sunday. Before this push started, there was a chance to get a little

192

breather and we all went off to a cute little place – Clermont-en-Argonne – and had a great blow-out – a magnificent fricassee – chicken I think – and the best pâté I ever ate in all my life – to tell you the truth I've had nothing worth opening my mouth for since then and I'm getting a bit peckish again. High time we all went back to Clermont –'

Her forehead creased. 'How do you – I mean, while all this is going on you can go off and – and have parties?'

'Not a party, exactly,' he said and laughed. 'Just a little supper in a village *estaminet* where the food was ambrosia and the wine was nectar – and the push hadn't started then, you understand. We all agreed we needed a little local colour so we kinda borrowed a truck from the French and off we went. We brought them back a few bits and pieces so they forgave us –'

'And he was all right then?' Poppy said and David took her arm and shook it lightly in a friendly, reassuring sort of way.

'He was fine, just fine. He's your fella, hmm? He never said he has such a great girl as you –'

'Oh, no!' She was grateful for the way the darkness hid her hot face. 'Of course not – we – it's just that his sister and I are great chums and he's a friend too, and I was naturally worried – I haven't been getting many letters lately, you see –'

'Sure,' he said, and there was a hint of laughter in his voice it seemed wiser to her to ignore. 'Sure, honey. Just a friend. Well, he's okay, believe me –'

'Where is he now?' she demanded.

'Hmm? Well, now that's a tough question. Where is any newspaperman at any time? He's where the action is, I guess. At the Front some place – he's a hard-working guy, is Bobby Bradman –'

'I know,' she said. 'I worked on the *Dispatch* once.' She hesitated, wanting him to think well of her for some obscure reason and then, ashamed of the momentary instinct to be less than truthful added, 'I was one of the typewriters, you understand. No one special.'

'No one special? Never believe it! The best people on the *Trib* are our stenographers, believe you me! So, you're a newspaper girl, hmm? Wow, I like you better and better. Listen, I've got all the pictures I need from round here right now. Come on down to the Square. There ain't exactly a lot of night life in this town any more – I doubt there ever was! – but there's a nice *cantine* the girls run and you can get free coffee and bouillon. There's a treat to look forward to.'

At once she was all compunction. 'Oh, God, I can't! I ought to be on the road again now. I'm heading out for another run – it was just that – when you took that photograph I didn't think at the time – I just realized afterwards, you see, that you must be a newspaper man and – anyway, thanks a lot. If you see Bobby again, tell him I'm based here, will you?'

'I would gladly, if I knew who you were,' he said gravely.

She laughed awkwardly. 'Poppy,' she said. 'Poppy Amberly,' and waited, hoping for one mad moment that he would say – oh, yes, of course, he's spoken about you! But of course he didn't. He just grinned at her and said, 'I can do better than that. Give me a lift back to the Front and I'll find him and let you tell him yourself, hmm?'

She stared at him in the dim light, her lower lip caught between her teeth, thinking. To take a newspaper man in the ambulance must surely be against the regulations? And would it be right to waste the space when a walking wounded man might need it?

She tried to explain that, but he shook his head at her, laughing again. 'Listen, Poppy, you don't understand what sort of guys we are out here! I've been here three weeks already, a whole lifetime, and boy, do I know the ropes! You just ride me up on the inside, hmm? Then I get a lift back on the tailgate – there ain't no wounded man alive can manage that, not even if he's only shot his toe off to get himself out of this mess. I'll be no trouble. Which of these little buses is yours?'

Still she stared at him doubtfully and he took her elbow in one firm hand and steered her towards the ambulances and the knot of her girls who were waiting for her, grateful to have this little respite before setting off again.

'Well, which one?' he said invitingly and she capitulated.

'*Queen of Flanders*,' she said. 'Flora, will you stay here and make sure the others are ready to take over this run when we got back? They can rest till then because all the men for the trains have been taken to the railhead, and then it'll be our turn. It's time you took a bit of a break anyway – I'm taking this newsman up – he can drive – yes, Mr Deveen?' And she threw him a sharply conspiratorial look and he nodded at once. 'So I can manage if I need a second driver. Which I won't – right, girls, we're on our way –' And she swung herself up into the seat of her ambulance and pulled on her gloves as David Deveen scrambled up beside her and began to get his camera ready.

'This is great,' he said with high satisfaction. 'I haven't been able to get any good stuff on the road, because no one'd ever let me ride up front this way. So I'll get some good pictures and you'll get to see your Bobby! It's not a bad deal, hmm?'

'Not bad,' she said, and pushed the gears hard and set out again, the klaxon at full throat, to push her way up the wrong side of the road towards Le Petit Monthairon. And perhaps to Bobby –

But he was nowhere to be found. When they arrived, David swung himself down to the ground and with his precious camera bag slung as ever over his shoulder went squelching away down the line of tents towards the section where the shelling seemed to be loudest.

'I'll be back in under the hour,' he bawled, needing all his energy to make himself heard above the bombardment. 'If he's in reach, I'll bring him with me. Or at least a message –'

She loaded her ambulance with a high heart, much less aware this time of the appalling nature of the injuries of the men she was looking after, helping the men aboard and checking that their dressings were in position for the journey almost mechanically. Bobby was here, where she was! After all these long months of wondering and watching for letters that didn't come, he was here; soon she'd see him and be able to hold on to him and tell him how glad she was he was unhurt and – she took a deep breath and smiled down at one of the less severely wounded men she was helping into the ambulance with such brilliance that he stopped the long tirade of grumbling in which he had been engaged and grinned at her and murmured, *'Merci, ma'm'selle –'*

She had been so sure that Bobby would be found that when David returned with a lugubrious expression on his face and the explanation he had garnered from one of the other Press men he had found up the line that Bradman had gone somewhere behind the lines in search of an interview with one of the French Commanders, it was all she could do not to burst into tears of disappointment. But she didn't; instead she was short-tempered and edgy with her girls as they came to report that they were ready to start the run back to Revigny and far less forthcoming with Deveen than she had been on the journey out, when they had chatted and laughed a good deal.

But he seemed to understand and curled up on the seat alongside her and tucked his chin down into his collar as they went bouncing their way back along the interminable ten miles of misery that was the Verdun-to-Revigny road and said nothing. And when they arrived back at four in the morning and unloaded their ambulances, with no interference this time from the Commandant, she bade him a curt 'Goodnight', and turned to make her way back to the stables and some sleep.

But he called her back. 'Look, I guess I'll find him tomorrow,' he said. 'I know how it is out here with friends and all – we all get pretty screwed up about things. Try to get some sleep, Poppy, hmm? He's been okay all this time you didn't know where he was – you can be patient a little longer now, hmm?'

She stood and looked at him and then nodded, and held out one hand to shake. 'You're right. I've been behaving like an ass,' she said frankly. 'It's just that – it's been such a long time, and I got so hopeful there for a moment. I get so lonely sometimes for a breath of home, and to see an old friend would be – well, you know how it is. And you're right. I am very tired –'

'Aren't we all,' he said with a heartfelt tone in his voice. 'Aren't we all! I'll look forward to seeing you again. And thanks for some great pictures – my editor owes you a pay packet, believe me!'

'I believe you,' she said and laughed. 'Goodnight, Mr Deveen!'

'David,' he said. 'Goodnight, Poppy. I'll be around to see you again. Just you believe it –' And he melted away into the night and left her standing there half-dazed with fatigue, but feeling better than she would have thought possible.

Some of the pressure seemed to be lessened the next day, and during the succeeding ones. The bombardment began to ease and the numbers of injured men coming back from Le Petit Monthairon had slowed to a trickle. There was time to clear some of the men from the bulging wards of the Urgent Cases hospital, as more and more troop trains came into Revigny and were converted into hospital trains by the simple expedient of removing all the seats so that the men could be packed in on stretchers on the floors of the coaches and taken back to Amiens, Reims and Calais. She was hectically busy, too busy to do more than give the most fleeting of thoughts to Bobby and that helped because in addition to dealing with the supervision of the ambulances taking the men to the railhead, she was heavily occupied in arranging proper quarters for her girls. It was becoming very clear they were to be here some time, and that the battle of Verdun would be a long one, and they couldn't go on sleeping in a stable, as she told the excitable little Commandant as best she could, trying to ignore the fact that he clearly loathed her after the other night's little episode. But he, too, seemed to have calmed down a little and at last grunted an instruction to his aide-de-camp, who gave her requisition forms to arrange for billets for her girls in the town. They weren't the ideal places to live but they offered real roofs and walls rather than the waterlogged slats that covered the stables, and above all real beds and wash stands. And the fact that now they could wash not only their bodies but also their hair cheered the girls enormously. And cheered Poppy herself too, who managed to give herself a half-day off before the week ended.

Flora was left in charge of the situation at the hospital, where the girls were being used to do some ward nursing, since there was at present no driving needed, and she walked the mile and a half into Revigny town to make the most of her free time. The roads were still filled with marching men, but all were going one way towards Verdun, and she looked at them as she passed them and they waved to her, feeling a deep sadness, for they were so very young, these *poilus*. Some of them looked to be no more than seventeen or so, mere fresh farm boys who had no experience of fighting. How would they cope with the hell that lay ahead of them in the mud and squalor that was Verdun? But she smiled at them and waved back, hiding her distress. They would find out soon enough what was to be.

The weather had eased a little today. It was Sunday and across the shattered fields there was a single bell tolling and she thought – church, I suppose. Imagine going to church in the middle of all this; and she tried to imagine what sort of lives the people of Revigny were living while their town, their very country, was torn apart around their ears. And couldn't.

Until she got to her billet and there she took a deep breath as she walked into the small kitchen off the little stone-built house where her room was, bending her head to make sure she didn't bang it, for the door was very low. Not surprising, she had told herself ruefully after her first attempt to walk through in an upright posture had resulted in a painful lump on her forehead; most of the people of the town seemed to be under five-feet-five. She felt very out of place with her own five-feet-ten.

Madame Corbigny, the widow who owned the house, was standing before her fire pinning on a rusty black bonnet as she peered into a small fly-specked mirror, and she threw a sharp little glance at her uninvited guest as she came in. It wasn't easy, Poppy thought, to be pushed on to unwilling townspeople, but what else could the military authorities do? She had tried to point out to Madame that she, as a woman, must surely be a more agreeable guest than noisy *poilus*, but either her French had not been up to making her point clear, or Madame would have preferred noisy soldiers, for she had just sniffed and said nothing. She never did say anything if she could help it, but even after only a few days under her roof, Poppy was getting used to her taciturnity.

But still she tried. '*Bonjour, Madame,*' she said now brightly. '*Il fait un peu beau cette après-midi, n'est-ce pas?*' For indeed a thin February sunshine was struggling to peer through the heavy grey clouds. '*Enfin, le printemps arrive peut-être! Deux semaines, ou trois, peut-être, et nous avons les jolies fleurs alors!*'

'Hmmph,' said Madame and gave her a withering glare and Poppy subsided, painfully aware of her shortcomings as a linguist. And the old woman marched to the door and pushed it open and stared over her shoulder at her.

'*Moi, je vais à l'église,*' she said pointedly and stamped out and Poppy felt herself well and truly set in her place. English and what was worse Godless in her hostess's eyes; and she managed to grin at the thought and went up the narrow wooden staircase that climbed up the far corner of the smoky little room to her own room under the eaves.

It was a pleasant enough room for all it was so small and so cluttered with massive furniture. A vast bed, in which Poppy slept buried in a deep goosefeather quilt, and an even vaster wardrobe in dark, richly polished wood, left little room for anything else. There was, however, a wash stand in pink marble with a large bowl and jug set on it, and it was in that that Poppy was most interested this afternoon. Her change of uniform was arranged neatly on the single chair that was the room's only other furniture, for Madame had made it very clear than on no account was she to use the wardrobe; not that Poppy could have done or would have wanted to, for it was packed tightly with Madame's deceased husband's clothes, all of which smelled powerfully of naphtha mothballs.

But none of that, she told herself again, now mattered, and she took up the jug and went downstairs to the kitchen to fill it from the vast black iron kettle which stood on the hob by the fire. When the jug was filled she carried it laboriously upstairs again and then came down and refilled it with cold water from the pump in the yard before punctiliously refilling the kettle too and setting it back on the fire to boil ready for Madame's return from church and no doubt need of it.

And then, slowly and luxuriously, she undressed and stood there in her little room, aware of the chill on her skin but not minding it, stretching blissfully. She could just see herself in the small mirror that stood over the wash stand, and she peered at her reflection, trying to see the Poppy she had always been, but quite failing. This Poppy was thinner than the one who had first come to France; still well-made enough, she told herself judiciously, with good breasts and rounded hips and almost flat belly, but still a lot thinner; and then she shivered as a draught of cold air curled in through the small window, and set to work to wash herself as thoroughly as she could, starting with her hair.

And when she was herself clean, she used the remainder of the precious hot water to wash out her underwear, leaning precariously out of the window to hang it over the sill to dry in the frail sunshine, and then brushed her uniform coat and skirt as thoroughly as she could. She might not be as smart as the FANY rules demanded its members should be – and especially as they were Britons working for the French forces – but she would do her best. After all, she told herself, once again hoisting round her the rather skimpy towel which was all that Madame had provided her, after all, I am in charge of the troop here until Mrs Brett arrives. And please let that be soon! It's too much to worry about altogether, being a driver and a first-aider and in charge of everyone else as well –

She ran her hands over her thick curly hair and wished not for the first time that she had cut it short at the start of the war. It was so very difficult to keep it as well-cared for as she would like, and now she spread the thick damp strands over her shoulders so that it would dry the quicker and thought about sitting down in Madame's kitchen beside the fire. But she would come home and find her there and be very nasty indeed no doubt, crashing her pots and pans about and muttering unfathomable French insults barely under her breath, and Poppy shivered at the thought and decided to remain up here in her bedroom to wait for her hair to dry in its own time. After all the entire afternoon was hers, so she need not worry. And the sheer luxury of sitting and doing nothing would be very agreeable –

She could not bring herself actually to get into bed under her quilt, weary though she was. To go to bed in the middle of the day unless you were actually ill was simply dreadful. That was a rule of life Mama had instilled in her long ago; so she pulled on the thin wrapper, which was the only one she had brought as part of her kit, even though it wasn't very warm, and threw the towel over her shoulders to spread her hair on it, before scrambling on to the high bed to sit with her back comfortably jammed against the headboard and her knees tucked up. She ought to write some letters, of course, but to just sit here for a while would be so lovely. And she closed her eyes a little just to relax, not to sleep, of course – just to relax while waiting for her hair to dry –

There was a sudden noise downstairs which made her jump awake, and she sat bolt upright staring at the open door of her room, her heart thudding in her ears and then slowly relaxed. How silly to get so agitated when it was just Madame, returned from church! And she took a deep breath and then felt obscurely that it wasn't polite not to acknowledge her hostess's return and called out, 'I am up in my room, Madame, *Je suis dans ma chambre. J'éspère que l'eau est chaude* – I used the first lot for my ablutions, you understand –'

There were footsteps then on the stairs and she sat up even more upright and frowned. Was Madame going to *speak* to her? Had her visit to church softened her in some way and made her willing to be friendly? That thought made her lips curve a little, and she stared at the door expectantly.

'Er – *J'éspère que la messe est agréable pour vous, Madame, et –*' she began, wanting to respond to friendly overtures in the proper manner, but as the figure of the person climbing the stairs appeared in her doorway the words died in her throat.

There was a long silence as she stared and then she said, 'Bobby? *Bobby?* Is it really you or am I – ?' And she actually reached forwards and pinched her own leg, hard, to see if she was still asleep and dreaming.

But she wasn't.

24

Never in her wildest and most torrid imaginings about Bobby had it ever been the way it turned out in reality. The whole of that afternoon was to become to her a mad impossible memory, and yet one which she knew to be true, and that was a paradox that she was always to find difficult to comprehend.

She had sat there on her bed, her wrapper barely pulled around her cold and newly washed body and with her damp hair spreading in wild tendrils over her shoulders, and stared at him in the doorway. He stood very straight and four-square, almost filling the small space but she could see that he was a good deal thinner than he had been, and considerably more lined. His hair looked dustier than ever and his face just as round, but there was a new air about him, a deep weariness that seemed to say – I have seen everything, done everything, nothing can ever again give me interest or pleasure. But then he had smiled at her slowly and that air had disappeared completely to be replaced by the old eager Bobby she had thought of so much and remembered so well, and she squealed like an excited child and scrambled off the bed and hurled herself at him, shrieking, 'Bobby, Bobby, Bobby!' at the top of her voice.

'Hey!' he cried and opened his arms wide, not attempting to fend her off and then holding her close as she clung to the lapels of his greatcoat with both hands, her chin tucked into her neck and her forehead thrust hard against his chin and wept with the relief and excitement of seeing him. 'Hey, what sort of welcome is this? David told me you were here at this billet and wanted to see me, so I just thought I'd stroll over – but all I get is this vague sort of, "Oh, it's you, is it?" reaction. This won't do at all! Where's the excitement? Where's the welcome a chap's entitled to get?'

She managed to laugh and lifted her face to him. 'Oh, Bobby,' she began and then stopped and without thinking stood up on tiptoe and put both hands round his face and kissed him hard on the mouth. At first he stood quite still, not seeming to respond at all, but she pushed herself closer to him and then indeed he became all she could have wanted, holding her very close with both arms hard about her, and kissing her as thoroughly as she could possibly have wished.

And then they drew apart and stood there staring at each other, she a little breathless with the suddenness and wonder of it all, and he looking rather dazed, and after a moment she laughed. It was a shaky laugh, a very uncertain one, but a laugh for all that, and he seemed relieved to hear it and managed to do the same, and she used the reaction to cloak her confusion and pulled away from him to return to perch on her bed.

'I'm sorry I can't offer you any better accommodation than this for your afternoon visit,' she said, trying to speak lightly, and annoyed with herself for the way her breathlessness showed in every word. 'But Madame doesn't go in for large rooms though she has a liking for monumentally sized furniture. There's a chair there, so shift those things on the floor and sit down! I'd ask you downstairs by the fire, but Madame looks so ferocious if I show any signs of being at all friendly, and I think she'd regard the use of her kitchen to entertain my friends as highly outrageous –'

He looked at the chair with its neat array of clean clothes and then grinned.

'I know better than to disturb such carefully spruced-up kit! No need to worry yourself –' and he pulled off his greatcoat, revealing beneath it a battered tunic and army-issue trousers and stretched luxuriously. 'Could you bear my shirtsleeves? I haven't had my clothes off for a couple of days – disgusting, isn't it?'

'Of course it isn't and of course I don't mind. Take off what you like! Would you like some water to wash in? I could arrange that –'

He looked at her over his shoulder and opened his eyes wide. 'Does a cat want cream?'

'I'll get it – hold on here,' she said and scrambled off her bed and pushed past him to the wash stand where she picked up the jug, now full of her dirty water, and then ducked under his arm to return to the doorway. 'I've only the one towel and it's a bit damp, I'm afraid, but do take it – I'll be as fast as I can –' And she went padding off down the stairs bearing the jug in front of her, as full of excitement now as she had been of weariness when she had first come into the house just an hour or so ago.

She went to the back door to carry the jug out to empty it, and then stopped as she realized that she was barefoot; but was suddenly shy about returning upstairs to fetch her boots so with her toes curling against the icy cobbles, she went out to the yard to empty and rinse the jug before coming back to refill it from the kettle. And all the time she went about these intensely domestic duties, she concentrated entirely on them; anything rather than confront her embarrassment about the way she had hurled herself at him. It had been so outrageous, so very much the opposite of all she had ever done, that thinking about it was impossible. Better by far to think of filling jugs and kettles.

She carried the jug upstairs carefully, and found him perched on the edge of her bed, his tunic off, his braces dangling and his shirtsleeves rolled up, and he stood up as she arrived and said joyfully, 'Now, that is what I call a welcome! In London a lady offers a gentleman a cup of tea. In France ablution facilities mean so much more!'

'There's soap over there and a flannel – do help yourself,' she said and carefully emptied her jug of hot water into the bowl as he came and stood behind her and took a deep breath of the steam.

'Oh, Poppy, the luxury! You are the greatest girl! If you only needed to shave, then I'd be home and smooth, wouldn't I?'

She giggled. 'I bet I *can* find you a razor – I'm sure I saw – just a minute –' and she hurried over to the wardrobe and pulled open its creaking old door. She had remembered seeing the case of razors and the big shaving mug and brush on the upper shelf and she pulled them out triumphantly and gave them to him and he shook his head in wonderment at the sight.

'Magic!' he said. 'I lost my razor when my kit was shelled in a mucky French dugout last night. The only thing I rescued was my notebook,' he patted his back trouser pocket in great satisfaction. 'I thought I'd look like an elderly cornfield for the rest of the week, till I could steal someone else's tackle –' And he rubbed his chin and now she could see more clearly that he was indeed rather stubbled, and smiled at him.

'Perhaps you ought to grow a beard.' she said lightly, and then picked up the jug again and made for the door. 'I'll get some more hot water – take your time, and enjoy it – I know what it's like when you haven't had a chance to wash for ages –'

Downstairs she dawdled over refilling her jug and then going out once more to fill the vast black kettle and return it to the hob, wanting to give him ample time to do all he wanted, and also took time to build up the fire more brightly and set the kettle firmly over it. There would be no hope otherwise of the water being ready for Madame on her return; but Madame's return was something else she didn't want to think about right now, so she didn't, and instead turned at last to make her way up the stairs with the jug.

He was standing with his back to her, and his clothes, she saw, lay on the floor to one side, except for his shirt which he had tied round his waist to cover his nakedness; for she could see that his legs were bare beneath it; and she stood and looked at the broad muscular back, which was also bare, of course, and felt her face redden with the impact of looking at him.

And there was something else too that affected her profoundly; the room smelled of him now, a strong very male sort of smell, for he was splashing mightily, one arm in the air and then the other, soaping himself all over his chest and arms and as far round as he could reach, with great abandon and obvious pleasure.

He looked over his shoulder then and she thought – oh, please let him think I'm red just because of the running up and down stairs – don't let him know how I really feel – for she indeed felt very strange. Excited and yet relaxed, heart beating like a little hammer and yet unalarmed – it was very strange indeed, but very enjoyable.

'Oh, Poppy, this is utter bliss! I can't tell you how much more comfortable I feel. Forgive the *déshabillé*, but I couldn't waste the opportunity.'

'Give me your trousers and tunic and I'll brush them,' she said, trying to sound practical. 'It won't really clean them up that much, but it should help a little –'

'Bless you,' he said with real fervour. 'Help yourself –' and leaned towards her little mirror, which he had propped up in front of him, and began to soap his stubbled face. 'These *poilus* are lucky to have someone like you to look after them, Poppy – you really know how to get the essentials sorted out.'

'We aim to please, sir,' she murmured and set the jug down beside him and scooped up his trousers and tunic, and went back downstairs, remembering this time to tuck her feet into her boots. They felt odd against her bare skin, but it didn't matter. It was all part of the madness of this impossible wonderful afternoon.

She took her time dealing with his uniform, brushing each seam as carefully as she did the main sections of fabric, glad to see that he had not succumbed to the greatest problems of Front-line life, the livestock that moved with such alacrity on to unwashed bodies, and then when she could brush off no more, went back upstairs.

He was sitting on her bed, the great goosefeather quilt wrapped over his legs and tucked firmly round his waist, leaning back against the headboard with his hands looped behind his head. His hair was wet now, too, and untidily rumpled on his forehead and he was smoking a cigarette, and he grinned at her round it, not taking it from his lips.

'I couldn't get dressed again as you had my trousers,' he said. 'So I thought I'd make a job of it. My shirt's out there on the windowsill, blowing in the breeze – it should help it a good bit – and so are my socks and underwear. The rest of me will have to make do with this excellent quilt for a while.'

'Your tunic and trousers are cleaner now,' she said, proud of the way she managed to keep her voice light. 'I'll let them air a little too, if you like,' and she went over to the window and leaned out, rearranging the now considerable number of items that decorated the sill, very aware of the way he was staring at her silhouetted against the light, even though he was behind her and she couldn't see his face or eyes. And then remembered that she was wearing a very thin wrapper indeed, and hurried to complete the task, pulling her head in and tugging the wrapper as closely around her as she could with the most natural and casual of movements of which she was capable.

There was a little silence then as she stood beside the wash stand and looked at him and he stared back at her. He wasn't smiling now. His eyes were wide and dark in his still face, but there was nothing forbidding about the expression she saw there and she took a deep breath, and felt as much as smelled the mingled scents in the room – damp and soap and dust and him, and from outside the earthy softness of the rapidly dwindling February afternoon – and suddenly her lips were dry and she pushed her tongue forward to dampen them, running the tip from one corner of her mouth to the other. And he seemed suddenly to look even more dark-eyed and pulled his hands down from behind his head and took his cigarette from his lips and very deliberately bent over and stubbed it out in the saucer that bore her night-time candle, and which sat on the floor beside the bed. And then sat up and held out both arms to her.

She hesitated only for a moment. She was a very young girl, only just twenty-one and she had lived in many ways the classic sheltered life of any well-brought-up girl from Bayswater, but the privations of the life she had been leading ever since she had joined the FANYs fifteen months ago (could it be so long and yet so short a time?), and the things she had learned from the giggles and chatter of the other girls with whom she now spent all her time, had changed her profoundly from the Poppy she had been when she had last seen this man. She knew what was on his mind now as well as she knew what was on her own; and she rejoiced in it. All she had been told in her girlhood about the right way for circumspect young women to behave with the opposite sex, all she had been led to believe about the sacrosanct nature of marriage when it came to dealing with the animal passions seemed totally irrelevant here in Revigny on this early springlike afternoon in February in the middle of a bloody war. Here, there were just two exhausted young people who had a need of each other, two people who were tied together by the bonds of a long-standing and very real friendship. After all, she thought, as she hesitated that one moment, we have known each other almost five years. Five *years*. And I've loved him so much all that time. I really have –

And very deliberately she took the few steps that carried her across the room and into his reach and sat on the bed and tucked her feet up so that she was curled up against him like a child. But not like a child at all, for after a moment of holding him very close she lifted her chin and opened her mouth a little, not knowing how she knew what it was she wanted to do but doing it all the same, and pulled his head down towards hers with her other hand. And kissed him with all the passion she had in her, which was so much that she was aware of a sense of amazement, as her tongue curved and then made a firm tip which she pushed towards his lips. And she felt an answering amazement in him as he responded, kissing her in return with equal fervour.

He did make some sort of attempt to control himself, keeping the quilt firmly tucked round him and doing no more than kissing her over and over again; but then the sound became louder; all afternoon it had been muttering in the background, a muffled obbligato in the bass, but now it seemed that someone had decided that the offensive was to be stepped up for what remained of the day, and for a while the shelling became louder and more peremptory and for a moment they lay there in the dimming light, clinging to each other, she with her face still raised to his and with her head bent back against his restraining arm, staring at each other. And it was as though they had the same unspoken thought: what does it matter what we do? We're alive and we're here, and soon we could be like all those other people who have been shattered to splinters of bone and muscle and shredded skin, face down in the frozen mud. We are here and we are alive and in such a need –

And he kissed her again even more urgently and slid his hand inside the edge of her wrapper and across her breasts and her whole body seemed to curl up into a tight enclosed object which then, as suddenly as though it had exploded, opened out and blossomed into a series of sensations that were the most delicious she had ever known. And she arched her back so that her body was pushed towards him, begging him with all her muscles to touch her in the same way again and again while clinging to him with her mouth, and he obeyed.

Later she was to know that on this first occasion he had been a deeply sensitive lover. She was to know that his own need was vast and almost all-consuming and yet he had been able to subjugate it to her need for time. And he took plenty of time, touching her, caressing her, kissing her on every inch of available skin – and there was a great deal of that for she had herself pulled her arms out of the sleeves of her wrapper – until she was whimpering at him through the kisses to do more and more and more and more, pulling at the quilt, which still lay between them, with urgent fingers.

And when he was as sure as he could be that there was no need to delay longer, he let the quilt roll away and they moved together with an amazing degree of certainty, considering Poppy's own ignorance and their still rather stilted feelings about being together, for it had been so very long a time since the days of that easy bantering friendship when she had first learned to love him. She felt no pain, no doubt, nothing but a delicious sensation of pressure and an opening to him which did hurt and yet didn't; for she enjoyed it so greatly, that sensation, and so relished the way it transferred all her awareness of herself from that place behind her eyes in which she usually felt she lived, to that place deep inside her belly where he was reaching and touching with his own desperate need, that it could be nothing but a delight.

And then it was over with the suddenness with which it had begun. The shelling from outside seemed to Poppy to have entered her, to have pounded her body with its rhythmic thumping, so that she could not be sure where her feelings came from, within or without. But she could be sure that they were good and that she had wanted them and that they had left her feeling sleepy and relaxed and completely right in a way she never had before. And she yawned and said softly, 'Dear Bobby – I do so love you –' and closed her eyes, not even knowing whether she was awake or asleep and not caring.

And he too remained so for a while, lying there with his arms about her and her hair lying damply against his face, but then the shelling again lifted its volume and that made him stir and touch her again, and begin to stroke her as he nuzzled at her neck, and she woke suddenly and lay there, startled, staring up at him, almost unable to see him in the dusk. It was as though she had forgotten all that had happened and was amazed to be there with him, as though she had opened her eyes to find a dream made concrete. But then she saw his face above her and lifted one hand to touch his cheek, and as he bent to kiss her again she laughed a little huskily and responded to him as eagerly as she had the first time.

And this time they took even longer, rolling about the deep old bed with an abandon that amazed her, and laughing a little and gasping a lot and muttering words to each other that seemed to make sense when they said them and yet which were disjointed and nonsensical in reality. But none of it mattered until they were both again flung into sleepy breathlessness by their peals of excitement, and lay side by side sweating and breathless and deeply happy.

And it was then that Poppy heard the sound of the fire below being riddled loudly by a poker held in an irate hand and she turned her cheek against Bobby's and whispered, 'Oh, my God! It's Madame! Now what do we do?'

25

She had always had a great respect for his abilities, for his self-confidence and the way he took charge of all situations, but never more so than that Sunday afternoon.

He kissed her briefly and slid out of the bed and dressed with a speed and economy of movement that was amazing and as she hissed her alarm at him, held one finger to his lips.

'My love, there are some things you can't hide, and a large chap in your bedroom is one of them. So, we deal with the matter directly. Don't worry – your reputation will emerge unscathed!' And he went to the door and with a firm step marched down the stairs. And she sat and listened to him go and then, galvanized by a sudden awareness of her own nakedness, slid out of bed and dressed almost as quickly as he had. But it took her some time to pin up her hair, which was being extremely recalcitrant in its newly washed state, and it was a good ten minutes before she ventured to follow him down the stairs.

She stopped in amazement as she reached the kitchen, for he was sitting beside the table, on which a large oil lamp burned cheerfully, and with his feet stretched out towards the fire which was now leaping high. Usually Madame guarded her stock of wood and coal most jealously and allowed only the degree of fire needed to boil her eternal kettle, but tonight she had piled on the logs lavishly, and the room glowed with unusual light, and pulsated with even more unusual heat.

But that was not all. She was herself sitting at the table facing Bobby, and in front of each of them was a small glass filled with deep ruby liquid; and she was smiling. Poppy couldn't remember seeing a smile on that dour face since the first time she had met her.

'Hello, my darling!' Bobby said heartily and winked at her. 'I've explained everything to Madame –'

'You have?' Poppy said as the old woman got up from the table and, chattering rapidly in totally incomprehensible French – for she had a thick country accent to add to the problems Poppy generally had in picking her way through the linguistic tangle – went to the cupboard in the corner to fetch another glass and a bottle and pour a drink for Poppy. '*Everything?*'

He laughed softly in his throat as Madame pushed the glass towards Poppy and beckoned her to the table. 'Not in detail, you understand,' he murmured. 'Just that we haven't been able to see each other since we got married last year and –'

She almost dropped the glass.

'What did you – married? Last – Bobby!'

'She understands fully now – about how we both joined solely and wholly to fight the war for Glorious France and all that – I think she thinks that war correspondents regularly kill Uhlans –' And he turned to Madame and launched himself into a stream of chatter which made the old lady nod and beam even more, and then turned back to Poppy. 'And that you of course are saving French lives at the rate of seven a day. So the fact that those *sales cochons*, the officers of the army, have dumped you on her without paying her anything like what they ought to for the rent of that palatial room upstairs, she has pushed aside – especially as she now understands that our union is blessed by Mother Church even if you don't go there much. She was a bit sniffy about that, but I explained to her that it's only because you don't understand Latin and anyway they expect you to go to Mass at the hospital, which you do – oh, Poppy, I've lied splendidly! Say you're grateful –'

She looked at him and managed to smile, but her face felt stiff. It had been absurd, of course it had, to let excitement and glory leap in her the way they had, absurd to think that he had actually been proposing to her. Why should she expect such a thing, here in the middle of a war? The way they had spent the afternoon was beside the point – wasn't it? No it wasn't, a secret voice deep inside her shrieked. Of course it wasn't. There was every reason to think he actually meant it –

'Yes,' she said and sat down. 'Terribly grateful.'

He looked at her sharply and smiled a little crookedly, and then turned back to Madame and started chattering to her again, clearly exerting himself considerably to pour charm over her like honey from a pot, and Poppy could only sit there with the glass of wine in her fingers and watch him, and try to put her thoughts into some sort of order. Her body ached in an agreeable way, and there were small sensations that came and went, echoes of the much more powerful ones she had known upstairs this afternoon, and she tried to push those down and away from her consciousness. That had been a mad interlude, no more. Hadn't he made that clear by telling her so triumphantly of his success as a liar on the subject of marriage? She had been caught by the unexpectedness of the situation, that was what it was; by his sudden appearance; by the silly circumstance of soap and hot water and clothes on windowsills instead of covering one up decently and –

She shook herself and he turned back to her and said quickly, 'Are you all right, Poppy?'

She managed a smile, and a show of equanimity. 'I'm fine,' she said. 'Fine.'

'I'll try to get rid of the old bat and then we can talk properly,' he said, and nodded brightly at Madame. 'Perhaps some supper, too – I could do with some real food –'

'Yes,' Poppy said, suddenly aware of how hollow she was. 'Yes – I think we might manage to get something at the *estaminet* near the station. They sometimes have room – though obviously they're always madly busy –'

Again he spoke to Madame, now clearly asking questions and she listened and nodded and then creaked to her feet as she threw her hands up and bustled over to the door to take her shawl and bonnet from the hook on the back, talking busily as she went, and Bobby listened and nodded and said to Poppy, 'We're doing well, Poppy! The *estaminet* is owned by her nephew, no less. She'll see to it he takes care of us. Get your greatcoat – and bring mine, will you, while you're up there?'

She went obediently upstairs, thinking almost resentfully as she swiftly tidied her bedroom by the light of the single candle which she had to use to find her way about that she might as well be a wife at that, the way he sent her on his errands, and fanned the little flame of her irritation with more thoughts of his perfidy in lying so glibly to that stupid old woman downstairs. After all, what did it matter what she thought? She was not so very important a person in Poppy's life; why be concerned for her opinion? But that didn't help, because Poppy could not deny it *did* matter; she wouldn't want anyone to think she was the sort of girl who – the sort of girl that always –

And she stood at her bedroom door with the two greatcoats over her arm, before blowing out the candle and thought aghast – but I am. I did. I was in this room this afternoon with a man who is not my husband and I – didn't I? And suddenly she thought of Mama and Lizah, and it was as though they had been here this afternoon, not she and Bobby, and she was staring at them and thinking how wrong it was to behave so. And then Bobby called her name up the stairs, and she took a deep breath and blew out her candle and came down to meet him. There was a lot to think about, a great deal. But not now.

'Rabbit!' Bobby said with great satisfaction. 'Madame says she knows for a fact that he has some excellent rabbits and she herself gave him her best *pruneaux* from last season – and I'll bet she charged him a pretty price for her gift! – and therefore there should be an excellent dish awaiting us. I've given her a few francs towards her wine to which she said, mercenary old bat, that she wouldn't dream of taking it while scooping it up so fast you hardly saw her fingers move. She's a horrid old besom, isn't she?' And he beamed at Madame and said something clearly very complimentary about her bonnet, for the old woman becked and bobbed her head and giggled like a girl; a repellent sight, Poppy thought fastidiously as she gave Bobby his greatcoat and shrugged on her own. Repellent.

By the time they were settled at a corner table in the noisy steamy *estaminet* that they had to fight their way into, and into which Madame had charged like a diminutive dog, snapping at everyone who got in her way and dragging them behind her, Poppy felt a little better. She had been absurd to be annoyed with Bobby because he had lied to that hateful old woman, she told herself. Hadn't he made life easier for her? To imagine going on living in that billet if he had just walked out and let the old woman think the worst was impossible. Madame Corbigny might even have demanded that Poppy be removed, and told the Commandant at the Urgent Cases hospital why – and Poppy shrivelled inside as she imagined the effect that might have had. No, it was silly to be angry with Bobby. And yet, and yet – and she leaned back in her chair as Madame's nephew arrived with a large steaming bowl of a fragrant dark stew and slapped it down in front of them.

The food was marvellous and for the next half-hour they concentrated on that, using quantities of the rough local bread to soak up all the gravy which was particularly delicious if a little pungent to Poppy's untutored taste, and drinking a rich red wine that was just as pungent in its own way and which made her mouth sting. And then the nephew brought them a plate of apple tart and coffee and Bobby leaned back and sighed deeply with satisfaction as he reached into his pocket for his cigarettes.

'Feeling better?' he said after a while and she looked up quickly.

She had been sitting with her head a little bent, looking into her coffee cup.

'Better?' she said lightly. 'Why better? I wasn't ill.'

'You know perfectly well what I mean,' he said quietly and leaned closer, setting his elbows on the table so that she could hear him, for the surrounding noise from the crowded tables was considerable. 'You were angry with me and furious with yourself, and then amazed and then glad and then sorry but overall you felt bad. Didn't you?'

She looked at him and felt the tears tighten her throat. 'No!' she said loudly and bent her head again.

'Oh, Poppy, don't be like that! Not after all that we've been to each other!'

'It was mad,' she said after a moment. 'It was just a – a combination of circumstances. Seeing you after so long and being there and being undressed and the washing and – and –'

'I wasn't talking about this afternoon.' His voice was very level. 'I was talking about home. About all the years at home. About the times we went to the theatre and suppers at our house in Norland Square. About the outings with Mabel and Chloe. About listening to *Schéhérazade* on the gramophone. About working at the office in Fleet Street and seeing each other across the newsroom floor. The afternoon was – well, this afternoon was something different. But after all we've been to each other before this afternoon you don't have to pretend to me. Do you?'

She had lifted her chin now and was looking at him and it didn't matter that there were tears in her eyes. 'Were they important to you too, those things?' she said, and even she could hear the wonderment in her voice. 'Were they really?'

'Important to –? Oh, Poppy, Poppy, you're part of my life! You were a lovely gawky schoolgirl who tried so hard to be grown up and sometimes managed it, and who made me laugh and was so sweet with my Chloe – and I know how frightful she can be, poor little scrap – and Mabel's such good friend – how could you not be important to me? I used to look at you and think – one day that child will be someone very special. Very special. And I was right, for you are. You're – oh, Poppy, you have no idea what you are!'

She swallowed hard and took a deep breath. She had to say it, even though it made her ashamed. It was something she should wait for him to say first. But she could not wait. Not now.

'I love you, Bobby. I've loved you for so long I can't remember what it feels like not to love you. Didn't you know that? Didn't you ever guess that?'

'Of course I did,' he said and he sounded a little rougher now. 'But I'm so much older than you, and there's Chloe –' He stopped and set his upper lip between his teeth and stared at her consideringly. 'You know she'll always be the most important person in my life, Poppy? You do know that?'

She blinked and then lifted both hands in an odd little gesture. 'Well, of course,' she said uncertainly. 'She's your daughter – of course she's –'

'It's more than that. Much more. There was her mother, you see. I loved her more than – I still do, Poppy.'

There was nothing she could say. She sat and stared at him, feeling as though she would never find words again.

'It's impossible to explain to someone who hasn't experienced it. A love that – and then the loss of it. I died too, really. The man I had been died, that is. I'm a different person now. Quite different. And the new person, the new Bobby Bradman – oh, Poppy, you're very important to that person. But you must understand there was another important person before you. And that means Chloe is more than my daughter. She's the bridge to the person I was, you see, and to all that mattered to me then. I don't want that person to die completely, because when he dies, so does Barbara. And I don't want that to happen. As long as she's remembered, she'll always be part of my life, part of reality. She won't be completely gone. And Chloe's there to make certain of that. Do you understand what I'm trying to say to you, Poppy? You're very special, and I think we could be happy together. We could – we could do a lot, you and the Bobby Bradman I am now. But there'll always be the other one there as well, and you have to understand that.'

At last her voice came back. 'I'm trying to understand, I know it's not easy for me. No one I've ever cared about has died, so I can't imagine what it feels like to be in that position. But the thing is, I'm not sure what it is you're saying to me. About me, I mean. I know what you're saying about yourself –'

'I'm saying that I know you love me, and I'm saying that as I am now, I love you in a sense. But it won't be the sort of love you feel. It won't ever be that, because I've given that away. It's Barbara's. I can share so much with you, and I know that you will be wonderful for me. But I'm trying so hard not to be selfish, Poppy! It would be so easy to say to you, "I love you, I want to marry you, please let's be married and we'll live happily ever after." But I'd be cheating you. You really have grown-up to be someone incredible – so alive and so passionate – it's not just because we're here in this stupid ugly war either. It's not just the – what was it you said? – combination of circumstances. You're a passionate woman and one who could gain so much from a man who loved you as you're entitled to be loved. The way I loved – still love – Barbara. But I do care for you. And God knows I want you –'

He managed a smile then. 'I imagine you can tell that, can't you? What you did for me this afternoon was – incredible.' He leaned forward and set his hands warmly over both of hers, which were clasped on the table between them. 'If you could settle for the present Bobby, who's a different person from the one I think you ought to have – well, you'd make me a very happy man. But be sure you know what you're doing, Poppy! If you say yes to this meagre proposal I'm giving you, be sure you know why –'

She was looking at him now with her eyes wide and dark with the heat of the feeling that was in her. She understood all too painfully what he was saying. At the back of her mind she could see Chloe, staring at her over her father's shoulder as he held her close and crooned to her, could see the knowing bright stare that had challenged her that first time she had met her. She could see, too, the shadowy figure of the woman she had never met, the woman who was her rival, and there was nothing she could do about her. And there he sat in front of her staring at her and waiting for her response to the question she had yearned for so long to hear him ask her. He wanted her to marry him – but on his terms.

And she laughed shakily and said, 'I don't think I have much of a choice, Bobby. I love you so much, you see. Of course I say yes. You must have known I would.'

His face creased into an anxious little grimace. 'Oh, God, if I thought that, I'd stand back now and say no – I had no right to ask you – forget it all – I truly didn't take it for granted, Poppy. I thought, perhaps, if I explained it honestly, told you how I feel, how it is with me, you might draw back and – after all, you have grown up a lot, haven't you? I haven't seen you for a year or so and the change in you is – well, it's incredible. But it's been like that for a lot of us out here. You can't live a war like this at first hand and not change quickly. You've managed to change for the better. Me, I'm not sure –'

He bent his head and stared down at his hands holding hers. 'Once I would have died rather than take advantage of a girl as inexperienced as you. I would have been able to set my own needs aside and protect you – but I didn't, did I? I abused you, really, because of my own needs –'

'Oh, stuff and nonsense!' Poppy said strongly. 'I was much more eager than that. You can't tell me that what happened this afternoon was some sort of seduction. It was just two people who needed each other and –'

He looked up at her, and managed that crooked smile again. 'You see what I mean? How you've grown up, Poppy! Yes, of course, you're right – but believe me, I didn't take you for granted. I didn't speak as I did to cheat you. I wanted to be honest, truly honest, I wanted you to know what soiled meagre goods were on offer here –'

She grimaced. 'Don't talk that way. You aren't buying and selling. I've told you, yes. I love you, so what else could I say? And once this hateful war's finished I want to marry you and look after Chloe and there's an end of it. I understand about – I know how you feel –' She couldn't say Barbara's name ' – about the past. But that's something I can deal with. I'll have to, won't I?'

And they sat and looked at each other, sitting there at a corner table in a smoky *estaminet* in Revigny while the guns at Verdun pounded their eternal bombardment away to the north and said no more. They were promised to each other, and Poppy should have been the happiest girl in the whole world.

But she wasn't.

26

But as the next few weeks went by and she grew accustomed to the idea of being an engaged girl she became more content. It wasn't easy to accept the fact that the man she wanted so much could offer her only part of himself, and she did, just once, think seriously about whether she had made the right decision. Wouldn't it be better to say 'No' altogether than settle for this promise of only half a love? But she pushed that aside with all the optimism she could find. He might think he was only capable of limited love for her, she told herself, but she knew better, oh indeed she did! He showed in so many ways how much he cared for her, how much he wanted to be with her; how could it not be because he loved her as much as she loved him? He would make every effort he could each day or certainly every other day to return to Revigny from his various sorties along the Front to get his stories so that they could curl up together and talk the long evening hours away after Poppy came off duty. Madame Corbigny, with elephantine and somewhat prurient tact, would build up her kitchen fire and go waddling off down the street to visit her cronies, clutching in her hand the francs that she regularly managed to extract from Bobby, and there they would sit side by side, watching the flames lick the logs while they talked interminably.

But they did not only talk, and it was that which gave Poppy her confidence that, after all, it would be wonderful once the war was over and they could be married. Sometimes he showed himself unable to keep himself from touching her, and she would slide into his arms and they would make love all evening until they were both exhausted. He had tried to demur at first, pointing out that they weren't married yet, and there was no sign of the war ending for some time. To make love now would be wrong – But she laughed that away.

'It's all a bit stable doorish, dear heart,' she said, and slid her hand inside his shirt and across his chest. 'If this was before that Sunday

afternoon it would be different – but it's after. So why shouldn't we?
And, anyway, who knows what will happen in the future? It doesn't
matter – there's just now and us and kiss me at once –'

And he succumbed with little more pressure and, for Poppy, those
weeks as February melted into the muddiness of a drenching March,
which gave the promise of a tender hopeful April, were idyllic. She
would spend her days on the wards at the Urgent Cases hospital
dealing with the care of the injured men who still came in steadily
from the Front ten miles away, or drive the mad bucketing run into
Verdun to fetch the wounded back, as surrounded as ever by the
stench of mud and pain and blood and death. But she had the golden
hours in her room or beside Madame Corbigny's fire to compensate;
hours when she discovered so much about herself and about Bobby,
about the way they could bring each other to a delight, even an
ecstasy, that never ceased to amaze her.

Sometimes she would try to remember the girl she had been, the
uninformed, the virginal Poppy, but she was unimaginable now.
There was just the new Poppy, eager, warm, desperate for love,
almost insatiably so, and Bobby who, slowly at first but then with
more and more delight, learned to match her in desire to give her all
that she wanted while giving himself even more.

They did talk about whether to write and tell the people at home of
their plans, and even once composed a joint letter for Mabel, but it
was Poppy who said at length, after they had struggled for some time
to find the right words, that it just wouldn't be right to deliver such
momentous news in a mere letter.

'I need to be there to see her and to see her face – and anyway –' She
had stopped then and looked at him appealingly. 'There are my
problems about my own family. I can't tell Mama in just a letter, can
I? And there's Jessie and Lizah, too of course –' And her voice had
dwindled away, as she looked at him from beneath her lowered lids,
trying to assess his reaction.

She had told him very soon after she had agreed they were to marry
about her family history, because not only did he have a right to
know; she had a need to tell him. It had been a long time ago since her
life in London had split into fragments; for the past year or more the
only strand of existence that had really mattered had been here in
France, except for that fiasco of a leave when two of her lives had
clashed so distressingly, and she had a deep need now to bring all the
pieces together to create a whole. And telling him about her parentage
had been the first step.

His reaction had been a little odd. She had tried to describe Jessie and Lizah as dispassionately as possible, but it hadn't been easy. They were both exotic people in her own eyes; in his they must seem positively bizarre, and as she had gone through her halting explanation of her Jewish relations he had sat watching her, apparently dispassionately, and said little. Only when she had finished by saying, 'I hope you'll meet them one day soon after we get home again, Bobby –' had he stirred.

'I'm sure I shall,' he had said and there was a hearty note in his voice that she hadn't heard before, and didn't like. He seemed to be trying a little too hard to be agreeable. 'I'm sure. But, after all, we aren't marrying each other's families, are we? Just each other –' And her heart had slipped down inside her a little, or so it felt, because it was clear to her that he was upset by hearing of her antecedents; and she had felt she had to confront him with that.

'Does it worry you that I'm half Jewish?' she had said challengingly. 'I have had no upbringing other than the one you know about – my mother is much the same as you are yourself, and as I imagine your relations are. But whatever sort of upbringing I might have had, being half Jewish is part of me. Does it distress you? Because if so –'

'Distress?' he had said and squinted at the fire, and she knew he was trying to be honest and suddenly, unaccountably, felt much better. The sense of sinking fear that had filled her hadn't been necessary after all. 'No, I'm not distressed. But I can't deny I'm startled. I'm ashamed to be, too. I've always prided myself on being open-minded and tolerant and to find that my first reaction to such news was – well, as I say, to be startled, shows I'm not quite as open-minded as I thought. Oh, Poppy!' And he had turned back to her and held his arms wide to offer a hug. 'You're so good for me in so many ways. You're going to teach me such a lot!'

And no more had been said about the matter until now and she watched him sharply as she said it again, 'There's Jessie and Lizah, too –'

But she need not have worried, for he only said, 'Yes, you're right. We'll wait till we get home and then tell everyone ourselves. That will be fun.' He'd stopped then and added almost under his breath, 'And of course I have to talk to Chloe –'

She was the one subject they did not discuss in the long spring evenings. They talked a lot about so many other people, however, often laughing a little over poor old George Pringle, though Poppy did her best to defend him.

219

'He's a dear good man,' she protested once when Bobby had launched himself on a particularly lively and somewhat unkind imitation of his pompous speech style. 'And he loves Mabel dearly. And she of course loves him.'

She had stopped then and tried to imagine not only George's but Mabel's reaction to hearing that her sister-in-law-to-be was half Jewish. She remembered suddenly sitting in the sunlit garden at Norland Square and trying to bring herself to tell Mabel about her father, and how Mabel had said sharply at one point when Poppy had made a feeble joke about the possibility of her father being a gypsy that 'You might as well talk of your Mama marrying a Moor or a Jew as talk of her marrying a gypsy – sometimes you go too far.' Oh, there were problems looming up about Mabel and George, she thought as Bobby, not one whit deterred by her reproof, continued his mimicry and then, in her usual way, refused to think about it. There was no point. They were not going to have to face the problem for some time yet. Wait till then to worry –

But then, suddenly, it seemed it wouldn't be so long after all. On the first of April, the new Commandant at last arrived, and the FANYs at Revigny were told that they now actually had a choice about what they wanted to do.

'The British Government,' announced Mrs Brett on her first day with them, 'has decided that women may now be employed close to the Front line' – at which there was some rather ironic laughter; where had they been all these weeks, after all? – and Mrs Brett had held up an imperious hand to stop them. 'So although you are now, properly speaking, members of His Majesty's forces, it has been agreed that since you have been attached to the French Army for so long, you may actually choose what you would rather do. They will be glad to have the troop here, or even a part of it, or you may choose to return to England when a new ambulance group arrives from Paris – it will be here in two days I'm told – and, after Blighty leave, be reassigned. Let me know what you want. You have only a short time in which to make up your minds, so think carefully.'

Poppy had of course told Bobby at once. She had hurried into Revigny that afternoon, getting Flora to stand in for her while she did, to ask his advice. Where once she would have been perfectly able to make her own decisions in the matter, now it was not just herself who had to be considered. If she opted to be a member of the British forces then that would mean leave and parting from Bobby – not to be thought of! But if she stayed and the French Army eventually sent her away somewhere else, then what? She badly needed, she felt, Bobby's guidance on this.

He was sitting in the *estaminet* with David Deveen, drinking cognac and coffee and they both greeted her warmly. Poppy was glad to see David. He was such a cheerful friendly soul, with his tangle of dark tightly curled hair and his narrow dark eyes that seemed to light up when he laughed, that it was impossible not to like him. And he was also such good company, and so willing and obliging, often taking the long run into Amiens to file Bobby's dispatches so that he would have more time to spend with Poppy, and generally being a good friend to them both in every way. And, Poppy thought, as she pulled off her cap and slid into the chair facing them, he might have ideas on the new situation too.

He did, for after she had explained as succinctly as she could he said at once, without giving Bobby a chance, 'For God's sake, kid, take the British shilling! You *are* British and the way these French are running the war – believe me, honey, you'll be better off. Go home and tell this guy of yours here it's high time he did too. He hasn't taken leave since God knows when. Such a sense of duty makes my teeth ache, believe me! If he gets any more clenched about the jaw with nobility, I swear I'll hit him.'

She had laughed but had slid her gaze sideways to Bobby, with a sudden hope lifting in her. To go home, now, together? Not to wait till the end of the war to be married, perhaps? To go now and share a leave in London and to see everyone and – she caught her breath at the thought of it.

'Oh, Bobby, let's! Do let's! Can't we?'

He had sat there for a long moment, clearly thinking hard and then to her delight had nodded. 'Maybe I should at that. It's up to me where I report from, after all. I've got a roving commission from the paper – and it's going to drag on and on, this battle. They're getting nowhere, just killing all the time over the same few yards. And there are other stories I ought to be covering. I've been thinking – there's a lot happening in Turkey –'

'Turkey,' she had cried, her eyes wide with horror. 'No, Bobby, you wouldn't go there, would you? It's so far and so –'

'It's all right,' he said soothingly. 'It's just a thought. There seems to be something brewing there involving Russia and so forth, but it's just a thought. Either way, I'd like to get some new stories to work on –' He had looked at her consideringly. 'Do you really feel you want to go home for leave, Poppy? The last time you were offered it, you told me, you turned it down.'

'It was different then!' she cried and seized both his hands. 'That was before I found you!'

'Spare my maiden blushes!' David murmured and set his hand mockingly over his eyes. 'And this lovebird stuff positively melts my virginal old bones —'

'Wretch,' Poppy said and cuffed him lightly, suddenly warm and deeply content to have this man's friendship. 'Come back to London too,' she said impulsively. 'It's a lovely place, our London, isn't it, Bobby? Beats Revigny hollow.'

'I know,' David said and laughed. 'It's got a zoo —'

'We've got that here,' Bobby said and jerked his head towards the motley collection of people at the other tables, battered soldiers and elderly toothless men of the town, and a gaggle of the highly painted women who always seemed to appear from nowhere when soldiers on rest leave appeared, and laughed too and a happy bubble of affection hung there between them and Poppy thought — oh, God, I'm so happy. Please don't let it be spoiled, ever. I'm so happy —

So, Poppy told the Commandant that she was taking the British choice — much to Mrs Brett's approval — and put in for Blighty leave, together with half a dozen of the other girls. Flora, however, had decided to stay with the French.

'I might get some more good work done out here now they're sending me to Paris,' she told Poppy dryly the night she left after the new troop had arrived to take over their tasks at the Urgent Cases hospital. 'Take care of yourself, Poppy. If you run across Miss Sylvia when you get back to London, tell her I was asking after her — oh, and give my good wishes to your friend Mabel. I hope she stays as friendly now you're marrying her brother. But you mustn't mind if she doesn't.'

With which cryptic words, she had hugged Poppy and climbed into her ambulance and gone off with the rest of the troop who were going with her, leaving Poppy a little put out by her words. But, she told herself as she went back to her billet to pack what few belongings she had, ready for her own departure, Flora was always like that. Strange girl —

On her own last night in Madame Corbigny's house in Revigny, she slept poorly, for the excitement that was building in her was becoming more and more intense. They were to leave the following morning at ten o'clock to connect with a hospital train that would take them up to Calais, and she and Bobby had made elaborate plans to meet there, so that he could come back on the same ship and do a story about it. His freedom of action made it a lot easier, he had told her, to fit in with her, and that was the best way to organize it. He sent a cable to the paper telling them that he was moving back to London to pick up a new assignment and that they could send a new man out if they liked. And he told them they needn't rush. This battle was well bedded in and would go on for a long time without much happening yet.

But for once he was wrong in his estimation of the situation, for Poppy had just fallen asleep in the small hours of the morning when she was woken by a sudden increase of the noise of the bombardment that almost literally shook her out of bed. She peered at her wristwatch and shook it in disbelief when she saw the time. It was just four o'clock and still dark; were the Germans starting a new bombardment now? Or was it the French who were taking the offensive? But she knew it couldn't be that; she had learned enough about the way the French Staff were running this battle to know how unlikely that was. But, whatever it was, it was a very intense bombardment for even here in Revigny, so many miles away, the din was appalling, and after a moment she slid out of bed and began to dress. There'd be no more sleep tonight, and after tomorrow anyway it would all be a lot easier –

Downstairs she found Madame sitting huddled in her corner chair, obviously terrified, and she tried to comfort her, though with little success, before slipping out into the chill morning air to make her way down to the hospital. She didn't know why she was going. Her tour there was finished. Only last night the patients had bade her farewell and she had said her emotional goodbyes to the rest of the staff with whom she had worked so long. They had all been tearful but very definite; their days at Revigny Urgent Cases hospital were over. Yet here she was, making her way once more down that rutted road towards the familiar gates.

The place was in an uproar. Already, ambulances from the new troop were arriving back from the Front and men were being unloaded, and she pushed her way through the hubbub to see if she could help. All her instincts were to join in the work, whether or not she was still officially on the staff of the hospital and she made her way through the crowd with all the skill of experience.

And stopped as she came to the back of the first ambulance. There was an odd smell in the air as the rear doors were opened, a smell that caught her throat and made her cough, and she wasn't the only one coughing. Some of the other drivers and first-aiders were too, but most of the sound of painful hacking came from the ambulance and she craned forwards to see what was happening.

These casualties were not the ones to whom she had become accustomed. These weren't men who had been torn apart by bullets or shell fragments; indeed many of those she saw as stretcher after stretcher was unloaded were quite whole. But they were coughing pitifully and some had eyes tightly closed against the flickering torch lights and tears of pain squeezing out from beneath their lids.

'Gas,' Poppy said aloud, not knowing she had and someone on the far side said grimly, 'Yes – gas – the bastards! Will you look at them? Oh, God, this is evil, sheer goddamned evil!'

'David!' she called and pushed her way past the people around her to reach him. 'David? Is that you?' For although the voice had been familiar, the face was not, for his eyes were gleaming pallidly in a black-skinned face and his teeth flashed oddly white as he spoke.

'David, what happened?' she cried.

'We got caught in the first blast,' he said and his voice sounded thick to her and he didn't look at her, still staring wildly about him and at the hurrying stretcher bearers and nurses. 'We thought it was just the usual gunfire, you know, and when I knew I wasn't hurt too bad – I just got a few grazes I think under here –' And he touched his cheek gingerly. 'I reckoned to see what else was happening and then we got separated and – then the gas started. The stinking lousy bastards! Gas, the bastards, the *bastards* –' And she saw the tears streak his face and put out her hand and held on to his sleeve.

'David, it's all right. I'm here – it's all right – come on inside and let me treat that face of yours. Let's see what really happened. Come on, David, please come on, now. I'll take care of you –'

He shook his head and then shook his arm to get rid of her restraining hand. 'No, I have to find him,' he said, almost distractedly and she knew that he was more than just superficially injured. He seemed shocked, not fully in control of himself and she said softly, 'It's all right, David. It's me, Poppy – look at me and you'll see –'

This time he did turn to peer at her, as they were pushed aside by the movement of the next wave of stretcher bearers, now carrying the men into the hospital as the ambulance ground its way out of the yard to go back to Verdun, and another one came rocking in through the gates with a new load.

'Poppy?' he said wonderingly and then, more urgently, 'Poppy!

224

Oh, thank God it's you! You can find him – Poppy, where is he?'

'David, what do you mean?' Something very large and cold had slipped inside her and was holding her belly in a tight grip. 'David –'

'Goddamn it, where *is* he? That bastard Bobby, where did he go? I saw him there and they said they'd shove him on the next ambulance and I was to come back on the tailgate and – where is he, Poppy? I just need to know the stupid bastard's okay. He pushed me out of the way and down into the dugout where I could find respirators but he – where is he, Poppy? Is the bastard with you? I want to kill him for being so stupid – he saved me, the stupid –' And then he was crying as Poppy held on to him and stared over his shoulder at the ambulance which was now opened at the back and round which the stretcher bearers were once again clustering.

And saw the first man pulled out and recognized the hair, that dusty rumpled hair, even before she saw that he was lying very still and with his eyes tightly closed.

27

At least now he was fully conscious and awake. She could talk to him, tell him to move his head *so*, put his hand there, and he would obey, and she would bend over him and wash him or give him sips of water or rub his lips gently with a swab stick dipped in olive oil to soothe the painful cracks there, and he would look at her, his eyes wide and dark with pain. But he could not talk to her, for his breathing was too laboured and his throat too tight and tongue too swollen for more than husky mumbles, although she was learning rapidly how to understand what it was that each guttural sound indicated.

How she had coped that first day she would never know. The new German offensive had sent such a wave of men into the Urgent Cases hospital that this time it threatened completely to submerge it and the situation wasn't helped by the fact that the seasoned FANY troop had gone and had been replaced by an inexperienced one. So Poppy had found herself not just looking after Bobby, which was all she wanted to do, but also helping care for other men.

But after two days it was a little easier. For once the hysterical little Commandant's demands for extra help had been heeded by his Staff and an extra detachment of nurses and orderlies had been sent in, and extra trains laid on to get as many men safely away to Amiens and Reims and Calais as possible; and Poppy was at last able to make her own necessary plans. Which were very clear in her mind.

She was to get her Bobby on to a troop hospital train somehow, back to Calais and then on to a ship for Dover. She was going to take him home and never mind the fact that he was a non-combatant and therefore had no right to be given the care and transport provided for soldiers. She wasn't going to let anyone know that, if she could help it; so she bundled up his greatcoat and his war correspondent's uniform and put it with her own kit and replaced it with a uniform taken from a dead British officer who had been in a unit which was fighting with the

French Army, hating herself for the deception, but determined that nothing could be allowed to stand in her way, and somehow had managed to get a place for Bobby on the next ambulance going to Revigny railhead, and then a berth on the train, in spite of the fact she had no Army papers for him.

She would have tried to get David on too, but he had refused. Once they had found Bobby he had seemed to recover some of his equilibrium, and by the next morning, when Bobby had regained consciousness and it was found that his only injuries were severe gassing and a broken ankle, he had seemed much better, though his grazed face was grim when he looked down at his friend's face, twisted with pain and with the gas-reddened eyelids closed against the stabbing of the light.

'Get him home and into the hands of a decent doctor, for God's sake, Poppy. The way he's breathing – it's dreadful –' And indeed it was, for every breath Bobby took was rasping and clearly agonizing, and his lips had that blueish tinge that showed how much damage had been done to his lung tissue.

'I will,' she said. 'I will, somehow. He's going to be all right, David. I promise you, he's going to be all right –' And she had stared at Bobby hard, as though doing so would push her own determination into him and make him fight his injury harder.

And perhaps it had, for by the time David came to see them off on the train at Revigny station, which he had insisted on doing, even though he was still far from well himself, Bobby seemed more comfortable. He lay on his stretcher, snugly tucked into a blanket Poppy had somehow managed to wheedle out of the quartermaster and with one of the few soft pillows that were available tucked under his head, and tried to say something to David, who shook his head at him and said softly.

'No, fella – not a word. I'll get back to London soon's I can – they're sending another guy out from New York to take over from me – and then I'll chew the fat with you as long as you like. Right now, you do as this little girl says and shut your eyes and sleep your way home –'

And he had put his hand on Bobby's shoulder and cuffed it gently and then turned to seize Poppy's hand, and had shaken it up and down like a pump handle, clearly not wanting to let her go.

'Promise you'll take care of yourself, David,' Poppy said. 'Promise me now. You've been so good to us – I do wish I could get you to come with us! If you got on the train now we'd find some way to talk them into letting you go to Calais – it's a real shambles in there, the paper work. That's how I managed to get Bobby on –'

'No, I've got to wait,' he said. 'Newspaper men – we're like that. A crazy lot. When my new guy comes, believe me, I'll be away like a shot, after this little lot. And I'll come to London on my way home. It's a promise. Goodbye Poppy. Take care of that stupid bastard there –' And suddenly he had let go of her hand and taken her by both shoulders and kissed her hard on the mouth and when he pulled back she could see there were tears in his eyes.

'G'bye Poppy,' he mumbled. 'You're a great kid and he's a lucky bastard – I'll see you –' And he was gone, loping away through the crowded platform with his camera case bumping at his side in its familiar way and she felt her own eyes prickle as she watched him go.

But now there was just the journey to think about, and for the next thirty sleepless hours that was all she did think about, that and Bobby. The train limped slowly through the burgeoning fields of northern France, stopping for long hours at wayside halts, so supplies soon ran out, and getting enough food and drink for the men on the train became hellishly difficult. Bobby's food, for he could cope only with soft gruels and broths and milk, was a major worry, but somehow she managed to beg and buy – at exorbitant prices – the things she needed from the local farmers at places where the train stopped, and at last at Calais, when they reached the hospital there, it wasn't so bad. They had a decent supply of invalid foods, and Poppy managed to get a large bottle of Brand's essence, and fed it to Bobby in patient spoonfuls, so glad to see the nourishing blandness of it slip into him that she could have wept.

The crossing was at least a smooth one, which helped, and by the time the cliffs of Dover could be clearly seen, she was able to think of other things, and most particularly about whether Mabel had been able to do as she had been asked.

Poppy had sent her a cable from Amiens, telling her as carefully as she could that Bobby was injured. It wouldn't be right, she had told herself, just to arrive in London and present Bobby's family with him in this state as a *fait accompli*. They had to be warned, and anyway, perhaps Mabel could be useful. In her last letter to Poppy – and her letters had become fewer and fewer as the months at Revigny had gone on – Mabel had told her almost as an aside that she had left the *Dispatch* office and was now working at the War Office as a typewriting supervisor, and Poppy, remembering this, had added a terse instruction to her cable, 'Arrange hospital care.'

The question was, had she done it? And she stood there beside Bobby's stretcher on the deck – for the ship was so loaded that every inch of space was occupied by wounded men – and prayed that Mabel had understood and obeyed.

And it seemed possible she had, for as the ship came slowly into the docks at Dover, there she was, a small figure down on the cobblestones, peering up at the sides of the steamer as it made its creaking way into its berth and Poppy leaned over and waved furiously and with enormous relief. To see once more that plump figure dressed in rather too tight and over-fussy clothes was so comforting that she felt a great wash of love for Mabel break over her head and she leaned over even more precariously and shouted, 'Mabel!' at the top of her voice. And Mabel heard her and looked up and then beamed from ear to ear and waved furiously.

The next hour or two were difficult, for now at last Army bureaucracy caught up with Poppy. The wounded men were being counted off the ship by a punctilious Captain and when he came to Bobby, he could find no record of him on any of the Army lists he was carrying so importantly in his folder. It took Poppy half an hour of explaining and wheedling to get anywhere with him and in the end she had lost her temper – much to the delight of the orderlies carrying Bobby's stretcher – and shouted at him, 'So what do you want me to do? Take him back on the next ship and dump him in Calais, or back in the trenches at Verdun? Don't be so stupid, man!' At which the Captain had bridled and gone brick-red and expostulated loudly. But he had taken her point and at last let Poppy and her precious stretcher off the ship.

And after that it was all much easier, for Mabel had indeed come up trumps.

'I've got an ambulance waiting, darling,' she had told Poppy after hugging her warmly and then crouching down beside Bobby to look at him with tear-drenched eyes. 'I pulled every string I could get my hands on. But if you can't pull well at the War House, where can you?'

'Oh, glory be!' Poppy said, and stood there on the dock and lifted her chin to the April air and thought – I'm home. I've got him home and it's all going to be fine – And she felt she had to say it.

'It's going to be fine now, Mabel. We're home and it's going to be fine –'

'Of course it is!' Mabel said stoutly. 'Once we get him looked after it'll all be wonderful. He won't go back any more and then we can all be comfortable again. Oh, Poppy, you do look dreadful! So thin and so – well, so dreadful!' And she peered at her, her plump cheeks creased with anxiety and her round eyes alight with concern.

And Poppy looked at her, at her smooth clean face and glossy hair and her pretty spring costume in yellow braided silk and thought – we were friends once, we two. We understood each other, and we laughed at the same things and had so much fun. But now we're like foreigners. After all I've seen and done, we don't even speak the same language any more.

'I'm sure I do, Mabel,' she said and managed a grin. 'But there's nothing a good bath won't make rather better, I imagine –'

And Mabel wrinkled her nose and said awkwardly, 'Well, yes – I rather think that might be a good idea –'

They had reached the ambulance now, a neat vehicle that was equipped for four passengers, so there was plenty of room for Bobby to ride in solitary style and Poppy was relieved to see it.

'Where are we going?' she asked Mabel as the orderlies carefully put Bobby in place on one of the waiting bunks. 'A chest hospital or –?'

'I've got him into the military hospital not far from Pirbright,' Mabel said, as with a lively display of frilled petticoat and silk stockinged ankles she too climbed aboard the ambulance. 'I was worried about the cost, you see – an ordinary hospital, well, I couldn't see who would pay the bills, could I? I mean, perhaps the paper will, but you can't be sure – so I thought – he was in the war, let the Government pay. And I pulled some more strings and there you are –'

Poppy followed her into the ambulance as the orderlies went away and the driver, who had been waiting patiently in his cab, revved up his engine. It had never occurred to her even to think about how she might have to pay for Bobby's care once she got him home. The only thing that had mattered was to find the right doctor and make sure he was properly looked after. How very practical of Mabel to consider the problem of costs, she told herself. How very sensible. It will of course be better if he is a patient in a military hospital which won't send in bills – but all the same she felt a little chill as she thought of Mabel's cool pragmatism, when it was Bobby who was so ill and in such need.

'It was dear George who pointed it out to me, of course. I dare say I wouldn't have considered the problem except for him. He is *so* sweet, and so caring of me, Poppy! I am so happy – we are to be married, you see, as soon as George has the practice precisely as it should be. He will not marry me, he said, until we can have the best of everything, a nice house and good furniture and so forth – isn't that lovely of him? I can't tell you how good it has been to have him to take care of me now Bobby has left me, and Goosey is so fussed over Chloe all the time. Without George I'd have been so miserable and alone –'

Quite a different language, Poppy thought. We speak quite a different language and she looked out of the smoked-glass window at the passing streets of Dover, and thought – not much longer now. We'll get Bobby settled in his new hospital and then I can get some sleep, have a bath and get some sleep. Somewhere –

And then blinked as she remembered and turned eagerly to Mabel. 'Where did you say the hospital was?'

'Mmm?'

'The hospital we're going to,' she said impatiently. 'Where did you say it was?'

'Oh! It's near Pirbright. In Surrey. Lord and Lady Middlemere, you know, they gave up their house for the war so that it could be a hospital. Frightfully good of them. They've built extra huts there in the garden so I'm told but there are some very nice wards in the house itself and I managed to persuade the Matron that my brother was a very important man as a war correspondent and that was why he had War Office permission to be a patient, and she believed me! Well, it's almost true –' And Mabel dimpled at her. 'I *am* in charge of the typewriting, after all, with thirty girls under me, so I can sign some requisitions quite legitimately. And I got my superior to countersign – he's rather sweet on me, to tell the truth, and that makes dear George so jealous, such fun! And it all helps. So darling Bobby will be in a lovely ward and be beautifully looked after, and then soon he'll be well and can come home and return to the *Dispatch* and everything will be just as it was before!' And she turned to look down at Bobby – who was lying dozing in his bunk, for Poppy had managed to persuade one of the Army doctors to give him a dose of morphia to ensure he suffered the minimum of pain during the disembarkation – and sighed gustily. 'Won't that be nice? And won't Chloe be pleased? I know I shall –'

'I think, you know, Mabel, that it won't be quite as easy as that,' Poppy said carefully. She had no wish to alarm her, but there was no sense in letting her nourish such false hopes. 'He's really had a severe case of gas, you know. It may take some time before he is quite well again –'

'What do you mean?' Mabel stared at her with her face suddenly crumpled with anxiety. 'You don't mean he's not going to – you aren't saying that – Poppy?'

'No, of course not!' Poppy said firmly. 'He will be well – I shall see to it that he gets the best nursing possible and – he'll get well. But I think it will take a long time. Months, maybe –' Longer, she thought privately, knowing a good deal about the effects of mustard gas from her lectures when she trained, as well as from direct experience of caring for such cases.

'Oh,' Mabel said and turned to look at him again. And then looked up at Poppy and said, 'Isn't it a good thing then that he is to be in a military hospital? It would have been bad enough paying for an ordinary hospital for a short time, but for a long one –' And she shook her head at the thought.

Once again Poppy pushed aside the uncharitable thoughts that came into her head about Mabel's practical attitudes and looked at Bobby herself.

'I'm awfully glad he'll be at Pirbright,' she said then. 'I was going to put in for my discharge now this has happened, so that I can look after Bobby all the time, but maybe while he's in hospital I can apply to join the training staff of the FANYs. Their camp's at Pirbright –'

'Give up the FANYs to look after Bobby?' Mabel seized on that. 'But Poppy, that would be so – I mean, how very good of you! I had never thought you would do anything so generous for us. I mean, I know we are old friends, and it is wonderful that you ran across each other there at the war and were able to bring him home safe after he was wounded but – well, you are very kind!' And she leaned forwards and hugged her friend warmly.

Poppy opened her mouth to explain and then closed it. And then opened it again and said, 'But –'

And could go no further. It wouldn't be right to tell Bobby's sister of their plans to marry until Bobby himself was in a fit condition to talk about them too. And yet unless Mabel knew, how could Poppy organize things the way she wanted to? She had been glad enough to use Mabel's services to get Bobby into the right sort of care here in England, but hadn't thought beyond that. Now, would she have to take a back seat and leave all decisions in Mabel's hands? Mabel's possibly foolish and undoubtedly parsimonious hands? Poppy closed her eyes to grapple as best she could with this dilemma. And finding no answer, did the only thing she could and put off the problem to a later date. Sooner or later she and Bobby would be able to talk to Mabel – and to her own family, of course – about what was to happen in the future. Now the important thing was to get Bobby well.

The hospital when they reached it was all that Poppy could have wanted for Bobby. A large and comfortable country house had been converted with considerable skill into a small hospital for officers and Bobby was ensconced in a bright three-bedded room that ran off the terrace, and which had large doors which could be opened to the garden.

'Oh, this will be wonderful for him!' she said fervently to the cool Sister in perfect white veil and spotless uniform who settled him in. 'He can breathe some decent air here and let his poor lungs heal –'

The Sister looked at her curiously. 'You've been working in France?'

'Working in France?' Poppy echoed and through her mind ran a jumbled tangle of images of the mud and the roads, the noise and the filth, the stink of death and blood at Revigny and the way her whole body had ached with the effort of it all – and smiled wryly.

'Yes,' she said. 'I've been working in France.'

'You'll need a bath,' the sister said practically. 'You can use our quarters if you like – you look done in, my dear, and that's the truth of it –'

'I think perhaps I am,' Poppy said and smiled again. Now the pressure was off, now she had managed to complete that appalling thirty-hour journey, now her Bobby was safely tucked into a warm clean bed in a pretty room in the April sunshine of England, now she could consider herself. And when she did she knew she was at the very end of her rope. So far at the end that she could hardly think.

And she looked gratefully at the Sister and then at Mabel, who was fussing happily over Bobby, who lay there very still with his eyes closed and not responding to her, though Poppy knew perfectly well that he was aware of all that was going on, so used had she become to his care, and tried to smile. And could only grimace awkwardly when Sister said, 'And something to eat, perhaps?'

'Oh, Sister, yes, please,' she said. 'But I think that first bath would be absolutely wonderful.' And then she looked again at Bobby and saw that his eyes were open and he was looking directly at her, and as though she had walked inside his mind she knew what he was thinking. He was remembering that Sunday afternoon, when he had used Madame Corbigny's kettle of hot water in her billet a million miles away, in another world. And just as he was crying at the memory, so was she.

28

They had put up the Christmas decorations by the time she arrived, and the place looked quite enchanting. Pieces of cotton wool had been stuck to each of the light shades to simulate snow and there were scarlet streamers and holly everywhere. The place smelled better, too, with the scent of pine needles overwhelming the usual smell of ether and carbolic because of a tree which someone had brought in and decked with glittering glass balls and small coloured candles, quite in a pre-war manner, and Poppy paused in the hall to admire it.

It was good to have the tree to look at. It was always necessary to stop and school her face into its jolly expression before going into Bobby, and to make sure she had her thoughts clear in her mind, and tonight she was grateful for the tree. It gave her something extra to talk about.

He was sitting as usual in the armchair at the foot of his bed, his head bent over a jigsaw puzzle. She had been so glad when, late in the summer, she had suggested he try doing one and he had become so absorbed that for a whole day he had not wept at all, but now she was not so sure. Lately he seemed to do nothing else, working his way doggedly through puzzle after puzzle, poring over the little cardboard pieces as though they were the most important things in the whole world. But at least it was better than weeping; he had done nothing but cry from the time in May he had at last got his voice back – or as much of it as he was ever to get back and the doctor had told him so – until the day in September when her gift of a puzzle had broken the pattern. All I have to do now, she thought with a flash of irritation, is find something to get rid of the puzzle habit and then something to get rid of the habit *that* will turn into –

'Hello, Bobby!' she said brightly. 'I've brought you some caramels! They're like gold dust these days, so hard to find, but Mrs Clarke in the village saved some specially for you. And I remembered your cigarettes, and last but not least, a divine blackberry tart one of our cooks did for you. There! Isn't that a lot of splendid loot?'

'Splendid,' he said and the thick guttural voice sounded dull and flat, and she yearned yet again to shake him, to tell him that it wouldn't sound so strange if only he'd stop being so miserable, that even those thick notes from his irretrievably gas-damaged larynx could sound warm and friendly. But she said nothing. What was the point? It only made things worse.

She sat down beside him and hitched her skirt a little higher for comfort; the uniform of the Training Commandant was not designed for lounging in, but she had learned some time ago that it was always wisest to visit him here at the hospital in uniform. There had been some attempt to dislodge him into an ordinary hospital, for he was after all only a civilian, but she had resisted that. Not because of any concern about the hospital bills elsewhere – now she had been promoted she was earning enough to cope with that – but because he was so settled here. He couldn't be called happy by any stretch of the imagination, but he was at least comfortable. He was used to the small room with its other two beds and their ever-changing occupants – for no one had been a patient at the hospital as long as Bobby had – and used to the nurses and the orderlies and above all the garden.

Sometimes, Poppy thought, the garden is the only thing that keeps him sane. He spent long hours just sitting on the terrace when the weather permitted, or inside the tall windows when it was cold or wet, staring out at the bushes and the flowers, almost watching them grow. Poppy had seen him do it, and had tried once or twice to coax him into conversation, but he had flown into such a temper that she had decided never to do so again. That was why she visited in the evenings now; once it was dark, it was easier to talk to him.

'I've brought a letter to read to you, Bobby,' she said now, and took it from her pocket. It had been lovely when the envelope had arrived yesterday with its now familiar American stamp and the spidery writing she had come to know so well. He was a good man, David Deveen, and never failed to send a thick wad of his closely written pages full of chatter. They arrived in the second or third week of each month without fail, and lit her long hard days with a touch of glory, for he told her so much of his life in New York, of what was happening at his paper, and how his neighbours were behaving that she felt she was there, sometimes, living it all with him.

He lived in an apartment house, he had told her right at the very beginning, on the East Side; 'not a salubrious neighbourhood you understand, but very quixotic. You meet people here that just don't exist in other places –' And he would weave long and funny tales about Mrs Levi and her deadly enemy Mrs Upstairsnik ('This cannot be her real name, but it's the only one I have ever heard Mrs Levi use for her, and it is always accompanied by a most vicious spit in the nearest gutter') and Mr Capitelli who kept canaries in the basement and was cordially hated by the janitor, Joe Fugg, in consequence, and Mrs Rodriguez who had no husband but did have nine children and never seemed to know what any one of them was up to ('and it's usually mayhem of a high order'). Oh, his letters were wonderful, and Poppy sometimes thought she couldn't have coped at all without them, for they were the only things that could make Bobby laugh these days.

David had been used to write to Bobby as well at first, but since Bobby never replied, seeming unable to bring himself to any sort of effort, Poppy had written to David and tried to explain that it might be easier if he wrote to her only and she would share the letters with Bobby. And ever since, as the months had pleated into each other and 1916 had dribbled away into more and more bad news from the Front as well as from elsewhere like Mesopotamia, he had written his letters to her. And they had been her lifeline to normality.

For there was little else to think of that wasn't work or Bobby. She had been accepted back to Pirbright with alacrity, for with her experience she was now a valuable trainer, and had after only six months been promoted to running the practical side of the training system. She took the raw girls who were now volunteering for the FANYs in considerable numbers, and turned them into well-drilled smart first-aiders who were also first-class drivers and all-round useful people, and sent them off to war ready to do the job she herself had done so well for so long. And if she sometimes wept into her pillow at night for the ones who she heard had died, no one else knew it but that pillow.

For the rest, she spent her evenings visiting Bobby, and sometimes went up to see her Mama and Jessie and Lizah. Mama had been her usual rather dry quiet self and had made no comment when Poppy had explained to her that she was going to be living in the camp at Pirbright from now on. She had just bent her head, and said, 'If that is your decision then it is. I am glad you were not in any way hurt by your time in France. You look rather thin, however,' and that had been all she had said that was at all personal. But she had asked Poppy to spend some time with her stepgrandmama.

'She is very distressed because both Harold and Samuel have left the house. Harold has joined the Army after all and is at Aldershot and chooses not to visit us, and Samuel cannot visit, for he has decided to live in Australia.'

She had lifted her brows then in a moment of sharp comment. 'He seems to feel he will be less likely to be forced into the Army there, and will therefore be safer. He also believes he can make a good deal of money from people as stupid as he says they are. I imagine he will find himself surprised on both counts.'

'I imagine he might,' Poppy had said dryly, remembering the few Australians she had met in the Army hospital at Calais, lively men with loud flat voices who were far from stupid, and who told her of some of the pressures that were being put on able-bodied young men at home to join the colours. 'And I dare say Grandmama *is* very upset. Of course I'll talk to her –'

And so she had, not that it had helped Maud much. She had clearly decided that life was no longer worth any sort of effort, and lay in her bed, lackadaisical and lachrymose, and had made small response to Poppy's efforts to encourage her. And when Poppy received the telegram to say that she had died of a heart attack in late July, she had not been at all surprised, though a little sad. She could not pretend to have loved Maud; how could she? She had hardly known her, except as a whining self-pitying wreck of a woman who always smelled of Chypre perfume with an underlay of brandy. It had seemed so wasted a life, her stepgrandmama's. So she went to the funeral and managed to speak the necessary civil words to Harold, who did at least put in an appearance, dressed exceedingly smartly in a field officer's uniform, and who was very urbane indeed, making no comment at all that showed he had any recollection of what had passed between them when they had last met. But Poppy, aware though she was of her mother's lonely state now, could not help but escape from the gloom of the house immediately after the funeral to go for comfort, as she so often did, to Jessie's shop.

There all was as it always had been, only more so. Clearly the war had led to greater prosperity for Jessie, and she did in fact speak of it in apologetic tones to Poppy.

'What can you do, dolly? You're in a business that people need and want, so comes a war and suddenly they need and want you even more! So I manage to get supplies for my shop, and I need to open out a bit. So I take the shop next door and then I need the one next door to that. And the more I try to please the customers the more they want and the harder I work and the trouble is, the more money I make! I feel a bit bad, you know? There's people around here only too happy to make the extra cash a war brings – I know trouser manufacturers and mantle makers gone into the uniform business, coining it – real swells they're turning into. Me, I ain't that sort. I just want to make a comfortable living for me and my Bernie, it's enough – but the way it is we make more'n's good for us. Or good for Bernie –'

And she had looked anxious suddenly, her large shining face creasing into heavy lines. And later, talking to Lily, still acerbic and still bullying the customers mercilessly, Poppy found out why. Bernie was as beautiful as ever, Lily told her, but he was also becoming more and more difficult to control.

'Three times we've 'ad the rozzers 'ere, owin' to him, us what never does nothing we shouldn't, watches the rationing laws like 'awks, the 'ole thing, and what 'appens? That bleedin' kid runs around the town getting into all sorts o' trouble. Three times the rozzers, inspector it was the last time, warning poor old Jessie as it'll be clink for the kid next time he gets collared. And she just says 'e's a good boy, just got a few wicked friends – you know what a fool she is for that Bernie! And all the time 'e's robbin' 'er blind, pinchin' food outa the shop, selling it for Gawd knows 'ow much on the sly – one of these days 'e'll get Jess into such tsoorus – all right – trouble – 'e'll get 'er into trouble – such trouble. She won't know what 'it her – you mark my words –'

And Poppy, uneasily aware that she was probably right, did all she could to comfort Jessie whenever Bernie's name came into the conversation, but it wasn't easy.

Lizah too, it transpired, was thriving, at least financially. His pub, Jessie told her, was always full, and he was making a mint in spite of the new DORA rules about pub opening hours. 'Some Dora that is!' Jessie had snorted in disgust. 'How can it come under the Defence of the Realm Act to fiddle with opening hours? I don't reckon it. But he's doin' okay. He does special parties for all sorts of well-off Army officers and the like. They want the best booze, and he can get it. I do the food and they gets a good value nosh-up for their money. It's a ridiculous thing how good a time a war can be for the people stuck at home. Hell for the likes of you and your friend Bobby –' And she had looked sharply at Poppy for a reaction and received none and, satisfied, had gone on, 'But all right for me and Lizah. Not that it's all wrong that Lizah should do well,' she had added with sudden fierce loyalty. 'Seein' as he sacrificed enough the last time around. A one-armed man – what sort of life is it? But now, he's gettin' a better share out o' things and no one can grudge him.'

It was odd when she went to see Lizah. He greeted her with all his old ebullient excitement, was full of chatter about her and how she looked and how wonderful it was to see her, but said nothing at all about her experiences in France. It was as though he could not bring himself to talk about it in any way and she had thought – it's because he knows what real war is like. He's been there himself. That's why he doesn't want to talk about it. He *knows* – and she accepted his unspoken wish and never mentioned her war experiences to him either.

Not that she talked to anyone much about that, except perhaps her students. They needed to know what they had to face in the months to come, and she would try to get across to them the awfulness of it, but without much success. They would sit there in the lecture room, their young faces smooth and full of the glitter and excitement of their youth, their energy, and the glorious business of being in a war, and listen without understanding at all the reality that lay behind the words she used. And how can I make them understand? she would ask herself wearily as she sent them off about their business at the end of her lectures. I wouldn't have believed it either till I saw it for myself.

The one thing that Lizah would talk to her about was her mother, and that was becoming ever more burdensome. She had hoped that by now he would have forgotten his obsession about meeting Mildred, about making a home with her for the three of them, but it burned as brightly as ever in him. Whenever Poppy went to see Jessie and he was there – as he so often was – he would greet her eagerly and ask after Mildred, and demand to know when Poppy was going to speak to her again. And Poppy would shake her head at him wearily and change the subject. But it wasn't easy, any more than trying to help her students understand what war was like was easy. Or trying to keep a jolly face with Bobby when he seemed so incapable of anything but the deepest gloom most of the time.

And that of course was the heaviest part of her burden – the fact that he was not totally incapable of controlling his misery, that he could, when he chose, seem to be cheerful, and make that thick new voice of his sound amusing rather than alarming. But he never did that for her. That only happened once every month or so, when Chloe came to see him.

They had slipped into a routine quite early in Bobby's stay at the hospital, she and Mabel and Chloe. Poppy visited every evening, and once a week telephoned Mabel to give her news of Bobby's progress, because as Mabel explained carefully, 'With my job at the War House, you see, I do work such very long hours that I get awfully tired. So I can't make the journey to Surrey as often as I'd like – but do phone me every week without fail, now –' And Poppy did, and once each month Mabel, with George Pringle to drive her in his small car, brought Chloe to Pirbright to see her father.

The first visit had been an agonizing one. Poppy had been there too, because Mabel, suddenly frightened, had begged her to be so.

'I can't deal with illness,' she had said fretfully to Poppy on the telephone. 'It does upset me so – I told George and he says I am very good to make the effort for it is a long journey after all, but I must bring Chloe, of course. So you will be there, dear Poppy, to help us? It won't be at all easy – you know how highly strung dear Chloe is.'

Indeed she was, for on that first visit she had taken one look at her father, and burst into tears and for almost the whole time there had wept and screamed and been impossible and had to be taken out in disgrace. But she had come back before the end of the hour, at Poppy's gentle insistence, and it hadn't been so bad then.

'Bobby, my darling,' she had murmured to him. 'If you don't somehow put on a show for her, she'll refuse ever to come again, and that would be so dreadful for you. You know how much you want to see her –' And he had looked at her from those still red-rimmed eyes of his and nodded.

Poppy had fetched Chloe, soothing her and crooning at her, and at length the child had sat on her father's lap and allowed him to hug her while he chattered brightly at her. And Poppy had been so hopeful and excited, listening to the change in his voice, seeing how animated he looked, how cheerful even. Perhaps this was after all the beginning of the end of his illness? Perhaps the shell-shock about which the doctors murmured was beginning to wear off?

But it hadn't been as easy as that. As soon as Chloe and Mabel had gone, he had lapsed back into his old ways, and only emerged again the next time his sister and daughter arrived. And Poppy bit back her own tears of frustration and tried to tell herself that it was an indication of Bobby's love for her that he treated her as he did. If he did not feel safe with her, secure in the knowledge that whatever happened she would still be there and caring for him, wouldn't he put on an act for her too? The fact that he didn't meant so much that was important; or so she would assure herself over and over again. But somewhere deep inside she remained unconvinced, particularly when he was in a very low state.

Now, as the Christmas decorations in his small room moved lightly in the draught from the door and the sound of a piano being played in the day room came drifting down the corridor, he seemed to be a little better than he had been, and leaned forwards to look at the blackberry pie she had brought and murmured his thanks for the cigarettes and caramels. Sometimes he didn't even do that, just sitting ignoring all she said and did, just sitting and staring. But tonight there was some animation in him and she said cheerfully, 'Well! Shall I read David's letter to you?'

'No, not now,' he said, and obediently she folded the letter and slipped it back into its envelope. There'd be time to re-read it and enjoy it herself before she went to bed tonight.

'Talk to me, Poppy.' The thick voice seemed to be less flat than it usually was, and she looked up sharply. Could it be that he was indeed coming out of it, this blank of cold misery that seemed to have enveloped him ever since that dreadful night at Verdun?

'Talk to you, my darling? Of course I will,' she said cheerfully and put out her hand and took his. It felt hot and dry under her fingers and she stroked it gently, glad he responded with small movements instead of sitting inert as he so often did. 'What about?'

'About – oh, anything. About leaving here. I've been here too long, haven't I, Poppy? It's time I left – time to try to get back to normal again. They told me today – the doctors, Armitage and that other one – Fletcher. They said I must go, I can't stay here after the year is out.' He managed a thin grin. 'I suppose Goosey will have to come back from her brother's farm to look after me. Will she, do you think? And will I get my job back at the paper, Poppy? It's all so easy, really isn't it? I just have to pull myself together and then everything will be wonderful –'

And he bent his head and let it drop on his chest and she thought – oh, no – please, not again. I can't bear it again. This stopped after the jigsaw puzzles. Not again.

But it was again. He was weeping those great sobs that had wracked him for so many long days and weeks and months at the start of his stay here, breaking his heart at his own inadequacy, his ruined voice, his all-enveloping sense of blank bleak misery. She knew how he felt, for she had been through every step of the way with him and now all she could do was slip to her knees beside his chair and hold him close, so that his head rested on her shoulder and he could cry into her neck.

And the hot tears slid down inside her collar and she knew that there was only one answer that would work. And he would have to be made to see it, no matter what.

29

'Do you think you can manage him?' Dr Armitage said and squinted at her over the smoke that rose from the cigarette that he had, as usual, clamped to the corner of his mouth. 'It's one thing dealing with a regular visit – even a daily one – to a man in his state, quite another to be with him all the time.'

'I don't know,' Poppy said. 'I only know I have to try. And why shouldn't I manage? It's not as though he's – he's not violent or irrational or anything of that sort –'

'Oddly enough, that can be less wearing than this constant depression. Violent people tend to be violent only occasionally and the people around them learn how to recognize the warning signs and act accordingly. But these depressed men –' He shook his head. 'I'm not ashamed to tell you, Miss Amberly, I find them exceedingly difficult to help. With a man like Bradman who has the added burden of breathing difficulties and that voice damage – well, that's why we have to let him go. We've done all we can. To keep him here longer won't help him, and there are the other men, of course –'

And he let the words hang in the air and bent his head to shuffle among the papers on his desk before him, and Poppy knew what he meant as clearly as if he had shouted it aloud. There are other men who can be helped, other men who may be healed. Bobby Bradman is a wreck and we don't want to waste any more of our valuable time on him – what's the point?

And at last anger began to move in her, and she was glad of it. All she had felt since Bobby had told her that he had been warned he had to leave the hospital, and that all that could be offered to him was a place in a Home for Incurables, was a constant anxiety tinged with cold fear. How could she cope if they took him away from here? How could *he* cope in a place like those so-called homes, which she knew to be filled with shuffling old men with dead, fishlike eyes and slumped bodies that shouted to the world that they were only there to wait to die? But now there was anger, cold clean anger, and she got to her feet and said crisply, 'It is very likely that once I do get him away, he will start to improve. After all, he has been given only the minimum of treatment over the past few months.'

'What treatment is there to give?' the doctor said and looked at her with that same squinting stare. 'You can't operate on shell shock, you know.' And she felt the hint of contempt in him; was he one of these doctors who, while paying lip service to the notion of shell shock, in fact regarded it as simply cowardice under another name? There were many such – she had herself heard them talk at the training camp for the FANYs – but she believed with all the passion she had in her that whatever might be the case with other men labelled as shell-shocked her Bobby was no coward. His experience that night in Verdun had changed him profoundly and physically; it was no mere quirk that kept him locked in his deep misery. He was ill, and he could be well again, with the right care. And she would give it.

'I'll need time,' she said now. 'There are arrangements to be made, and I must apply for a compassionate discharge myself. You understand that I can't take him until then –'

'As long as we know that plans are afoot, then we won't push you,' he said and rose to his feet, his hand held towards her. 'And try not to think too harshly of us, Miss Amberly. We are, after all, a military hospital and we've done the best we could for your civilian friend – or should I say fiancé?'

'Yes,' she said. 'Fiancé. And yes, I do understand your difficulty. It has been a long time and I dare say that – well, anyway, thank you for all your efforts. At least he's alive and that is something to be deeply grateful for in these dreadful days. I'll let you know what is to happen as soon as I can.' And she turned and went, marching down the long parquet corridor with her head up, listening to her own footsteps and knowing that a much harder interview was to come.

Because it was not as though the subject hadn't been discussed between them before now. Back in June, once she was sure he was over the worst of his chest illness, and it had become clear that any further progress would be slow, she had said to him firmly that they would be married; but that had thrown him into an even deeper despondency.

'What good am I to you?' he had wept at her, howled at her, almost spat at her. 'What good am I? A wreck – I'm not going to let you marry me in this state. When I'm better, maybe –' And had refused to say another word. And when, in later months, she had tried again to return to the subject he had blocked her just as successfully. But this morning was to be different. She would interrupt his obsessive garden watching and tell him how it was to be. She would not ask. She would *tell*. There would be no argument, no blocking this time. It simply had to be –

And if somewhere deep inside her made her feel heavy and miserable as though she were thinking not of the glory of marrying the man she had loved for so long but of some sort of prison sentence that had been passed on her, she was not prepared to admit it to her conscious mind in so many words.

He was sitting by the window when she came in, and one of his room mates was lounging on his bed behind him, reading. Poppy stood hesitantly at the door for a moment and then the other man saw her, opened his mouth to speak, and seeing some expression on her face that she herself did not realize was there, slid to his feet and tied his dressing gown cord more firmly round his waist.

'I'll go and see what's happening in the billiards room,' he murmured. 'Knock a few balls about before lunch, hmm?' And he smiled conspiratorially at Poppy and went out of the room and she thought – oh, God, will it always be like this? That look of pitying understanding on other people's faces when they see us together? Will it always be a matter for misery that we are together, rather than the joy it used to be?

And refused to think such thoughts any longer and went over to Bobby and knelt at his side and set both hands over his on his lap.

'Bobby, I have news – wonderful news,' she said loudly and willed him to turn his eyes away from the dripping winter landscape outside the window, with its dead rose trees and sagging grass and weeping trees, to look at her. And at last he did, and stared down at her with the blank eyes that she found so much more disturbing than almost anything else. If he had looked at her with more expression it would have helped so much.

'Darling, we're getting married,' she said and as he opened his mouth went on rapidly so that he couldn't get a word in edgeways. 'No, it's all arranged. There are things to be done – banns and so forth, you understand, and arrangements to be made at home, but it's all in hand. Be happy darling – I am. We shall leave here and everything will be as it should be. We shall be happy and be together always and then you'll start to get well. You'll see. It's being here that has made you so low, I'm convinced of it. You've been here far too long – it's made you miserable, and made you feel like an invalid. Now it's time to start feeling like a well person. And then you *will* be –'

He went on staring at her as she chatted on, hardly knowing what she was saying now, painting a roseate picture of the way life would be, how they would be contented all the time and how she would learn to cook properly from Goosey, for of course to start with they must live in the house in Norland Square, and how jolly she was feeling, and at last, slowly, she began to see a response in him.

And as she watched his eyes lose that glazed stare and begin to be more alert a part of her mind thought, as still her tongue ran on and on – perhaps I was right? Perhaps I can make it all right for him? – and the elation that suddenly filled her seemed to invest her words and so shift itself to him, and he began, amazingly, to smile. And she put up arms to him invitingly and waited, her own eyes almost pleading with him, and at last he moved. He leaned forwards and put his arms about her and held her close and after a moment she turned her head and with one hand pulled his face down and kissed him just as she had in her little room at Madame Corbigny's, with all the passion she had in her.

And he responded. For the first time since he had been here at Pirbright, he moved out of his misery towards her. His lips were hot and dry on hers and there was a mustiness about him that smelled quite unlike the way he had been when they had first made love, but none of that mattered. She only knew he was kissing her as a man should and she pushed her whole body towards him with all the strength she could and clung to him.

There was an apologetic little cough then, behind them, and she pulled away from Bobby and looked over her shoulder. The man from the other bed was there, standing in the doorway and grinning widely.

'Far be it from me to spoil an idyll,' he murmured. 'But there are already three chaps playing billiards down there and three others waiting and not so much as a corner for poor little me. So I came back – I know I'm *de trop*, but if you could carry on as though I weren't here, I'd be as quiet as a mouse, I do promise you!'

'Ass!' Poppy said joyously and looked back at Bobby. 'You can be the first to congratulate us. We're getting married soon. Aren't we, Bobby? He's leaving here and coming home with me and we're going to pretend hospitals never existed –'

'And about time too!' the young man said and clapped his hands together like a schoolboy and then put his head out into the corridor and shouted, 'Hey, you chaps! Come here! We have a celebration going on!'

There was a clatter of feet in the corridor as people came running from adjoining wards and more cries and laughter, for so little happened here in the general way that any change in the smooth routine was an occasion for enjoyment, and within minutes the small room was crammed with people, all pumping Bobby's hand up and down or patting Poppy on the back, and threatening to kiss the bride, and Poppy, while she laughed and fended them off amiably enough, watched Bobby anxiously. But it all seemed to help, for he sat there bemused at first but then seemed to catch the spirit of the moment, and laughed and nodded too. And bursting with gratitude and for the first time with real personal excitement about the plans she had been forced to make, she hugged him again as one of the men went off to search for tooth glasses in which to pour, as he put it, 'The mildest little celebratory tot before lunch.'

After that it was all much smoother than she had imagined it could be. It was as though everyone wanted to co-operate as much as they could to help Bobby. She posted the banns at the local church and the vicar there was as delighted as though they had both been his parishioners for ever, instead of for just a few months, and then arranged with the Commandant of the FANYs that she would resign her commission.

She could not pretend she did that without a pang. She had come to Pirbright to train as a raw girl with no experience of the world, even of herself. She had been as coltish and awkward as a pigtailed schoolgirl and wide-eyed with her own ignorance. And now she was a slightly wary and definitely battle-scarred woman, one who could deal with emergencies that once she could not have imagined occurring and one who had lost all her fear of her fellow men and women. There had been traces of shyness in the old Poppy; there were none in the new one. There had been a scatterbrained quality about the girl Poppy but there was not in the woman Poppy, who was calm and sensible and generally poised for all eventualities. And she owed all of that to having been a FANY and having trained here at Pirbright.

She tried to say as much to her Commandant when she explained to her why she had to apply for discharge from the Service, and she, a wise and sensible woman, listened and then nodded and agreed. Poppy did indeed owe the FANYs a debt of appreciation.

'But not so much,' she said firmly, 'as we owe you. You've worked exceedingly hard and given back to us far more than we ever gave you. We shall miss you, Miss Amberly, very much. But there it is – when you run a women's service, you have to expect these losses. It's all wrong, isn't it, that a man may marry and maintain a career and a woman can't?'

'Yes,' Poppy said with feeling. 'Oh, yes! It would be so good to stay on and – but it isn't just because I'm marrying that I have to leave. Bobby is still ill, you see and –'

'I know. But you'd have left anyway, wouldn't you? We don't have many married women in our ranks – a few, I do agree, but they are the special cases –' And neither of them said more, though Poppy knew she was referring to the FANYs who added an extra role to their ambulance driving and first-aiding; they worked as messengers carrying important dispatches, and, it was sometimes whispered, acted as secret agents at times. But it was not done to speak of them, so they didn't.

'And it isn't easy for a woman to run a home and to do a job as well –' the Commandant finished.

'I shall have to,' Poppy said quietly. 'Bobby can't work, and we have no income to speak of. He has some, of course –' She hesitated, feeling a little disloyal at speaking of their personal concerns to someone who was after all a stranger in their lives, but she needed a confidante and the Commandant had been her mentor and guide for some time now and was a sensible and reliable woman. So she went on hurriedly, 'He was married before you see, and his wife died in childbirth. So his little girl – Chloe – she has to be considered. And most of Bobby's money is taken up in providing for her. And soon she must go away to school, for she is getting on for nine. Bobby feels he wants her to have the best and that means a good boarding school and they're rather expensive –'

The older woman looked at her sharply. 'I see. What will you do?'

'I'm hoping to go back to the *Dispatch*, where I worked before. I was a typewriter there –'

'Ridiculous waste.' The Commandant almost snorted. 'You have learned to be a most capable officer. You are able to organize splendidly and run complicated affairs. You should be a manager of some kind –'

'A manager?' Poppy stared. 'What of?'

The Commandant lifted her brows. 'My dear, how can I say? A shop, perhaps, a business, an office? Somewhere where there are people who need to be taught, supervised, encouraged, made to put their shoulders to it – you are excellent at such tasks, as I well know. And I will know even more sharply in the coming weeks when you have left us, no doubt! Still my dear, I wish you every happiness. You want to leave in February, you say?'

Poppy nodded. 'Please, Ma'am. And I do thank you. I have so much to organize – it helps greatly to have you so – so amenable to my needs.'

'My dear, under this amenable surface I am positively shrieking my disappointment like a furious cat! But all the same – good luck, my dear.' And she had actually come round her desk and kissed Poppy on both cheeks.

It had been much harder to tell the family of her plans, so much harder that she waited until there was just a fortnight to go to the day they were to walk up the aisle at the parish church. She started by telling her mother. In some ways she was the hardest to face, and in others the easiest. Certainly there would be no emotional fireworks to deal with and that was one comforting thought.

And there were not. Mildred listened to Poppy's account of her plans and said nothing at all until she had finished. And then lifted her chin a little and said, 'Are you sure this is what you want?'

'Of course I'm sure, Mama! I have thought most carefully about it –'

'As long as you are not acting out of pity,' Mildred said. 'That is so bad a basis for any life.' She stopped then and her eyes slid away from Poppy. 'That was why I came back to this house. I pitied my stepmama – and you –'

'You pitied me?' Poppy stared and felt the back of her neck tighten with irritation. 'What a strange thought,' she said with a laugh that had no humour in it. 'How can one pity a child? I was not after all ill-treated in any way before we lived here, was I? Such memories I have of my life before this house are good and comfortable ones –'

And suddenly there rose in her mind's eye that image she thought she had lost so long ago, of the small warm kitchen with its cake-laden table and the fire burning in the grate and Mildred, her face glossy with sweat, and wrapped in an apron, pulling puddings boiled in great greasy cloths out of a steaming copper. And shook her head to rid herself of it as Mildred said dryly, 'Perhaps they are. But the place you lived in as a child was not so – suitable as it might have been. So I came here and brought you to live a better life. However, that is not the matter we were discussing. All I ask is that you are sure you have chosen your husband well. It is a difficult decision.'

There was a little silence and then Poppy said in a sharp voice, 'Is that why you never made it?'

Mildred was equally silent for a long moment and then she lifted her chin and stared at Poppy with her face quite still and expressionless.

'That is an impertinent question, Poppy,' she said. 'And you have no right to ask it.'

'No right?' Poppy said and hated the shrillness of her own voice. 'No right when I have Lizah begging me every time I see him to persuade you to see him again, to let him tell you that –'

'The remedy for that is simple,' Mildred said and got to her feet, making it clear that the conversation was ended. 'Do not see him.' And she went out of the room with her back very straight and without looking again at Poppy.

After that talking to Jessie was like a balm. She wept with delight first that there was to be a wedding, and then with distress that her dear Poppy was to marry 'such a man – a cripple yet –' and then with compunction when Poppy was sharp with her for describing Bobby thus and then with excitement as she launched herself into plans for the wedding celebration. At which Poppy had to lift both hands in the air and cry 'Stop!' and then explain to her at careful length that she was to be married in a church in Surrey and that the sort of East End celebration Jessie had in mind would not be at all suitable.

'Then what sort of wedding will it be, for Gawd's sake?' Jessie cried. 'A glass of wine with water and a dry biscuit to match it? Some celebration!'

'It will be a small and quiet party,' Poppy said firmly. 'Just immediate family – which includes you of course – and a few people from the hospital and the camp. We shall have a simple wedding breakfast which the Camp Commandant has told me she wishes to provide for us, and that is *all*. I wouldn't spoil your fun for the world, dearest Jessie, but I do assure you that I cannot have a big party. It wouldn't be right in these hard times anyway. I understand that it is easier for you, working as you do in a food business, to make a spread, but I could not hold my head up if we had the sort of lavish party I know you would arrange. It would embarrass me –'

'Embarrass, phooey!' Jessie began and then stopped as she saw Poppy's face, and threw her arms about her. 'All right, dolly, all right! Not another word. You want a tuppenny ha'penny wedding, *have* a tuppenny ha'penny wedding – what can I do? But I wish you all the joy in the world and please God your nebbisher fella'll get better and be the sort of real husband a girl like you deserves.'

And Poppy did not ask her what nebbisher meant, for she had a shrewd idea that it denoted pity for helplessness, and that was something she did not want to consider.

'I should tell Lizah –' Poppy said then and Jessie threw her hands up in irritation. 'That one!' she said. 'The way he plans things, he always gets 'em wrong – he's only gone to Scotland, hasn't he? There's a chap up there who says he can get me salmon, only he won't deal on the phone naturally, and he won't put nothing in writing. So Lizah had arranged a holiday for himself, up there in the snow and all that, I ask you, because he thinks not only can he fix up my salmon for next year, he can do a deal on whisky. Any time he could have gone, but punkt! he had to go now. So he's up there and won't be back till Gawd knows when – I'll try and phone him and –'

'No,' Poppy said swiftly. 'Let him be, dear Jessie. It's going to be hard enough to arrange things – if he comes to the wedding there'll be problems with Mama – really, I can't deal with that. Say nothing. When he comes back, I'll present him with a *fait accompli*. He might be a little upset, but he'll see why in the end –'

'That he never will,' Jessie said succinctly but agreed at last to say nothing to Lizah yet. Which left just Mabel to talk to.

Why Poppy should feel uncertain about telling Mabel of her plans she was not quite sure. The two girls had quite lost the old closeness of their pre-War days when the world had been a simpler, easier place, where giggles and clothes and poached egg lunches were all that mattered. Now with Mabel so aware of her importance at the War Office as supervisor of so many other typewriters, and with her absorption in her George, it was all very different, and Poppy went to see her to give her the news with some trepidation.

But Mabel seemed pleased enough to hear what she had to say. She was not as effusive as Poppy would have expected once, and as the old Mabel would have been, but she seemed contented enough and hugged Poppy when she had finished outlining the wedding plans, and wished her well.

'Where will you live, Poppy?' she said then, watching her sharply with those bright eyes of hers and Poppy flushed a little.

'It will have to be here, at Norland Square,' she said. 'At least for a while. I would not wish to make life difficult for you, dear Mabel, but to ask Bobby to seek another home now would be – well, he is still not better. And –'

But she could not bring herself to add, 'And it is Bobby's house, not yours,' even though that was the truth. Mabel knew it perfectly well, after all; what need to be provocative?

Now Mabel nodded slowly. 'I see. Well, perhaps I can persuade George to arrange our own wedding soon. That would be the best really. Then you and Bobby – and Chloe of course – can live here. Goosey must decide for herself, of course, to whom she will go.' And she had smoothed her hands over hips encased in excellent grey broadcloth trimmed with emerald braid and smiled at Poppy. 'Her wages are not so very high, after all, even though these days domestics do ask the most ridiculous sums. They are so hard to come by, you see. Running a house is a difficult task, as you will discover, Poppy. I, of course, have had so much experience –'

And that was that, Poppy told herself as she sat in the corner seat of a compartment in a slow train rumbling its way back to Pirbright. Everyone had been told, the wedding had been arranged and she was to be Mrs Bobby Bradman. The one thing she had wanted for as long as she could remember – well almost as long – was to happen. She should be the happiest person alive.

But all she could think about was Chloe. For Mabel had told her firmly that she and only she, her very own aunt, should speak to the child on the matter, and Poppy had been forced to agree. And now, as she sat and stared out at the lowering January sky outside the train, all she could think of was the deep foreboding that filled her. For being Mrs Bobby Bradman meant also being Chloe Bradman's stepmother. And she wasn't at all sure how she felt about that.

30

It had been blazingly hot all week, and that hadn't helped anyone's tempers at all. Small irritations seemed major and big anxieties massive. Goosey snapped at Poppy and Bobby shouted at Goosey and Mabel sulked whenever she was in the house, which was as rarely as she could manage, and Chloe was totally impossible. Altogether it was a horrid time, and Poppy, standing by the piano and dusting the ornaments on it with a lackadaisical hand, felt the sweat trickle down between her breasts and felt more edgy than ever.

She picked up the photograph of their wedding last, as she usually did, rubbing the duster over the elegant engraving of a drooping lily which ran up the side of the silver frame, and then set it back in its place and stared at it.

It seemed an eternity ago since she had stood in the trampled snow outside the church at Pirbright, wrapped in that cream cloth coat and carrying the spray of lilies and stephanotis that hung almost to her kid-shod feet. She had been right to refuse to wear the usual kind of wedding dress, she told herself now, staring at her own image, at her smiling face under the wide brim of her fur-trimmed hat. She'd been so proud of that fur trimming and the way it had been repeated on her coat to look so very stylish, and how the matching cream silk dress she had worn underneath had made it all seem so special. Just as good as a cloud of satin and lace and veils, she thought, just as good and much more suitable in wartime. And then she looked at Bobby's face as he stood there beside her, his face and his posture so wooden and so still, and tried not to wish he had smiled a little more that day. Six months ago, now. It didn't seem possible it could be so long, and yet so short a time. She had been married all her life, it seemed sometimes.

She lifted her head and listened. Voices were raised somewhere downstairs and then a door was slammed, and another shouting match could be heard, muffled but very loud, coming from the kitchen and she thought – shall I go down and intervene? And decided against it. If Goosey needed help with Chloe she'd soon come and ask for it. She usually did –

She moved over to the window and stared down into the square below. There were some boys playing with a bicycle down there and she watched them there for a while, glad to have something to look at to distract her thoughts, but it didn't help for long, for eventually they went off in the direction of Holland Park and the pavements below were left to their usual deserted Sunday morning calm. And she was unable to dodge her thoughts any longer.

A decision had to be made, that was the thing of it, and as the words came into her mind she had a sudden image of Lizah, leaning forwards over Jessie's kitchen table and saying earnestly, 'She needs you, that's the thing of it, Poppy. Apart from what's in it for you – and believe me, it won't be bad. Jessie'll see you right, she's a good girl, is Jessie – but she *needs* you –' And she moved away from the window sharply as though physical action were needed to banish the vision.

Yes, a decision to be made and she lifted her head again to listen, but all was silent now. Clearly Goosey had managed to settle Chloe and Bobby hadn't been disturbed, and she was grateful for that. The last thing they needed now was for Bobby to lose his temper and to come rushing out of his room growling at everyone and getting more and more agitated because his voice would not make the sound he wanted it to, until he was left a gasping wreck who needed to be taken back to his desk and soothed and given camphor on his handkerchief to inhale. But it hadn't happened this time, and she took a deep breath of relief and picked up her duster and after one last look round the drawing room went down to the kitchen to help Goosey.

Chloe was sitting at one end of the kitchen table, her head bent over a piece of paper, drawing busily, and Poppy stood and looked at her for a moment. Her hair was shining a dull gold in the sunshine that was slanting in through the area window, and her cheeks were soft and downy under the long downswept lashes. A pretty child, she thought, so very pretty. And so delightful when she wants to be. If only she didn't behave so disgustingly when she's thwarted, we could all be so much more contented here.

Chloe looked up and caught her eye and scowled, but Poppy did as she always did with her and smiled sunnily. She had vowed to herself from the start that this child was not going to win her battle with her, and the best way to prevent such a victory was to refuse to fight at all. With Chloe Poppy was always sweet reason, calmness and pleasantness personified. The more the child shouted, the calmer Poppy was. Never could Chloe do to her what she did to her aunt and her father and to Goosey, which was to reduce them to red-faced shouting travesties of themselves. Poppy wasn't going to play that game, no matter what. And her determination seemed to be starting to pay some dividends, for Chloe had for some time now given up trying to irk her and saved most of her bad behaviour for Goosey who was very vulnerable to her attacks, and to a lesser degree for Mabel. She seemed a little nervous of her father and never deliberately provoked him as she did the others; his anger at her was always a by-product of her naughtiness with other people. And she did not try to provoke Poppy either, any more, finding it no satisfaction. Now she looked at her with that scowling stare that was the usual with her, but then her face cleared and she returned to her drawing, saying nothing.

'I came to help, Goosey,' Poppy said. 'You must be exhausted.'

'Exhausted! I should say I am, dealin' with that imp of Satan there, an' –'

'So, what are you doing now, Goosey?' Poppy rode over her smoothly. Would she never teach the silly old woman how to stop goading Chloe? Complaining about her was the best way to make her fractious. She came across the kitchen to stand beside Goosey and look over her shoulder. 'What's that?'

'An aspic. I'm doing that there chicken from yesterday into a bit of *chaud froid*. I found one egg and I made a bit o' mayonnaise – seemed the best way to use it fair like, between us all, and with this 'ere aspic, I can glaze the chicken nice enough and no way to tell it's left-overs. An' boiled potatoes and that bit o' lettuce and radish from down the garden. Though 'oo'd ever have thought we'd 'ave to grow our own in a decent 'ouse like this one, for all the world like we was no more'n a muddy farm like my brother's – well, there it is. We live in wicked times –' And she lifted the heavy iron pan from the stove with a twist of her gnarled old hands and thumped it down on a mat.

'May I finish that for you, Goosey?' Poppy said. 'Or is there something else you want me to do?'

'Something else? Well, you said as we was to 'ave a bread and butter pudding, and I've done that, and it's coolin' nicely in the larder. There's a few raisins in it, and more than you deserve, Miss Chloe and so I tell you, stealing 'em from me that way, and me queued over 'alf an hour for them down at Shuttleworth's last Friday! And I got a bit o' treacle saved up, we can put with it for a touch o' sweetness. And I done the jellied consommé for Mr Bobby – it was a good idea, that, you 'ad.' And she looked at Poppy a little grudgingly but with respect all the same.

Finding things that Bobby liked and which were easy for him to eat and never made him breathless as some hard-to-chew foods did, wasn't easy, and consommé, well-flavoured and heavily jelled, was one that he greatly enjoyed, especially when it was laced with a spoonful of the last bottle of good sherry they were nurturing. It was getting harder and harder to find the sort of food they wanted as the threat of rationing came ever closer and luxuries became harder to find. Poppy knew she could get any amount of extras just by asking Jessie, but she never did. It seemed to her wrong, and it made her uneasy to try to get something to which the family weren't really entitled, even though Bobby was an invalid, but she had accepted the big bag of bones Jessie had pushed at her last week. That hadn't seemed too selfish or wicked, and it was a delight to see how Bobby wolfed his consommé.

' – so there's just this and I'll do it after it's cooled a bit. I got the beds to deal with now, and the drawin' room –'

'I've dusted that already,' Poppy said. 'I hate to see you so overworked – it's fine now, Goosey. Look, I'll deal with this if you'll let me and then you can rest before lunch once the beds are out of the way. I'll set the table too. Maybe Chloe will help me –' And she looked at her over her shoulder, but Chloe kept her head down and the only response she showed to the words was a deeper hunching of her shoulders.

'Well, I won't say no, Mrs Poppy, and that's a fact,' Goosey said, and stretched her back a little. 'I can't deny as I'm tired. I didn't sleep a lot last night what with the heat an' all –' And she went creaking away, leaving Poppy and Chloe silent in the kitchen.

I didn't sleep much last night either, Poppy thought. It had indeed been hot, dreadfully hot, and she had thrown off the covers and propped herself up a little against her pillows, moving as gingerly as she could to avoid waking Bobby, but he had been restless too and had woken, and that had been the end of sleep.

At first, when they had come back to Norland Square after their wedding, and Poppy and he had started to share the big double bed in his room at the front of the house, she had been startled but deeply gratified at the suddenness and depth of his physical passion. She had deliberately not thought at all about lovemaking for a very long time. That had belonged to the past, to the ridiculously happy days in Revigny in her small bedroom over Madame Corbigny's kitchen, not to the present with a depressed and breathless Bobby. But she had been wrong and he had seized her with a hunger that had left her breathless and, at first, deeply happy.

But only at first. She had realized within a month that there was less of tenderness and love in his frenzied kissing and caressing than fear and hunger and, somehow, a search for peace. For the pattern was always the same. He would kiss her furiously, running his hands over her body and kneading her flesh as much as caressing it, and then, without stopping to discover whether she was ready for him, or how she felt – without so much as a word, usually – he would be on her, crushing her beneath his weight and his frantic pushing so that all she could concentrate on was breathing, keeping her head set hard to one side and her face tightly clenched as she prevented herself from crying out, for often he hurt her, though he never seemed to notice.

And afterwards, when he had reached his own peak he would roll off her and fall immediately into sleep, and she would lie there waiting for her own body to relax and give her peace again, glad at last to hear that stertorous breathing beside her. For while he slept he was happy.

But last night had been different. Last night he had not slept afterwards but lay awake staring out at the trees beyond their window until, when she had turned to another position to sleep, he had roused himself and, as though they had not shared that frantic effortful experience just an hour earlier, had started again. Only this time it had gone on for so long and been so painful that in the end she had not been able to prevent herself from weeping and then he had been distraught with guilt and had cradled her head in his arms and murmured at her. And perhaps it had been worth it for that, for now she did feel he loved her, and that he was concerned for her rather than just himself, hurling himself at her in a totally self-absorbed search for his own peace of mind and body.

They had slept at last, but not until it had started to get light, the August morning creeping over the trees in the square and waking the birds to shout their dawn chorus, but the heat had woken them early, and now Poppy felt her eyes red and sandy between swollen lids. But tired or not, she had to make a decision.

'Chloe, while I wait for the aspic to cool, come and help me set the table for lunch. There'll be us, of course and George too, so you bring the five glasses and the table napkins and I'll fetch the cutlery.'

The trick with Chloe was never to ask her a direct question. Just take it for granted she will do as you want and she is much more likely to do it, she had told herself long ago, and it was surprising how often she was right. It worked this morning too, for Chloe scowled at Poppy again, but threw down her pencil and got to her feet and went to do as she was bid.

They moved round the dining-room table together, the small girl in the white frilled pinafore over a blue ninon frock, and Poppy in her workmanlike cambric blouse over a black, heavy cotton skirt and Poppy tried not to be aware of the relative costliness of Chloe's clothes as compared with her own. She dressed very carefully and sensibly these days, and not just because of the difficulty of finding elegant clothes. Her small salary had to stretch a long way, what with the rates on the house and Goosey's wages and the grocer's and butcher's and everyone else's bills so there was little left over for gewgaws for Poppy. But Chloe, who was dressed out of her father's income, never had anything but the best. That rule still applied, even now they were on such short commons, and even though the *Dispatch* had made it clear that they could no longer offer their former correspondent any more work and certainly did not feel they owed him any sort of a pension. And Poppy tried not to let it rankle, but it did sometimes.

It was Chloe who broke the silence. 'When I go to school,' she said suddenly, 'I will need a bicycle.'

'A bicycle? Why?' Poppy looked at her, puzzled. 'There's no bicycle on the list of things they sent for us to get for you –'

'Oh, the list!' Chloe said contemptuously. 'No one pays any attention to the list! I asked Mary Challenger and she said this year everyone has bicycles. If you haven't got one you just have no fun at all. So I want one.'

'They're awfully expensive, Chloe,' Poppy said. 'And hard to get. All the steel and iron and so forth is needed for munitions, you know and –'

'I don't care!' Chloe's voice rose dangerously and she stood with a glass in one hand and a folded napkin in the other and stared at Poppy, her lower lip thrust forwards ominously. 'Everyone has bicycles! Mary Challenger said so!'

'Oh, yes?' Poppy said and stopped setting forks in place. 'And what else did Mary Challenger say?'

'She said that all the best people there at Buckley Priory have leather tuck-boxes too, and that their people send them cakes and all sorts of delicious things every week to put in them,' Chloe said and looked sideways at Poppy. 'Shall I have one?'

'I see,' Poppy said with a fine judicious air. 'Are Mary Challenger's people war profiteers, then?'

Chloe went very pink. 'Mary Challenger's daddy is in the Navy! He's a captain on a warship.'

'I see. Then I don't suppose he'd be very happy to think of people having war profiteers' food instead of the sort of rations they ought to have, would he?'

Chloe stared, her lip still stuck out, but there was an uncertainty about her now. She knew about the sort of people who were labelled as war profiteers. Only last week Mabel and George had launched themselves on a lively denunciation of various of their neighbours in the Square who were suspected of illicit food buying and hoarding, and Chloe had heard all of it.

'Shall we ask Captain Challenger, then, Chloe dear? What do you think? When is he next home on leave?'

'I don't know,' Chloe said after a moment and her voice was rather smaller now.

'Well, I'll tell you what we'll do then,' Poppy said heartily. 'When he does come home we'll have a word with him about whether or not people ought to have bicycles and tuck-boxes in wartime and see what we should do. Will that be all right?'

But Chloe said nothing and bent her head and began again to set the table, and Poppy sighed softly, glad to have avoided another crisis over Chloe's constant demands, and started again to try to think about her decision.

Should she ask Mabel? – No that wouldn't help. There was no question that Mabel would have strong ideas about what she should do and would express them forcibly. But they would be based on what Mabel thought was best for Mabel rather than on what might be best for Poppy and Bobby. So she couldn't ask her. Anyway she had become so very tense and irritable lately. Oh dear, Poppy thought, as she fetched the cruet from the sideboard and set it neatly in the middle of the table, if only George Pringle was less organized and set in his ways. It will be at least a year before he has the money and the house and the practice he says he has to have before he can be a married man and by that time Mabel, I swear, will have died of her own frustration and fury. It's been four years those two have been courting now. High time the wretched man made her Mrs Pringle and set her up in her own home. Then Bobby and I –

Then, a small voice deep inside her whispered, then you'd be even worse off than you are. For you know that once Mabel goes and you can no longer call on her salary to stretch the budget you'll be in bad trouble. You can't work every day, and there's an end of it. You can only work every other day, with Bobby as he is, and heaven knows it's bad enough on the days when I'm not here and Goosey has to manage alone. If Mabel leaves us then it will have to be an everyday job for me, and then what will happen? Decide, Poppy, for heaven's sake, *decide*.

And now she could not put off thinking about it any longer. It had hung over her all through this past blazing week, while the weather got hotter and hotter and the news from France worse and worse. The battle of Passchendaele news and casualty lists chilled every heart, and now the French were pushing again at Verdun everyone was sunk into the deepest gloom. To have this problem of her own as well had been almost enough to make her crumple. But she had not, and now she set the last knife in place and cast her eye over the table to make sure it was all as it should be, and led Chloe back to the kitchen.

She sat down on the other side of the table from Chloe as Chloe too sat down and said abruptly, 'Give me a piece of your paper, Chloe. And another pencil.'

'What for?' Chloe said truculently.

'Because I want it,' Poppy said simply and suddenly Chloe grinned and gave her what she asked for. This was the sort of language she understood and Poppy grinned back at her and for a moment there was a delicate strand of liking between them. And Poppy cherished it. It wasn't easy being Chloe's stepmother, heaven knew, but sometimes, just sometimes, there was a hint of a reward for all her efforts.

She set the piece of paper in front of her and chewed the end of her pencil for a moment and then began to write. She made two columns and headed one with the letter 'J' and the other with the letter 'M'.

Under the 'J' column she wrote first 'Money'. Then, after a little thought, she added in swift succession, 'Fun', 'New Interests', 'Use of my Training'. And then she shifted her eyes to the blank column and the letter 'M' and thought for a long time. And at last, a little tentatively, wrote 'To Please Mama'. And after another pause, shifted her pencil to the first column and added to it, 'To Please Jessie'.

And then sat and looked for a long time, thinking hard and at last managed to find another few words to add to the 'M' column, 'Comfort' and 'Money'.

After another long pause she set down the pencil and held the piece of paper in front of her and studied it. She knew really. She hadn't needed this exercise to make up her mind, but she had felt she had to go through it, to salve her conscience.

For that was the hardest part of it all. Mama had made her an offer that would solve many of her immediate problems – but which she would hate.

'Come and live here in Leinster Terrace,' Mama had said to her, actually bringing herself to use the telephone to do so. 'I am alone and the house is really much too large and empty for me. It would please me greatly to have you and your husband and your stepdaughter here. Queenie will manage us perfectly well, and you will have every consideration. I will pay all bills, of course, including the little girl's school fees, if you wish.'

It had been an amazing conversation to Poppy, who had stood at the telephone in Bobby's little room, where he spent his day sitting at his desk writing and reading in a desultory sort of fashion, and had stared out of the window as she held the earpiece close to her head and listened to the thin, clacking little voice. Go to live with Mama in Leinster Terrace? She must be very alone and unhappy to have asked her to do that. Did she really miss Maud so much? Did it really matter to her that Harold and Samuel no longer lived there? Clearly it did. Why else would she have held out so lavish an olive branch?

And yet, and yet – Poppy had tried very hard to imagine living there again, had tried to see Bobby in the great cavernous rooms among all that heavy, expensive – if rather old-fashioned – furniture. And had tried to see herself there as Mrs Bobby Bradman, stepmother to Chloe rather than as Miss Poppy, most juvenile member of the household; and could not. If she was there, she knew she would always be her mother's daughter, a watchful person who had to be careful at all times to keep her own counsel and hide herself away from her mother's sharp eyes. It could not be borne, it really could not.

And then Jessie had offered her a lifeline. So casually, so cheerfully, and yet a lifeline.

'I tell you, Poppela,' she had said at the end of a long hot afternoon, when Poppy had managed to persuade Mabel to stay at home to keep her brother company so that Poppy could slip away to visit the East End once more. 'I tell you, I'm nearly ruined by work. I always said hard work never hurt no one but I ain't so sure any more. Me, I'm so exhausted, I don't know what I'll do next.'

And indeed she had looked it, for her face was drawn, even seemed haggard in spite of its plump contours, and her eyes looked bruised and red. Poppy had never seen the ebullient Jessie so low.

'If only I had someone like you here to watch over it all, oh, what a difference it'd make!' Jessie had said then. 'Here I am, the wholesale side growing like it's a tapeworm or something, and more orders'n I can deal with, as well as all that War Office stuff I gotta do, and what I need is someone with a bit of sairchel – oh, don't look at me so puzzled! Don't you know that word by now? A bit of common sense, a bit of energy, a bit of what it takes, that's sairchel. I need someone with a bit of it to manage it all for me. Me, I can only do so much. I could pay you well, believe me, I could. And you could have a nice office and afford someone to sit with your Bobby, a nurse, maybe. It could all be so *nice* – and I really need you, Poppela.' And she had looked at Poppy with an expression of mixed hope, wishfulness and lugubriousness that was so absurd, Poppy could almost have laughed; almost, but not quite.

And Lizah had leaned across the table and said the same thing. 'The thing of it is, she needs you, Poppy –'

Goosey came creaking back into the kitchen, muttering beneath her breath and Poppy, moving a little abruptly, folded her sheet of paper into two and then tore it very deliberately into several pieces and then took them to throw them into the stove.

There could be no question about what she had to do, could there? She knew the answer. All she had to do now was tell everyone. And that was going to be the hardest part of all.

31

'That'll be seventeen pounds of butter,' Poppy said again into the telephone. 'Yes, that's right. Seventeen pounds. Yes, of course I have the necessary coupons! Would I order if I didn't? And how about margarine? Hmm? Well, I suppose that'll have to do. But I hope you can do better for me next month. I've got a special priority rating, you know, because of the War Office work we do –'

By the time she'd hammered out the details about the cheese and the soured buttermilk and hung up it was past one o'clock, and she looked at her watch and bent her head again to her ledgers. Too much to do to have time to get out and do that shopping for Bobby after all. He had wanted her to spend an hour at the big bookshop in Cheapside digging out the maps he needed to finish his thirtieth chapter, but it was going to be impossible today; these orders had to be in, all of them, before five tonight or they wouldn't have their necessary supplies for next week in the restaurant, let alone the wholesale side. Bobby's maps would simply have to wait till this evening. Maybe if she phoned the shop they'd agree to wait for her? After all, she had been a very good customer this past year, as Bobby's demands for background material for his book had doubled and redoubled.

She stopped working for a moment to stare out at the patch of blue sky that was framed by the grimy window of her office and thought – but it's worth it, and her lips curved a little. She had been so worried that he would slip backwards when she started working full time here at Jessie's office, and had told him of her plans with much trepidation. But somehow it had all slipped into place so beautifully that at first she had thought – this can't last. It's a dream, too easy to be true. But it had been true, and had stayed that way.

Chloe had gone off to school in a high good humour and to everyone's intense relief had actually liked it and still did. When she came home for holidays she prattled all day about the school and the friends she had there and showed no interest whatsoever in anything at home, making it clear she rather despised anything that wasn't part of Buckley Priory, and was eager only to get back, and that had a profound effect on Goosey. She had dreaded losing her last nursling, even as difficult and noisy a one as Chloe had become, and Poppy had feared the old woman would lose her energy and interest in living altogether and have to be retired. But instead Goosey found a new lease of life in fussing over a somewhat older ex-nursling and he, far from disliking it, as Poppy had been sure he would, relished her coddling.

Within a month of Poppy starting at her new job, after explaining to him as tactfully as she could how useful the extra money would be, he had started to work on a book. He had been writing all sorts of odds and ends ever since they had got married, none of which he had submitted anywhere for publication, but now for the first time he was engaged on something purposeful; an account of the War as he had seen it in those first two years. And Poppy had watched his absorption and been deeply glad of it, even though it meant he hardly ever talked of anything else. He seemed, at last, to be getting better. His voice was as thick as ever, his breathing as laboured and wheezy, but he was no longer so tense and miserable. Now he was just obsessive about his work, and with Goosey to tend to most of his physical needs all day, and Poppy to cater to the rest of them most nights – for he was as voracious as ever in bed – he seemed a happier man. Not the man she had once known and loved so deeply, but still a happier one. And for that she was grateful, and knew contentment.

It was as well that life in Norland Square had been so much easier during the year since she had started working with Jessie, for it had been far from easy at Cable Street. She had found herself pitchforked into a business structure that had grown so rapidly and in so *ad hoc* a fashion that it was an incredible tangle. Successful it was, undoubtedly; the original small shop was buried now within a much larger establishment on one side of which was the restaurant, a sizeable place which held thirty tables, all pushed rather close together, and all capable of accommodating four diners.

It was not a beautiful place, having plain cream-painted walls, which often ran with condensation as did the big plate-glass windows, a red linoleum-covered floor and marble-topped tables at which bentwood chairs were set. It looked what it was, plain and workmanlike, and was often wreathed in steam from the kitchens as well as tobacco smoke from the customers; but yet it had a lively, indeed vibrant, atmosphere that made it a cheerful and comfortable place to be. It clattered with activity from morning till late at night, for Jessie opened to provide breakfasts for the many local workers who, now they were earning such war-swollen wages, could afford to eat in commercial establishments, reached a crescendo of busyness between twelve and two when all the factory owners and their various business contacts poured in to eat vast lunches, bustled all afternoon with passing tea-hungry trade and finally exploded into a stylish venue at night. Somehow the word had got about among fashionable Londoners that '"Jessie's" in the East End is a *divinely* amusing place to eat, my dears, you *must* try it, madly decadent and one *never* knows with whom one might rub shoulders.' And Jessie was hard put to it to accommodate all the eager would-be customers who besieged her.

But that was not all. On the other side of the original small shop she had started a wholesale section, where some of her best-loved dishes were prepared and packed ready to be taken away by those who could not get into the restaurant but still wanted the food. The wholesale side also supplied large offices and shops, as well as the important War Office connection which was not so lucrative, and some other shops in places such as Golders Green and Hampstead, where richer Jews had gone to live, leaving the East End behind them but not their taste for East End food.

So Jessie made her own special salamis and Vienna sausages, bright red and luscious and reeking of good garlic, and pots of chopped chicken livers and mashed eggs and onions (a highly indigestible if delectable dish which drew its *aficionados* from as far north as St John's Wood and Maida Vale) as well as her more familiar standbys of sandwiches and filled rolls, cheesecakes and sponges, honey cakes and the soft rich biscuits she called kierchels. She had added to this side of the menu the delicate pastry filled with apples and raisins known as strudel, and also baked little shortcrust concoctions filled with the stickiest of plum jam. And all of it sold out in vast quantities very fast indeed. However much Jessie baked, however many extra girls she took on to slave away in the small hot kitchens, she could never produce enough.

'Listen dolly,' she had said to Poppy when after just a week of working in Cable Street she had tried to explain to her aunt just what a tangle her business affairs were in. 'You want me to explode already? O' course the books are a mess! O' course it's all a mishmash. How else should it be, with me workin' the way I am? Why do you think I need you here at all? Would I ask you to sit in that ferstinkeneh little office all day if I didn't have to?'

And Poppy had laughed and hugged her and gone away and never complained again. It wasn't Jessie's fault at all; this wasn't like dealing with poor Miss Jessamy, the vague and helpless FANY Commandant at Calais who had needed Poppy to organize her. Jessie was a shrewd and sensible woman, but even with her considerable organizational gifts (and she ran the kitchen and the shop and the restaurant with great skill) even she could not manage to deal with banks and records and ledgers as well. So Poppy worked long hard hours at the small desk in the cluttered little office, slowly imposing order on Jessie's chaos. And when she had done that, took over the task of ordering supplies as well, much to Jessie's gratitude, for it was a difficult job at the best of times and almost impossible now that official rationing of foods had been imposed by the Government and supplies of almost everything were dwindling alarmingly.

Her telephone pinged and interrupted her reverie and she picked up the earpiece and tucked it into her neck, bending her head to hold it, so that she could continue to use her writing hand. But after a very little while she set down her pen, and sat up and concentrated wholly on what she was hearing.

'Jessie Braham's,' she said. 'May I help you?' It amused her sometimes that she was more than just the bookkeeper and the manager of the whole accounts department of the business; she had to be clerk and receptionist and typewriter as well. 'I beg your pardon? Oh, yes, this is Mrs Bradman – Yes – No, of course not! Oh!'

And now she sat more upright and stared at the window again as the little voice clattered on tinnily in her ears, but she was seeing nothing.

'Are you sure? Yes, I see. How much do you say? Oh. Yes – well, look, Mr Doyle, I'll see that a cheque reaches you before the close of the bank tomorrow. I doubt I can get it to you this afternoon – Mmm? Oh, yes indeed, it will be covered. You should know that! No, no need to say more. I'm sure you will. I appreciate your indulgence. It's good of you to be so – considerate. And, after all, it could be just one of those errors that happens. Well – no – perhaps not. But I'm sure we'll soon sort it out – Good afternoon.'

And she cradled the phone and sat and looked at it for some time before carefully totting up the last column of figures in the ledger before her and then closing it and getting to her feet. At this time of the afternoon Jessie would be in the wholesale kitchens, leaving the restaurant to the care of Barney, a lively if somewhat elderly man who had come to Jessie as a waiter and stayed on to become her chief support there. Lily still ran the shop almost single-handed, and between the three of them, and with an ever-changing gaggle of girls who worked as cooks, as waitresses and as general hands as the need arose, they somehow managed to keep it all ticking over.

Poppy stopped as she reached the door of her small office and then after a moment turned and went back to her desk to rummage in a small drawer and eventually found what she was looking for and returned to the door, but with an expression of distaste on her face. It deepened as she went out and locked the door after her; she had never needed to lock anything ever. It was horrid to feel now that it was necessary, and for such a reason.

She found Jessie, as she had expected, in the kitchen of the wholesale side. Around her three girls were busily working; one dealing with a vast bubbling pan of pickled salt beef on the gas hob, which she was skimming, and which filled the whole place with aromatic steam, and the other two in rolled-up sleeves and well-dusted with flour working skilfully with the very fine pastry needed for the strudel. Jessie herself was working over a great sheet of carefully rolled-out pastry almost as thin as the strudel dough, which was laid on a thin cloth, and which she was cutting into the finest long shreds before arranging them on another cloth which was draped over the back of a chair.

'Look at that!' she cried triumphantly as Poppy came in. 'Just look at that! Lizah said as how there was nothing new I could put in the range and I swore there was and here it is! I'm doing bone broth soup with lockshen – you know, noodles? And after that I'm going to try 'em on kreplach – that's a sort of dumpling only it's got stuffing in, meat and so forth – I'll show him whether I can put anything new in the range!'

'I'm sure you can,' Poppy said a little abstractedly, for she was not quite as interested as Jessie was in the details of cookery. 'Jessie, there's something I have to talk to you about. It's really '

'Later dolly, later.' Jessie was still bent over her pastry, cutting long strips with sweeps of her sharp knife which were so rapid that the blade seemed to shimmer. 'I got to get the kreplach pastry made and –'

'This is important, Jessie,' Poppy said firmly. 'I have to tell you now, because I must finish the books this afternoon and I can't until – and then I must get away on time because I need to do some shopping for Bobby. Please, Jessie, I don't bother you unless I must, you know that.'

Jessie sighed gustily. 'All right, all right – what does she want of my life?' she demanded of the three girls who just grinned at her and said nothing, and with one more pass of her wicked little knife finished the last of her noodles and set them to dry.

'All right, I'm coming, I'm coming. Kreplach I'll have to make later, what can you do? Come on then and we'll pop inside and see if Barney can make us a cuppa tea. I'm parched –' And she wiped her gleaming face on her apron, leaving her cheeks comically streaked with flour and stomped away to the back of the wholesale kitchen to the door that led to the passage that had been constructed to link the rambling premises that were once four shops and which were now one business.

Following her, Poppy thought – she needs a holiday. As soon as this hateful war is over, I'll see she gets it too. She's looking tired, even though she's so cheerful all the time. She wheezes a bit now, too. Not good for her, all this hard effort – But there was no sign that Jessie herself was at all concerned about her well-being as she ensconced herself at a corner table in the restaurant, where the lunchtime trade was at last beginning to ease off, giving Barney and his two helpers a little respite.

'So tell me what it is,' she demanded. 'Am I making too much money?' And she grinned cheerfully, well aware that she was indeed making a good deal of money by dint of all her hard work.

'You're doing very well,' Poppy said and then leaned back as Barney arrived, unasked, to bring two glasses of lemon tea and a plate of hot crisp rolls filled with steaming salt beef and mustard. 'No, thank you, Barney. Just the tea for me –'

'Lunch,' Jessie said firmly. 'Everyone needs lunch. You're looking ridiculous, you're so thin. Eat your lunch or I can't listen to nothing you got to say.' And Poppy grimaced and obeyed, knowing from long experience that Jessie meant precisely what she said. And found she was, after all, quite hungry and that the beef tasted delectable.

They sat and ate in silence for a while as Poppy tried to think of the right words to use when she spoke of her telephone call, but it was impossible. The words Mr Doyle had used to her had been uncompromising in their directness, and she couldn't imagine how her own could be any less so. But how would they affect Jessie? And she stole a glance at her and caught her eye; and Jessie grinned companionably and chewed the last of her roll with gusto.

'Have you heard about my Bernie?' she said as soon as her mouth was empty enough to permit speech. 'Got a marvellous job he has. Marvellous.'

'Oh?' Poppy said guardedly. 'A job?'

'I told you he would, no trouble at all! Only left school a coupla weeks ago, and already he's earning good money!'

'What is he doing?' Poppy needed to know before she went on to talk about what she was concerned about, and she lifted her eyes to watch Jessie's face as she explained and felt her own determination melt away as she saw the glow there. It wasn't often Jessie looked as completely happy as she did now.

'He's a personal assistant! How's that then? Personal assistant to Mr Joe O'Rourke! You heard of him? Most of the people in these parts know him. He's a bookie – well, calls himself turf accountant, but in anyone's language that's a bookie. I wasn't best pleased at first, believe me. I thought, the sort of people my Bernie'll meet, it can't be good. But Mr O'Rourke comes in here to eat regularly and he's a decent fella. Irish, o' course, but as decent as they come –'

Poppy felt her lips curve for a moment at the unconscious class labelling of these clannish streets where she now spent so much of her time. To belong to the wrong group could be a major handicap in Cable Street, but Jessie was broader in her views than many of her neighbours. Although some of her Jewish friends and relations would never even speak to a non-Jew, Jessie counted many among her friends. And clearly Mr O'Rourke was one of them.

'He's been in business around here since before the South African war. Well-established man, excellent sort. And he's taken on my Bernie as his personal assistant! He promised me he'd see the boy right, and I trust him – he'll take care of him –' And she stirred some more sugar into her tea with such pride and satisfaction that Poppy felt her eyes prickle.

'I'm delighted,' she managed and then bent her head to stir her own tea, although she had put no sugar in it. It was all getting a little more clear now. What Mr Doyle had told her made a different sort of sense and she bit her lip, as she tried as swiftly as she could to work out what to do.

'So,' Jessie said comfortably and leaned back in her chair and stretched a little, looking round her restaurant with a practised eye and nodding cheerfully at some of her more familiar regular customers. 'What was it so urgent I had to leave my kreplach?'

'I – it's the cheques,' Poppy said, improvising rapidly. 'I have to keep coming to you to sign them – I thought, it might be easier if you arranged with the bank to take my signature for the run-of-the-mill stuff. I could fix up a document this afternoon and get Barney to witness it, and then take it to the bank when I go tomorrow. But I have to sort it out today, to get it fixed up this week –'

'Is that all?' Jessie stared at her. 'For Pete's sake, Poppy, I could ha' agreed that over the kreplach! You didn't have to make such a performance out of *that*!'

'This way I made sure at least you got some lunch,' Poppy said and Jessie leaned forwards and pinched her cheek affectionately.

'Better than any daughter could ever have been,' she said and then lumbered to her feet. 'I'm a lucky woman, hey, what with you and my Bernie? Listen, I got to get back to the kitchen – arrange what you like, dolly. You're in charge, when it comes to the office,' and she went away leaving Poppy staring miserably after her.

Well, she told herself as she waved at last to Barney and turned to make her way back upstairs to her own little eyrie, at least I know what to do now. But I have to speak to him – and for the rest of the afternoon she worked flat out to complete all her ledger work, and to get ready the new document which she had promised Jessie, and then get away in time to do her shopping for Bobby. It was a tight afternoon and by the time she at last climbed on to the bus that would take her home her head was aching a little from the tension. But it would ease up in time, she promised herself as the bus made its lumbering way through the crowded shabby streets, heading westwards. Once I can get this office running completely the way I want it – and once Bobby finishes his book and – but she didn't want to think about that.

At home Bobby was absorbed in his work, and flatly refused to leave his room for supper, seizing the books of maps she had brought him so eagerly that he hardly even looked at her, and she took herself off to the kitchen to eat there with Goosey ('only a little something with toast, Goosey,' she said. 'I ate a huge lunch –') a little hurt but at the same time relieved. Tonight was the one when she had to take her weekly walk along the Bayswater Road to visit her mother, and knowing that Bobby was happily occupied with his chapter thirty at least made sure that she need not feel guilty about going out and leaving him again, which was something to be grateful for.

But, as she went along the Bayswater Road, her blue cotton dress flopping a little over her calves with the speed of her walk, and her neat straw hat pulled tidily over her now bobbed hair (for she had gladly seized on the new fashion for short hair as soon as she had heard about it) she felt less than comfortable.

It was good that Bobby was happier than he had been, very good. That was a major anxiety off her mind. It was good that her mother was becoming so much more pleasant to visit, as indeed she was. As long as Poppy did not talk at all of her East End connections and pretended that she was just a happily married lady who stayed at home as such ladies should, Mildred seemed content. Visiting her was less of an ordeal than it had once been, and sometimes even real pleasure could be found in her Mama's company, such as when she made one of her waspish but perceptive remarks about her more affluent neighbours who weren't ashamed to flaunt the fact that they were food cheats and hoarders, by giving parties. But now she had something else to worry about this evening, and worry she did.

It would be easy enough to get Bernie out of his scrape this time. Mr Doyle had made it clear when he had told her of the fact that a suspicious cheque drawn on Jessie's account and made payable to Mr J. O'Rourke had been brought in by the young man, that he had no intention of making a police matter of it. So long as the bank was reimbursed, he added, for once he, Mr Doyle, had scrutinized the cheque accepted by one of his cashiers, he had realized it was a forgery, possibly on a cheque stolen – ah – *taken* – from the young man's mother's desk, he had of course protected Mrs Braham's account. But he could not carry the burden of his care for her; the bank must be given funds to cover its disbursement. And with Poppy's new power to sign Jessie's cheques that was a simple matter.

But it could not be the end of it. The boy had to be confronted with what he had done and prevented from doing it again – and from betting again, if that had been the source of his debt – and that was not a task that Poppy relished. In the last year Bernie had grown at a remarkable rate and now stood a strong six foot and an inch and had a well-muscled body to match. It might have been better for him, Poppy thought as she crossed Palace Gate and could see the corner of Queensway ahead, if he had done as some beautiful children did and grown up plain. But he had not; quite the reverse in fact. Where he had been an exquisitely pretty child, now he was an incredibly handsome youth. Even though he was not quite sixteen, he was already attracting glances – and more – from a wide range of young women, many of them considerably his senior. And Poppy could understand why, for his melting dark eyes with their long lashes and the neat straight nose and the firm chin with its hint of a central cleft was very beguiling.

But she wished most fervently that people weren't so taken in by his looks, for it made him more headstrong than ever to be so popular. No doubt Mr O'Rourke had taken him on to attract the women he dealt with; it made good business sense to do so. But it made very bad sense indeed from Bernie's personal point of view, or so Poppy told herself worriedly as she at last reached the end of Leinster Terrace and turned into its all too familiar stuccoed length.

So, what shall I do about him? I shall have to see him in the morning, of course, and make it clear he's been caught, and also make it clear I expect him to repay the money, because I'm not going to falsify the books to please the scallywag. But can I force him to see the sense of it? That was the problem. If he chose to dig in his heels and say he didn't care what she did, her bluff would have been called, for he knew, as she did herself, that his mother would do anything to keep life smooth for him.

But, Poppy told herself firmly as at last she ran up her mother's front steps, I shall do all I can to make sure she doesn't. The sooner life gets hard for Mr Bernard Braham the better for him and the better for Jessie. And Jessie was the one who mattered most.

32

'So that's the last of it,' Bernie said and grinned at her and almost against her will she grinned back. It was hard not to respond to that glint of even white teeth and the way his smile creased his cheeks so engagingly.

'Make sure it is,' she said and scooped up the three banknotes he had put on her desk. 'Don't think I shan't be watching you as carefully as ever, because I shall be. And don't think I won't do what I said I would if I have to –'

'Ah, phooey!' Bernie said and stretched, so that his neat waistcoat with the fine gold chain across it lifted over his flat belly and displayed a rim of white shirt. 'You wouldn't say a word to my Ma. You know you wouldn't. Just like she'll do anything to keep me happy, so you'll do anything to keep her happy –'

'And so should you,' Poppy said sharply. 'You're the only son she has and she should be as precious to you as –'

He lifted his brows. 'So who said she wasn't? Believe me, I got a lotta time for the old girl. I'm just sayin' that you won't tell her nothin' that'll upset her, on account of you don't *want* to upset her. Just like she is with me. That's all I said.' And he smiled again, winningly.

But this time it didn't work and Poppy said as sharply as ever, 'There's still Joe O'Rourke. I can still tell him what you did, and warn him off. He's a straight dealer, and if he thinks there's anything the least dubious about you, out you'll go and you know it.'

But he still smiled cheerfully at her, still sat there stretched back in his chair with his hands linked behind his gleaming dark head. 'Joe O'Rourke? I should worry. I got plans o' my own. I don't need O'Rourke and his penny-ante business –'

A wriggle of anxiety slid under her ribs. 'Bernie! What are you up to now? I tell you, if I find out that you've –'

'Oh, pooh, pooh, pooh, dear Cousin Poppy, pooh, pooh, pooh!

273

What's to get in such a lather over? Have I said I'm doing anything I shouldn't? I just said I got plans for my future – is that so terrible? A chap has to think about the future, you know – seventeen next birthday – not much time left –'

She laughed then, a sudden scornful little sound. 'Oh, of course, so old –'

He looked serious for a moment. 'I mean it. I intend to be very, very rich by the time I'm twenty-one –' He unlinked his hands and stretched his arms wide, embracing in one comprehensive gesture not just Poppy's little office but also the shops and the restaurant and the kitchens below and the whole East End beyond that. 'I'm not staying here in this lousy place a minute longer than I have to. A house in Park Lane, that's what I want, and cars and yachts and – oh, everything! *And* I'm going to have it –'

And then he caught the look on her face and laughed again and leaned forwards so that the chair crashed down from the back legs on which he had been balancing it and made the room shake a little. 'Don't look at me that way! I'll have it legal, believe me! It's a mug's game to play crooked. You get caught.' He grimaced. 'If even that old fool Doyle can catch me so fast, then it just ain't worth it. My talents are different anyway. You'll see –' He got to his feet in one long lithe movement. 'So there it is, Poppy. It's all shipshape and straight, okay? No more naggin' and watchin', eh?'

'You've paid back what you owed, yes,' Poppy said. 'But that doesn't mean I'm not still concerned about you. You're –' She made a little face and then leaned forwards, wanting suddenly to get across to him some of the complex feelings she had about him. 'Look, Bernie, I know we never have got on terribly well, but you were a dreadfully spoiled child and – well, that was the way it was. But you're almost an adult now. You said that yourself. Let's try to behave like adults, and be good friends, can't we? I think so highly of your mother, you see, and it would be so agreeable to be close to you too. And once I can be sure you've – well, let's say grown out of some of this foolish behaviour then it would be so much easier. But I do need to be sure –'

He looked back at her with a smooth half-smile on his beautifully shaped mouth and an air of friendliness on his face but his eyes were as hard and expressionless as pebbles.

'Of course, Cousin Poppy!' he said heartily. 'Of course! Well, I must be on my way. Got to see a man about a dog,' and he winked outrageously so that the shadows of his long lashes stroked his cheek for a moment, and got to his feet. 'See you around!' And he turned and went, leaving her alone in the dark little room.

She sat there for some time before at last she got to her feet and went to light the gas. It plopped into life with a soft sigh and the room lifted its golden cosiness around her and she went over to the window to stare down into the evening street below. It was cold for October, a sharp biting chilliness filling the air, and she shivered a little and pulled the jersey she was wearing more tightly around her shoulders. It was no small wonder so many people were ill in such weather; that as well as over four years of war and everyone so exhausted and food so short – it was inevitable that people should be catching flu so easily. Jessie had had it and had been really miserable for a week and was now only just getting over it, and Goosey had been ill too, for much longer than a week, and needed long hours of care night after night, which had stretched Poppy badly, for she had had to deal with Bobby during the day and fit in her essential office work as and when she could. It was no small wonder she felt so tired herself, she thought, and then lifted her shoulders pettishly at her own self-pity and turned back to her desk.

At least Bernie had repaid in full the debt he had owed the books for that forged cheque and she believed him when he said he wouldn't try such a thing again. Being caught was not at all to Bernie's taste. The main worry now was what he would get up to next. That he had all sorts of schemes going that paid him well was clear; that gold chain he wore was the real article and he was generous with gifts to his mother; and she, poor fool, thought Poppy wearily, never asks where he gets his money from. She just takes it for granted her clever Bernie can earn all he wants. Oh, Jessie, Jessie, when will you learn what he is? But Poppy had other things to worry about now; and she pushed Bernie to the back of her mind and flipped open her engagement book.

And then muttered an imprecation beneath her breath. She had meant to send a message to Dr Dixon to tell him she would like to make an appointment for tomorrow morning, but she had quite forgotten. There would be no chance now that he could find time for her, and it had been – how long? She totted up the dates in her mind and muttered the same imprecation again. She should have seen him in August, and here it was the end of October, and she still hadn't. Well, never mind; there was no real need to be concerned, for it was just a routine visit, wasn't it? Of course it was nothing to worry about. But all the same, her secret little voice whispered, do make sure you visit him soon. He said he wanted to see you every three months to check all was working as it should, and it's been much longer than that. And the last thing you need now is any sort of trouble in *that* department –

But she refused to think about that, too, and rapidly dealt with the last items on her desk and set it tidy for Monday morning. Ever since Jessie had been ill it had been agreed that Poppy would not work on Saturday mornings in the usual way, but would go over to the Isle of Dogs to see Lizah; he too had caught this wretched flu, and been unable to visit Jessie, and since she in her turn had been unable to make the journey down to Lizah's pub, it had fallen to Poppy to make the regular eastwards trek, and Saturday was the best day to do it.

She turned off the gas and made her way down the dark staircase to the shop. Her back was aching and she felt a little sick, but that was just fatigue. I am not, she told herself fiercely, as she reached the door at the bottom and pushed it open to reveal the brightly lit restaurant, I am not going to get ill. I have not caught the flu and am not going to. And there is an end of it. I'm just very tired, that's all –

Jessie was sitting in her usual corner, a steaming cup in front of her and Poppy made her way over to her past the full tables with the chattering noisy occupants, and slid into the chair opposite her.

'Well, darling, how are you feeling?' she said cheerfully, making it as clear as she could this was just a rhetorical question, that she knew Jessie was feeling fine, just fine. And Jessie picked up the message and smiled widely and said, 'Feeling as right as ninepence. A real old fraud, that's me –'

But she wasn't. She had indeed been very ill and looked it. Her body seemed to have fallen in on itself. She was still a big woman – it would take more than a battle with a bout of flu to reduce her – but the power that had always been there seemed to have drained away. Her face was drawn now, where once it had been rubicund, and her skin had a greyish tinge that was sharpened by the red-rimmed look of her eyes. And her spirit seemed to have left her, too; when she spoke it was with an effort, and the eager bright-eyed glance that had been used to take in very swiftly indeed whatever it chanced upon seemed sluggish and dull. But she was still Jessie, for all that, still trying however low she felt, and now she grinned at Poppy, a tight little grimace that made Poppy want to weep suddenly and said again, 'A real old fraud, that's me –'

'No, you're not,' Poppy said stoutly and leaned across and pinched her cheek affectionately. 'You were thoroughly ill, and you need all the rest you can get to be sure you're well again. Look, I can go over to Lizah in the morning tomorrow – I know I said I couldn't till the afternoon, but as it turns out – what shall I take to him?'

Jessie's brows creased and she leaned forwards. 'Listen, Poppy, I'm that worried about him. I phoned, you know? He's got a phone there now – nothing but the best for our Lizah, hmm? But he wouldn't talk to me. That was what that girl said – silly cow –'

Poppy patted her hand. 'Now, don't upset yourself, Jessie,' she said soothingly. 'I'm not too keen on this new one either, but there it is – Lizah doesn't change, does he? And she has looked after him well, you know –'

'Looked after him?' Jessie snorted, an odd sound that seemed to come from the depths of her belly. 'That lazy – looked after him? He needed *me*, that's what he needed, poor old Lizah – she ain't got a notion about lookin' after ill people. And when we phoned this afternoon and she said he wasn't fit to talk on the phone, I thought – I'll show you, madam – I'll show you – I'll go over myself with you tomorrow, Poppy –'

'You'll do nothing of the sort,' Poppy said firmly. 'You're not fit. You've only been out of bed yourself this past two days – and ought to be there now, if you ask me. I only agreed to let you sit in here to cheer you up, you were so miserable –' And indeed she had been constantly dissolving into the ready tears of the convalescent; at least since she had been allowed to spend her days in the restaurant she had been a little happier.

Poppy frowned then as a thought came to her and turned her head towards the cold passageway at the back. 'You say you phoned this afternoon? While I was at the bank, was that? Did you go struggling up those stairs yourself?'

'No, no –' Jessie shook her head pettishly. 'I sent Barney – he told me –'

'That's all right then. Look, stop worrying, Jessie. I'll go along to see him tonight, if you like – not even wait till tomorrow. How will that be? And then I'll come and see you in the morning and I'll tell you how he is. Now, what shall I take him? You won't want me to go empty-handed –'

She left Jessie happily making a list of the food and drink she wanted taken to her sick brother, while Poppy went to talk to Barney. And she came back to pick up the list and to reassure Jessie that all would be well; but she was anxious for all that. For Barney had told her that the girl presently resident in Lizah's pub had been far from obstructive, as Jessie had thought, but very much alarmed.

'Seems as Mr Lizah ain't fit to talk,' the old man said lugubriously as he polished forks busily. 'Lorst 'is voice, that Nellie says, and breathin' very thick – didn't want to tell the missus that, though, did I? Be as well if you do go over tonight at that, the way Nellie was goin' on about 'im –'

'I'll go as soon as I can, Barney,' she told him. 'I have to sort out some things at home first, but I'll go after that. Pack up the things Jessie wants me to take to him, will you? I'll collect them on the way back. But I have to go home first –'

Indeed she did. There was Goosey to see, to make sure she was still progressing well, and Bobby's supper to be arranged and if possible her own. It would be much easier just to take a cab now to travel out to the Isle of Dogs and then go home; to make the journey the way she was going to would be much more tiring, and every bone in her ached to crawl away into bed and sleep. But there it was, she told herself as stoutly as she could; Lizah had to be visited tonight to give Jessie peace of mind, and she had her own tasks to deal with first. And deal with them she would.

The streets were quiet when she came out and began her sharp walk to Aldgate Underground Station. It was easier to travel home this way than to take a cab or bus these days, for so many people had become nervous of crowded places that the trains were much less busy than they usually were, and also cabs were hard to find; not only was the demand for them great from those who wanted to be alone and hoped to avoid the flu contagion that way, but also many of the cab drivers were ill, so there were fewer hacks to be found. So she sat in the half-empty train, swaying through the dark tunnels and staring out at the way the cables that lined the walls swooped and swung in the passing rush of air and tried to marshal her energies. Perhaps, once she got home tonight from the East End, she would have the Saturday and Sunday to herself, to rest a little? And then her heart sank as she remembered that she had promised to visit her mother at some time; and she could not break that. Not when Mama had been behaving so reasonably.

She bit her lip as she thought of that, staring out at the dirty walls of the blank tubes through which she was hurtling. Mama was being reasonable, yes, but there was a reason for her reaonableness. She had seemed to take it well enough over a year ago when Poppy had told her, as kindly as she could, of her decision to take Jessie's offer rather than her own, and for a while Poppy had thought she had accepted her *congé* with philosophical calmness. But Poppy had been realizing for some time that it was not so; Mama had not at all given up her hopes. She wanted Poppy to come and live with her, if necessary with her husband and stepchild, and even with her sister-in-law. That had stopped being an issue when Mabel had at last married her George in January of this year and had gone to live with him in his splendid new house in Brondesbury, that most elegant of modern suburbs, but Mildred had not given up her general plan. Which was to lean on Poppy in so many subtle ways that eventually Poppy would decide for herself that the most sensible thing for her to do would be to close the pokey little house in Norland Square and come to live in her mother's much better establishment in Leinster Terrace –

It had been some time before it had dawned on Poppy that this was what Mildred was trying to do, and from then on she had been as watchful as it was possible to be but, even though she was aware of Mildred's efforts, she was sometimes beguiled by them. When the house in Norland Square seemed particularly small and noisy – when Chloe was home, for example – or when Goosey was being particularly fractious, the thought of that cool and roomy house where her mother sat in solitary state was very seductive. To have enough space to call her own, Poppy would think sometimes. To have a room for Bobby so big and so sensibly furnished that he would never have to lose his temper and shout himself hoarse because he had mislaid one of his precious papers in the maelstrom of documents and books that littered his small study; to have servants to take the burden off old Goosey so that she would not nag and grizzle quite so much – oh, it could be so agreeable!

But it would not work, she whispered now to the dark tunnel walls as the train rocked her furiously towards Bayswater Station. It could never work, Mama and Bobby, or Mama and Chloe –

It would work for Chloe, she thought then. Chloe who was always so scornful of her home and made so many scathing comparisons of it with her friends' much richer houses; she would like to live in such a house as Mildred Amberly's. She would like to have more servants, and to peacock about in those large stuccoed streets – and Poppy took a deep breath and closed her eyes against the images that thought conjured up. She was not going to give in to Mama on this issue, any more than she had on previous ones. And she would go to visit her as she had promised she would, and somehow would manage to avoid the subject entirely. That was the only way to deal with such difficult matters. Don't talk about them. Don't think about them. Let them sort themselves out.

She let herself in with her latch key and then, startled, stood in the hall with her head up and sniffing. Someone was cooking and she frowned sharply. Goosey was still not well enough to do any such thing. Only this morning Poppy had told her firmly she must stay in bed all day, until Poppy came home when she might be allowed up for a while for a little light supper. But now someone was in the kitchen making – and again she sniffed and thought in wonderment – sausages? Who went out to the butcher and queued for sausages in this bitter cold weather? Bobby? Could it possibly be Bobby who – and she pulled off her coat and her knitted woollen hat and hurried along the passageway to the kitchen stairs.

And when she got to the top of them, stood there staring down, her face blank in amazement. For it was Goosey who was standing at the range, her hair in its bedtime pigtails down her back, and an apron on over her nightgown and wrapper. She was bent over the fire, her face glistening with sweat in the heat and she was shaking the big pan in which several sausages were spitting cheerfully.

'Goosey!' Poppy cried. 'What on earth are you doing? Go back to bed at once! You aren't fit to –'

Goosey turned her head and stared at her, and Poppy hurried across to her for the old woman's face was pallid behind the glow the fire had set there and her eyes looked red and anxious.

'My dear,' Poppy said more gently. 'You really mustn't. Now come along, do –' And Goosey without any argument at all managed to pick the heavy pan off the fire and set it to one side before turning and, leaning heavily on Poppy, coming to sit down at the scrubbed wooden table in the middle of the kitchen.

'My dear old soul,' Poppy said, keeping the scolding note down, but unable to suppress it entirely. 'What *are* you thinking of? You know you've been very ill and you need time to be well again – why did you –?'

'She wanted to make some supper for me, that's why!' The voice was loud and resonant in the big kitchen and Poppy, startled, turned her head and peered through the dimness, for the gas had not been lit and only the firelight illuminated the old dresser and its winking dishes and the big shabby armchair on the rag rug – and then felt her face go smooth with amazement as she saw Chloe appear from the direction of the larder. She held a large slice of cake in her hand – and Poppy registered without thinking that it was a piece that had been meant to provide a slice for each of the three of them, she and Bobby and Goosey – and her mouth was full. She looked sleek and content and well pleased with herself as she grinned at Poppy and took another large bite of the cake.

'Isn't she a duck?' she went on. 'As soon as I got here and told her they'd sent us all home from school, to stay until this stupid flu thing is over, she was so pleased to see me! And when I said I was dying to have sausages for tea she said she would fetch them and cook them. Wasn't she naughty? She just put her coat on over her nightie and went. Such a villain, dear old Goosey!' And she came across to stand on Goosey's other side and hug her, staring over her head at Poppy with bright-eyed insolence, daring her to say anything at all.

33

And for the first time in all the years since she had first set eyes on Chloe, Poppy took her dare and said all she wanted to. She stood there for one long dazed silent moment but then opened her mouth and let it all pour out: her scorn for the child's selfishness, her loathing of her snobbery, her wilfulness and her stupidity. It was not like speaking to a child of not yet eleven; there was nothing childlike about Chloe in the way she used and abused her elders, Poppy told herself, so there need be nothing of concern for a child's feelings or lack of ability to comprehend in Poppy's blistering attack on her. She had behaved with a degree of selfishness that quite overcame any pretence of lack of understanding, Poppy told her; she must have seen what was perfectly obvious to any person's eyes – that Goosey was ill. Yet she had demanded of this sick old lady, who had for so long loved her and looked after her, that she put on just a coat over her flimsy nightdress and go out in bitter weather in a manner that could have a positively fatal effect.

'Yes, fatal –' Poppy said, and glared at Chloe. 'Do you hear me? It could be fatal to treat a sick old lady so!'

And she seized Goosey by the shoulders and actually pushed Chloe away, and then very gently tried to lift the old lady to her feet. But she wouldn't move; indeed it seemed she couldn't, for she sat there with her head bent and her shoulders shaking and Poppy realized with a great wave of compunction what she had said and how she must have frightened her and fell to her knees beside her.

'Oh, Goosey, of course it won't be so bad,' she whispered into her ear. 'You won't die just because of going out in the cold – but Chloe had to be told, you must see that she had to be told. She can't go on all her life doing as she wishes and no one to say her nay ever! She has to understand if she is not to grow up to be a monster.'

'I can't bear it, I can't bear it,' Goosey said in a cracked voice, and then coughed and said it again. 'I can't bear it –'

'Please, Goosey, let me take you to bed,' Poppy begged. 'You really aren't well enough to sit here – and you're so cold! I can feel it – and yet your face is so hot. Oh, you must have a fever again. I shall call Dr Martin right away – come to bed, Goosey, please –'

She became aware of the fact that Chloe was crying, and probably had been for some time, and she lifted her head to look at the child and saw her standing there, her face streaked with tears and her mouth open in an unlovely grimace to show the remains of the cake she had been eating.

'For heaven's sake,' Poppy said, allowing all the disgust she felt to show in her voice as well as on her face. 'For heaven's sake stop that bawling and help me take Goosey to bed. She's ill and needs immediate care –'

'It's not my fault, it's not my fault,' Chloe howled. 'I never told her to go out! It was all her idea, she said if I wanted sausages she'd have to go and get them but I never told her to go, it was all her own fault, it wasn't me at all –'

'Be silent at once,' Poppy said loudly and reached across Goosey's bent shoulders to take Chloe by the arm and shake her. 'Stop that stupid caterwauling at once and come and help me –'

But still Chloe went on howling at the top of her voice and after one more furious shake of her arm, Poppy let her go and moving with all the gentleness she could, but very firmly, she pulled Goosey to her feet and began to lead her towards the stairs. The old woman leaned against her heavily and her feet dragged and Poppy thought with desperation – this flight and then two more – I'll never manage it alone – I've got to manage it – 'Oh, Chloe, do be quiet! And come and help me!' she called over her shoulder. 'Don't just stand there shrieking like an idiot – come and help me –'

'What the devil's going on here?' The voice came loud and thick from the stairhead above her and she lifted her head and peered, cursing herself for not turning on the gas before she had started to take Goosey upstairs; it was going to be hard enough without having to struggle in virtual darkness.

'Chloe, stop that noise and tell me what's happened, for God's sake!' the voice came again and Poppy in amazement thought, Bobby? And then said it aloud, 'Bobby? Is that you?'

'Who else would it be?' His voice was thicker and rougher than usual in the darkness and she felt rather than saw him come down the stairs and pass her and heard the snap of a match as he fumbled to turn on the gas; and then the kitchen sprang into full light and the flickers of flame from the fireplace seemed to dwindle in response and Poppy stood there blinking at him.

He was wearing his old rough brown robe, the one he always wore to work in and his hair was rumpled as though he had been tearing at it, and he turned and glared at her and then at Chloe. Poppy stared back at him, her head spinning with her confusion. Bobby never left his study except to go to their bedroom or to the bathroom or, in hot summer weather, to go into the small garden at the back of the house. He certainly never came down into the kitchen. If there was anything he needed he raised his head and shouted in that thick voice of his and always someone heard and always someone came running. But here he was and she felt a great wash of gratitude overwhelm her as she looked at him and thought – he heard it all and he's come to help me.

'Oh, Bobby,' she said and then again, 'Oh, Bobby –' and reached one hand out towards him, partly in gratitude for his presence and partly to call him towards her so that together they could take Goosey, now drooping even more beside her, up to her room.

He stared at her for a moment and then, as at last Chloe's bawling dropped in intensity to become a heavy sobbing said abruptly, 'What on earth is all this din about? A man can't hear himself think. I'm trying to work –'

'I – I'll explain later,' Poppy said and thought – I know I won't, I've never told tales to him yet about Chloe's awfulness and I don't suppose I shall start now, even after what she has done. 'Just help me take Goosey upstairs first –'

Chloe was no longer sobbing so heavily. She was gulping and sniffing in a singularly little-girl fashion and now she held out her hands to her father and said piteously, 'Daddy –'

He stood there for what seemed to Poppy a long time, although it was little more than a second or two as they both stared at him, she and Chloe and even Goosey who, with an enormous effort, lifted her head and looked at him as she leaned even harder against Poppy, who braced herself against the weight.

And then moving abruptly Bobby turned towards Chloe and set his arm across her shoulders and looked at Poppy.

'I told you, I'm trying to work,' he said gruffly. 'What's all the noise about?'

It seemed to Poppy that his voice was coming to her from a long way away and she moved slowly, turning away from him, trying to lead Goosey towards the door and the long climb to the haven of her bed.

'Goosey is ill,' she said dully. 'I have to get her to bed,' and now Goosey seemed to take over some of the effort needed and began to walk more upright.

'I can manage well enough, Mrs Poppy,' she said gruffly, and her voice sounded even more hoarse than it had. 'I'm sorry to have been such a trouble to you all. I'm just a stupid old woman and I don't know no better than to make trouble for you all. Never you fret, Mrs Poppy – I can get to my bed on my own feet. I can manage –'

'No,' Poppy said firmly. 'I'll take you –'

'That you will not,' Goosey said and moved away from her and reached for the banisters of the stairs that led up to the ground floor of the house. 'I knows my place and it'd give me satisfaction if you knew yours. I'll get myself to my own bed soon enough, I thank you. Miss Chloe, don't let those there sausages go to waste, now. You eat 'em. They're as near done as makes no matter. Another minute or two on the range there and they'll be just as you likes 'em.' And moving with infinite slowness the old woman went up the stairs.

And turned her head when she reached the top and said to Poppy, 'You come up in a while, Mrs Poppy, when you got all sorted out 'ere, and you'll see I'm well enough –' And then she pushed on the door and went, and they could hear her footsteps dragging across the passageway floor over their heads as she went towards the staircase that would take her up the remaining two flights to her bedroom.

'Well!' Bobby said after a moment. 'That was a great deal of noise and fuss over nothing!'

Poppy whirled on him and cried, 'Nothing? Over nothing, do you say? It was over a great deal, and far from nothing!'

She could not remember ever feeling quite as she did then. Her belly seemed to be churning with fury, a vast almost uncontainable fury, and she could not for the world have said why she felt that way. It was not only because Chloe was still standing there in the shadow of her father's arm, leaning against him and watching her with that blank-faced stare of hers that was so familiar. It was not only Bobby's uninformed attack on her, either. It was something more than either of those, something that held all the frustrations and disappointments she had ever known and she felt the churning increase and lifted her head and closed her eyes, trying to control it. She would not give in to this tide of feeling, she would not. She who had seen so much in the war, who had been through so much, to give in and shriek and weep just because of a ten-year-old child's manipulations? She could not. She would not – and she stood there and pushed the tide of tears that threatened to engulf her down and down, and said nothing.

'Then what was it about?' Bobby said irritably. 'I heard you shrieking from the other side of the house, from my room with the door closed. It was a disgusting sound. I had to come and see why and yet you don't say.'

Still Poppy was silent but now she lowered her chin and stood there looking at him, aware of Chloe's continuing stare but refusing to catch her eyes.

'Well?' Bobby said and his voice was rising now as his irritation increased. 'Are you going to explain, or is it possible for me to return to my work? I for one have better things to do than stand here and waste time with a pair of foolish creatures who won't speak to me! Chloe! *You* tell me what all the fuss was about!'

Now Poppy did look at Chloe who stared back and then said in a small voice, 'Poppy was angry with me, Daddy.'

'Then I dare say she had every right to be,' Bobby snapped and held her away from him so that he could look at her. 'You've not been in the house an hour and already you're making noises and fusses! Is this to go on until you return to school? For if it is, I tell you, I for one shan't put up with it.'

'I didn't mean it –' Chloe said and now there was a whine in her voice. 'I didn't mean it! Goosey said she wanted to give me sausages for tea and Poppy called me names. She said I was a selfish creature and wicked and she said I was a – I can't say the word, Daddy –'

Poppy stared at her, blankly. Had she in her rage used language she should not have done? She tried to think back, and couldn't. It would not be impossible, of course; her years in the FANYs and now her daily occupation in the East End had ensured that she had a much wider and indeed coarser vocabulary, some of it highly regrettable, than the average young lady of her class, but all the same – had she used such language to Chloe? And she frowned as she tried to remember the words that had poured from her in rage, and could not.

And Chloe, seeing the frown, misinterpreted it and shrank back against her father and began to wail again. 'I'm not, Daddy! Tell her I'm not – I didn't mean to hurt Goosey – she said she wanted to make my tea – so I said thank you. I didn't know she was ill – I haven't been at home to know she was ill – tell Poppy to leave me be, Daddy, tell her to leave me be –' And she burst again into noisy tears and buried her head in her father's robe.

It was all too much for Bobby. He pushed her away with a pettish gesture and marched across the floor to the door. 'For heaven's sake, it's like a kindergarten here! I'm going to work. I don't want to be interrupted again tonight. I just want peace and quiet and no more shrieking! Poppy, see to it if you please –' And he stamped away up the stairs and again the sound of footsteps retreated over the passageway above their heads.

There was a long silence and then Chloe took a deep breath and said softly, 'So there.'

'What did you say?' Poppy turned her head to look at her.

'Nothing.' Chloe seemed to quail under the sharpness of Poppy's look and slid across the floor to the range. 'I'm going to have my tea. Goosey said I was to have my tea, so I shall –'

'Chloe, that is not the end of it. You understand me?' Poppy said quietly. 'We cannot go on like this. You are indeed a very selfish little girl and you must learn not to be. You cannot go on treating people so badly –'

Chloe looked back at her over her shoulder, all winsome dimples. 'But I am not bad at all! Daddy didn't say I was, and Goosey said she was sorry for making trouble for us and so she had! It was all her fault for going out. So I am not naughty at all! And don't you dare to say so, so there!'

And she turned from the range and carrying the heavy pan in both hands, very carefully, put it down on the kitchen table.

'Don't do that,' Poppy said automatically and snatched up the pan. 'You know it marks the wood and that makes more work for Goosey –' And indeed there was a dark burned ring on the pale scrubbed wood.

Chloe looked at it and shrugged her shoulders. 'It'll come off well enough, I dare say,' she said indifferently. 'Goosey'll get it off. She always does, however much she moans at me –'

'That is what I mean!' Poppy banged the pan down again on the range and using the heavy fork that hung there beside the fire put the sausages on to a plate which she took from the dresser and then slammed it down on the table. 'You care nothing for how much work you make for others, and this must stop! You must be more thoughtful. It is too much to expect Goosey to do everything. She is an old lady now, and it is too hard for her to work so much. She needs consideration from you, from all of us –'

'Then get some more servants to help her,' Chloe said calmly and plumped herself down at the table and began to eat the sausages with every appearance of relish. 'Then she won't have to work so hard –'

Poppy took a sharp little breath in through her nose, using all the control she had not to shout at the child again. 'We cannot afford that,' she said in a tight voice. 'Servants' wages are expensive and we simply cannot –'

'You Jews can afford whatever you want,' Chloe said in her clear loud treble, and pushed another piece of sausage into her mouth. 'You're just too mean to spend the money.'

There was a long silence broken only by the sound of Chloe chewing and then Poppy managed to find her voice. 'What did you say?'

Chloe threw a sharp little glance at her, her eyes bright and knowing, but only shrugged.

'I am not –' Poppy began and then stopped. Why should she deny the fact that half her heritage was indeed Jewish? Why should it be regarded as a taunt that such should be the case? And she leaned over the table and took Chloe by the shoulder and said in that same small tight voice, 'Why do you say that?'

Again Chloe threw her that bright, too bright, little glance. 'Well, it's true, isn't it? Auntie Mabel says it is. She says that's why you hang about the East End. She says it's a great shame that we should have to put up with such things. She says that –'

'I don't want to know what she says,' Poppy said dully and straightened her back. 'I never want to hear what anyone else says. Finish your supper and then go to your own room, Chloe.' And she went to the stairs and climbed them wearily. 'I'm going now to see after Goosey,' she said. 'And after that I am going out. You must send yourself to bed. There will be no one else to help you. Goodnight –'

And she left, with the small satisfaction of seeing the dawning horror on Chloe's face as she realized that she would indeed have to take care of herself at bedtime; she who had always been waited on hand and foot by Goosey. Well, tonight, and for many other nights, she would have to manage as best she could. A child of almost eleven should be able to wash herself and put on her own nightdress without supervision. And if she couldn't, well, Poppy thought, as she climbed the last few steps before Goosey's room, well, that is an end of it. I shan't help her – and she knew that some part of her long battle was over. She had tried so very hard to love Chloe, but now she had to admit she had failed. It was an impossible task; all she could do now was try to live with her in what amity she could and wait as patiently as she might for the child either to grow up into a more agreeable person

– which seemed at this moment to be very unlikely – or to leave her father's house to live elsewhere. And who, Poppy asked herself bleakly as she tapped gently on Goosey's door, who will want to marry such a woman as this child is likely to become?

Goosey, to her great relief, was better now she was in bed. Her fever seemed to have abated, for her forehead was not unduly hot and she seemed much more comfortable now she was lying down and she refused sturdily to permit Poppy to call the doctor to her.

'I'll be well enough, come morning, Mrs Poppy,' she said from her pile of pillows. 'Just you see how well I'll be – and it's wrong to call the doctor and him so mortal busy rushing around. There's so much of this here flu about it fair frightens me. There was three died on the other side of the Square last week, three, would you believe it! And the doctor called to all of 'em. But I ain't going to die, not this time, any road. I'll be fit as a flea again soon – just you see if I ain't. It was because I felt that much better and that glad to see Miss Chloe safe at home away from that nasty school as I popped out like I did. I shouldn't have done, I dare say –' She gave a little chuckle then. 'When I told the butcher as 'ow I wasn't properly dressed, got off me sick bed like, 'e served me in front of everyone and gave me extra too! Nice bit o' liver I got in the larder now for lunch tomorrow! So don't you fret, Mrs Poppy –' and she hesitated as Poppy turned to go to the door and then went on in a little rush, 'Don't you fret any over Miss Chloe and her naughty ways neither. She'll grow out of them, I dare say –'

Halfway down the stairs Poppy stopped again. The door to Bobby's study was firmly closed and she stood and looked at it for a long time and then took a deep breath and marched in. It was absurd, the outside of all limits, to stand outside her own husband's door like a frightened child! She would tell him all was well with Goosey after all, and ask him to listen out for her, because she, Poppy, had to go out. He was so much better now, so much more in control of himself, surely he could carry some of the burden of the household for tonight? And she remembered Chloe's stricken look when she had been told she must take herself to bed and felt a moment of compunction. Dreadful child though she was, she was still, after all, a child –

'Bobby,' she said as she came in. 'I am sorry to disturb you, my dearest, but I have to –'

He threw down his pen in a rage and whirled in his chair. 'For God's sake!' he shouted, and his voice had never sounded thicker or more ugly. 'Am I to get no peace in my own home? I told you, I am working – I am at a difficult section of this chapter and I need – I *demand* peace and quiet. Go away, Poppy! You're worse than Chloe with all your interruptions!'

She felt her face flame and then lose its colour and she stood there and stared at him for a long moment and then said stiffly, 'I am indeed sorry if I disturbed you. I am well aware of the fact that you are working. I have been doing the same all day – indeed every day – and I know how difficult it is to concentrate sometimes. But some interruptions are inevitable. I must go out, Bobby, and I wished you to know this, and to know also that Goosey is not so bad as I feared and I shall not need to bother the doctor tonight after all. Chloe has had her tea and –'

'Go out then!' he roared. 'Go where you like! What do I care for such nonsense? Leave me in peace, you hear me? Just go away and leave me alone –' And he whirled again and picked up his pen and hunched his shoulders, leaving her standing there behind him as though she had been dismissed like a recalcitrant servant.

But she did not stand there for long. As soon as she had caught her breath, she turned and went downstairs and put on her coat and little round woollen hat and let herself out of the house, closing the door firmly behind her.

34

At first she was quite determined she would never go back again. She took a cab to Cable Street, reckless of the cost and feeling a need to indulge herself, and sat in a corner of it, her head against the dusty leather squabs as it rattled through quiet streets emptied by the tedium of war and the darkness of the late October night, and thought hard and angry thoughts about everyone at Norland Square.

Why should she care at all about any of them? No one there cared for her – well Goosey, a little now, grudgingly, though heaven knew it had taken her long enough to lose that early suspicion and jealousy of her she had displayed – but no one else. Most particularly not her stepdaughter, who was undoubtedly the nastiest and most hateful child who had ever drawn breath, and now, not even her own husband.

And she felt tears prick her eyelids and then brushed them furiously away. She would not weep because Bobby had been so nasty, she would not. She deserved better, heaven knew she did; had she not for this past two years tolerated his moods and his miseries, his rages and his tears and soothed him back to some semblance of peace, over and over again? What other wife would have worked as hard as she had, running the house on very short commons indeed, and putting up with his imperious and ill-mannered child and bad-tempered housekeeper, while at the same time doing a difficult job helping to run a large business with her aunt? How else could they have managed unless she had worked at Cable Street, for wasn't her salary the prop and stay of the household while Bobby earned nothing? And how could her old friend Mabel have turned out to be so duplicitous? To speak as she clearly had to her niece, to use insulting words about her – it was a wicked cruel thing to have done and, Poppy told herself furiously, I shall never go back there again, or speak to any of them again. I shall never go back there to be insulted and slighted and misjudged. Altogether Poppy indulged herself in a welter of self-pity and anger and hatred, and did so very thoroughly.

But by the time she reached Cable Street much of her ire had dissolved away. She felt tired and dispirited but not so angry. What was the point? People were what they were, after all. Bobby could not help being so unbearable sometimes; it was the effect of his war experience. To be angry with him was like being angry with the guns that had blasted him or the gas that had so nearly choked him, or even with the German soldiers who had used them. Such things and such people were all victims, just as Bobby himself was a victim of a dreadful world in which horrible wars could happen. And it was the same with Chloe; to hate her because she had been made the child she was by her grieving father and nurse was stupid. Poppy might just as well blame Chloe's mother for dying and leaving her grief-stricken family to rear the child the way they had. It was all due to Providence, not to human activity. Or so she tried to convince herself as she told the cabbie to wait for her and ran in to collect the parcel of food she was to take to the Isle of Dogs for Lizah from his anxious sister.

Jessie herself had gone to bed, leaving Barney in charge and he was standing yawning at the back of the almost empty restaurant, and Poppy realized with a little shock that it was much later than she had thought. Past nine now and still a long journey eastwards to be undertaken. For a moment she thought that the best thing after all would be to go home now and sleep and to set out for Lizah's first thing in the morning; but then Barney gave her a long carefully written note from Jessie full of detailed instructions about what was to be done with the food she was sending him and repeated thanks to Poppy for going there tonight, and she shrugged in resignation and took up the box of food and went back to the cab. After all, she was on her way now, late as it was. She might as well go on and be done with it. The fact that she was tired and feeling not a little queasy again, even though she had not eaten since lunchtime, was to be ignored. Tomorrow she could rest; that would be soon enough.

Schooner Street was very dark, for the pub seemed to be closed; certainly there was no cheerful light pouring out on to the pavement from its single large window and the cabbie peered round suspiciously as she called to him to pull up.

"Ere, Miss? What are you doin' in a place like this? You want to be careful, now – there's people down 'ere 'as'd eat yer for ninepence –'

'I'll be all right,' she said impatiently, and climbed out of the cab. 'But I want you to wait to take me back. I shouldn't be too long, I hope

– there's someone here who is ill with the flu, you see, and I must deliver some food to him. But then I'll be ready to go home and I'll never find another cab at this time of night. So will you wait? To take me back to Leinster Terrace in Bayswater?' The man seemed to hesitate and she went on wheedlingly, 'An extra half-crown on the fare if you do –'

'Done,' he said and turned off his engine. 'But no longer'n 'alf an hour, mind. It's a cold night and I got better things to do than sit in a rotten slum, freezin' –'

She had to knock on the door to get in, for it was locked and she stood there puzzled, trying to peer through the dark glass while she waited, but there was just a scrawled sign there that read, 'Closed due to illness,' and silence. She knocked again, harder this time, and at last there were shuffling footsteps and the bolts on the door rattled.

'Nellie?' Poppy said, as she tried to see who had opened the door. 'Is that you?'

But it was not the thin-faced girl who was Lizah's latest in the long string of girls who shared the pub with him, but a boy with rumpled hair and sleepy eyes who stood and gawped at her.

'What's going on?' she said sharply. 'Where's Nellie?'

'Gorn,' the boy said succinctly. 'Said she was too scared to stay no more with 'im so poorly.' And he jerked his head back towards the darkness of the pub. 'An' I said as I'd 'ave to stay on account of I 'aven't been paid this week and I want my rights. Pot boy, I am, an' I wants my fair dues. 'An' I ain't goin' 'ome till I *am* paid – my Mum'd slice me up if I did. So 'ere I am –' And he turned and went shuffling back into the pub and Poppy, with a backward glance and reassuring nod at the cabbie, followed him.

'How has he been?' she asked as the boy reached for the gas jet over the bar and lit it and the untidy room sprang into being. 'I thought he was picking up a little last time I saw him.'

'Don't ask me,' the boy said. 'I ain't no nurse. Told yer – just the pot boy. I kep' out of the way, I did. I'm just waitin' 'ere till I get my pay, that's all. Then I'm off to get another job. Can't be doin' with this. My Mum'll slice me up if I don't get a proper job –'

'For heaven's sake –' Poppy muttered and pushed the box at him. 'Go and put this in the kitchen, will you – in the cold larder. I'll go and see for myself what's happening.' And she pushed past him and into the little room at the back. Here the sense of neglect was even more pronounced, for the fire which was usually burning so cheerfully was quite dead and the room was cluttered and untidy. She looked round and then went to the glass-fronted door on the far side that led to the staircase and climbed its narrow treads to the single bedroom at the top.

Here at least the fire was still burning, though fitfully, and the gas was turned low. Lizah was lying on his side, his head deep in his pillows and breathing heavily and Poppy tiptoed over to him and peered down; but she could see little, for his face was obscured by the bedclothes. And after a moment she stepped back and took off her coat and hat and began to tidy the room. She made up the fire which began to cheer up immediately, greedily consuming the fresh coals she put on, and then moved around quietly, picking up discarded clothing and folding it and putting it into the drawers of the big tallboy which was set against the far wall, and collecting soiled cups and plates and taking them to the landing outside ready to be carried downstairs.

Clearly the loss of Nellie as a nurse was not to be regretted too much; she had been as sluttish in her efforts in caring for Lizah as she had been in her own person, and her loss was no tragedy. Poppy had looked in the wardrobe and seen that half of it was empty and assumed that had been Nellie's half; and thought how glad Jessie would be to hear of her departure, even though she had abandoned Lizah when she was most needed. And then frowned. Clearly, Lizah would still need some care before he was quite fit again, and who was to give it? With Jessie herself ill and Poppy needed at Norland Square –

She hesitated and then, very gently, turned up the gas so that she could see Lizah better. One part of her, the well-trained nurse part, wanted to leave him to sleep peacefully, but the other, the practical part, knew that she could not stay long, and must return to her own home. And she could not go until she had at least spoken to Lizah and made sure he understood that Nellie had gone. She would find someone else to send somehow – perhaps one of the girls from the shop would rally round – but he had to be warned.

It was then that she realized just how ill he was, for rousing him was extraordinarily difficult. He lay there, breathing thickly and yet rapidly, and now she could see him more clearly, fear trickled into her, for his face was drawn and tinged with a faint blue and his lips were even darker. And she thought – pneumonia? Has he developed pneumonia?

For all the signs were there, the dry mouth, the shallow painfully hard breathing, the flaring of the nostrils as he took each breath and his starving lungs struggled to collect more and more air, and she took a deep breath herself and using every atom of skill she had, slid one arm behind his back and hoisted him up, holding him so that he leaned against her while she piled his pillows up into an armchair shape behind him.

And the fear inside her thickened and clotted, for now she could smell how ill he was, could inhale the all too familiar acrid odour that had always seemed to cling to those of her patients in the past who had not been able to get well. But she refused to think such thoughts, and with a last great heave she lifted him so that he was sitting almost upright against the pillows and then pulled the covers up to his waist. Then she went down to the kitchen and found a basin to fill with water and a towel and brought it up and bathed his face; and after a while he began to respond and at last opened his eyes blearily and peered at her.

'Millie?' he said hoarsely and then peered again. 'It is Millie, isn't it? I knew you'd come, dolly, I knew you would. Been telling everyone that you would –' He closed his eyes again sleepily and Poppy said urgently, 'Lizah! It's me, Poppy – Lizah!'

Again he opened his eyes and stared at her and this time there was some understanding there rather than the distant glazed look that had so alarmed her and he said softly, 'Poppy –'

'Yes,' she said. 'Poppy. Listen, Lizah, dear. You're not at all well – I have to fetch a doctor to you – I'll have to go away and –'

'No!' He pulled at her wrist then, clamping his hot dry hand over it so tightly she almost winced. 'It's Millie as I need. You fetch Millie to me. I kept tellin' you, didn't I, as it was Millie who had to come and then I'll be all right? I've been saying it all the time to everyone –' He began to roll his head restlessly on his pillow and let go of her wrist and started to beat his hand on the covers instead. 'I keep on tellin' everyone – Millie – it's Millie I got to see –'

'I – she can't come, Lizah,' Poppy said gently and put her hand over his to try to still that awful restless beating. 'You know that – let me go and fetch the doctor –'

'Millie –' he said again and turned his head and opened his eyes and looked at her and there were tears there and she watched, horrified, as they spilled over and ran down his cheeks; and then he was weeping bitterly, each sob pulling at his chest painfully and she could hardly bear to look at him. And again he said, through his tears, 'Fetch Millie – just fetch Millie and then I'll be all right, I promise I will. I can't think of anything at all, only Millie – fetch her –'

She stood and stared down at him, her own face twisted with

distress, and tried to think. In all those long months at the Front, looking after dying men, she had learned a great deal about the behaviour of the sick. She knew only too well how persistent a delirious man could be about what he wanted, and there had been so many times when she had had to sit there with a man begging her to fetch his wife, his sweetheart, his mother, and been helpless to do anything for him. And had watched him die, miserable and lonely, and hated herself for her own uselessness.

But now she was not useless. This man could have what he wanted. She had only to send a message to her mother on the other side of London to fetch her here. That was all. And then he could die in peace –

For there was no doubt in Poppy's mind now that her father was dying. She had too much experience to think otherwise. The blueness of his lips, the way his chest developed that awful concavity between the ribs as he struggled for every breath, the uneven threadiness of the pulse beneath her fingers as she held his wrist, all told the same story. Pneumonia, which had killed so many wounded men in France, was killing this man, wounded only by a flu germ, but desperately ill all the same. And she could let him die in peace. Or at least could try –

'All right, Lizah –' she said then, and leaned forwards and stroked his forehead. 'I'll fetch her. Just lie quietly and rest now. I'll fetch her –'

He turned his head on the pillow and opened his eyes and stared at her. 'Poppy?' he said and again his voice was thick and laboured. 'You'll fetch your Ma – you'll fetch my Millie?'

'Yes,' she said. 'I'll fetch her,' and smiled and gratefully he closed his eyes and she thought – not so delirious after all, and felt a little surge of hope. Perhaps he could weather the crisis when it came? She looked closer at his face, at that familiar forehead with its tracery of lines which always made her think of Paddington Station and the dark curly hair frosted at the tips with white and tried to see the grey blue skin lose its threatening tinge and become a happier pink; but stare as she might she could see only what was there: the collapsed and struggling face of a man whose lungs were barely able to maintain their function. The crisis would be soon, she told herself. Very soon. And I promised him, I promised him –

Downstairs she found the boy sitting in the kitchen eating a piece of Jessie's strudel and he stared at her over the piece held in his fist and said truculently, 'Well, I ain't ate for two days – no one brung any food in and what was I to do? I couldn't go out and leave 'im, could I? Anyway my Mum'd slice me up –'

'Never mind what your Mum'll do,' Poppy said crisply. '*I'll* slice you up and worse if you don't do as I say. Now take that piece of strudel and another if you want it, and put on your coat and go out to that cab there. There are two things you have to do, and when you've done them, I'll –' She looked at him and his suspicious little white face peering at her and said with resignation ' – I'll pay you what's owing to you and then you go home to your ferocious mother. Will you do that?'

His face cleared miraculously and he jumped to his feet, a scrawny little creature who looked no bigger than a properly fed eleven- year-old would be, but who was probably past sixteen, and whose face looked even older with its expression of weary watchfulness that was never far away.

'You're on, lady,' he said. 'Just tell Fred what you want, and Fred'll do it. I'm known for that, for doin' things, I am. Just leave it to Fred.' And he grabbed another piece of strudel from the box he had already rifled and ran to fetch his excuse for a coat from the hook on the back of the kitchen door.

Poppy found paper in a drawer of the kitchen table and a pencil too, and wrote her notes hurriedly. One to the casualty department of the London Hospital, begging them to find a doctor to send to Schooner Street, since the landlord of the pub there was extremely ill – and she went on to write a careful if rapid account of his symptoms according to the way she had been trained to describe a case in her FANY days – and ended with detailed instructions for finding the address.

And then, with more effort and her face creased with anxiety as she did it, she wrote a note to her Mama.

It took two false starts but in the end she managed it. And folded both notes and went out with Fred to the cabbie, explained to him what was to be done and sent them on their way. And then went back into the pub to climb the stairs and sit beside Lizah's bed in the small cluttered room above, as the fire settled in the grate and the ships on the river beyond the window hooted their muffled mournful notes. And all she could do was wait and watch and listen.

Mildred stood in the hallway with the note in her hand and stared at the boy standing four-square and sulky in the middle of her polished floor, his filthy boots making tracks on its black and white tiles, and then looked down again at the note.

At first she had thought it some sort of stupid hoax and had begun to say so, but then she had looked again at the handwriting and known it to be Poppy's, even in pencil and in that hurried scrawl. But how could Poppy expect her to do anything so ridiculous as to go at this time of a bitterly cold night out to the Isle of Dogs of all places, to see a man she had told her resolutely for years that she had no intention of ever seeing again? How could Poppy possibly imagine it? And she crumpled the note in her hand and lifted her head to tell the boy peremptorily that he must return to whence he had come and deliver that message.

And then stopped and stood and stared at the boy again. He was dirty, with his face streaked as murkily as his oversized boots. His coat, a thin rag that had clearly belonged to at least two other people before it had found its way to his scrawny back, was thin and tattered and small comfort on so cold a night. His face was narrow and peaky, but his eyes were bright enough as he stared back at her, and suddenly, it was as though she were living two experiences at the same time. This had happened before. Long ago, she had stood on a dark night at the door of this house and read another note given to her by a bright-eyed boy, demanding she go with him in a cab to the East End of London; and though that boy had been tolerably well-fed and full of cheerful chatter and this one was painfully thin and morosely silent, and though the message that time had been sent to her by her brother and this time had come from her daughter, the situation was so much the same that she could not help it. She lifted her chin and she laughed aloud.

The boy was stung into speech. 'What's so bleedin' funny?' he demanded, pushing out his lower lip at her. 'If I laughed when I got messages saying as 'ow people was dyin' my Mum'd slice me up, she would.'

'I wasn't laughing at that,' Mildred said. 'It was something quite different –' She stood and looked down at the boy for a long moment and then smoothed out the crumpled note and re-read it. Poppy had written shortly and very much to the point.

'Lizah has pneumonia. I doubt he can live the night. He wishes only to speak to you. Will you come?' And she had signed it simply with a 'P'. That was all. No pleas, no begging, just facts.

At first Mildred had doubted the truth of it; not that Poppy ever lied, as far as she knew, but Lizah, the Lizah she had known would say anything, she had told herself, anything at all to get what he wanted. Well, almost anything. But now the boy had confirmed it and she looked at him again and was amazed to hear her own voice.

'Wait there. I'll fetch my coat and hat –'

Poppy woke suddenly and lay there curled in the big armchair staring round in amazement, confused and alarmed. Where was she? And she struggled to sit up and winced a little, for her foot had gone to sleep and the pins and needles of returning sensation were agonizing. And then remembered where she was and why.

The room was cold, for the small fire she had lit when she had come downstairs after taking her mother up to sit beside Lizah had long since spluttered out, and there was frost riming the small window-panes behind her. And she looked at the frost and thought with a sudden stab of anxiety – it's morning. Oh, God, it's morning. I've been here all night and no one at home knows where I am –

But there was no point in fretting about that now. She would explain when she saw them, as she would soon, and she lifted her head to listen to see if she could discover what was happening upstairs. But there was silence and after a moment, as her feet became fit to bear her again, she stood up and went out to the kitchen to wash and tidy herself as best she might, trekking out to the little iced lavatory in the yard beyond and feeling the morning air on her face and in her lungs like a shock of water thrown over her. She stood out there for a moment or two, staring up at the hard blue of the sky as the small bushes that struggled to survive in the asphalt patch that was the yard whispered in the breeze as their frozen twigs moved and thought – it's good to be alive. She felt better than she had last night, that was certain.

But then, even as she thought it, the unpleasant sensation came and she felt nausea lift in her and thought – it's hunger, that's all. I didn't eat enough last night. But even the image of food was too much to cope with and she had to run to the lavatory to get there in time, and then stood bent over it, retching painfully. She could not be truly sick, for her stomach was empty, but it was just as unpleasant and when at last she was able to stand up and make her way back to the kitchen she was pale and sweating and felt dreadful.

There was still silence there and she sat in the armchair by the dead fire, her head thrown back, and waited for the nausea to subside, and thought of anything, anything at all but how she felt and what it might mean; and conjured up the face of the doctor who had arrived last night, just half an hour before Mildred too had come, and heard again what he had said.

'You're quite right, my dear. Pneumonia and in both bases I'm afraid. The right lung is consolidated as far as the apex, though there is still some function that can be salvaged. But we must just wait to see what will happen. Crisis or lysis – you clearly learned about that when you trained, hmm? This war has brought strange skills to unexpected people, indeed. And now it is almost over, glory be, although we have this dreadful epidemic to deal with. We are indeed a wicked world, Miss Amberly, and we must be wicked people that God should find it necessary to punish us so harshly.'

And he had sighed and given her a bottle of expectorant medicine to give her patient 'should he survive the night, and I must warn you it is possible he may not – should he survive the night –' And had gone away, a weary little figure who had at least given her some comfort, even though it was clear he could do nothing for Lizah.

And then Mama had come and Poppy had led her, wordlessly, up the stairs to the bedroom and stood back as Mildred moved to stand beside the bed and look down on Lizah's sleeping face. She had said nothing at all to Poppy, not a single word, and Poppy had been grateful for that. She had come and that was good enough, and as she stood there and looked at her mother's straight unyielding back in its well-cut and expensive dark grey merino coat and then at the tousled head and the tired face on the pillow, she had tried to visualize them together. Not as lovers – to imagine such a scene would be a repellent exercise and unworthy of her – but just to see them walking side by side perhaps or facing each other over a dining table, talking and laughing and eating –

But it was an impossible image to conjure up and she had given up trying and had only said aloud. 'Lizah –' And he had stirred and turned his head and looked up and seen Mildred standing there. And had smiled.

It had been that which had made Poppy weep. His face had creased into that familiar map of pleasure that she had come to know so well in the past few years, and he had looked, for all his blue lips and his sallow cheeks, a happy man, happier than she had ever seen him. A triumphant happiness, a sureness of delight that had never been there on his face before, and that had been more than she could bear. And she had turned and made for the door and said in a choked voice, 'I'll be downstairs in the room behind the saloon bar, Mama. Come and fetch me if you need me. If the crisis comes – fetch me,' and had curled up in the big chair beside the struggling fire and wept herself to sleep.

But her Mama had not wept. She had known that before she left the room. She had just pulled the chair closer to the bedside and sat down in a composed way and said to Lizah, as she pulled off her gloves and laid them neatly on her knee, 'Good evening, Lizah. I am sorry to see you so ill.' And that had been the last thing Poppy had seen or heard of that room as she closed the door behind her and fled downstairs.

Now she lifted her head again and thought – it's so quiet. Perhaps Mama has fallen asleep too – and got to her feet. She couldn't just sit here and wait. It must be late? And she looked at the small clock on the mantelshelf, but it had stopped. So she looked out at the sky beyond the little window. It must be close on seven, she thought and wished she had worn her wristlet watch last night. But Mildred would know the time. She always wore a watch pinned to her bodice; and Poppy began to climb the stairs, telling herself that she had to ask Mildred the time. That was all. Just to know the time.

She opened the door gently, and stepped inside and then stood very still, staring at the bed.

It had been carefully arranged to be smooth and perfectly neat. The counterpane corners fell tidily to the ground in even folds, and the surface was unmarred by the least mark. But it had been pulled right up to the head of the bed to cover the face of the shape that lay there, and Poppy closed her eyes and then opened them again and looked once more.

And then, moving her head with a great effort, looked at her mother who was sitting very still and straight beside the bed, her hands clasped on her lap.

'Mama?' Poppy said and then more loudly, 'Mama?' for Mildred had not moved, still sitting there with her eyes fixed straight ahead. And Poppy, moving a little awkwardly, came and knelt in front of her and set her hands on her mother's, and looked up into her face and said again, 'Mama?'

And this time Mildred did look at her, and as Poppy gazed up at her she saw something that she had never seen in all her life before.

Her mother was crying.

35

There were many times in the ensuing weeks when Poppy remembered just one small event of that long and all too eventful night: the little doctor standing beside Lizah's bed and looking down at him and saying, 'We are indeed a wicked world, Miss Amberly, and we must be wicked people that God should find it necessary to punish us so harshly.' For it seemed to her that one misery after another piled on to her in such profusion and with such crushing effect that there were times when she feared with all the depth of her being that she would collapse under it.

It did not seem so at first, of course. She had arrived home on that Saturday morning at almost eleven o'clock to find Bobby in a towering rage because of her absence, a rage that was based as much on his fear as on anything else. It had taken her some time to comfort and reassure him, but once she had explained what had happened and how she had had to remain at the pub in Schooner Street until the necessary officials had come from Lizah's synagogue to deal with the matter of burial, and how she had been needed to make arrangements for registering his death, he had calmed down.

Chloe too had been easy enough to deal with; she also had been alarmed by her stepmother's apparent disappearance, and in consequence was subdued and much more biddable a child for several days; so much so that Poppy told herself a little sourly that perhaps she should regularly make dramatic gestures and so deal with Chloe's tantrums that way. But pushed the idea away as unworthy of her. Chloe had to be tamed by other means, and somehow she had to find them.

But she had little time to consider how to deal with Chloe and her needs, for her own were suddenly pushed firmly in front of her eyes. Lizah's funeral at Plashet Grove Cemetery was arranged for the Monday of the following week in the usual Jewish manner. 'We always have our funerals quickly – in the old days when we lived in a hot country what else could we do?' Jessie had told her, her swollen red eyes bleak in her ravaged face as she sat in the corner of her living room on a low chair, wearing a dress that had been ripped at the bodice by a functionary of the synagogue. 'Another thing we do – we rend our clothes and weep – what else can we do when the people we love leave us?' Poppy insisted on her right to attend it. Jessie had tried to dissuade her, because 'women never go to the burial grounds, Poppela – it isn't done –' But she had been adamant, and in a sober black costume and wide-brimmed hat had made the long journey out to the far eastern side of London, the only woman among many black-clad men.

And that had made the whole matter so much worse; for when she fainted after the interment, collapsing on to the cold earth to lie there dazed and sick for a long moment, no one knew quite what to do to help her. But one of the men had at last had the sense to take her up in his own car – for he was a rich man who had been a gambling crony of Lizah's – and had taken her to the London Hospital in Whitechapel Road to be cared for.

And there she had been told what she had long suspected; she was pregnant, and she had lain there on the narrow consulting couch in the small cubicle in the casualty department and closed her eyes against the matter-of-fact tones of the doctor who had examined her, and tried to understand her own feelings.

'I am sure your husband will be a happy man, Mrs Bradman,' the doctor said heartily as he packed up his stethoscope and put it in his pocket. 'Your first baby, I take it?'

'He – he was injured in the war,' Poppy said in a tight little voice. 'He was gassed. He's an invalid. I work myself for our income –'

'Ah,' The doctor said noncommitally. 'I see. You – er – did not consider taking steps, then, to –?' And he stopped, the soul of delicacy.

'Oh, of course I considered it,' Poppy said with some bitterness. 'I saw the gynaecologist Dr Dixon – he told me what I should do if I did not wish to become pregnant just yet, and gave me the necessary equipment. I was to go back to see him but I missed the appointment – too busy –' And her voice trailed away.

'Well, there it is,' the doctor said even more heartily. 'Nature will have her way! I wish you well, Mrs Bradman, and suggest you visit your own doctor as soon as may be to make arrangements for your confinement. I estimate the child will be born about June the eighteenth, next summer, you know. Had you planned this birth you could not have done better! Babies do thrive in summer months, with good care. And since you are clearly not one of the residents of this neighbourhood, I am sure yours *will* thrive.' And he went away followed by the swishing starched skirts of the carbolic-scented nurse who had accompanied him throughout, leaving Poppy to continue to think about how she felt regarding her situation.

Which was, she decided, confused. She ached with pain to think that Lizah did not know. It would, she was certain, have made him very excited to be told that his daughter was herself to be a mother. She could imagine just how he would have laughed and bustled over her, making her sit down and rest and – and again she closed her eyes at the pain of the tears that filled them.

Would Bobby be so pleased? She tried to think but could not. Bobby and Chloe. All his child-loving energies had always been concentrated in her. Would he find room in his life for another child? And she felt her old enemy, fear, slide into her, for Bobby now was not the Bobby she had once known and loved so dearly. The Bobby of today was a selfish man, wrapped up in his writing and in his own needs and desires. He had long since stopped showing any real concern for anyone but himself and Chloe. How would he deal with this new development? And she decided not to tell him for a while. He was not observant of her and her body's rhythms. He would not know until she told him, and there was time enough for that. It would be easier not to think about it now. As she so often did, she would leave the matter aside to see what effect time would have.

And she made the same decision about telling Mama – she had her own feelings to cope with. She had responded so amazingly, in Poppy's estimation, to Lizah's death, that it would be asking too much of her to expect her to handle such news as her impending grandmotherhood now. Let her grieve for her own lost past, as she was so clearly doing. Time enough to think of the future and such babies as it might bring.

The only person Poppy could imagine being unreservedly glad was Jessie, and so it proved. When Poppy told her she clapped her hands and laughed and then burst into tears and then laughed again, and then, to Poppy's mixed amusement and embarrassment threw her hands up to the heavens and loudly thanked her God for bringing her such a gift to comfort her after her so terrible loss. Jessie, Poppy told herself privately, could exaggerate exceedingly sometimes –

And then suddenly it all became dreadful. Late on a Friday

afternoon in the first week of November, Goosey, who had at last recovered from her feebleness after her flu, telephoned Poppy at the office. As soon as she heard her voice, Poppy knew that there was something very bad happening; Goosey regarded the telephone, which was in Bobby's study, as an instrument of the devil and hated it cordially. That she should be using it must mean that she was very alarmed indeed, and Poppy held the earpiece to her head with so tight a grip that her knuckles whitened.

'What is it, Goosey? No, don't shout, my dear – just tell me quietly – no, *quietly*. If you shout I can't hear you properly –'

'It's Mr Bobby, Mrs Poppy,' Goosey managed and she was weeping and that made her almost as incomprehensible as her shouting had. 'He's that poorly – oh, Miss Poppy – He was as right as anything this morning when I gave him his breakfast – you saw that yourself – and now he's sitting here in his chair and he can't breathe proper and I can't get him to his bed and I don't know what to do –' And she burst into such a wailing that all Poppy could do was hang up and run, seizing her coat as she went, and not stopping to tell anyone what was happening, to make for the Underground. It was the fastest way to travel and she could not risk wasting time finding a cab.

Bobby, unable to breathe properly – it had been her ever-recurring nightmare ever since this dreadful epidemic had first taken hold, that Bobby would catch it. With his lungs and throat so badly damaged already, how could he cope with such an infection? Goosey had been kept well away from him during her own illness, and only allowed near him once it was clear she was no longer an infection risk, and there had been no visits allowed at Norland Square for many weeks. But somehow it had happened, and she fled down the long corridor towards the train platform, her heart beating in her chest like a hammer, and coldly certain that the worst had happened.

Goosey was sitting on the stairs, her apron over her head and weeping bitterly when at last she got there, breathless and sweating, and Chloe was sitting behind her, her face white and pinched, and Poppy pushed past them both and ran to Bobby's study.

He was sitting bolt upright in his chair, his head held at an unnaturally rigid angle and breathing very noisily indeed. She could hear him even before she went into the room and knew then, deep in her mind, what the outcome would be. But didn't want to face it. And managed not to do so, for the next dreadful days.

The doctor came and fetched oxygen for Bobby to breathe, and advised that he should not be moved to his bed.

'He'll do better sitting here, Mrs Bradman,' he said soberly. 'And it will be easier for you to care for him. Fetch a commode in here and let your housekeeper or daughter bring up all the items you need. You must take care of yourself too, of course. In your delicate condition – oh dear, oh dear, this tiresome epidemic! It makes it all so difficult for us all –'

And he went away, leaving Poppy sitting beside Bobby as the cylinder of oxygen hissed gently and he lay against the pillows she had set behind his back with his eyes only partly closed so that a narrow rim of the whites of his eyes showed, and struggled for every breath.

There were times in the ensuing days when she became confused about who she was sitting with, whose breaths it was she was counting as they rasped in and out of those tortured lungs. Was it Bobby, her beloved Bobby, or was it Lizah? Or was it herself? For there were times when it seemed to her that her own breathing was as painful and effortful as that which she was watching, when she longed just to stop trying, to close her eyes in oblivion and just stop trying.

But she could not do that, and she sat on doggedly, watching him, sometimes taking off his mask so that she could feed him sips of water, over which he choked, or massaging his cracked lips with scraps of cotton wool dipped in olive oil, and lost count of time.

There was suddenly a great deal of noise from the street on one day early in his illness and she looked up blearily when Goosey came creeping in, and stared at her with stupid blankness when Goosey told her, with tears running down her lined old face, that the war was over. The Germans had signed an armistice and it was all *over*. And it was to Poppy like that time a few months ago when the Government had announced that women of property over the age of thirty were to be given the Vote. It had seemed so irrelevant somehow, even though it had once been so desperately important to her, something for which she had yearned so much. So it was with the Armistice; she had yearned very much for peace too, very much indeed, but now it just did not seem to matter. None of the excitement reached her, only the noise of klaxons and shouting people outside. She just sat the long hours away watching Bobby slide out of her fingers as his breathing became ever more erratic and his awareness of her presence ever more blank.

For he never spoke to her at all. She would murmur to him, speaking of the long-ago days in Revigny when they had been so happy, when the guns had crumped around them, when they had been surrounded by mud and death and the stink of blood, and been so very happy. Or she would make plans for the wonderful days to come when his book would be finished and a great success and the baby would be born and they could be rich and happy and just live peacefully, sitting in the garden in the sun –

Bobby died late in the afternoon of 15 November, slipping from life into death so silently and with so little sign of change that at first she did not believe it had happened; and then as she sat there with the soft gaslight over her head plopping a little and the firelight dancing on the ceiling, she saw that he had left her. The struggle to breathe was over. He had fought long and hard, God knew; for a full week he had used his gassed lungs and his ruined throat as though they had been made of iron. He had tried, how he had tried to live.

But he had failed, and she bent her head and set it against his hand, so that the remaining warmth of it filled her brow and thought wearily – lucky Bobby. No more fighting. No more misery. Lucky, lucky Bobby –

It was inevitable that she would catch it herself, of course. Even before Bobby's funeral she was herself in bed, propped up against pillows, only hazily aware of what was happening to her. Goosey came and went, her face appearing over her and seeming to be as vast as a map of the world, and as lined, and then dwindling to nothing and becoming a terrifying pinpoint of light in a black world. Dreams came and refused to go away, visions of the trenches and the ambulances bucketing along the Verdun road and the shouts of the men in the Urgent Cases hospital and then there was Bobby, but not Bobby as he had been this past two years. A joyous happy Bobby who cried out to her and waved to her and called her to come to him, and she tried to run after him and could not, feeling herself tethered to the bed in which she lay. And she knew she could not follow him, however much she wanted to, for it was not her own body which kept her tied here in these hot sheets and rumpled blankets, but her baby's body, which lay there heavy as tomorrow within her and would not, could not, let her follow Bobby.

And then there was Jessie, a soft-faced Jessie who murmured at her and set cool cloths on her head and gave her things to drink that she could swallow and slowly it got easier. Until at last the dreadful dreams stopped and the noises in her head stopped and she was lying exhausted but well aware of what she was and where she was, in her own bed in Norland Square.

It was then that she learned of what had happened to Bobby. How his sister Mabel had come to see him in spite of the fact that she had a feverish cold, and had spent a long afternoon with him. Goosey hadn't told Poppy, she said with desperate, almost grovelling apology, wringing her old hands almost in despair, because Miss Mabel had told her not to. 'She said it was stupid to fuss over Master Bobby so, and her his only sister, and I wasn't to say nothing to you – and so I didn't – and oh, Mrs Poppy, but if only she'd ha' known, she'd never ha' done it. I'm sure she'd never ha' done it, for hasn't she died too of this dreadful flu? And I wish to God I had myself –' And she had wept so bitterly that even in her weakness Poppy had to drag herself upright to comfort her and tell her it was no blame to her.

It was February before Poppy was quite well again. There had been long weeks of the deepest, blackest depression during which she had wanted only to die, but Jessie had been a stalwart, refusing to let her sink under it, spending long hours with her. And had cheered like a child when Poppy had at last demurred at the time she was spending with her – 'because who's looking after things at Cable Street if both of us are away?'

'That's what I like to hear!' Jessie beamed at her. 'If you can worry about business you're getting on all right. It's fine, dolly, fine. Lily and Barney and the girls are coping great, and there's my Bernie looking after the office, bless him –' At which Poppy had closed her eyes in horror and opened her mouth to remonstrate, and then decided to say nothing. For what good would it do? Wait till she got back to work herself. Then she would sort it all out, whatever that young villain had done.

By now, her pregnancy was making itself visible. Poppy herself had become much thinner while she had been ill, so the five months of development showed as a visible bump; soon she would have to tell her mother and Chloe. Some things could not be hidden for ever, after all. But now it remained still mostly her own secret, and Poppy would sit beside her fire in the drawing room staring at the heaps of coloured cushions and Diaghilev-inspired decorations Bobby had put there and think dreamily of how it would be when he or she was a real person, someone who could crawl about among these pretty things and see their father's gift to their future. Oh, that would be a splendid thing, she would think; almost as splendid as the fact that she was still safely pregnant. For as her doctor had told her, she had been very lucky.

'Many of my patients in your condition lost their hopes completely because of their fever. But your infant seems a sturdy and determined one –' And he had patted her hand and gone away, well satisfied.

Chloe had gone back to school after the Christmas holidays, since she too had had a mild attack of the infection and it was now considered unlikely she would have another. That was a great comfort to Poppy who still found the child's company difficult, though she felt a deep and abiding pity for her. Both her father and her aunt dead; it was a tragedy indeed and she would look at her and think – poor child with only a stepmother to care for her. And had tried to reassure her as best she could that she was still loved, was still safe, still had family to call her own.

But Chloe had listened to her halting words with eyes as opaque as pebbles and said only, 'Yes, Poppy. Can I go now?' And had turned and left her as soon as she had finished speaking, and Poppy had looked after her and felt the ready tears of her convalescent weakness fill her eyes. It was going to be a miserable business, rearing Chloe. But there was no one else to do it. Just Poppy. And do it she would.

'And me,' Jessie told her stoutly, when she confided in her her fears for the future. 'You've got me, dolly. And your mother – for she's easier now since Lizah died. She's let me visit her twice, you know, since the funeral. Twice! It'll all get better now, you'll see.'

She went to the window then, and looked out into the Square, where the thin February sunshine lacquered the first of the snowdrops in the small front gardens to a glistening white.

'Listen, dolly, we've had a bad time, you and me. We've lost a lot. My Lizah and your Bobby and – well, that was last year, hey? There's this year to live now. The first year of no war. A new year and a new baby – that's what we got to think about now. A new year and a new baby. From now on, it'll all get better, won't it? It's *got* to.'

'Yes, Jessie,' Poppy said, and smiled at her. 'Yes. It will all get better.'

And she believed it.

ZOYA

Danielle Steel

One woman's odyssey through a century of turmoil . . .

St Petersburg: one famous night of violence in the October Revolution ends the lavish life of the Romanov court forever – shattering the dreams of young Countess Zoya Ossupov.

Paris: under the shadow of the Great War, émigrés struggle for survival as taxi drivers, seamstresses and ballet dancers. Zoya flees there in poverty . . . and leaves in glory.

America: a glittering world of flappers, fast cars and furs in the Roaring Twenties; a world of comfort and café society that would come crashing down without warning.

Zoya – a true heroine of our time – emerges triumphant from this panoramic web of history into the 80s to face challenges and triumphs.

SPHERE BOOKS
GENERAL FICTION

ISBN 0 7221 8315 1

Mary Rose-Hayes

The Winter women have everything!

ARRAN a bestselling novelist with a social conscience, waif-like beauty, and an unbelievable sex-life . . .

CHRISTIAN the elegant jet-setting hostess, with a string of famous consorts and lots of money . . .

ISOBEL screen idol of millions, beautiful and gifted actress and devoted mother to her enchanting twin children . . .

Yes, the Winter women have everything: talent, fame, beauty, wealth – and a lot of secrets. Secrets that none can share until their father's shocking death: secrets that bar them from one thing they all truly want. Love . . .

bright, vivid, well-written . . . oodles of action and a sense of humour – Kirkus

SPHERE BOOKS
GENERAL FICTION

ISBN 0 7474 0135 7

All Sphere Books are available at your bookshop or newsagent, or can be ordered from the following address: Sphere Books, Cash Sales Department, P.O. Box 11, Falmouth, Cornwall TR10 9EN.

Please send cheque or postal order (no currency), and allow 60p for postage and packing for the first book plus 25p for the second book and 15p for each additional book ordered up to a maximum charge of £1.90 in U.K.

B.F.P.O. customers please allow 60p for the first book, 25p for the second book plus 15p per copy for the next 7 books, thereafter 9p per book.

Overseas customers, including Eire, please allow £1.25 for postage and packing for the first book, 75p for the second book and 28p for each subsequent title ordered.